T0368772

The Tree

& The Panzaic Plea

2nd Ed.

R A Brown

THE TREE

& the Panzaic Plea

2nd Ed.

R. A. BROWN

iUniverse, Inc.
Bloomington

The Tree
& the Panzaic Plea

Copyright © 2010 R. A. Brown

All rights reserved. No part of this book may be used or reproduced by any means, graphic, electronic, or mechanical, including photocopying, recording, taping or by any information storage retrieval system without the written permission of the publisher except in the case of brief quotations embodied in critical articles and reviews.

This is a work of fiction. All of the characters, names, incidents, organizations, and dialogue in this novel are either the products of the author's imagination or are used fictitiously.

iUniverse books may be ordered through booksellers or by contacting:

iUniverse
1663 Liberty Drive
Bloomington, IN 47403
www.iuniverse.com
1-800-Authors (1-800-288-4677)

Because of the dynamic nature of the Internet, any Web addresses or links contained in this book may have changed since publication and may no longer be valid. The views expressed in this work are solely those of the author and do not necessarily reflect the views of the publisher, and the publisher hereby disclaims any responsibility for them.

ISBN: 978-1-4502-7185-1 (pbk)
ISBN: 978-1-4502-7187-5 (ebk)

Printed in the United States of America

iUniverse rev. date: 12/16/10

Authors Introduction

To teach how to live without certainty and yet without being paralyzed by hesitation is perhaps the chief thing that philosophy, in our age, can do for those who study it.

Bertrand Russell

A note to those who have read "The Tree or the Panzaic Plea": this is an updated, condensed version of that book. Since I published "The Tree...." In 2005, I have received many recommendations that the philosophy is very important, and to get it to a wider audience by editing to produce a thriller with some philosophy.

This book of anticipatory historical fiction raises one likely possibility for the future given our history. It also considers the idea that although life can be exciting and satisfying day to day, everyone at some point asks themselves what is the meaning of all this stuff surrounding us — the earth, the solar system, the universe and time? Is it all meant just for Homo sapiens? This book explores the best answer that science and/or faith can deliver at this moment. It is the answer that you most likely would have arrived at if you had decided to become a tediously overeducated scientist as an occupation. As such, it is enlightenment, and meant to be intellectually stimulating.

Start with what we know about this planet and its flora and fauna including that special species, Homo sapiens. For the latter I use the metaphor of the vanity of Don Quixote versus the humility of Sancho Panza. They correspond to the two sides of: "This world is a comic tragedy to those who aspire to greatness, a tragic comedy to those who accept it as it is." In this context we can examine ways to enjoy life; given a healthy respect for our limitations. This helps explain our cultural successes and failures. It helps us come to terms with what we are.

Most of this was written before 9-11-2001 --- much of it, way before. The first full draft circulated after a stay in Paris in 1996 allowed me to complete the product of 25-years of sporadic work. In that era, topics such as science versus religion were politically incorrect to discuss; largely unpublishable. Right after 9/11 I submitted Op Ed pieces in which I suggested that we should examine the role of faith in such acts of man's inhumanity to man. They were rejected with comments like; "You have insulted every Arab, every Christian." Since then there first were a few editorials in this vein, then a torrent of best-selling books. I suppose that like all good ideas, it is at first rejected, then gains acceptance as obvious.

But given that just about all concepts for running a society have been failures, even catastrophes, and science based knowledge often has been used for warfare, we are left with the question; what is the meaning of this life; and what should we do with it? Our life? Can science accept that all the cosmos is there just to make our lives more comfortable? Did that redwood tree grow there just for you to chop down to make into a house? Is there some other reason for its existence? How does one best go about finding the answers to these questions? And does your answer have any merit?

You may or may not get answers from this book but when you're done you should have a better feeling about it and be alert to the ability of current scientific knowledge to help in addressing these questions. As of today 9/8/2010

Acknowledgments: Thanks to Wayne Burns for introducing me to the Panzaic Principle; and in memory of Vivi Brown and her comments and Marcia for being there.

Part I
Incident in the Mountains

©1998 R. Brown all rights reserved

There are many events in the womb of time which will be delivered.

William Shakespeare

Chapter 1.1 Alpine Lakes

The abrupt purr of rain jerked J's attention from reading about his deadly encounter in the New States, back to his daily concern with survival in the Serengeti. He had been digging into his memoir of the tumultuous years after he found the unexpected loot. This sudden weather shift drew him up to the high view surrounding his Captain's chair.

.

He marked his place in the manuscript and moved to the big window. He could see plains forming an amber carpet all the way to a distant, dark wall of trees. Above him a steel gray ledge of cumulus clouds extended to the forest edge. The late afternoon sunlight peered under the western edge and gave the billowing clouds a yellow hue. They heralded the edge of the storm enveloping him from the east, from the mountain.

.

Bright sunlight still splashed across the golden grass of the savanna. The wind-stirred grass undulated with flashes of darkened gold. An occasional crack of lightning lit the five kilometers between J and the dark of the forest.

This was a daily event at his African home as regular as the number nine bus in Seattle. Towers of cumulonimbus would generate on the hot slopes of the mountain and amble down like a gardener watering the high plains.

A grill admitted sounds of the wind raising a heady wail as it buffeted his towering view room. He'd been so into his past adventure he had missed the first drum roll of this march of dark cloud. A flash of white took a picture of the plain in front of him and thunder vibrated the air in the room within seconds. The discharge was not more than a kilometer away. J moved swiftly back to the chair as it was insulated and the walls were conductors. He was sitting at the highest point in his vicinity. Two minutes later the next crack of thunder was simultaneous with the lightning. The sizzle of the electric charge flew down the conduits in the walls and J could detect the sharp smell of ozone.

He welcomed thunder and wind as nature's attendants heralding the imminent arrival of a torrent of rain. What a treat — there was a warm feeling to be safe in the midst of one of nature's dangerous productions. J always rooted for the storm to pass directly overhead. This was much easier to survive comfortably when he was ensconced in the Tree.

When he was out on the plains his fascination with the green hue of the thunderstorm sky and the mamma clouds, looking like their namesake loaded with water, made him a sitting duck for the oncoming deluge. Several times he had been caught out in one of these storms and despite his intimate knowledge of their dynamics, the close up roar caused a surprisingly ingrained and abiding fear.

The smell of ozone and the rising humidity combined with his earlier reading to take him to a previous storm in a prior world. He picked up the journal and flipped to the events that had caught him up in the deluge of that distant day. His curiosity and impulsiveness had launched him along a crapshoot path that led to this insulated moment. J looked around his African aerie --- living in a protected pocket amid a sea of danger, the world all changed around him. Back then he had been in the high forested lake country of the Puget Sound region.

♦

There was no wind. Below, the mountain lake was a mirror reflecting the tall peaks on the other side of a narrow valley. A loon call drifted its low-high note across the quiet, celebrating the stillness of the afternoon lake. The sky was blue in unpolluted splendor. It had taken a two-hour drive plus a four-hour climb for J to get here from his home, but it felt like a world away.

He was on his own in this remote region of the alpine wilderness. It had been a family tradition to come up each October and backpack into the high Cascade Mountains. They had found a place to pause, marvel at nature and contemplate J's favorite topic — the meaning of existence. Or as his wife had liked to put it, they wondered about the existence of meaning.

Surrounded by granite cliffs, deep blue lakes and green forests, it was the ideal place to reflect on meaning. Almost everyone who sat here and looked at the view had the same thing to say; "It's beautiful." J the scientist always asked, "Why is it beautiful?" What, in their inner mind made them all think this was beautiful. After all, it was just nature. His wife's answer was "They just *knew* it was beautiful. If you're a Homo sapiens, you *know* it's beautiful. Even *you* know it's beautiful." Perhaps this had something to do with the 'meaning' of the existence before them. They felt lucky to be able to take these few days from the daily treadmill to explore these questions, and the merit of their lives.

Their favorite place was the Enchantment Lakes - where large rock ledges, mountain cliffs and larch forests surrounded alpine lakes. J and his wife had often climbed the ten miles of switchback trail up the narrow valley side. The trail was as difficult this time as he remembered. But he reveled in the exertion and the aching muscles. This was the price to pay for solitude. Without the arduous journey myriad people would have loved such a beautiful place to death long ago. It had been well on the way to being worn out until regulations were instigated to limit the number of visitors.

J had difficulty with the regulations --- he couldn't forecast the weather enough in advance. He was capable of planning but he also exhilarated in spontaneity. Life should be an adventure. Too often the choice was between that and nothing. Once he had followed the maxim 'You only live once.' It turned out this idea converted too easily from an excuse to do something dangerous in his twenties to a conservative 'be careful' rationalization as he passed forty.

His practical bent, tied to his idealism like a tail to a kite, allowed him to conform to regulations when they were logical and only marginally intrusive to his freedom. He could ask and follow directions. In certain situations he was even addicted to ritual. More than once his wife had wondered aloud how a non-superstitious scientist could wear the same socks for a three-day tennis tournament just because they were 'lucky'. He had shrugged, 'it was OK as long as he knew they were simply rituals'. He could give them up in a flash if they interfered with logical life. The smelly socks were borderline. No doubt they improved his confidence and made for positive thinking.

In a contradictory fashion — characteristic of his entire personality — J didn't adapt well to the alpine reservation system. He did not like to invest the work in backpacking into the mountains when the skies turned ugly. His vocation provided him with the knowledge of the weather a few days in advance so this soggy strait was not necessary. But month-old reservations often had to be abandoned due to storms, and many glorious days were unavailable for instant reservation.

Fortunately, after the summer season and the first big chill the number of hikers decreased dramatically and the park service did not concern themselves with the rules. These days the forest rangers had their hands full trying to save the forests from timber rustlers. Renegade loggers would grab a patch of timber from the national forest and vanish before anyone came near. There were many unemployed loggers and ample idle equipment to make this viable. Traditional logging had disappeared with traditional forests. The price of clear or tight knot lumber from the oldest, tallest timber tempted even the most moral of the loggers. On the eastern slope this problem had evolved with the new border at the Columbia River. In the post-revolution alignment of states the region east of the river that skirted the mountain range was now another state with fairly elaborate border checks. One of the few things they were not severely rigid about at customs was people bringing in valuable lumber.

J came to the Enchantments alone for the quiet and the memories. Also, the basic questions had yet to be answered and he liked to think that he was getting there. His occupation in the sciences provided regular input to feed a fundamental curiosity about the planet and the life it sheltered. He was lucky to lead the good life in the tumultuous world of the early twenty-first century.

Like the late winter storm in the midst of spring there is often a warm, tranquil period in the Northwest Autumn. Recently it had become a certainty — a warm extension of summer. High pressure moved into the Puget Sound at the beginning of October and settled in, locked between the two mountain ranges like a fat robin snuggling in its nest.

J came up to see the larch forests. The larch was a peculiar tree. It looked much like the many other evergreens of the forest — the cedar, the fir, the hemlock or spruce. But the larch was deciduous and just before the needles fell they turned golden. The adventurous hiker who dared to flirt with the first serious winter storm was rewarded with a magnificent show of flaxen forests. The color splashed across the amphitheater of the mountains and lakes. The closer a larch was to the high tree line the better the colors. This year a drought had squeezed the finest colors into every dying spike. The glorious show brought J into the backcountry where a chance meeting would change the direction of his life.

The heavy rains just ending last week made the trails quiet. He had seen a few young couples, all less than thirty. J called the fifteen-year gap to his age the 'the wisdom gap'. When he was young he had followed the 'never trust anyone over thirty' adage. Now he would add 'never trust anyone under thirty.' This because the pre-frontal cortex often did not gain control over the untrustworthy brain stem impulses until later; if indeed it ever did.

This was a polemical opinion for a professor, where most students were under thirty. He chose graduate students who had spent a few years 'out in the world'. They showed a better ability to detect the differences between meretricious and meritorious, between the domain of hormones and that of cerebral contemplation. J had borrowed Cervantes' contrasting characters from the story of the Man of La Mancha to illustrate these two attitudes. He enjoyed the dichotomy between the easy-going practicality of Sancho Panza and the quest for perfection by Don Quixote.

The hikers had all disappeared into the vastness of the area, each with their own private site. J thought the couples would probably spend most of their time in the elaborate tents that practically sprang to full erection when placed on the ground. Much like the young men.

J was glad that the push of passion had slid away behind him. The loss of his wife was certainly a factor. Still, instinctive interest in sexual matters teased at him, and probably would to the grave. At least this primordial drive could be more easily diverted these days.

He yanked his thoughts back to the glorious view in front of him. He didn't come up here to dwell on the sorry state of mankind. That was too much like work and would return soon enough. Time now to concentrate on the beauty of the environment. Otherwise it was like many pleasurable experiences — you knew you had done it but you couldn't remember any of the particulars.

He planned to leave today. Early in the morning he had collected his cooking gear, compressed the pot-skillet-plate combination into a tidy cube. This followed the stove into the bottom of the pack next to the still folded tent. The hard work added to his trip by the tent made him shake his head. The added weight and volume had been justified only once or twice in several years, when caught by surprise storms. Fortunately, over the years technology had decreased the size and weight of backpacking necessities in direct proportion to his own decrease in strength and energy. Having invested so much money in the tent he always brought it along. It was great when it actually did save him from getting soaked in a downpour.

When he looked at his watch it was still early. He slept deep but not long in the mountains. Four hours would be enough to get him down by dark, so he had six hours to explore. He left his pack hidden in some bushes and headed for a spot on the opposite canyon wall.

The climb up was difficult with many detours and turned into a strenuous hour. Finally he made the spot he had picked out and could lean back on a Cadillac-size slab of granite. He had a solid backrest of stone with an Ozymandias view of the valley. On the other side of the lake were the invisible campsites scattered here and there and glimpses of trail as it passed along the lake.

J scanned the valley from his left, starting in at the southern boulder-strewn chasm that terminated in a rock wall. This vaulted upward to the source of the stones far above. It was a dead-end canyon with shear granite walls on three sides. The trail continued upward in switchbacks at the northwest corner of the canyon. A hidden waterfall snaked down the end wall.

Another lake was above the rock cliffs, starkly beautiful above the tree line. There, in the spare landscape, boulders as big as city blocks lined the lake. On the slabs of smooth granite slanting toward the bottom of the lake only a thin dark line marked the boundary between the air and crystal clear water below. It looked like a gentle walk down into the depths.

Beyond this lake was a long valley that rose into a high pass. This valley led to the Columbia River and the new Federation State.

To the right of the switchback trail he could see along the length of the lake in front of him. The trail was largely visible before it dropped over the giant step down to the next lower lake to the north. That lake was much like the one he sat above now.

Three men appeared over the crest and were slowly moving off the trail toward the lake outlet heading for a resting spot. From there a magnificent view of the lower canyon could be seen.

Much as he was inclined to dislike spying on other people J never failed to do so in the mountains. It seemed incongruous to watch people when so much natural beauty was available; but one of the exciting things about being in the wilderness was viewing the animals. The living things provided dynamic phenomena compared to the static eternity of the surroundings. Fellow humans were something natural to watch.

J's present surroundings in the mountains constantly reminded him of his species lowly position. At night the blue-black sky full of shining bright stars gave testimony to the tiny scope of his domain. Some sparkling spots of light were galaxies whose light began the journey to his eye long before the solar system was born.

When he looked at the granite slab he sat on he could see rivulets of black and white gneiss that formed a billion years ago when the rock had plunged deep into the mantle and warmed. A hundred million years later it had warmed once again and there were pink and brown veins where new minerals had melted and flowed through the semisolid mass under pressures that he could barely imagine. It was a table of time as disconnected from his state as the distant stars. It gave him a feeling of satisfaction to know these things. The self-effacing feeling of being such a small cog in the big picture was comfortable. There was so much to learn. There was great job security in his profession exploring the environment. It would never be completed.

Another reason to pay attention to the new hikers --- he had a new toy in need of amortization; luxury compact binoculars bought especially for this trip. He had always been fascinated with telescopes and binoculars. During his raising-a-family period he always had several pairs of cheap binoculars and had built a decent telescope out of mirrors, pipe and a coffee can. These days he could afford the best available.

The binocular scene quickened J's pulse. There was something strange about these guys. The three men wore identical backpacks; brand new, completely enclosed back huggers. They were dressed like hikers, but their gear and their attitude didn't fit

It was possible they were fishermen — either not very bright or very new to the sport to be here at this time of year. The lakes were stocked in the spring and the steady march of fishermen had surely caught all but the very smartest of the gorgeous lake trout.

The only clear thing was they were very tired. Their packs were instantly shucked and two collapsed on the ground without giving consideration to the view. These two looked under thirty. The third man was older and acted like a leader. He walked to the rim a few meters beyond and contemplated the view for a few minutes before he found a nice log seat. The other two seemed grateful to sprawl on the heather. Two days ago J had stopped there. He had passed up the soft ground cover for the panoramic view.

While they rested J surveyed the area through his field glasses. There were two young men on their way down, passing the inert trio. He could see evidence of one or two other parties camped in the mile of forested pine needle carpet between the lake trail and the cliffs. He had chatted briefly with one of the passing hikers yesterday. But the mountains weren't like a camper van campground; nature was the main attraction here. People didn't socialize with strangers all that much.

He met an amiable young student on the trail to the upper lake yesterday. They had hiked together for a while. Junior — J had a habit of assigning new names to passing acquaintances — reminded him of himself in his earlier, naïve years. As he described to Junior his reasons for coming to the high country, Junior had been moved to explain his attitude toward life. "I'm accumulating knowledge. I still have the luxury of youth, years to learn about everything before I begin to pontificate."

J laughed to hear this echo of his own ideas, "I know the feeling. But I've reached the point where my knowledge is enough to begin pontification on certain subjects."

Junior thought about it, "I suppose my time for that will come. What good is it to have a lot of knowledge without spreading it around?"

"It should be manure for productive conversation," J was thinking that he didn't miss the intellectual 'luxury of youth' any more than he missed Junior's creamy complexion. His own facial crags and creases and even the first traces of bags beneath the deep-set blue eyes added a measure of character, in his opinion. He and 'Junior' parted ways soon, natural loners venturing deeper into the lake country.

Movement at the base of the lake brought his attention back to the three men. The older man was up and getting a drink from his water bottle. The man next exhorted his friends to activity. By the way he hefted his pack it was evidently lighter than the other two. That probably explained why he was the first to recover.

The other two each sipped from the lake outflow stream. This was another sign of their high-country naiveté. The stream looked clear and pure, but it could contain giardia, a pathogenic bacterium. A drink of crystal clear water could result in a year of dysentery. Those two young fellows also left their resting stop without taking the few steps to the rim to look down at one of nature's better efforts. They evidently didn't come up here for the scenery.

J moved back into the shade and shelter at one side of the rock seat. It was an instinctive movement. When he stopped to think about this he realized his pulse rate was up and his palms were slightly sweaty. The unusual nature of the three men set into motion his physiological signs of uneasiness.

The feeling that something unusual was happening was reinforced when the three rapidly moved past the camping area. It didn't seem likely they could be planning to continue up to the next lake. That was another exhausting mile. It was a smaller basin with fewer campsites, much colder and more exposed. It was definitely only for high country aficionados. J had spent a day up there with only his daypack.

These men were tired, judging by their long rest stop, too tired to have traveled only from the first lake three miles below. They must have started at the parking lot. It had taken J the whole morning to get up to this lake and he was in better shape than any of these three, judging by their bulk and their step. They had been climbing for hours and they were continuing determinedly past this lake. He moved very slowly to a less prominent position on his lookout ledge and kept his body out of the line of sight of the men. He felt a little silly for doing so but he did it nonetheless. They probably wouldn't spot him without binoculars, anyway.

To teach how to live without certainty and yet without being paralyzed by hesitation is perhaps the chief thing that philosophy, in our age, can do for those who study it.

Bertrand Russell (1872–1970),
British philosopher and mathematician.
A History of Western Philosophy

Too much sanity may be madness. And maddest of all, to see life as it is and not as it should be!

Miguel de Cervantes (1547–1616),
Spanish novelist and dramatist.
Don Quixote

Chapter 1.2 The State of J's World

It is fair to wonder why J was sitting on this cliff high in the mountains. He was alone now, but he hadn't been for most of his life. He had participated in a traditional family unit that included all of the pleasures of falling in love, marriage, security and children. He had his share of acquiring — new cars, a new house, a wine cellar and a telescope observatory; and joining — a swim and tennis club, half dozen Save-the-World groups and the University Faculty Club.

He had started slowly in life; his shyness and slow maturation had postponed social distractions to scholarly study so that he possessed a degree in engineering before he had gotten around to thinking about what to do in life.

He fell in love and married the girl he was going with at college graduation. His training had already set in motion the questioning of his every action and "fell" struck him as a remarkably apt term. They were compatible - she laughed heartily at his jokes, he thought of her before anything else, and they merged smoothly on the dance floor. Their coming together was a melting pot of genetic attraction and intellectual jousting to a draw. Half chance, half decision.

♦

Both J and his wife had been born in Southern California and spent their teens in the stable hedonistic aura of the glorious and gruesome twentieth century. They had both attended San Fernando high school although they were just passing acquaintances then. Both had shy genes. He first registered her existence when they met on two successive weekends in their junior year of college. The first was at a Zuma beach party, the staid nature of which could not be understood by a subsequent generation.

It had been a warm evening and a grunion run was predicted for some time that week. These small fish spawned at high tide on the beach. If you were there at the proper moment, and the proper place, the beach was carpeted with wriggling, screwing fish. Hundreds could be caught and thrown in a gunnysack. J never knew what for. His father had buried them in the garden. No matter, the pleasure was in the doing, and the actual disposition of the fish was an anticlimax.

This particular night the grunions were absent, probably because another biological phenomenon had graced the scene. The plankton bloom was full. These microscopic creatures invisibly saturated the water. Whenever agitated they fluoresced sea foam green. Of course the wave action agitated them and each crashing roller glowed like a mile long neon light.

J discovered that when he ran on the beach his footprints would be filled with angry green, and he had run for half a mile in the darkness testing the sand for bright footprints. His future wife passed him on his return, running by, saying hi, sharing a sigh of amazement, and passing on into the night. There was no thought to intruding into her reverie on this vacant beach anymore than to giving up his own.

The next weekend they crossed paths skiing. The San Fernando Valley was one of these places on earth where one could get in the car in the morning on certain days in spring or fall and go sunning on the beach or skiing in the mountains, depending on which direction you pointed the car.

On this day the snow at Big Bear was hard packed and the sun was shining. The first hours in the morning were the best, before the sun had worked its way on the chilled surface. This was J's second attempt at skiing and his experienced friends had convinced him to get a 10-run chairlift ticket since this was by far the best buy and the most sensible thing to do.

He was in the process of nearly killing himself in order to use his full ticket. Since he hadn't yet learned to turn, this meant the steep parts had to be sidestepped down, a slow and embarrassing process. Or he could traverse in a switchback pattern with a full stop and careful kick-turn at the end. There was another way that gave him a terrifying exhilaration; simply schussing straight down, provided an appropriate slowing down area existed. But usually these conditions didn't apply and overall it was a tedious learning experience and J was working hard not to waste his ticket.

He met his friends on one run and they laughingly urged him to follow as they plunged over a ridge. He impulsively did, realizing its steepness only after he was over the hump. His friends had turned immediately and traversed off to a lesser slope at the side. Turning was a skill only to be learned by J years in the future. Looking down in a moment of terror he saw this was the final hill above the long line of skiers waiting for the chairlift below.

Very quickly he was heading for the center of this line, picking up speed by the instant, soon sliding even more ignominiously on his stomach. He used his trailing skis as an anchor and was lucky enough to stop short of the line. His greatest injury was acute embarrassment. A ski instructor helped him up, "The Nose is for experts only. You don't look like one."

"I haven't learned to turn yet," was greeted by an incredulous look tinged with some respect-- which made J feel a little better.

"It takes lots of nerve, and little brains, to come off the nose with so little skill," the guy looked down at him from his superior height. A small smile began at the corner of his mouth. "I'd better give you a free lesson as part of my duty to protect everyone else on the mountain."

The best part was cutting into the front of the line with the ski instructor's authority, but he regretted not having his ticket punched.

On this run down with the ski instructor J met his future wife again. She stopped near enough to hear a few comments from instructor to pupil and then decided that the level was too fundamental for her and skied on. But there was another moment of eye contact and a very generous smile.

In later years J reflected on how these chance meetings in romantic settings probably registered deep in subliminal chambers. When they met again a year later at a college social the aura of these places must have emerged to enhance the occasion. In any event, the combination clicked, the timing was right, and love, marriage and children followed. With an engineering degree he was well on his way to a comfortable existence.

But then he attended a special seminar on 'The Economics of Evolution' while pursuing a misguided master's degree in business. A young physics professor lecturing outside his field presented the talk. This was stimulant enough to produce a room full of experts in each of the specialties suggested by the title. The speaker was well organized and convincing to J, although he seemed to lack any hint of humility. J had been taught that this was an important part of interpersonal communication and he was mildly offended by the speaker's attitude.

However, the vital result of the evening washed over J as he strolled across campus toward home. The question and answer period had been long and lively, a brilliant show. The pedantic questions that bombarded the speaker were dispatched with knowledgeable and erudite answers. Finally, only the most confident were left to parlay with the speaker. And to J the speaker always seemed to win the contentious discussions. He even had the audacity to point this fact out at the end and offer a simple explanation.

He was a fundamental scientist with a long and difficult program of training in his cranium. Many of the audience, however, were specialists in fields that required so much study that it impinged on their training in scientific fundamentals. There is just so much that one can learn in four or five years.

Here, he did exhibit some modesty, stating that he was not inherently cleverer than they but simply blessed with a demanding and thorough scientific education. He claimed to be just an average physicist with an unusual interest in economics and evolution. It was convincing to J. During the talk J's engineering training kept him on the fringe of understanding while his last year in Business was of no help.

The evening changed J's life. He changed majors and spent the next four years getting a comprehensive scientific education, with a Ph.D., the union card for academia, thrown in. Also, he lost some respect for humility — it too often was a front for incompetence.

◆

J had been blessed to exist near the apex of a century of industrial civilization in a country that revered this process. However, in recent decades a decrease in almost every aspect of culture had made it evident the current period was one of decline. Whether it was temporary or not was not clear. It could be a minor dip, although it had the feel of a major trend.

By the end of the century the bulk of humanity around the world saw American consumer society via the movies, satellite TV and the Internet. They were astonished and envious of the possible level of material human existence, and yet they realized they had little chance to reach those goals. They wouldn't be able to attain the lifestyle Americans on television seemed to take for granted. It may be called materialism, affluence, collecting cargo, or simply the accumulation of things. But it seemed to be a universal human addiction. As the economic and educational gaps between countries became stronger there was global unrest, revolutions reacting to inefficient despotic rule, envy of the rich nations, and disgust at naïve attempts at leap-frogging a feudal society into a democratic one. When religious zeal was added the great terrorist travail began.

About the time the kids were in high school J had 'retired' to an academic career with a lucky published paper, a carefully planned obsequiousness to tenure, and a University professorship. J and his family rode not the crest of the wave of prosperity but the tide of spilled over wealth. His job was scientifically challenging and fairly prestigious. He was positioned within the upper echelon of wage earners, though still far below the enlarged corps of elite rich.

It was a comfortable life- with time for contemplation, gardening, skiing, sailing and reading. It would have been a perfectly satisfactory drawn-out ending. He could have sat back in his comfortable digs and observed the turmoil in society that was inevitable as the population exploded. At times he wondered what it was all about, but intuitively felt the answers were beyond his ken.

Of course he would occasionally complain about the decrease in air and water quality He observed climate change and the decay in general comfort level as crowding increased. But this was a complex issue; there were no easy solutions and he finally didn't expect any. Particularly with the New States alignment, where despite the reduced federal power there had been a continued diversion of money to national security.

It had become evident that global climate was changing as a result of human activity. What was obvious to most scientists in the last century was now clear to the general public. J had early heard the impeccable theory, seen the disturbing data, and embraced the threat of global warming. His only regret was that he was too conservative, along with most scientists, to accept the more dire predictions. These had been correct. Many politicians and fringe scientists who had argued against concern for the anthropogenic influence on the planet warming had their careers and reputations consigned to the trash-heap. They had facilitated a disastrous delay, eagerly grasped by politicians who had little concern or understanding for the future, and it was too late to do anything about it now. J figured the biggest crisis would probably occur a little beyond his lifetime. He was okay with that. But the theory of Chaos — that small perturbations in seemingly stable systems could explosively cause large changes to completely different situations — was set to operate during J's lifespan.

The first convulsion struck when, on a fine morning, his wife boarded a plane that was hijacked and crashed into a tall building as a religious statement. She was just one of thousands to be sacrificed on the altar of terrorism for the sake of terrorism. The trauma of this loss lasted a very long time and troubled him continually; he fell into depression. Eventually his intellectual side helped him prevail over the emotional weight that was dragging him down.

He and his grown kids had huddled together for a long time. Finally the kids grew into their own lives. J moved on to another mode. There are many comfortable slots for people in a well functioning materialistic society. The USA in the form of the weakened New States was still among the world's prosperous economies. His work became his main interest. He went back to studying. He had always been drawn to philosophical subjects like 'the meaning of life'. Now they became a consuming passion.

On this day high in the mountains another perturbation was about to give J a change in circumstance that would have several long-term effects on the tableau of his life.

I do not intend to tiptoe thru life only to arrive safely at death.

Anon.

Chapter 1.3 A stash

The early afternoon sunlight, undiminished by the dense atmosphere that occurred mostly below this altitude, made it uncomfortably warm for J on his perch in the rocks. But he could observe the men better from there. They were slowly moving to the upper end of the lake. J would be able to move back into the shade and lean against the back wall to watch them as they climbed the zigzag trail up toward lake three.

There was movement on the trail near the center of the lake. Junior was cautiously moving behind the men. His curiosity must also have been aroused.

The show got very interesting when the three reached the point where the trail curved upward into the switchbacks. Here, they stopped to rest while the older man consulted a paper. Then, instead of going upward, they took off along the lake end, clamoring slowly over the rocks and fallen logs. For a short distance there was little room between the lake water and the cliff wall and their progress was slow. He could hear their progress when he couldn't see them, as the occasional thump of displaced rock echoed clearly across the stillness of the valley. He could also hear the noises of other campers as they broke firewood. Otherwise it was completely silent.

J felt a tsunami of excitement tempered with a ripple of fear. They were in a dead-end canyon, filled with rocks calved from the cliffs. The rocks could loom as large as a house. There were no level spots for camping. J had explored this short canyon in the past. The river ran down the middle, invisible under the rocks. Although the picture was of a dynamic rock precipitation from the shedding cliffs above, in the decade of J's observations there was no obvious example a recent fall. This erosion had a time-scale out of direct notice by his short-lived species.

There were many caves and niches. The men were probably headed toward one of these. The purpose could be any of a dozen possibilities flitting through J's mind. He knew that it was not likely a legitimate purpose. And he knew that he was going to find out. The increased pulse and signs of flowing adrenaline returned. Logical thoughts of danger were ignored, and J's lassitude since his wife's death was buried under the immediacy of the intrigue in front of him.

He did a quick jump back to the shadows at one point. He had just decided that a drop of some kind was being made. If so, a pickup was likely. He hadn't seen any likely candidates in the past three days. There was another person involved - Junior. J guessed that he too was just curious about the three men and their strange destination. He was now disappearing into the canyon, still following them.

The men stopped to rest about two-thirds of the way up the canyon. J was leisurely surveying, alternating between the men and their surroundings. When he ranged back to the group after a glance away, he was startled to find the older man looking up with a pair of binoculars. J instinctively ducked back into the shadows, simultaneously remembering that motion was most perceptible. He praised himself for his caution in not showing much more than his head. Some measure of paranoia was certainly in order. He regretted the motion though. If he was in the field of the man's binocs, it would have been noticeable. If so, the man was probably carefully studying J's area right now. He didn't dare check.

He considered his position. While it wasn't polite to spy on people he had done nothing illegal. On the other hand, he had already formed the opinion that these men could care less about legality. They couldn't reach him here, but he couldn't leave without being seen. His pack was near his campsite. It wouldn't be hidden from someone doing a little searching.

About two minutes passed. Not long, except when filled with anxiety. J resolved to wait one minute more then take a careful look. He heard a sharp report, possibly a rock falling from the cliffs. J, perhaps in heightened mode, thought it sounded like a gunshot. He quickly moved to the edge of the rock and very slowly edged his head out. No sign of the men or Junior.

Had they hidden to observe him? He sat back and wondered. Finally, he decided- what the hell, and peered with the glasses toward where the men were last seen. There was still no sign of them. Just as his worry was causing him further anxiety one of the men emerged from behind a large boulder perilously close to the hidden river. Soon all three were making their way up through the canyon.

This canyon dog-legged back toward the cliff so the men could not be seen from the west lake trail from the time that they were a hundred feet in. It was clear that they were attempting to be quiet, as once, when one of the pack carriers displaced a rock, producing an echoing thunk; it was followed by a curse, each noise carrying clearly to J's side of the lake.

When they were about three hundred yards up the canyon the leader took out his paper and looked up. He appeared to be lining up a distinctly phallic rock in front of him with some feature on the cliff. He moved slowly to one side, sat down with his binoculars at the ready- this time J was ready to duck if they were pointed his way. He was relieved to see that a sweeping search of the cliffs on his side was begun far from him. He had plenty of time to slowly duck before his area was scanned. When he looked back a minute later the leader was talking to the others. They shucked their packs with a relief that seemed to make it the last time. They made themselves as comfortable as possible amongst the rocks.

After fifteen minutes J had to duck again as the leader made a complete search around the area. When finally the binocs were put away J was certain that he was seeing something not meant to be seen. The carriers hoisted their packs without fastening them on their backs and followed the leader as they all disappeared behind a very large boulder in the area toward the distinctive spire. For the next quarter hour there was nothing. J kept his glasses on the area as much as possible.

He occasionally surveyed the valley and the ridge above. The couple on the promontory had a fire going, and a low layer of stable air caused the smoke to fan out about ten meters above the lake like an inverted glass of spilled hot chocolate. Another couple had walked down to the lake, apparently exploring the shoreline.

When he next saw the men they emerged and moved quickly to retrace their steps. Their packs were on, but lively movement betrayed a lack of weight. They were clearly intent on leaving. The leader was still surveying the area but didn't bother with binoculars.

J could see that the exploring couple was moving on a collision course. Their progress was slow, as they were picking their way along the lakeshore. They would meet the men before the trio regained the trail juncture. J thought that meant trouble for the couple. He felt impotent sitting up so high, like an observer of a chess match with a perfect move in his head, unable to take part.

The girl slipped from an unstable rock at the shoreline and fell into the water with a shriek. Her companion grabbed her hand and pulled her out of the near freezing water quickly. J could hear her raised voice --- the young fellow was apparently in trouble for the sin of laughter.

The men had frozen at the noise. They waited. The leader edged forward to a point where he could see the couple, now walking back along the trail toward their camp.

When the couple was out of sight the men moved on to the trail and assumed the attitude of tired hikers. Within a few hundred yards they passed by the couple at their campsite with no apparent interchange.

The couple was preoccupied with getting her warm and having a lively discussion. She was making recriminations and he was making some kind of justification. Their body language was clear. The leader apparently assessed the situation quickly and the couple was providentially spared the suspicion of forbidden knowledge. That would not likely be the case for a single person roaming around the cliffs. J was not going to move yet.

The men moved rapidly along the lake. They paused at some point as they passed two campsites. J noted with satisfaction that they didn't pause as they passed his campsite. He glanced at his watch and calculated that the men could reach the trailhead down at the parking lot at an hour before dark if they continued at a moderate pace. They would do it. They weren't prepared or inclined to stay. They were clearly out of their natural environment and anxious to leave.

After the three had passed over the ridge J sat still for a few minutes contemplating events. He decided to move to the end of the lake to a position where he could observe the men on the trail below. After a careful look around he emerged from his lookout and moved down to his right, working along the steep cliff toward the north end. He knew that his progress would be evident to the campers across the lake if they should glance up. Consequently, partly as an exercise and partly in the spirit of his mood, he moved with stealth. He shook his head at his own galloping paranoia.

He had not traveled far when he abruptly stopped. His gaze had constantly referred to the trail exit from the lake where the men had recently disappeared. He noticed movement at the top of a rock near the outflow stream. J slowly moved to cover, keeping his eye fixed on the spot of movement. When he trained his glasses on the rock he recognized the leader, just settling into a comfortable prone position, binocs in hand. He was making a final survey. From the rock he could look over the lake to the canyon head. Several minutes passed as he made certain that no one was in that area.

J's heart rate moved to high gear as the leader's glasses swung slowly in his direction. He didn't move as he was buried in shadow, and he remembered his recent lesson. The lead man's scan continued on to the far end of the cliff and then back to the main area of interest. He then backed off the rock, apparently satisfied.

A few minutes after the leader had vanished J worked his way to the north end and fifteen minutes later peered down the canyon. He caught a glimpse of the men, already 1000 feet below. This time they were definitely leaving. J felt a rush of exhilaration at this realization. All thoughts were now turned to searching the area. He moved quickly across the logs bridging the outflow and along the lake trail even running at times. It did strike him that this would appear as odd behavior and he tried to moderate his enthusiasm, his need to know what they had been up to.

He slowed and concentrated on the trail as he passed the campsites. One party waved and J waved back as he moved on. He didn't want any conversations. At the point where the men left the trail J continued on up two switchbacks and then sat down and repeated the leader's survey of the area. Satisfied, he left the trail and retraced their steps to the approximate spot. Although he had concentrated on the layout from his lookout, the ground level chaos made it very difficult to determine exact locations. It was rock jumble everywhere.

When he recognized what he thought were the boulders that had occupied the men earlier he decided to investigate the area. At best he figured to find evidence of a toilet stop. At worst he feared he would find the missing junior.

The rocks were huge with crevasses and narrow passages. Soon he could hear the river below. At this point he noticed a red smear on a sharply descending boulder. Close inspection convinced J that it was blood. Peering down into the dark fissure he could see more blood but no body. There was the babble of water from below. There was no way he could get down to the river. There was such a roar. The boy would be long gone by now. J stared into the depths for a long time. A life reduced to a smear of red on a rock, soon to be erased by the weather.

There was nothing he could do for Junior. The friendly young boy was in the wrong place at the wrong time in an increasingly dangerous world. His body would never be found. From his conversation J knew that the youngster's friends didn't know where he was. His car, perhaps his tent, would be found. His relatives would be notified. But the trail would probably end there. J felt a stirring of rage at the gratuitous death.

There were several options for him. He could notify authorities. Junior's parents would learn a lot more beyond the fact that he disappeared in the mountains. But that was it. These days there was slim chance that the police would catch the criminals. It was even possible that any police he would approach were corrupt, since the tax revolt decay had hit all public services hard for decades. The crooks might even get to hear about J reporting how he had witnessed an apparent murder. And they would know he had seen them make their drop. Then he would be fair game. J scratched that idea. He tossed the paper with Junior's address into the dark recess.

Then he had to consider whether to continue investigating a situation that was obviously fraught with danger. He could just go home. There was a silence all around him. There was no easy answer to this one. It felt relatively safe.

He clamored slowly back from the river grave to the junction wondering which direction he would go. Right was to home and safety, perhaps. But that wasn't going to fly. He was consumed with a need to know what was going on. He turned left.

Soon, the tall spire appeared, even more prominent then he remembered. After ten minutes of searching, broken only by nervous checks to see if anyone was coming, he had found nothing. The sun had dropped below the mountain. The quality of light was going even though it was hours to sunset. Was this all going to come to nothing?

Sitting down, he noted that below and to his right was a rectangular, man-sized rock supporting a much larger boulder that had its rear edge resting against the flat top of another very large rock. J reflected that if a cord were tied to the narrow smaller rock it would resemble the box trap propped up by a stick that he had used to catch birds in his youth. Only this would be a crusher, not a catcher. J was not a fatalist, but the place was just appropriate enough to be a hiding place. He moved to the rock and edged around the supporting pillar on his hands and knees. He had to wait a few moments for his eyes to adjust to the darkness.

Slowly, just five feet beyond him, a rectangular package emerged from the shadows. He looked as carefully as possible at the surrounding area. He worried that there was some kind of an invisible cord tied to the stick on his trap. Caution finally prevailed over his very strong desire to get the package and he backed carefully out of the open wedge.

J reluctantly spent the time to go back to his camp and get the long length of nylon cord that found so many uses in the wilderness. He heard the nearby couple moving down to the lake.

When they continued on up the lake trail J had no recourse but to wait. He used the time to set up his tent since he was delaying his departure until tomorrow. When he was finished he moved to a spot where he could see the couple and watched as they proceeded along the lake edge parallel to the popular route of the day.

J cursed their curiosity, his luck, and life in general. They could spend an hour in there, and it would get dark early in the canyon. For a moment he wondered if it was possible they were the intended receivers of the drop.

He was just about to move up to spy on them when a loud peal of thunder rolled through the canyon. Sharp edged cumulus clouds were rapidly springing from behind the cliffs. J apologized to his luck as he got his rain fly, put it over the tent, and ducked inside just ahead of the overhead thunder and a large raindrop on the fly.

The rain noise was a steady roar when he heard the couple running along the trail toward their tent. He dug out the seldom-used raingear and wished it were better. It wasn't going to keep him dry. But he really wanted to know what was in that package.

Fifteen minutes later, in a leaking poncho, he moved slowly back to the cache. At least his hat was sturdy leather, channeling the rain into a cascade a few inches from his nose. He had his headlamp in his pocket. The rain was thinning as he arrived back at the catch location. He shimmied into the wedge shaped opening with his headlight strapped on his forehead, surprised to see there were two packages, one nearer than the other.

The closer package was wedged against the rock. The back package looked easier to get since he could easily slip a loop over it. He tightened the slip around the package carefully, so as not to move the bulk while he was under the huge weight of that giant boulder. He backed out of the cave to the side, got behind a rock and slowly pulled on the rope. It was heavy. The package was binding on the rough surface. Finally it slid out to the side. J heaved mightily and let the package bound the two feet off of the lower rock. Nothing disturbed the quiet except the rain. The package was tightly bound in oil-impregnated paper so the rain formed globules of water on it. J looked at it, reluctant to touch it.

Finally, he stooped to lift the package. It must have weighed about a hundred pounds. Now he understood why those young macho males were so pooped. No wonder it slid so hard.

One such package was all he could carry. He placed it under his poncho and started back to his tent, carrying it in front of him. He only made it about fifty feet when he had to rest, placing the package on a convenient boulder. His pulse was pounding in equal parts from exhaustion and excitement.

He had to stop and rest every few hundred feet and he worried about his back. He considered getting his backpack, but the package was too large to fit into the main compartment. So he just hugged it like a lover and made his way in spurts. No one was out to see this strange sight. When he reached his tent he slid the package in and followed it. It was dark, he was soaked to the skin, and the rain was a degree or two away from snow. Despite all this a sense of euphoria soaked him thoroughly. He felt infinitely secure in his flimsy tent.

The package wrapping was heavy paper sealed at the ends with tape. It was only a moderately neat job, sort of like the Xmas packages that he wrapped. Adequate but unaesthetic. He was nervous about the contents. It could be a number of things, from drugs to securities, which would be of little interest to him.

He quickly opened the end, peeled back several layers of paper and saw the one thing that deserved the risk. Anonymous money. He was looking at the ends of bundles. J carefully pulled out two of the packets. They were twenties, not all new. All arranged with Jackson facing upward. He figure about a hundred bills times twenty equaled two thousand dollars in this one little stack sitting in front of him.

He felt a leaden disbelief and the sense of impending danger. He briefly considered putting it back. That would be impossible without raising a lot of questions. He instinctively calmed himself and listened to the still air. The usual animal sounds were going to really be heard by him tonight. He tried to figure the volume of cash — thirty times six times four was seven hundred and twenty packets. This times two thousand dollars was well over a million. A hundred pounds of paper was about a million dollars. J knew that many people had this amount in cash, even thousands times this amount in stock. But he had never really let himself calculate exactly how much a million dollars was worth in buying power. Lessee, at ten percent interest this would earn his salary each year just sitting there. If he lived thirty more years he could spend a hundred and fifty thousand a year. A lot of money. He was looking at it, beginning to feel that he was committed to keeping it, even a little possessive. Those men probably had a similar feeling about it.

He slipped out two more packets. He idly stacked the blocks of money as a child plays with building blocks. He pulled out another stack of bills to put a roof on the building. Then he noticed that these were hundred dollar bills. Whoa, he needed to multiply the above total by two, maybe four, maybe more. And the same multiplication for the level of danger. J sat back on his heels, debating his odds.

He had no doubts that the owners were mobster elements. Legitimate business doesn't get transacted this way. Not to mention that they had evidently killed a camper whose only sin was curiosity. Like J.

The fact that they were vile creatures was good- any reservations about taking their money eased. It was bad, though, since the price of getting caught was evidently fatal. He had to consider putting it back.

Escaping with the money would be a formidable challenge. He didn't even think about spending it. Instead, he thought about how it would be a welcome change from mourning the loss of good times past. Anyway, he seemed to be unalterably committed by his genes. He couldn't step back and be detached. He recalled a book by a long-time war correspondent with the thesis that Homo sapiens goes to war because it's in the genes — there were many drawbacks to being tied to your gene line. Taking a foolish risk motivated by greed might be one of them. He tried to be objective about his choices but he remembered the other package that he hadn't touched yet. Underneath the rock. He multiplied by two again and his options dimmed. He wasn't going to be able to walk away.

It was too dark to go outside; it had taken a while to outwait the storm and unpack the loot. He would have to wait for morning to get the other package. J made himself rest during the dark hours. He didn't sleep much, even though he knew that alertness and strength would be needed the next day. That night he stuffed a half million dollars in his sleeping bag sack and used it for a pillow.

Ch 1.4 The Morning After

Dawn arrived early in the mountains around the lake. The tips of the peaks were lit first as if by a searchlight. The granite glowed brightly, promising warmth in another hour or two.

It was a clear dawn. A morning that soothed the body and mind. It nurtured an awareness of life, joy at simply being a part of it all. This was why he came to the mountains and why he was always up early.

Today was somewhat different. J knew that he had hours before the other campers crawled out of their double sleeping bags. They had good reason to dally he thought, wincing with the memory of yesterday morning when he had heard soft moans drifting down from the tent on the edge of the campsite above him.

He had spent ten minutes boiling his tea water listening to the sounds of lovemaking. They were over a hundred feet from him and invisible. But the soft moans and whispered directions kept his interest as he struggled to leave his listening post. He wondered at the impulses that kept him in camp listening when a perfect daybreak was offered down at the lake. The woman's humming turned to moaning and finally climaxed — he thought that was the right word — in shouting pleasure. It had been an expert performance and he learned something about the variety of human nature from it, though peeved at his slavery to his hormones.

This morning he frowned as he thought that another interest had displaced this innate drive today. Was the new one avarice? No, it was much more than that. It isn't avarice that provides the thrill from tweaking the tail of a lion. It was the same genetic predisposition that promoted Homo sapiens into war. It was exposure to a banquet of hormonally pleasing action. This continual subservience to his hormonal impulses really peeved him now. He should sit back and think, evaluate, maybe reconsider. But not right now.

He quickly dressed and made his way back to the stone vault with his nylon cord. The second package looked very similar to the first, just taller and narrower. He resisted an urge to move it a bit to slip the lasso over it and instead carefully slipped the cord around the back, tied a knot and backed out to his shelter behind the side rock. When he pulled on the cord it was just like pulling the string to his bird trap.

There was a loud report of what must have been a directed blast at the supporting column in front of the package. The blast noise was followed by a low, loud crunch as the roof met the floor. It wouldn't have been much different if he had been between them.

He was genuinely startled. Despite all his precautions he wasn't really ready for a bomb. Only his innate caution had saved him. His hearing was stunned and his heart jumped all about inside his chest. He had the feeling of terror that came from making a fatal error. Maybe he hadn't, but it still felt like he had. The close call punctuated the danger and activated chemicals in his gut that must be related to the survival instinct. Or the birth of an ulcer.

The sheer relief as he patted himself, still whole and alive, faded in place of concern about the noise. He briefly wondered whether the intended recipient of the package was within hearing range.

The noise was probably confined to this level of the canyon. Most people would assume that it was a rock fall or sonic boom. He never even thought about someone at the upper lake. He cut the remains of his rope from leading to the new rock debris, so nothing showed.

He moved out of the box canyon, pausing only briefly to say goodbye to Junior. He was walking quickly toward his camp when he met the couple from the watery escapade standing in the middle of the trail.

"Did you hear that bang?" as though he could possibly not have.

"Yes, apparently it was a big boulder crashing to the floor from up on the wall," hoping they didn't ask how he would know such a thing and how he got there so quickly.

The boy assumed this knowledge immediately, "Yes, that's exactly what I thought it sounded like."

J liked this boy's fresh simplicity. But the girl was frowning slightly so J sought to turn their interest, "Did I hear a shriek and a splash last night?"

The boy was J's perfect foil, "Yes, Marie fell in the lake."

"I was afraid of that and started to investigate, but there was laughter so I guessed that everything was OK," to pour fuel on the fires of distraction.

The girl's frown changed focus. She wasn't quite leaving it; she still had questions, but the reminder irked her.

"Well, it's getting late, and I've got to hike out today. I hope you enjoy this lovely day." This finished it off on a friendly note as J moved along the trail toward the money.

Back at his camp he placed the package and packets of money in the center of the tent next to his backpack. The pack had one big compartment and three moderate ones on the sides and back. The package wouldn't fit in the big compartment. It would have to be broken down and stuffed into the separate compartments. He was not going to panic and rush out of the mountains. He resolved to spend the time for thorough packing. He would break camp carefully and make certain that there was no evidence of who had camped here.

When he broke open the entire front row of the package by ripping the paper from the end the packets of money spilled over the tent floor. It was hard to reconcile the feelings he had as he surveyed the money. The bundles seemed to expand like a sponge when released from the tightly bound package and J had doubts about fitting them all in the backpack. He hadn't given it a thought, but now he was glad that he didn't have a second package.

As he began carefully stuffing the pack he noted different bills. There were many packets of hundreds and an occasional five hundred. He wondered what kind of people carried five hundred-dollar bills. He had never even seen one, and here were hundreds of them. If the average packet was fifties then the total value was in the millions. His apprehension grew. He no longer felt even the psychological security provided by his cozy tent.

J spread his slightly damp rain fly on the ground and emptied his backpack onto it. The clothes, extra food, butane stove and other basic survival gear occupied more than half of the volume of his pack. He mused that survival gear in the future might take the form of more elaborate things.

The extra weight of the money scared him a bit but he would be going downhill. And he was truly motivated. It would be a lot of work --- but damned good pay for the effort.

The cover-up of his trail would begin here. He suspected that it would be just the beginning of a long process. It would be prudent to be extremely careful at this point since any errors now would undoubtedly cause much more effort later.

He went through all the material that had occupied his backpack and placed it in a pile. Anyone finding this cache would know his name from its inscription inside his bulky winter jacket. He realized that even without these connections they would know a lot about him. His size, the stores he frequented and his food and reading preferences. Heck, what about fingerprints? A fire was built and most things were burned. He was made acutely miserable by the odor of his clothing burning. A breeze flowed away from his neighbors camp sites and he was thankful for that.

He moved the pack against a tree and began breaking camp. The tent was unstaked and everything in the camp was dumped into the center. He wasn't going to bother cooking breakfast and he ate all of the dry food he could hold. Dehydrated fruit and some candy were all he could carry in one of the pockets of his army field jacket. The money had not fit entirely in his pack and he was congenitally incapable of throwing away thousands of dollars. About six bundles bulged the pockets of his jacket. He tied up the tent with rope and surveyed the area.

Finally, he threw the tent sack over his shoulder and made his way back up to the area of his find. There was no movement from the other campers. It was still early. It didn't even occur to him he was leaving millions of dollars alone in an abandoned camp. For some reason the hillside, the lake, the cliffs felt serene. Poignant. As if the danger would catch up with him later. Not yet.

He hated to go near the drop site again, but only in this area could he find a safe disposal place for his gear. He found a foot wide crevasse between two huge boulders and dropped the gear to the dark bottom. It shouldn't come to light ever again. The waste of some of his cherished and expensive equipment bothered him. But none of it was worth its weight in twenty-dollar bills.

His pack was where he left it. The sight of it made him think what he would have felt if it hadn't been there. He knew he was going to have some trouble with this. It was making a personality top heavy with 'possession' right now. He shrugged, and got ready to don the pack. He found that the only way he could get it on his back was by setting it on a ledge and backing into it. The pack was well designed and the weight was distributed on his shoulders and hips. Still, this was the biggest load that he had ever carried. He started down.

J paused at the end of the lake and looked back at the primordial stillness of the amphitheater. This would be his last look at this precious place. Always before, he knew that he would be coming back. He supposed that his wife had thought she would return on her last visit here. There was something special about knowing that something will never be seen again.

Movement high on the switchbacks leading to the upper basin caught his eye. A quick look with the binoculars revealed two men with backpacks near the top, rapidly descending . This scene gripped J like a cardiac arrest.

With sudden insight a likely reason for the money drop became clear. Its face value increased significantly by simply moving a hundred miles east across the border. But money could not be transported safely across the border between his state and the next. These men were probably heading for the drop site. They would mean to transport the money back up and then down the remote canyon and across the border without benefit of a custom check. J wondered what they would think of the mess they were going to find. Their presence was terrifying.

A new course was set and he suspected that many old and dear pieces of his life would now change. A fearsome prospect, really. Then he relaxed. This was the same motivation that caused men to happily exchange a plowshare for an army rifle. And many who enlisted sought the perceived adventure. Then he remembered that they almost always regretted it, if they survived.

◆

Movement on the far edge of the savanna jerked him out of his reverie. He reached up and swung down a large pair of binoculars fastened to an expandable arm that held them steady. Peering at the point of a grove of trees a kilometer away, he saw a small herd of impalas grazing in the rain near a large area of trees. Inside the green was a popular watering hole. The line of green brush leading away from the acres of water marked the river from the pond, flowing in J's direction. The green vein on the plain stopped where the river vanished underground after about a kilometer. He followed its invisible course to a point thirty meters away, where it rose from an underground spring and fed another pond in his own oasis.

This water hole was much smaller, about half an acre. It was currently serving the thirst of a cheetah and cub, seemingly oblivious to the rain. The torrents of water plastered their fur to their skin, so they both seemed scrawny.

The pond was too small for the hippos that lived in the big water hole across the plain. Hence it missed the nutrients provided by the dung and occasional dead bodies that made the distant pond a very well fertilized and active ecological niche. That pond was the largest source of water for a hundred kilometers. J thought of it as the zoological garden, since just about every type of animal in East Africa appeared there at one time or another.

The flora lasted longer at the local pond, only succumbing completely to the occasional visit of elephants. But this too was a well-visited watering hole, with all kinds of tracks leading in from both sides. J spent hours watching the animal interactions.

His gaze swung over to a tree where six weeks ago a hornbill had cemented herself inside, leaving a small hole through which the male fed her regularly. J checked frequently for the event of her breaking free from her nest. This morning he saw she had begun, and was now emerging. He watched for an hour as the young chicks inside slowly resealed the hole with slug slime. They would stay there, safe from poisonous snakes, fed by both parents, for four more weeks before beginning the chore of freeing themselves. He kept watching the baby hornbill chicks in their labors until they had reduced the hole to the size of a bottle cap.

He empathized with them, with the comfortable feeling of being enclosed in his own fortress.

If we didn't live venturously, plucking the wild goat by the beard;
and trembling over precipices, we should never be depressed, I've
no doubt; but already should be faded, fatalistic and aged.

Virginia Woolf

Chapter 1.5 The Way Down

It was still early in the morning when he passed through the lower lake campsites. Of the dozen locations there, only one showed any activity. Two men were preparing to move, probably upward, busily breaking camp and looking up to see him only at the last moment. J was making a debonair effort to make the heavy pack seem light. They asked the usual questions about conditions ahead and J cheerfully answered. He waved perfunctorily, unable to raise his arm above his waist for fear of setting himself off-balance.

He returned to a casual pace, at least as casual as was possible with close to a hundred pounds on his back. He sneaked a glance back and was pleased that neither man was looking curiously at his inflated burden. A good thing too, as the twist from the turn in his body unbalanced him, and he lurched like a drunk, saved from falling only by bouncing off a tree. He leaned against the next tree to rest.

Near the foot of the lake he spotted a woman down near the water. He was happy that she was too far away for any interaction. But then he looked up and was startled to catch the full gaze of another young woman. She was silently sitting on a rock participating in the morning scene and evidently curious about passersby. She smiled, J gave his short wave, forgetting his balance problem in a fluster, teetered, recovered and hastened on, impersonating the white rabbit. He didn't look back.

He remembered his theory that these kinds of eye contacts provoked sets of genes that locked the incident in one's memory. She would remember his eyes, probably even the blue color from an across-the-living-room away. He hoped that she was sufficiently interested in his face to not notice the bulges in his pack and field jacket. She would probably remember him most for two things, his lack of balance and his lack of interest in her. Lovely women like that were not used to being ignored. If anyone should ask her 'was there someone with odd behavior' up here, he would spring to her mind quickly.

He thought about the men descending to the valley from above. They were high on the ridge, evidently just beginning their descent, and it was unlikely that they heard the explosion. They would not be anxious and wouldn't reach the money site for an hour. Regular cell phones didn't work up here, although a satellite kit would operate all right at certain times of the day. He hoped that they were unprepared for this what they would find. They would want to return the way they came. Even if they came down his way he had well over an hour head start.

Recalling the booby-trap, he wondered why was there such a lethal trap as protection for just a day? Why had the pick-up team made it so closely after the drop-off? There was probably an interval allowed to make the pick-up and they decided to hit the earliest time? He didn't know it then but the prediction of the arrival of the first big storm, usually not expected for a couple of weeks, had unexpectedly moved up to tomorrow. He had a weather radio that he normally would have checked today but it was residing at the bottom of the canyon. Quite possibly they were two independent units that weren't even in touch. Underground activities tended to work that way. It really made the timing dangerous for J.

He wondered if the pick-up men could even tell if the money was still there, or if a body lay under the big rock. There was a possibility that they couldn't. He supposed they might blow up the rock to see. It would be risky for them to draw that much attention to themselves. There was so much that he would likely never know.

J didn't expect to see the three men who deposited the money since they obviously had no camping gear. The remote possibility occurred to him that they could have been camped here as part of a large group, with others carrying the camp stuff. The idea reestablished the fearful caution that had served him well the day before.

He had three hours of hiking to work on his escape plan. He realized that everyone who visited this region would be suspect. He sifted through his memory to see what things might connect him to this area. There was a signup box at the trailhead. J wasn't inclined to sign in usually. But this time….hadn't he? He recalled thinking that compared to the other problems the hiker was leaving behind for a few days — pollution, rampant crime, economic instability and compounding confrontations in the international terrorist game — signing in and out was a small imposition. He might have fallen down a cliff, after all, and required rescue.

He closed his eyes in a reflective wince as he recalled passing the box and thinking why bother, and then he had signed in anyway, under the same impulse that pushes a dog to urinate on a tree. Now, he really regretted this action. It would be a simple matter for the owners of the money to get the register slips. He would have to get back the slip. That should be simple; it wasn't a locked box.

This led J to his main concern, how to handle the parking lot. The lot was the narrow part of the funnel. It would be easy for someone to maintain a loose check on people entering and leaving the area.

The worst thing was his VW bus, conspicuously parked with his very own vanity license plate. He had been mildly repulsed when he received it as a gift from his prosperous daughter in sales. It was the type of thing that fitted her lifestyle but conflicted with his. She was devoted to making a lot of money. This was not done purely from greed but from a rather sophisticated understanding of the futility of idealism in a crass world.

One thing about the license plate, it was a rather obscure reference to his interest in Cervantes' hero, DONQ. Still, it was memorable, and traceable, and a clue leading directly to him. The car had to be removed smoothly.

By late morning J was in the heavily forested floor as the trail ran beside the creek. In most areas of the country it would be called a river. This Cascades creek was twenty to thirty feet wide and generally uncrossable except for the few bridges and occasional fallen trees. It probably seemed fortuitous to those using a log for a footbridge, as the trail did a couple of times. Considering that the tree probably lasted fifty to two hundred years and trees were continually falling, it was to be expected.

J remembered one spectacular fallen tree near the bottom of the trail. It was a four-foot diameter cedar that spanned the river at a point where it plunged through a gorge fifty feet below. He had always forbidden his athletic kids from crossing it, as it presented its siren call in partial view of the trail. J realized this natural bridge offered a way to avoid the highly visible last quarter mile of the trail, and the spectacle of his overloaded pack and jacket to anyone in the lot.

Rounding a bend, J was startled to face a young man. He was instantly relieved to recognize that the Levis, wool shirt and a bruised nylon pack marked him as Northwest indistinguishable. They exchanged hellos and J discouraged any further conversation by briskly walking by. He was aware that his own appearance was also backcountry modern, but the bulk in his pack and jacket would not escape a prolonged observation.

As soon as the hiker had passed out of sight around the curve, J moved to the side to take a break. The pack was heavy and it was an effort placing it on the forest floor. He didn't want to just drop it. He gently lowered it on a slope by the trail, draped his field jacket over it and stretched out using it as a headrest, looking over his weary feet at the trail.

A few minutes later another young hiker came along closely followed by another. J had tipped his outback hat over his face and feigned sleep until enough time had passed to convince him that there were no more in this party coming along. The mornings were always the busiest time for the trail.

J rolled over and looked around for a ledge to assist in getting the pack on. There were none nearby. He reluctantly put on his jacket. He would have been warm in the jacket alone and considered discarding the wool shirt. There was no question about losing the jacket since it was carrying over a hundred thousand in bills. However, there was no safe place nearby to strip off and ditch his shirt and he was not about to leave his pack near the trail now.

He stood the pack upright on its aluminum frame, sat in front of it and, reaching backward, slipped his arms through the straps. When he tried to stand up the weight made him fall backward. The image flashed through his mind of the monkey trap in India where cashew nuts were placed in a weighted jar with an opening big enough for the monkey's hand, except when it was full of nuts. The monkey was caught when it refused to release the nuts. At the time he had thought it an interesting example of how dumb a monkey could be. But since then he had seen enough analogous situations with human beings to understand that it was a common malady across the board. And here he was in the midst of his very own version.

He lifted the pack like a box in front of him and carried it to a fallen tree that allowed him to get under it. As he shucked on the pack and turned to the trail, there was the fourth, overweight, out of shape straggler smiling at him.

"They get heavy don't they?"

"Yes, they do," answered J, smiling as he walked slowly past him, he added blandly, "Have a nice hike, you're half-way there --- though it gets steeper." The best defense was a good offense. No matter how clever he was many things were going to be unpredictable.

In the lower part of the trail the canyon changed in nature from the sharp V of the past three miles to a broad U. Forests thrived here, providing a canopy a hundred feet above the trail, which became a gentle walk on the spongy pad of a millennium of deposited fir needles. There were only a few campsites cleared near the river in this section. One was occupied by a couple saving the cost of a motel room. J did not have to see them to guess this. No one else used these low camps. This area was a slum compared to what was above. He figured that he was only about a quarter mile from the trailhead.

He soon reached the tree-bridge that he remembered. He had often imagined crossing the various natural bridges, including this one. However, as he actually proposed to do it, what looked easy in speculation became difficult and dangerous in actual intention. The log seemed more slender and at a steeper angle than he recalled. On the other hand, the canyon was not as deep as he had imagined. But it was deep enough to place life in serious jeopardy if he should tumble in.

This was the last crossing point before the sturdy bridge that crossed to the parking lot. That lay in full view of the lot, fifty feet above the river. J considered that he was being too extreme with this measure of caution. The effort seemed to outweigh the chance that an observer was in the parking lot.

But he recalled the cautious nature of the leader around the drop site. It seemed that leaving an observer at the parking lot for a while was consistent. And most of all many tricky decisions were going to come due in the near future; he resolved to always answer them on the cautious side.

He continued walking past the risky log crossing to a point where he could see a piece of the trail below him. He leaned against a tree and listened and watched the trail for two minutes then quickly went back and began his river crossing. He walked the first twenty feet easily. He was a natural athlete and his balance was good. But he was aware of the awkward weight on his back and felt antsy and nervous.

Thoughts of a disastrous slip crept into the corners of his mind, threatening his equilibrium. He had to kneel, and then carefully sit astride the log, slowly scooting along in a sitting position. It took a few minutes and J frequently looked back to see if anyone was passing to witness this apparent folly. Near the opposite side the log widened but began to slope upward toward the exposed roots. He could hear nothing above the roar of the water flowing beneath him.

On his last glance back with a scant two meters to go, he caught the movement of a bright red backpack on the trail not fifty feet below an open spot from which he would be obvious.

He pushed up to his knees and then to his feet with a Herculean effort.

He ran, in what looked like a slow motion replay, a few steps to where he could drop to the ground beside the log. The adrenaline surge had given him strength to move; however the weight on his back made leaping a strictly downward proposition.

His short jump had landed in soft mulch. He twisted to the side so that the weight of the pack struck the ground. But the dirt was loosely laid on a solid slab of granite. The heavy pack made gravity's pull strong and he started sliding backward towards the chasm. He grabbed a bush and then another and wrenched his load under the log, where it caught on a snag.

He was still visible to anyone coming down trail, but fairly well sheltered from those going up except to a backward look. He sifted through explanations for being where he was as he watched the hikers move on up the trail. It they looked back he would present them with an extraordinary sight. The roar of the water masked their steps as he watched them go by. Luckily, they kept their eyes on the ground in front of them, trudging steadily on.

He was going to have to perform a bootstraps pull out of his present position on his own, and before anyone came down the trail. In his jacket pocket was always a short length of strong nylon cord and a Swiss army knife. He fished these out. Tying the knife to the cord end he swung it in a bolo up over a tree branch wedged long ago into the bank when the tree fell. The knife slipped back down to him along the smooth granite apron. He removed the knife, pocketed it, and tied a slipknot on the rope. He thought of it as a rope now, as it was going to have to do a rope's duty.

A tug and a test on the line showed that it was securely anchored to the branch. J tied the other end to the top of his right shoulder strap, slipped his left arm out of the pack strap, wrapped his left hand around the rope and rolled to his right. Now his right arm was free, and he used it to keep a grip on the pack. He inched up, trying to distribute his weight equally between two frail anchors. It worked. He paused only a moment before doing the hard work of hauling his pack up. When he was safely up and over a small ridge, he fell exhausted to the damp forest floor to rest for a few minutes. He felt some imperative to be safely gone as soon as possible.

Two groups had appeared on the trail so early in the morning. He figured that wasn't bad. He checked his watch for the day. Since he had been alone, he often needed to use the day of the week indicator, something he had thought superfluous when the watch was purchased.

It was Friday, and he recalled that this was a three-day holiday coming up. That was why he had originally planned to leave yesterday— to avoid the large influx of people on such a nice weekend. But now that he was off the trail he began to feel grateful for this circumstance. The more people the better for him. He hoped for dozens of prospects in this theft. Unfortunately, the weather prediction was working against him.

His destination was only a half-mile away. Yet off trail hiking in the Northwest was not easy. The fallen timber and undergrowth was densely packed. The carpet of ferns could hide crippling holes, and some plants, like the Devil's club, had sharp barbs. Some areas had to be circumvented as the stinging hairs could penetrate even his tough clothing.

Twenty minutes later he heard a car passing not far in front of him. He found a depression by a log and deposited his pack. Walking to the road he cautiously peeked out of the foliage. The road was clear and narrow with no distinguishing features. J found a branch that was covered with a distinctive chartreuse moss and placed it by the road to add a good visible mark. He went back to the pack and unloaded the bulk of the money into the depression and covered it with debris.

With a light load he made it back to the log crossing in a short time. He waited a minute without seeing anyone before attempting his balancing act across the river. With the money off his back he felt light in spirit as well, and the crossing was relatively easy. He removed his jacket and used it to stuff his deflated backpack before he descended to the bridge that crossed to the parking lot.

There were a couple of groups preparing to hike in, and J dallied on the bridge until he decided that no one would be at the trail box when he arrived. He walked quickly up the steep switchback to the sign-in box. He was about to raid it when he noticed a man sitting about twenty meters away on the tailgate of a pickup truck, gazing steadily at him.

J figured that he could have been looking at him for most of the past five minutes. Even from this distance J could tell this guy was Lean-and-Mean, a universal diagnosis from his sharp features. The steady regard was enough to cause J to continue past the box along the edge of the lot farthest from the man.

He did not look closely at anyone in the groups preparing to go in. He went straight to his beat up van. Opening the sliding door he was happy when there were no signs of vandalism. The local branch of hooligans often visited the temporarily abandoned cars in the hiking lot. The odds were even. The old bus was a relative eyesore and minimized the risk --- even though he wasn't fond of driving it. It was noisy, climbed the mountain like a middle-aged smoker, which it was, and sported high visibility ugly orange. His wife had read that accidents were far less likely with such paint jobs. This time the color might lead to an accident of a different sort for him. J was glad again for the weekend crowd.

He lifted the rear door and tossed in his pack with just the right amount of effort to make it obvious that it wasn't empty, but neither could it contain a few million dollars. He thought to drag a tarpaulin lying in the back out a bit as he casually slammed the rear door down. The license plate was covered. He hoped it wasn't too obvious. As he drove out of the lot he could glance around from within his one-way sunglasses. The man was now looking at a group of young women who were busy signing in.

He turned west on the road and slowed down only after a loud acceleration to fifty-five miles per hour. Almost immediately he spotted the marking branch. It was so obvious it was the type of prized decoration that could have attracted a passing driver. That would have been funny, and time consuming.

There was little shoulder to the road at this point and he had to drive a hundred meters further to park. He sorted through his stash of clothes and emergency supplies in the van and changed into his emergency outfit. It included a large felt Australian outback hat to help disguise him. He was glad he always had his ancient daypack in the car. He filled it with junk from the van including food from a cooler left over from a picnic on the way up. It finally looked like a complete backpacker outfit.

There was also a can of black spray paint in the footlocker. J applied the black mist like cologne to his beard, turning it from brown to an inky black. Dirt to his face darkened his complexion and he was satisfied that he wasn't recognizable as the earlier packer.

He hitched a ride from a young man in a very old, pre-gas rationing, 8-cylinder, 4-barrel, chrome-lined libido enhancer. The man looked sidewise at J's appearance, which didn't do too well close-up. He seemed chagrined when J asked to be let out at the parking lot, after a journey of less than a mile. J wasn't concerned with bad impressions on strangers; he was concentrating on making no impression on the lean-and-mean stranger in the parking lot.

The man who J thought of now as a guard was rummaging inside his truck when he had to walk by. J went on to the trail register box and opened the lid as if he was preparing to sign in. There were several people moving around the lot, probably day hikers, but none were beginning the trail at the moment. J stopped and pulled out a new registration slip. He pretended to sign it, folded it and sneaked a glance back as he placed it in the slot of the box. Lean-and-Mean hadn't emerged so he quickly reached around to the nail inserted to keep the box closed. He had done this before just out of curiosity.

Quickly he rummaged through the few slips, then grabbed them all, squeezing them in his fist, closing the box, replacing the nail and leaving the box in one quick movement.

He moved across the bridge and up the trail before glancing back. What he saw gave him pause. Lean-and-mean was walking down toward the box. J turned back to the trail and moved quickly on. The next juncture where he could look back at the lot was several hundred meters farther on, and what he saw from there rumbled his stomach.

Lean-and-mean and a rather large dog of a noted tracker variety were just leaving the lot, having decided to climb the trail at this moment. Must have some questions to ask. Or maybe he had gotten a satellite phone call. Maybe there was a pincher move afoot. This shot a flood of adrenaline into J's system, which enabled him to move very quickly up the trail to the log bridge.

Fortunately, no one was around at the log crossing. J dug around in the provisions from the van he had stuffed into his pack. He found a peppershaker. There was a half cube of partly melted butter. He moved across the log this time very easily, he was getting good at this. Halfway across he turned and smeared the butter over a smooth, bark free section of the tree. He then liberally sprinkled the pepper over the butter and tossed the shaker into the chasm. He was hoping the combination might give the dog a problem, maybe cause a slip into the creek.

J wasn't waiting around. A glance at his watch indicated that just a little over an hour had passed since his last crossing. He moved quickly but carefully in the same direction as before. If Lean-and-mean was trained as a tracker he would easily follow him, particularly with the dog. As a hobby J had learned to trace the small scuffmark, the bruised limb, and the displaced pebble. This helped him disguise his trail, but he knew it would never fool a talented tracker.

Moving away from the creek, he was making good progress, despite the work of trying to leave an invisible trail. He was distracted and caught his breath when he heard a yelp, and perhaps a scream of anguish.

Lean-and-mean would be mad at losing his dog. J was fairly certain they weren't smoothly crossing the log. Now he could transfer the money to the van. The main threat would be from lean-and-mean trying to work out what J was doing. Perhaps he would figure correctly and run back to search the road. J was getting tired but speed was still essential.

◆

Back at the chasm of the tree crossing, lean-and-mean's dog sat on the steep bank and watched the water crashing over the falls into the pool below. A body bobbed to the surface. J would never know this; weather conspired to keep the body hidden until the next summer. Then it was just a minor back page note in the paper, unnoticed by J.

Meanwhile up in the mountains, the two men from the upper lake discovered the pick-up point mess; with satellite cell phones they had notified bosses in Seattle and put lean-&-mean on alert, sending him to his fate. They passed by the bridge log without seeing lean-&-mean's dog. When they reached his pick-up without seeing him, so they took advantage of the keys left in the car to accelerate rapidly in the direction of Seattle.

◆

The money was hurriedly recovered and loaded in the back of the van. J had just turned the ignition to start the car when he heard a car approaching from his rear. He could never move out in time. Perspiration from a different source now joined the large amount from his recent work as he trained his sight on the rear-view mirror.

His relief was immense when an elderly couple shot by in the left lane without slowing a beat. He whispered thanks to the driver for being his harmless self and for providing vehicle noise to mask his own. He accelerated gingerly to the speed limit and concentrated on the road. There was a juncture only a mile ahead where he would turn to take a little used pass to the south. It would be longer, but not the one a pursuing avenger would take.

No traffic tickets or accidents on this trip. He turned on the radio, shifted the dial until 'King of the Road' appeared. This was a favorite tune. And appropriate. J relaxed and permitted a smile of satisfaction to replace the furrowed brow of the past twenty-four hours. The smile cycled on his face until he drove into his driveway hours later.

When he picked up the newspaper a headline said 'Earliest big snowstorm in decade to hit the Cascades'.

*Believe me! The secret of reaping the greatest fruitfulness and
the greatest enjoyment from life is to live dangerously!*

Friedrich Wilhelm Nietzsche (1844–1900)
German philosopher and poet.

Chapter 1.6 Home

The roof of the van scraped the lilacs and the fir tree branches that formed
a canopy over J's driveway. Even with a fortune in his pack J paused to
survey his own patch of nature — a half acre of it. The abundantly watered
flora of the Northwest formed a wall around his property made of leaves,
pine, fir and flowers.

He hadn't been interested in pruning these past two years. His
passion for natural plants was beginning to wane as he confronted their
inclination to take over. That's probably why they were natural. The ivy,
salud, blackberry, fern and morning glory bindweed would soon be all
there was. The beautiful and expensive nursery plants were all frail losers
in the long run. Except perhaps for the rhododendrons. They stretched and
craned to gain a place in the sun, and set their display every spring. But
even they were hardy only to the degree that they were the native purple.

His wife had coveted privacy, and his instincts responded to planting.
The result was a completely private half acre — a rarity within the city.
He paid the high property taxes to prove it. The patch of land, the view of
the lake and mountains, and his comfortable house were what kept him
here. Within an easy bike ride of the University campus, a short bus-ride
to city center.

He parked on the driveway apron since the van wouldn't fit in the
garage, greeted the old dog, extracted the burglar alarm key from the dog's
house, and leisurely unloaded the car.

Two hours later, he was sitting in the living room, surrounded by a
carpet of green and gray currency. There were large neatly stacked piles
of Andrew Jackson twenties and Franklin hundreds, the most common
currency thanks to money machines. There were also a few casual stacks
of McKinley (five hundred), Cleveland (one thousand) and even Madison
(five thousand). These had been rare since they had all been withdrawn
from circulation in 1969. However, as rampant inflation eroded the
value of the dollar, the hundreds had gained in popularity. And as anti-

counterfeiting techniques were perfected the large denominations were put back in circulation. There were a surprising number of these, all looking fairly new since they had only been in circulation for a few years. There were piles containing a thousand, ten thousand, even some with a hundred thousand in one pile.

Although much of the money looked new, most was used. It weighed in at eighty-seven pounds. He shook his head in amazement at what the adrenaline rush allowed him to carry. The crystal display on J's calculator glowed 3,498,000. He wondered where the other two thousand dollars were, and considered recounting.

J opened the fireplace doors, put in some newspaper, a crushed egg carton and wood. He lit the fire using a twenty-dollar bill to pass the flame. He threw in the spare wrapping, checking for spare bills — a calculated extravagance was one thing, a careless waste, another.

He got a plastic garbage bag and filled it with the money, keeping a few hundred out for his wallet. The bag was stuffed in the wood cabinet just to get it out of his sight. He wanted everything to be the same as it was before this windfall.

Lying on the couch watching the gray lake turning white under a rising southerly wind he tried to recapture the wonderful feeling of contentment that this environment always gave him. To be snug and warm while watching the huge maples and firs dance and bend in the wind and hear the rain against the windows and skylights. After the initial ache subsided J had accommodated fairly well to living alone. This was contentment independent of money and he was glad that he could feel it untainted by the presence in the wood cabinet.

He was a little afraid of this monster. He believed that absolute power absolutely corrupts. He had seen good people turn petty as they accumulated a lot of money. He didn't need much money. He'd never gone out of his way to make a lot of money. So what was he doing risking his contented life for this chimera in the closet?

Of course his generation could afford to be blasé about money. His old house was bought for a tenth of its current value just fifteen years later. It was a readily available middle class acquirement then. Now, people settled for a condominium, some of which he could see in rows far across the lake. Or else couples worked long hours as highly paid professionals to make the house payments on a palatial single family residence in the nearby suburbs. Many of them had the view or a place right on the lake, but only the ultra-rich had this plus privacy.

He was wondering why he had opted to gamble his comfortable life for money that he didn't need. Using this money without arousing suspicion would be difficult. And just thinking about it was already occupying too much of his time.

When the previous owners discovered their loss they would likely be checking for sudden affluence. He went over this possibility time and again and the only link to him compared to the million other people in the area would be the car. He wished he knew whether the man in the lot had recorded license numbers. If they had those they would have a limited number of people to check for large expenditures. He was sorry to expose the others to danger but none of them would be acting like they came into a fortune. If the crooks didn't have licenses they might be looking for an orange van. He resolved to leave the car in the well-hidden yard on his dead end street where it wouldn't be seen even with its high visibility. This was not much of a strain since he rode a bike to work and had a small electric car for shopping trips.

He resolved to hide the money at his house. He had a big house and lots of land. It would have to be a very good hiding place because there was a good likelihood that the losers would burglarize every parking lot participant. That would hardly be noticed in the daily action. In the past twenty years the numbers of jobless and homeless had increased despite the new governments' best efforts in his state. This was simply because they never could address the root reason --- population explosion. The crime from this pool of surplus Homo sapiens had increased even more rapidly. When state authorities declared that they just couldn't keep up and cut back the social service programs --- a supply of poor, disgruntled citizenry had been created. J had to protect the house from random burglary and already had an elaborate system. But he figured that it would be a small deterrent for any visits from the former owners of the money. So he couldn't hide the hoard in the house. He figured correctly.

◆

The doorbell rang. With a quick glance around, J nervously opened the door. He was relieved to see his friend Deman, a neighbor and colleague. Deman was Dean in the college of Arts and Sciences. He had all the accoutrements of his craft; a handsome countenance, bountiful hair now tastefully grayed; he was tall and athletic in appearance.

"Have a seat, Deman. Would you like half a beer?" He made his way to the refrigerator and opened a bottle of the local microbrewery products. Demonstrating restraint was his way of combating the easy availability of liquor.

He glanced at the fireplace. The twenty-dollar bill had been placed on the edge of the fire to watch it burn, and it hadn't burned completely. If Deman saw this he would surmise that something extraordinary was about, since it was so uncharacteristic of him. He quickly thrust the beer into Deman's hands and grabbed a section of newspaper from the table, moved to the fire, blocking the view of the smoldering bill. But Deman was quick and grabbed the newspaper before he could put it in the fire over the bill.

"What's the rush to dump this paper in an already burning fire? Something I shouldn't see?" He took the paper and moved back to his seat, smoothing it out and looking for the article that was about to be censored.

J smiled to himself as he reached in with the poker and stabbed the twenty, now down to its last dollar, into the flames. The skeptical mistrust that he shared with Deman sometimes misfired. Although they were friends and avid conversationalists, they were more opposite than alike. J was nice-looking in a craggy way, a Siberian Husky compared to Deman's Borzoi. J had the lively deep blue eyes, an average nose, full lips that a woman would envy – except for the evident scar on the lower lip where it had met a fist in a teenage rite-of-passage. He had just enough dark brown hair, average height and didn't look particularly athletic. The last aspect was false, as he could run circles around Deman in any sport. And that was fine with Deman.

J settled back into his chair and they talked about the article that Deman was serendipitously reading, on the efforts to diffuse the mayhem in the streets by banning bullets.

Deman began amiably, "Of course anything newsworthy has been long-gone from the newspaper. Way back when the news and entertainment departments overlapped, there was some, but then the entertainment industry won the ratings war, and the news departments were history. I know you fought hard for better news, hell, I may have even written an email in support, but laissez-faire capitalism triumphs over all."

"All includes a lot. Like everthing that makes a civilization viable."

"Civilization seems so fragile. The conservative tide washed away two hundred years of civil liberties and trust in government. The first terrorist strike worked so well into the new administration's agenda that I even thought they might have planned it; finally concluded that it was just dumb luck. Good for the conservatives, bad for the nation --- usually the case. There was positive feedback of the negative slide. Naturally, domestic terrorism rose in defense of terrorism, all heavily armed. Pretty soon one couldn't trust anyone who looked different or had a different religion; or finally, anyone they didn't know."

"Feels like it was yesterday." J stared into the fire.

"You must have been happy when the government became convinced that the people had to be protected from themselves. When domestic terrorists launched random sniper attacks, the lack of any gun or bullet identification — all blocked by the NRA — had made it hard to catch them. So your enlightened liberal government required marking bullets and passed a huge tax on their sale."

J grimaced, anticipating Deman's attack, "Yeah, I was naively happy. But the undermining of our Democracy was too thorough. There is an innate tendency in homo sapiens to fear change."

Deman adds, "To fear death."

"Yes, and get around it by believing in eternal life. But then it was extended to fear climate change, and so deny it." J is always back to fundamentals.

"I accept some of the blame. It was stupid to provoke the gunnuts, and thereby the conservatives. But other factions of the population contributed to the revolution. The gun people had a cozy relation with the religious right — often the same people — and controlled many legislatures. The religious puritan ethic that the country's forefathers had so carefully kept at bay with their remarkable document finally rose and laid siege to the government. It began in the eighties, briefly faltered, then revived in 2000 and exploded as fear triumphed. It cumulated in the appointment of the intellectually challenged majority to the Supreme Court. They blatantly empowered the superrich, who successfully manipulated the conservatives. They had a lock on government. Turned out to be a fatal flaw to our democracy."

"Did you think it was that dramatic? Was it obvious to you? I was a busy grad student and it didn't impact me."

J shook his head, "Nobody saw it. The process took decades. We finally got the records of the big-oil secret meeting of 1978, where they recognized that global warming would cause their business to collapse, decided they needed to suppress all mention of global warming and could only do it by controlling government; and finally formulated an inspired plan to take over the Republican Party via its soft underbelly, the religious right."

Deman was there, "Yes, we know it now; though we hadn't a clue for decades. The anti-war students, liberals all, let the 800-pound gorilla out of the cage."

"But it was not obvious; it just appeared to be a conservative movement. Then a razor thin margin changed the world. One vote on the supreme court in the first stolen election. Then --- we found only years later --- a second election was stolen with manipulation of ballots in brilliantly chosen critical swing states."

"And a third; then a fourth --- it became so easy" Deman was almost proud. "Due to the concentrated political money of the superrich and the deficit education of the electorate. They had positive feedback --- elect a conservative, get more money for the rich, less for education."

J said; "While the dangers of global warming were successfully suppressed for 28 years, it came on like thunder this century, and the general environmental deterioration and "sending our money to middle eastern countries that hate us to build their militaries and fund their wars against each other and then us", became so obvious that the population rose up against big oil, the military-industrial complex and big greed. An intelligent group was elected, but their openness policies revealed the deep sins of the past administrations, the CIA and the military. The damage to our democracy was just too deep and fatal. Conservative reaction was strong and armed. It did become a jungle out there, on the international scene and then down to the local tribal level. Guns were back. Local justice, vigilantes, wanted dead or alive — the Wild West was again the rule."

Deman struck, "Finally, that Supreme Court, with a narrow majority of pedestrian thinkers, did us in. Instead of more regulation of the financial sector we got Corporations recognized as persons, followed by a swing vote of a 'liberal' appointed by a liberal president, abiding by "a higher order", reversing Roe versus Wade, and finally they reversed all bullet banning since 'We have a right to bear arms'. The trigger was pulled."

"What a shallow bunch." J was there.

"Maybe they reasoned: we opened the floodgates of population explosion, we need to free-up a means of population control?" Deman's cynicism was symbiotic with his embrace of the Panzaic Plea. He couldn't ignore the ill effects of the quixotic shortsightedness. "You liberals didn't foresee the cascade effects. The new congress thumbed their nose at the

Supremes by passing a gun law. Then the NRA was able to convince its members to boycott the government — to not pay taxes. When their fines mounted, their spines stiffened and they led a well-organized national movement to refuse to pay taxes. It was a bad example. Other segments of the society stopped paying taxes that helped support the latest Mideast oil war, the military, abortions, genetic research, climate research, foreign aide, and every picayune function of government. And then we just followed the example set by the Soviet Union and split into parts."

"Yeah. We got a revised states' alignment with a weakened national government still in charge. Some semblance of stability was retained." J was grateful for small benefits.

"But it is an undereducated, fearful, conservative society out there." Deman slapped the newspaper article as if to punish it for the stupidity.

J returned to the good aspects, "At least there was little bloodshed. We divided on logical, ideological lines. We got to change our name away from the confusion with Washington, D.C." Such a little thing to be happy about, but in the present world liberals had to grasp at small things.

Deman tilted the empty beer glass to his lips again, frowned and quickly got up. They were frequent verbal combatants with a relaxed friendship. Deman knew his way to the refrigerator where he proceeded to get himself another, full beer. "You're sure digging deep to find some good. Many felt Cascadia was chosen to highlight the huge mountain range that constituted the boundary between the West and the Midwest."

"Could be. Voters here were never completely logical. At least this region was still a ways from anarchy — but it was peeping over the horizon like a polar bear on the old pack ice." J recalled those days well. He and Deman were most comfortable when engaged in bantering reminiscence.

But that was in the past now. J continued, "At least after the break-up of the country it was easy here compared to other states where the fear and ignorance triumphed. There they blame science for the failure to maintain a great civilization. Education became the whipping boy while concepts in evolution, genetics and biology were suppressed as they strained to maintain a past that plagues them."

Deman nodded, "They hate their life and yearn for a better after-life. At least they have hope if not education."

J shook his head at the futility of it. He was a bit amazed at his ability to concentrate on this philosophy without being distracted by the fortune in the closet. Now the thought struck him that his newfound cache might let him escape this stalemate and the concurrent decaying culture and environment. He bid Deman good night and retired to begin thinking about it.

◆

The grumble of the rain had become a roar as the storm front passed the Tree. The air was so thick with water that he could no longer see very far. J pushed a button on the console by the chair and camouflage covers slid over the windows. He rose and with a slight push the chair swung to the side, revealing a spiral staircase. He bounded down a steel frame cylinder through an area used for storage. A second spiral stair passed through his bedroom. Finally he arrived at the kitchen, still over twenty feet above the ground.

This room, like the library and the bedroom, had circular windows — tinted glass covered and black now, and slanted ceilings for the top two feet with occasional sections of window glass. The glass was camouflaged most of the time by the outer cover that moved electronically, or from backup cranks in the wall. They were opened only by a process that included checking the outside through small portholes, then a single open slit, and finally only a few could be opened at once. The delays were built in to waylay any of his impatient inclinations. They also closed automatically if there was no sign of his body heat in the room for more than five minutes. It was possible to over-ride these automatic defenses with switches that were on identical consoles in every room.

J followed the slow window opening process, finally exposing a large square of window looking at the pond. The slanted upper windows served as skylights, now covered with rivulets of rain. He grabbed a packet of dehydrated soup, dumped it into a cup of water and put it into the microwave. Lunches were usually this type of fast food. He reserved gourmet cooking for dinners.

Sitting on the stool at the table that was a shelf in front of the window, he could see the waterhole where some gazelles had replaced the cheetahs, drinking unmindful of the downpour.

When his lunch was done, the dishes found a place in the compact dishwasher in the center of the room. J went into the downward spiral stairs. This time he dropped over thirty feet through steel framework with color-coded pipes exposed up the sides and center. He was several yards below ground when he entered the 'gym'.

There were two workout machines, a treadmill, and electronic and mechanical arcade games, a shuffle board and strangely, a bridge table, covered in green felt, with a lovely green glass shielded light suspended above at about eye level. There were four chairs, as though waiting on a foursome for bridge.

J headed for this table. He felt like a game of bridge. Hoping he would draw a decent partner this time. He cut the cards, placing each on a rectangular glass scanner in front of the four stations. "J plays with Marilyn, against Michele and Marie" intoned an electronic voice.

He dealt the cards; real cards. He could have programmed a random dealer and visual display, but derived pleasure from the tactile sensations. He placed each card face down on the scanner so the computer could read it. A lively game began.

J won easily and reflected that he hadn't reprogrammed this computer for a while. He had read a few more books on bridge so that by now he had an advantage over his own expertise of a year ago. He was getting better. Needed better competition. He resolved to bring the computer program up to his present level as soon as he had a spare afternoon.

He walked to the other end of the room, opened a soundproof door and went down a straight staircase, into the 'engine' room. A large door stood to the side at the bottom of these stairs, for waterproofing the room in case of a flood. It had never been needed but once J had closed it to button up the room as a precaution when the river was flooding the plain unusually high. That day the river had emerged above ground for the entire distance as it crossed the plain. At the high water mark the river had lapped at the bottom of the Tree.

Most of the time the plain was hot and parched. But in the rainy season, because he was within thirty miles of the plateau leading up to the high mountains, an unseen rain in the mountains could swell the river quickly without prior warning. Once or twice a year it would pop out of numerous cracks in the savanna and in a moment becomes a wide river several feet deep. Caution was advised as the rise was as quick as a man could run, the current was swift, and there were numerous predators working the fringes for the drowned or hapless creature trapped in mud. The water drained quickly, usually within an hour.

J found that the best way to guess when the water would rise was to observe the animals. They seemed to know what was going to happen, probably from superior hearing ability, possibly from some other sensing connection not available to their human neighbor. He was becoming an expert on the animals — prudent knowledge for his position in the scheme of things- sometimes predator, sometimes prey.

Part II Life on the Edge

And that inverted Bowl we call The Sky, Whereunder
crawling coop't we live and die, Lift not thy hands to It
for help—for It Rolls impotently on as Thou or I.

Omar Khayyám (1050?–1122),
The Rubáiyát of Omar Khayyám (1859).

Ch 2.1 A Class in Fluid Dynamics

It was three years after J's heist of the money. He was beginning to feel confident that the former owners of the money had discovered no connections to him. After the first few nervous weeks he had slowly begun to relax. He thought the only way he could assure his innocence in case there was some obscure connection was to act exactly as if it hadn't happened.

His life style was identical to before. The money was hidden carefully on his property. It was clear that he lived totally within his means.

The college campus where J worked was a beautiful place; insulated from the surrounding bedroom and business communities. It was landscaped Northwest natural with English gardens tucked in here and there. There was still open space. Broad meadows were interspersed with tracts of rhododendrons reaching for the rationed sun beneath groves of fir and cedar. The smell of cedar was strong as thousands of students trod the shortcuts through fresh-clipped lawns. Ten million red bricks artfully arranged into paths and planters, walls and buildings. There was an ethereal comfort connected to the gothic design of multi-paned and leaded windows with soaring rooflines above. Older buildings sometimes merged into modern additions in a fairly reasonable way.

Hanging overhead like a vulture there was always a crane or two. The building program was incessant, befitting one of the state's most successful businesses. The campus was really beautiful decades ago.

From an open window high in one of the older buildings J's voice could be heard. "And so they gave it a wavelength and a period and named it a gravity wave. It was born out of disorder but, having been described, could no longer be called turbulence." There was a strong accent on the next to last word.

"Why a gravity wave?" From the class.

"I don't know. I suspect it is because the motion is perpendicular to gravity so it was assumed, correctly, that gravity must play an important role in keeping the wave motion going up and down. Consider an ocean wave. Now that's a gravity wave familiar to us all. When a name relates to a familiar property then it has a good chance of catching on. It doesn't need to explain anything. This is just another case of form over substance."

"If it's popular why don't we use it?"

"We are not going to be satisfied with just a name in this class. We question where the wave came from, what caused it, and check the mathematics to see if gravity is crucial or just peripheral. Here we always want to know the physical reason behind the observed wave, or any phenomena for that matter."

The same voice, low-pitched, but definitely feminine — sultry was the term that registered in J's mind — persisted, "OK. What's the reason behind gravity?"

J became alert to his questioner. This was a provocative, even aggressive query. It was unusual in these classes. The inquisitor was vaguely familiar. In fact, he only now recognized her as his own new graduate student. This wasn't so strange — first year graduate students were totally occupied with classes and seldom interacted with their research professors. Her gentle smile diffused the aggression in the questions. A classic face bore the burden of distracting beauty.

J had to kick-start his brain to get on with the answers. "I don't know. But I don't feel bad about that since no one else does, either. They are spending a lot of time and money over in physics explaining gravity in terms of relativistic space if you are really interested. Einstein's general theory gets you half way there. If that doesn't do it, try the math department and string theory."

J directed his words toward his student, "But your point is well made. There is always a level where our knowledge just doesn't allow us to see any deeper into the basic reason behind things. At that point we must assume some hypothesis. Pluck it out of the ether."

"That sounds risky."

"It is. But that's not a problem. Try everything. If it doesn't work, toss it."

J needed to elaborate; students expected it. "Remember that we're not working in a complete vacuum. We try to choose a hypothesis that relates to something that has been observed. For instance, a few observations suggested the first law of thermodynamics and it was easy to design experiments to test this assumption. Then, each time it was successful in describing or predicting an observation it merited a bit more faith. Only after a century of reinforcement did it secure a reservoir of faith sufficient to call it a law."

"Do you mean that our laws are faith-based?" His student Kay arched her eyebrows.

"Yes I do. That's a risky admission because of the misuse of the word faith. I use it to indicate 'an acceptance of relative certainty'. There's never a total faith. We have to remember — constantly remind ourselves — that everything is built on a basic assumption that may be wrong. Most certainly it is wrong at some point. And when that assumption fails we can graciously switch to a new hypothesis." J often rises to the bait.

Like most students she wanted to be told the truth by her instructor — given a firm foundation from which to build a better future. Her comment was slightly petulant. "So even our laws are not absolute?"

"Right. As far as we know there are no absolute truths, only relative truths. We just hope that one holds well enough in the domain of our applications so we can use it to our advantage. Consider, it's not unlike any other business gambling on a new invention or a software program."

"How do I gamble on gravity?" Kay had picked this day to make herself known to J.

He smiled. "For our purposes we will bet that gravity as proposed by Newton is a good enough hypothesis to get us to our next goal. In the case of a rocket scientist that would be that a missile would land within a ten feet of the target a thousand miles away. In your case a successful theory that leads to a thesis. In my case a text book on dynamics. In my son's case the bottom of the hill in the next Slalom ski race."

"I like that." She could smile at the success of her foray.

"Gravity is simply defined as a constant of proportionality that occurs in Newton's Law for motion. So far, it has worked pretty well in geophysics. Fortunately, in this class we don't have to mess with general relativity, quantum mechanics or string theory."

The students relaxed. They didn't have to memorize philosophy. They appreciated the break as long as it wasn't too long. They knew that they couldn't be tested on philosophical musings, and J was frequently distracted in this direction.

True to form J continued, "Too many people start their analysis of a problem by beginning at a high level of derived knowledge and thereby assuming the considerable baggage of other, often second rate, hypotheses. Much of the published work from academia is started right at the top, where the last analysis — often that of the author's professor — left off. We get a small perturbation on a small perturbation ad nausea.

"This has led some pundits to claim that most academic publications are simply imitations of previous work. I won't let you get away with that, which means that you have to get scientifically fundamental. Your workload is going to be large. On that happy note class is adjourned."

Amongst the students filing out, a young man jostled a classmate; "For an expert in the field he certainly begins a lot of answers with 'I don't know'."

"Yes. He is hard to pin down and addicted to bullshit. He talks like the whole scientific establishment is a house of cards ready to tumble down when some genius blows. I've just got to get him specific enough for me to begin on a thesis topic before that happens." The second student was the source of the questioning voice, emanating from a very feminine face — small precise nose, dominating green eyes under sharply defined eyebrows, a ready-to-pout mouth and a delicate chin with perhaps a hint of an overbite — atop a feminine body that couldn't be hidden despite dungarees and a fashionable rugby shirt.

Her friend peeled off while she continued down the hall to catch J. "Professor J, will you be able to look at my outline of possible research topics this afternoon?"

J was startled. First-year graduate students were universally consumed with preparing for the end-of-the-year exam that would determine their academic future. He usually had to coax thesis prospects out of second year students. "Yes, of course. But I will have to cut it short to prepare a lecture for the 'Friends of the Faculty' dinner tonight."

"I saw that announcement. You're going to talk about 'The Environment, Chaos & Complexity'. How erudite." This was said with that same smile to soften the possible sarcasm.

"And probably misleading. No one there will understand much about these topics. That's fortunate, since I don't know much myself. I have a bit of work to do to fluff out the bit of substance with entertaining bon mots. But I would much rather look at your stuff."

J winced inwardly at this. He was quite aware of the double entente that flowed when interacting with female students. Generally, he just relaxed and tried to ignore them. His students quickly learned to attach no importance to them — whether they would be offended by them or happy to pursue them. It was never obvious that J was aware of them; although they could be reasonably certain that he was, with faculty information sheets full of "sexual harassment guidelines." He had carefully read them but lost interest when he found that they were not guidelines on how to do it. They were a subset under the University rules for 'politically correct/ incorrect statements. These tracts had many of his colleagues feeling that their lectures, papers and even their conversations were in straitjackets. J chose to disdain the dialogue; feeling that what is said will be interpreted according to the situation, by the people involved, colored with their own agendas.

"I've heard you called an expert on chaos theory." She vaguely remembers that maybe it was J himself who provided the opinion.

J smiled. "The trouble with chaos is that it has no principle. It is a misnamed phenomenon. It isn't even new. I recognize old stuff from nonlinear stability theory with new names. Its popularity with the public came from a movie director who gleaned some scientific insights from it and made it a celebrated cause in a popular movie about cloning dinosaurs in a Jurassic Park. I'm not complaining; there is a lot of value in this process. For one thing, it made it easier to get our last grant.

"Anyway, most science has an innate fascination waiting to be revealed. The problem is that scientists don't know how to celebrate it. The unfortunate result is they can't sell it to the public. I really can't understand why everyone doesn't want to learn science."

K was sympathetic to the feeling, but easily understood the why. "It has a bad reputation of being very difficult — all that math and stuff. Maybe they don't need to know the basics of anything, let alone chaos theory."

J registered that she was provoking another philosophical discussion. He continued, "OK, if you're really interested, I'll ramble on, because it is helping me create tonight's lecture. The Chaos concept is a manipulation of turbulence theory. Strangely enough, it describes order amongst disorder. So it has a lousy name. It is a semantic laundering of well-known mathematics processes for instabilities and nonlinear solutions. It is full of sound and fury, signifying nothing.

"Now the more honest study called 'Complexity' is a well-named concept. It is what chaos should have been called. The phenomena in question are complex and ordered, but not chaotic. And there we are again, the naming word is so important." They had reached J's office.

Kay nodded, as if she understood his thoughts. "Sounds like you can just use one of your class lectures."

He shook his head. "This is different from a class of graduate students.

Sometimes a layperson unrestrained by a hierarchy of knowledge on the subject can ask a crucial question that exposes a superficial premise. She just needs to be mildly intelligent and possess abundant self-confidence.

"My audience tonight will be comprised of contributors to the University. Not necessarily correlated with university education or even graduates. But they are all rich. My bias expects their knowledge to be broad, not necessarily profound and usually lacking science. That's fertile ground for growing over-confidence. The familiar barriers of classroom timidity and fear of saying something stupid will not be present. The rich do not get intimidated even when they should."

Kay knew more about this than J could imagine. "So you are going to be careful and entertaining."

J smiled at her insight. "Yes, that is what it is all about. Since you aspire to this profession, it's not too soon to realize this fact: Success depends on an ability to entertain.

"The professor is motivated, rewarded, and paid to stand before other members of his species and entertain them. I don't denigrate this. In fact, it might be the most fundamental accomplishment desired or attained by Homo sapiens — performing before fellow members of the species. Probably just an elaboration of the mating ritual."

Kay said, "Of course athletes, priests and show people do that pretty well. They get a lot of reward from our culture." She had abilities in these disciplines and had thought about the possibilities.

"You're right on that. And the professor and the politician don't even readily admit to pandering to this basic stimulus. But they do." J was pleased with this conversation. "So it should not be too difficult to use this rather catchy term, chaos, to describe our ineffective efforts at managing environmental/cultural decay in the past few decades."

She nodded as she took the seat facing his desk. Such statements were a given these days. No one questioned the obvious fact that Homo sapiens had botched the job of maintaining a decent ecological balance and that the disastrous cultural aberrations that currently played across the planet were somehow related.

"OK, but before you get into it, how about giving a quick look at this idea and tell me if I know enough to begin the problem."

"Of course." J kicked himself for not showing proper interest. The professor-student relationship was a delicate, carefully cultivated partnership. J painstakingly selected the students that he agreed to support. It took about six years if they finished the program, a considerable investment.

This particular student had all the basic background that J looked for. She survived well in a good school to attain a respectable degree in physics. Her graduate record exam scores, which J treated as simply an advanced aptitude test, were excellent. Most importantly, she had been out in the world working, getting mature, and had exceptional letters of reference.

He remembered now a phrase used in one reference. "Surprisingly mature intelligence coming out of such a youthful, attractive person." Physical attributes were universally deemed irrelevant and any reference to them suggested they were really worth mentioning. This same professor had also remarked that he had offered her an opportunity at his school for graduate work. J wondered if the implied sexual appeal had influenced his decision to ask her to stay.

He looked again at this student. She had been here half a year and he had only spoken to her personally a few times, generally motivational, as she followed the usual regimented course to the gigantic exam at the end of the year. It was time to get to know her.

He uncharacteristically continued eye contact. This was enjoyable. She looked back, probably realizing that this was the first time he had actually looked at her without complete academic detachment. She had learned that such gazing bouts inevitably worked to her advantage.

J diffused the moment, "Let's see if this is worth pursuing," as he picked up her work. He was grateful to see her name on the paper since it had escaped his memory.

As he read the outline his nods and smiles gave Kay some confidence that he liked it. But then he said, "Congratulations, all you have to do is inflate this succinct outline into a sesquipedalian, sonorous production to assure that your PhD is in the bag."

She wasn't yet familiar with J's sense of humor. Since she turned red and seemed about to explode, J quickly added, "Just kidding. It is a well thought out proposal. Not pedestrian, but not too exciting. It will be a good topic to pursue and I'm confident that you'll avoid those pedantic adjectives."

"They're not part of my bag. My father taught me to cut straight to the essence, fill in the details later. I've been able to focus sharply since I learned to walk at ten months. So don't worry about padding."

"OK." J resolved to reign in his wry humor when dealing with this young woman. He handed the outline back to her and seemed to turn his attention to his desk.

She might have liked to continue the conversation but was grateful to end on a high note. She felt guilty about imposing on his time and quickly departed.

The words for the lecture flowed smoothly into J's computer. Several trips to stored files rounded out the lecture. Then, a search through his files of overhead slides provided the visual imperative, and essential crutch — perhaps simply as an excuse to turn out the lights. This, and a resolve to not drink too much wine this evening and J was ready for his talk.

Ch 2.2 Lecture to the Lions

The campus at night; the faculty club is warmly lit; old, wood and elegant. Old is revered at the University. J had mixed feelings in the case of the campus design. The traditional old gargoyles depicting academics that graced the library buttresses were dear. The modern new glass and concrete buildings were relatively cold and ugly.

Despite a reputation for liberal thought amongst the general population the institution is a bastion of conservatism, in its architecture and many of its intellectual attitudes. Conservatism had its usual effect; it was a great leveler and competent mediocrity was served.

Fortunately there existed a tradition of tolerance for the eccentric. J felt that it was these people less encumbered by tradition, often dismissed by the outside culture as mentally bushwhacked or 'bipolar-disordered', who might be able to see the flaws in the present and divine the future — and thereby have a chance to improve it. This tolerance was the saving refinement of the institution. As usual he found himself on both sides of the conservative/liberal dichotomy.

Ivy blanketed several of the buildings. J hated it as an invasion, but appreciated the color briefly when it turned red in the first fall chill. Then it merged with the wood and bricks like veins of blood. Ivy was lovely when tightly controlled as it was here. They had tamed it to be innocuous nine tenths of the year and brilliant at Showtime in the fall. Ivy is like Homo Sap, J thought, using his fond nickname for the species. He was always looking for metaphors for the human dilemma. Someone took the care to thin the ivy or it would leave behind the esthetic complimentary role and smother the building. What will do the thinning for Homo sapiens smothering earth?

♦

There is periodic laughter from within the faculty club this evening. The audience and J are having a good time so far. "So we have looked at the math concepts of Chaos and Complexity from the perspective of Cervantes' characters Don Quixote and Sancho Panza. We have looked at the environmental degradation of the past decades as being so pathetic that it was laughable. That's what you have to do with pathos, laugh and forget, or be profoundly pained. We have chosen to laugh, but let's spend the last few minutes thinking about what we, you and I, have gotten ourselves into.

"This quandary in which the world finds itself seems to be mostly caused by us, the dominant species. We are the significant perturbation that is upsetting the global balance and possibly sending the world equilibrium toward another chaotic state. We prefer the state that we are in because we have invested our wealth, our culture and our survival in this specific environment. We've been nurtured within it for thousands of years. But we can see that we are overloading the system. It seems to be adjusting.

"Currently Homo sapiens' main importance in the ecosystem may be his tendency to destroy species. In this we are following one of my favorite mottoes: a thing worth doing is worth doing well. We're doing it so well that historians recognize the unprecedented mass extinctions of species brought about by us as the end of an era. We are even more potent than a two-megaton meteor strike.

"But it kind of gets you in the ego when destruction is your forté."

J was impressed with his audience's attention. He figured that they had come prepared for a lecture, tanked up on coffee, and were being polite. Like when they went to church.

"Of course we would like to proceed under an assumption that Homo sapiens are a particularly valuable item in the store — we assume that the store is useless if it doesn't stock this item. You are all willing to make that assumption, right?" Sure they were, but he couldn't avoid expressing his opinion. "I might note that I think that it is a far out notion requiring some kind of leap of faith, but I'm willing to make it, as a hypothesis.

"Of course there are liabilities even where we have the best or the most. We are master of the territorial imperative, breeder magnum opus, powerful brain-stem virtuosos with potent opposing cerebral hemispheres and carry a big reproductive tool. We suggest that God is great — and he looks just like us.

"I know, many of you are saying, 'but these are our assets, not our liabilities'. I'll agree with that. But maybe this is a case of 'too much of a good thing.'

"The need for territory to call our own is motivating, and satisfying, but incompatible with a successful dense-population sociology. It motivates us toward construction of elaborate habitat and to war to defend it. There is no more satisfying feeling than being ensconced in a secure fortress. But we want to share it, even advertise it — a mating incentive. We are in extreme competition over limited space, a solitary nesting animal that is tending toward a beehive type habitat.

"We are certainly the most successful breeders on the planet. In the early days this wasn't a problem, probably even a necessity when we were sharing habitat with saber-toothed tigers. But it has lately – in the last millennium — become a liability. The existing methods of population control — war, pestilence and natural catastrophes, are a rather unsatisfactory condition."

"Don't forget the fourth characteristic." From a stylishly dressed young woman.

"Yes. I can't forget it. We've the biggest penis for our body size. I suppose many will have difficulty seeing why this is a liability. I put it in the same class as the Peacock's tail — potent in the mating ritual but a drag to carry around.

"Finally, there's our flagship characteristic, our brain. In it resides our egotistic overconfidence. Let's get great things done, we say, and do. But it's usually done under an illusion of what's great and often yields an unexpected result. What's great on the short time scale may be catastrophic on the long time scale. A basic Don Quixote mistake.

"The make-up of the brain has to be our singular asset, but therefore it has to be blamed for our failures too. The terrorists' use their brain to destroy or damage huge numbers of their species."

J was pleasantly surprised at the interest in his audience. They were smiling at times and actually nodding in agreement. He was ready to bail out at any time that he felt they were restless but it didn't seem that that time had come yet. He knew that it would.

He was inspired to describe the institution that they were supporting in a way they had probably never heard. Certainly not from the administration. "Let's consider this situation some more. Many people feel that here in academia is a citadel where the intellectual attainment of Homo sapiens prevails.

"I'm here to tell you it isn't necessarily working. The University was supposed to provide a nurturing environment for the cerebral aspects of the brain, and for the innovative ideas that at times can spring forth from this audacious orb. There is evidence that this is not being done very well. And I'm not even talking about the fact that the biggest and most expensive building is the football complex and the highest paid faculty member is the coach.

"The power of the brainstem function has made insidious inroads here. Sometimes we are limited even more than elsewhere because of our respect for tradition and pomp. Many of the major breakthrough concepts have arisen outside in the free market. The transistor, computer, internet and multi-level-marriage ideas all came from independent thinkers in the market driven sectors." They should love this, thought J, and indeed many of the Captains of industry were nodding.

That seems to have gotten their attention. They don't expect me to tear down my own house. He had more. "Memory banks are god. But brain cell bulimia keeps the mind slim. Imitation of what's been done in the past and what is expected of a tightly controlled future keeps it narrowly focused. Also, the inane cultural bias toward the physically big or beautiful prevails here too. Our deans are tall with bountiful hair. They build buildings, not ideas." J gave a glance at his friend Deman, dean of his college, sitting in the front row to the side. He was holding his beautiful head of hair and looking down.

"It has been a long time since the dominant forces in our culture have been bothered by or even noticed a university intellectual. The conservative forces noted the liberal bias in academia and successfully emasculated its influence by the turn of the century. The independent thinkers still exist – in their safe ivory towers. And they frequently predict the calamities that befall our society; like the inevitable failure of military intervention in the Middle East, the inevitable economic crisis of lassaiz faire capitalism, and the likelihood of revolution when the ratio of rich to poor increases for long periods. Not to mention the obvious global warming calamity. But they are ignored. Currently, they're irrelevant to societal changes.

"But at least the respect for the higher cerebral functions hangs on at the University --- by its fingertips. The University is the main place where science is sometimes allowed to flourish unfettered by material justification. Yes, we study obscure topics, like the mating habits of the gibbon — and learn valuable insights about humanity. What seems obscure can have profound applications. Knowledge of a certain fungus leads to penicillin. Ignorance of this leads to clear-cutting of the forests from whence it and the next antibiotic are obtained. Studying ants leads to the understanding of their critical role in the ecosystem and the understanding of biology in society.

"Of course there are limitations. Even I might question a study of the sex life of a ping-pong ball. But the point is that the ultimate value of what is studied is often not apparent. Serendipity must be a modus operandi. Unfortunately it is difficult to append to a proposal for funds."

And now thought J, I'm going to discuss another innate premise of these beautiful people. "Outside the University our society gives large rewards to the beautiful people and those who entertain them. A genetic emphasis is placed in this evaluation. As a result people are getting better looking, taller, and more athletic. We are producing superior singers, musicians and specialized athletes. In short; we are in general terms, sexier. Now you are thinking, 'What's wrong with that, I like it.'

"Well, I like it too. But these are all meretricious characteristics, useful in the mating game but of little value for survival of the species into the next era. This is too much the 'fitness' that Darwin talked about --- that of producing more progeny. The thing that makes us 'fit' is success at attracting a mate and reproducing.

"Oh, the others still can breed, though they must be clever. This is fortunate since the genes still need the diversity. Almost incidentally the genes that favor good brains also manage to survive. This may be the thing that makes us long-term fit. The university is a good place for the skeptics with the burden of Quixote's mantle to seek refuge from a crass, simplistic culture. It serves like the medieval monastery storing the books for the future despite the fact that almost no one in their cultures could read. People did learn to read. Maybe it's not too much to hope that someday they will learn to read science and learn to think beyond their immediate space and time."

J was carefully watching his audience now. These were provocative statements and the prevailing good mood could easily turn. He didn't see any outward signs of hostility. So now he was going to push it. "However, the current trends indicate that Homo sapiens hasn't learned to contemplate broadly enough for the species to survive. And as long as the universities have been corrupted by the baser motives of our culture funding for the real thinkers will remain few and far between.

"They must hide, since their real thoughts brand them instantly as misfits and often block the career roads paved with conformity. What we need is a new university free from these bonds. I have a format if anyone has the means." There was general laughter, mainly because everyone needed relief from this pounding. Deman looked particularly excruciated.

"In the right environment the brains might develop in their sanctuary, and someday they might break out from that university into the general culture. Homo sapiens will then have a chance to seek its destiny." Simply put, this was J's goal in life — looking for just such a chance.

Now it was obvious that there was disagreement shown by stares and glances at watches. Well, no matter, J's mission was not to find agreement, but to plant a tiny seed of doubt in this complacent comfortable class.

"The current situation has the University harboring pragmatic Panzas and idealistic Don Quixotes. They are not the real Sancho Panza, who is more in touch with his native impulse. Nor are they real Don Quixote, who honestly believes in the righteousness of his cause. The imitators are armed with proper credentials, guided by public opinion polls, motivated by self-serving ambition, directed by the establishment. And, like Don Quixote, they often leave in their wake a situation far worse than before their arrival.

"These people have marched under the banners of many religions, communism, supply-side economics, laissez-faire capitalism, and sundry simplistic polyisms." There was a stirring in the audience; scattered laughter seemed to be of the nervous kind. J noticed a young man sitting in a side seat who nodded seriously. He tried to determine through the man's horn-rimmed glasses whether he was simply sleeping.

"You would have thought that after the failure of Communism and then the crash of unfettered Capitalism, both impaled on the horns of an idealistic concept of Homo sapiens' character, we would have taken heed. No, Don Quixote always picks himself up, battered and bruised, and then moves on before the tenuous system that he erects catches him in its collapse."

The silver-maned gentleman in the first row asked a question. "You say you have a format to remedy this?"

J recognized that it was time to inject some hope. "In the debris of lost cultures, indeed in the nooks and crannies of academia hide a very few really sharp Sancho Panzas. They find practical solutions. Like the Good Soldier Sweik, who played dead immediately when confronted with combat, they've learned the art of hiding their attitude and knowledge so they don't stand out. They have the idealisms too — but they have tempered them in the cauldron of the real world. They know and respect the limitations of Homo Sapiens as the building material for social solutions.

"These people suggested the solutions to avoid all of our ecological disasters years before they became crises. They are often scientists because science is a perquisite. But they are often without the combined essential features of bureaucratic entitlement — height, hair, sonorous voice box, good connections and an aura of certainty. The last is the essential virtue of those perceived as knowledgeable. Both the bureaucrats and the public take its absence, an attribute of Panza, as a sure sign of weakness.

"Perhaps it is necessary to completely redesign the University environment before meaningful intellectual progress can be made."

The questioning Captain clearly wasn't satisfied, but J noted that the young man on the end of the row was definitely nodding agreement. It was particularly notable because most head motion was in another direction. At this point J took his own advice and finished with a caveat to ameliorate the antagonistic feelings, "Please accept these speculations for what they are, polemical theories meant to stimulate the gray matter, on the cutting edge where we want to be this evening, and possibly wrong. Any questions?"

The myopic young man who nodded had the first question, "If the solutions to our problems are already known by the scientists as you say, why haven't they been enacted?"

J was grateful for this question. He had pondered the answer long and hard. "Knowing the solution is only half the problem, marketing it is the other half. I think this is well known to most of you here. The marketing department needs to be as big as the research department. Here, it doesn't even exist.

"The innovators can only develop and promulgate their ideas away from the well-regulated mainstream media. The media is preoccupied with popularity, a great leveler of culture, and generally unable to understand science. Consequently the solutions to environmental disasters haven't been understood, publicized or enacted soon enough.

"But the solutions have always been there, sitting on the shelf. They usually contain changes that are anathema to the voters. These include increased taxes for infrastructure, universal health care, environmental regulation and protection, and at least double the education budget, with an emphasis on universal scientific literacy."

J critiqued himself. "Wow, talk about Don Quixote. I can't spell it, but I am one. Still, remember, we need both, the spiritual vision of Quixote and the earthy wisdom of Panza.

"The public can be swayed by a smooth talking scoundrel to buy almost anything, from a swamp to a war. This has been our experience.

Unfortunately, we just haven't found enough scientists with charisma who could sell the scientific method. Apparently it is too much work to develop a scientific capability and a political touch. So the solutions just sit there unused."

The Captain Silver head of industry injected a question in a commanding voice. "Why is science so important? It could just be a source of facts and figures to be used by those skilled in politics and marketing. The scientist is just another of the many staff experts with another piece of information for the leaders of society."

J smiled at the supercilious insult in the question. It was a fair counter to his own pompous position. "Yes, in our culture we have usually gone under that assumption. It was worth trying. Scientific advisors are the closest we've come to integrating science into government. Some measure of this attempt has been a facet of many failed cultures. The problem is, the advice is often not understood, frequently ignored, and in the case of global climate change, suppressed. When it was addressed by an enlightened president, it was disastrously compromised by anti-tax elements in congress. As a result of the misapplication by people who didn't understand the science the long-term consequences of most scientific development has been a greater unforeseen disaster down the line." J realized that such elements were sitting in front of him.

"What hasn't been tried is for the leaders themselves to be socially and scientifically adept. The need is the same as that perceived by Plato with his philosopher king. But in the intervening millennium the need has become for a philosopher/scientist king. The science part is to ground the philosopher in reality, foresee the repercussions of change and gain some independence from market forces. Philosophers are often Quixotes; they need a basic understanding of the huge forces they play with.

"Note that it has happened fortuitously on one occasion. Several of our prominent founding fathers were scientifically adept. The Panzaic sensibility of our Constitution was a result." J was not above injecting tidbits that he knew would please this crowd.

"But this was before the rigor mortis of cultural institutions was well set. We don't get that kind of leaders anymore." He had to point out painful truths.

A female with a leadership aura had a good question. "Why should we go to the extreme bother of studying science when it isn't needed in our profession?"

"Yes, it is a lot of work to learn science. Maybe you don't need science to maximize your bottom line for next year. But, a successful democracy depends on an enlightened electorate --- that's you. If you want to consider long-term issues --- and I'll not mention the survival of your species since it is too long term for most --- recall the plagues when knowledge of sanitation was absent; or the vulnerability of the financial system when safeguards against human frailties such as greed were not in place. Science is an important facet of the solutions to most complicated problems, environmental or sociological. But needed tax measures have often failed because they are very long-term. The voting majority is too ignorant of the scientific aspects to understand many issues beyond the impact on their immediate income. And the CEO seldom looks beyond next year's profit statement.

"The trickster politicians exploit this character and substitute their own self-aggrandizing agenda. They even have the audacity to promote tax cuts in the face of monstrous national debts and infrastructure decay. If you want democracy to work you need education of the electorate."

J was talking to the lions in their den. He wanted them to know that they were part of the problem. But a glance at Deman, whose head was buried so far in his hands that he was in danger of falling forward, stopped J. Panzaic prudence kicked in; it was time to get back to academic detachment.

He gratefully acknowledged a question from a silver-haired woman in front. Remnants of her beauty-queen days could be seen in her dramatic features even as she eased into the matriarchal role. But she remembered well her most frustrating experience at the required science classes in college. "Just what is this mystery method of science?"

"That's a good question. Science seeks truth as a relative characteristic attached to some hypothesis proposed as a theory and substantiated by observations. The process of science is a balance between statements of observations and predictions of theory. There are no rules to limit the hypothesis. But every idea must be treated with skepticism and subjected to the rigors of observational or experimental verification. The hypothesis gains stature with positive reinforcement. It is debunked and discarded by negative observations. In science it must all hang together. The mystery of science is there are no mysteries, just the unknown, which is best handled by an open minded approach."

She seemed to like that. "That seems simple. But what about the statement: 'The exception proves the rule'?"

"Evidently that should be, 'The exception proves the rule doesn't work.' Time to modify the rule."

There were other hands in the air but J looked at his watch, "At this point I need to conclude. We've seen Complexity at work in some simple science and tried to apply it to sociological problems. It puzzles the mind, and makes us 'bear those ills we have rather than fly to others that we know not of', as Hamlet would say.

"It is fuel for the instabilities that lead to Chaos. How can we know which Chaotic solution is right for us? Who's to say what the right direction is? Perhaps materialistic aggrandizement and power over the earth is Homo Sap's peak destiny. Maybe we're simply meant to vector greenhouse gases into the atmosphere to bring on the next millennia in global evolution."

The Captain would not let him off so easily. "You begged the question earlier. Just what are these obvious solutions to our great problems that are being ignored?"

Ah well, thought J. Nearly made an escape. He couldn't avoid it. The truth as J saw it just had to come forth. His genes had hard-wired the connection between his cerebrum and his mouth. "We don't have time for the details. To let you escape I will answer that there is one key element to every solution. It is the only part of the solution to any environmental and cultural disaster that is easily understood — population control by Homo sapiens.

"It is so obvious and simple an answer — a typical Panzaic solution — that any novice can see it. It is so complex a solution, requiring abandonment of our breeding based religions and control of our brain-stem functions, that no quixotic bureaucratic genius can enact it."

This 'answer' was given as J walked off the stage.

It was still early evening when J left the club soon after finishing his dessert. At the social he was popular but no one seemed anxious to talk to him about anything beyond the perfunctory. It was as though he hadn't said anything challenging or worth thinking about. Discouraging.

♦

In the basement of the Tree J serviced the generator, ticking off each step on a checklist as he did each duty station. He enjoyed the machinery; keeping the generator, compressor, heat exchanger and a couple of exotics in a gleaming and well-lubed state. For electrical power he had numerous backups. The solar array worked well in the constant sun of the subtropics, despite the serious compromises in exposure necessary for security. He had several types of generators from traditional to the latest miniaturized technology. This occupied him for an hour and he was ready for an afternoon nap.

He slept briefly in the cool of the lower bedroom. Here, there was no likelihood of an animal screech wakening him. Most nights he was in his 'master' bedroom, high above the ground, with good ventilation and access to the sounds around his place. This was a prudent defensive requirement at first.

There was always the automatic security system with sensors and alarms. At the monitoring panels he could read the weather outside and look around with a surveillance camera. He was the local Big Brother watching over all. He cracked a grim smile when he thought of the philosophical debates he'd had with Deman on similar systems set up by governmental authorities under the auspices of homeland security. All moot now.

The lower bedroom looked like a Parisian hotel room with half as a marble lined salon. In fact, he had remodeled it over the years to resemble a hotel reception area that he fondly remembered. He straightened the bed and moved to the door at the end of the room.

The next space was for storage and another door led to a long corridor lined with bottles of wine. The room was kept at optimum temperature and many of the wines wouldn't reach perfection for another decade. Along with me, thought J.

He selected a bottle, went back to the bedroom, set the wine on the nightstand, and opened the floor to ceiling wood doors of a closet. He changed into outdoor gear. He was anxious to walk the plain soon after the rains.

Ch 2.3 A Conversation with Deman

J parked his bike in the corner of his office and flicked the computer keyboard to check his email. Only one new message sent late yesterday. It said 'The Dean would like to talk, please come over at eight a.m.'.

J wondered if Deman knew that he usually arrived before eight, an hour before almost anyone else. He decided that this was unlikely. More likely it was a standard ploy to put a little pressure on the invitee who would be forced to show up late. 'One-upmanship' was an academic disease.

J enjoyed the walk to the administration building. One of the pleasures of his work was the environment. It was a lot nicer early in the morning before the hoards of students flowed through. There was a lot of grass, trees — singular and in groves — vistas at every corner. It seemed to him this environment was soothing, like the womb, and probably necessary for his psyche. It was definitely one of the advantages of working on a University campus.

The administration building was in early gothic. There was something about the brick and ivy that made an academic feel comfortable. It felt nice to J. He smiled at the secretary. "Deman's expecting me" and failing to notice her dismay walked into the empty Dean's office.

So the gamesmanship extended to the confidence that the summoned faculty member would not be available at eight sharp. J wondered how long he would have to wait, and relished the opportunity to be sitting in the office when Deman arrived. He did five minutes later.

Deman was made from a mold. His parents were academic historians, tall, slim and hirsute, and they bred a perfect 'classic Dean'. He had a precious tool in his radiant smile. He used it constantly to disarm and diffuse. It was said that he could make an employee feel privileged to be fired under its afterglow.

Although J often talked with Deman he never responded to the smile. As a result, Deman had turned it off in their relationship. Except for the frequent truly funny exchanges. J noticed that in those cases the smile was quite different. The eyes became involved. It reflected rather than encompassed, spontaneous and not cultivated, quick to appear and quick to disappear. There was no evidence of either version this morning.

A point already made by his presence, J eased it with a quick question, "Well, how'd I do?"

"You offended three-quarters of the President's contributor list."

"That's peculiar, where did I go wrong? The other quarter must not have been listening."

Deman paused a moment, appreciated the humor, then the audacity, and quickly passed to petulance. "You're giving a lecture on the environment with a couple of new buzz words thrown in. You're trying to educate them and give them an idea of what you do for a living. You end up telling them that the world is a basket case, overpopulation is the root cause and implying that those of them who have religion are the leading cause of the overpopulation. Not to mention the over-moneyed class who only care for themselves."

"Charlie Darwin, did I say that? Well, I know you've got to keep it simple. I tried to reduce it to the simplest factor. At that level I'm trying to save the world for, or from, mankind. I note that you are looking at capitalism as a religion."

"The point is; you have to tailor your lecture to the audience. They aren't scientists so they don't see a lot of the connections. You have to lead these buggers, not bugger these leaders." Deman had his own sense of humor buttressed by degrees in History veneered atop an anthropology degree.

"These people are rich. They're each a success story, something not just unappreciated, but probably not even comprehended by you. Their devotion to education keeps this place going. You sorely taxed that devotion last night."

J shook his head, "Yes, most of them successfully chose the right parents. I do agree some of them are success stories. Mostly consisting of being in the right place at the right time."

J appreciated Deman, probably because he had a decent understanding of science, unusual for administrators. Deman was obviously startled to encounter a scientist well versed in history and literature. It quickly became evident that one of J's favorite characters was the simple Sancho Panza, also seen in literature as Falstaff, Camus' Sisyphus or the Good Soldier Sweik. Deman's favorite was the fatally complex Don Quixote. These character types were all over classic literature. In fact, they would agree that their presence defined classic literature. Each recognized their favorite character in the other.

J was surprised that Deman was as well versed as J in the ironies and satire of Cervantes in Don Quixote. Deman had readily accepted the metaphor for life — that those imbued with the highest, purest idealisms cause a lot of trouble for Homo sapiens. Those 'helped' by them often ended up worse off.

They agreed that idealisms fuel the engine that drives Homo sapiens to the next town along the road to upper eternity. And that if that idealism is untempered with understanding of evolutionary and genetic realities it is doomed to failure. Sancho Panza was a better administrator, a better person then Don Q, proving that the humility of simple fairness is better politics than the haughtiness of perfection. Or perhaps it was just that it was more in tune with the capabilities of the species.

They even agreed that sociobiology — the concept that mankind was merely the gene's way of making another gene, with the keystone, evolution — was as sensible a religion as any. But from this point they went in different directions.

Deman frowned, "Look, once again, let's review. We agree that you're just a Homo sapiens, most talented of the species on this planet, but still, just one of the myriads of known life forms. You're lucky if you live eighty or ninety years, sixty of them enjoyable. This is the minutest part of a blink-of-an-eye in geological time. Your chances of influencing anything in the future beyond your single blink are minute. But your chance of influencing the next thirty years of your own life is large."

"I know that, Deman, but toward what end? What if it gives me pleasure --- enriches my life --- to dream about a better world?"

"The problem is that you frequently choose to sacrifice your personal environment for some quixotic ideals about the distant future of 'your' species, and 'your' planet. I do not understand 'your' naiveté."

"What you call naiveté may be understanding possibilities that you don't entertain."

Deman rose and walked around his desk. He wanted to talk man-to-man, not administrator to teacher. "That's true. Suppose that I grant that you have contributed to the better understanding of the place of the species in the scheme of things and its contribution to global nest fouling. This contribution would be a bigger help if we were a more intelligent species. As it is, that knowledge just sits there like scum on a pond."

"I feel better for having done it."

"Yes, that's the quixotic reward. You are less famous, less important, and far less paid than the average rock singer, movie star, charlatan politician, professional athlete or successful entrepreneur. This should be proof to you that the species doesn't care if it survives a thousand years. Don Quixote is a fool. "

Deman was wound up. "And it wouldn't be so bad, you pinning yourself on the cross, even entertaining, but you don't have to imply that those of us who don't must occupy a level somewhere beneath you. Your attitude is a criticism of everyone who takes charge of their life."

"And the lives of as many others as possible." J felt himself falling behind.

Deman was happy in his self-satisfaction. He scolded J, "I have been through the same thought process as you have. I cannot see any good prospects in your quest for surcease of sorrow for human-kind on this obscure hunk of rock. We have good jobs, intellectual stimulation, and a comfortable environment. Why can't you be content with survival as a goal?"

"So I am. The difference between us is you are totally content in your existence, while I gain more contentment by working to assure that we muddle through to the next way station, where perhaps there will be a better perspective." He listened to the quiet for a moment. "I can't just let it go."

Deman had made what J called the Panzaic Plea. Once you accept that Homo Sap is simply the current most talented animal species on this particular planet and realize that this is an insignificant hunk of dirt circling a humdrum sun in an average galaxy — then it is a small step to this Palliation of Panza. Since there are is no evidence of rewards attainable beyond our meager reach and tiny life span, one's actions should be directed toward optimizing the quality of one's life interval. Energy expended to improve the lot of future generations of Homo sapiens was mostly wasted effort — Quixotic. In this philosophy, 'Good' behavior was sometimes defined as that which does the most to enhance one's own existence. Altruism, that genetic appendix, is suppressed. It's just another attempt by the gene at manipulating the species toward their own agenda, survival and propagation of the species. However, Deman would be quick to recognize that consideration for one's fellow species, --- do unto others as you would have them do unto you --- was simply a sensible formula for a happy existence and such behavior qualified as 'good'. Correspondingly, gross self interest often leads to catastrophic consequences for one's own life. The CEOs and traders whose hedonistic ignorance produced the turn of the century financial melt-down and ultimately the collapse of the US system were good examples of this.

Deman stated it: "We are but the most talented animal species on this planet, an insignificant piece of dust in the cosmos, so don't expect anything exceptional from us".

J shook his head, "I can't deny it. But I'm disturbed by the noxious results when this conclusion is innately adopted by the greedy. Their inference is that it is illogical to worry about the future, the present environment or anything that gets in the way of taking everything you can for yourself. This truism is behind the collapse of most societies." J knew Deman realized that J's quixotic trait was a veneer on a logical panzaic attitude. To J, without this layer he would be resigned to hedonism; this was a deadly flaw of the Panzaic Plea. Some concept of fitness attached to long term survival of our species was needed, but it wasn't obvious.

Deman looked at J sympathetically. "Again, I must remind you that the destiny of the species, of our ecological niche, of the whole damn planet, is determined on scales far removed from the realm of the individual organism. It's out of reach and out of sight— might as well be out of mind."

J looked Deman in the eye. "A lot of people get to this conclusion without your intellectual luggage. There must be a hundred popular slogans based on this paean, from 'Carpe diem' to 'Good ole boys drinking whisky and rye, singing this'll be the day that I die'. There are so many such panzaic exhortations that the quixotic concept of sin had to be invented to keep Homo sapiens in line."

Deman shrugged, signaling that he knew it was a hopeless argument. "And that certainly didn't work. Why do you have to tag us with guilt or laziness or lack of vision. I pay taxes, vote, teach idealisms, and love my neighbor. And I really enjoy my good fortune at being at the top of the food chain. I don't need eternity."

"Hah. Since your politics triumphed you've paid less and less tax. You helped elect leaders with the same cynical philosophy as you, although in their case it was arrived at with none of your intellectual rationalizations. Their first thought is, 'Will it help me or please me?'"

J had tweaked Deman in another direction. Possibly he wasn't interested in why Deman had called this meeting. They were addicted to cerebral contest and Deman was now on the introduced topic. "You should try it. Perhaps it is better than, 'Will it benefit mankind?' You've worked for laws and movements to guide the poor, the homeless and aimless to a more 'meaningful' life. They are quixotic concepts of redemption with a little welfare thrown in. I thought this was a noble occupation."

J raised his well-defined eyebrows to the inevitable. He knew the fate of 'noble' enterprise.

Deman looked at the ceiling as though reading a prompter. "Never mind the statistics of decades of attempts at rehabilitating the aimless with a success rate of about ten per-cent. They found out that some people simply don't want to, or cannot, work to improve their education, marketable skills, or even basic sanitation."

J looked at the same spot for inspiration. "Yeah. But even when we understand this, a whole new concept of helping these discards of laissez-faire capitalism can be found. Welfare helps the system to survive. Homo sapiens need to purchase the insurance policy, public welfare, with some sensible goals. Look, we both agree that stabilizing population at about a tenth of what it is would have produced a much better world for all, including you and me."

"But I say you are fighting the impossible fight. The uneducated protoplasm lives to breed. The jungle is our natural state. We just have a very sophisticated version. Learn to live in it." Deman rose, suggesting a summation. "All right. We agree on a lot of fundamentals. But here you are, still astride your white horse and blathering what for you and me is axiom. Your lesson is like a lance without a target. Do you want to save somebody? Something? What is the point? How about saving me?

"Save me from the self-righteous. There is no greater threat to the establishment of intelligent civilization than that of the true-believer, and they exist in every ideology. Oh sure, we're suffering under the Fundamentalist Right now. But I do include the Quixotes of Capitalism and Communism, Humanism, Greens and Sociobiology for treating their theories under the banner of religion. They are just pseudo-intellectual versions for those who cannot stomach the banal simplicities of the supernatural faith based religions. This was Cervantes's' pure cry."

J was impressed at how fired-up Deman had gotten. Pressures must be building. He just said, "I hate it when I agree with you."

Deman was looking through the wall, lost in his own analysis, "Of course when I am forced to think about it, it depresses me. The weakness of these aspiring thinkers — they have at least engaged their brains — is that most often they do not even have a sense of the overall problem.

Their concerns and understanding are local and short-term. Solutions to problems are applied midstream and within the system. There are too many limitations. Inevitably, as you and I constantly note, consequences they have failed to see crop up and devastate their solution — usually to the point where their actions and the unforeseen outcome are a disaster. Why is it that Quixote can never see the real truth, which is — there is no God-given truth? It's not that hard to see."

J couldn't disagree. "The layman with no formal analytic training hasn't a chance of avoiding a critical flaw in almost any social enterprise. At least the scientists and engineers are trained to constantly be aware of the assumptions behind any application. They accept these acts of faith that must be made- to reduce the important factors in a problem to a manageable number. They anticipate likely failures; but it's our best shot."

"I think our 'best shot' is a dud."

"Could be. But as I pointed out, a scientist, and this includes you, often knows good basic solutions — with all the caveats. We have discussed them, to my frustration and your boredom. We both can see the fatal faults in most respected efforts to achieve justice for all. So why not try to fix them?"

Deman scoffed, "Because you can never convince, or even fool the masses into suppressing their brainstem marching orders long enough to establish the solutions. And worse yet, for those of us with all the education and understanding our culture can provide, there is this quandary over motivation. You have this ephemeral urge. I don't." Deman at last had J in the mood where he could deliver most mercifully his doomsday warning. "So why don't you just realize your quixotic position, face a Panzaic reality, relax and enjoy your station in life? You would soon move into administration, double your salary, and attain nirvana on earth in your little time remaining."

J smiled at the proposition and offered the frail answer, "It's tempting, and logical, and probably pleasurable. But is there a sense of meaningful existence?"

"Is this a trick question? Philosophers debate if there is existence. And we probably don't agree on what constitutes 'meaningful'."

J smiled painfully. These were practically his wife's words. "I know you think that I still have that last appendix of faith; that there must be some reason for it all. When I shed that remnant of illogical charm I will be the same as you. Qualified and capable of the easy hypocrisy that lets you manipulate everything that constitutes your immediate environment.

"Still, I could do it. I imagine it. But in that sleep of ideals, what are the rewards? We both know that we already have enough wealth to accumulate material possessions unknown to history's greatest kings. Lust, to an educated mind, is soon satiated. Leisure, or just surfeit from the rat-race, is desirable, but perhaps not in comparison to participating in fascinating work."

J seriously considered Deman's suggestion. "I probably could surrender to Leisure. Just to concentrate on immediate surroundings, provided they were rich enough with nature. Just provide me with a sunset view, an occasional glimpse of deer and eagle and a quiet walk, and I could make Panza's Plea. I could drop out and no longer harass you with reminders of the mysterious meaninglessness of your life. No raise, just arrange for my salary to be sent to me and I'll be off." It was like J was floating a trial balloon.

Deman was considering. For a moment, J realized that it was possible that he actually could grant him his fanciful wish. The manipulative smile was back on Deman's face, "I'm tempted. But what would I think about if you were gone. My greatest amusement is in your quixotic aspirations. My strongest faith is in your panzaic foibles.

"But you're a lot of work. To keep you as entertainment I have to think about how to make amends and hypocritically manipulate the rich bastards you provoked last night."

J had to agree that he was indiscreet. He was persuaded that he was not just impolitic but impolite. He wasn't certain yet that he should be sorry.

Deman concluded, "You know, a few of them have the power to terminate your career. And mine. Think about that. Maybe you should give serious consideration to the solution that you've just been toying with. Let me know what you think."

J was a fighter. "I wonder if they consider that when I'm working, doing science, I'm content and have little time to criticize them. If forcibly retired, I will have full time to write letters, articles, and books to try to bring them down."

"They probably realize that. You and I both know that if you get too bothersome they have other ways to take you out. Besides, would you really have an impact on them with a few written words here and there? They probably don't fear you at all. They'll do whatever they want." With that, he abruptly turned his attention to the inbox on his desk.

J realized that once again he had been manipulated into presenting the case for exactly what Deman had probably invited him here for. It was time to think about all of this.

When he got home that afternoon he found that he had other things to think about. He had almost forgotten the money.

God pity a one-dream man.

Robert Hutchings Goddard
(1882–1945), U.S. physicist.

Ch 2.4 Moving Money

For long periods of time J forgot about the 'appropriation' he had made in the mountains. Still, it was always in the back of his mind like a rock in the stream of consciousness. He was always waiting for the first shoe to drop.

As part of his cover-up, this year he had driven the orange VW bus to Los Angeles in the new state of Calzona. The only nervous time was at the border going down. He forgot that they routinely checked cars — no problem — and recorded license numbers in the process. He was checked, but he didn't give it much thought. Not enough to change his plans anyway.

He removed the license plates and left it where he expected it to be stolen soon. He got rid of the license plates and took the train home. It didn't work out quite like he wanted.

When he checked the LA newspapers the next day he saw a picture of his van. It had been stolen as planned, but then used in an escape from a robbery. The story mentioned the bright orange color and the lack of plates.

It was two months later, after the conversation with Deman, when J biked home to a surprise. After he disarmed the alarm system he found that burglars had visited. Sophisticated burglars. The alarm hadn't been triggered. Since J had installed some of the motion sensors himself, he figured that his monitoring agency had been compromised.

As he surveyed his house he became increasingly alarmed. Valuable items were left beside ripped open possible hiding sites. There were holes in the walls. Some flooring had been ripped up. When he checked the attic crawl spaces it was evident that they had been visited. If a large item like several million dollars of cash had been in the house it would have been found. Very little was taken.

J resisted running outside to check his hiding places. Most of the money was under large Rhododendron plants, but one stash was readily available under an annual. This was the active 'bank' where he steadily converted the smaller bills into large ones. The volume and weight of the original had been cut in half. Fortunately he had recently 'deposited' a stack of five hundred dollar bills here, so there were none in the small safe in the house that served as a way station. It had been taken. In the evening he casually walked outside and noted that everything was undisturbed in the yard. He was confident that there wasn't proof of anything. But it wasn't good. They would keep their eye on him.

He reported the burglary to the police since that was the normal thing to do. They did their usual survey. The policeman remarked on the professional nature of the break-in and unusual search while looking long and hard into J's innocent blue eyes. Then he said how busy and understaffed the police were and J would probably not hear from them again, particularly since there was nothing significant stolen. They probably decided that they didn't want to get involved in this action. J figured he got himself into it after apparently escaping notice. It was a little sickening. Sometimes precautions shot you in the foot.

He figured that his place was likely set up with surveillance equipment. This was a problem because he didn't want to make them aware of his suspicions. Since microelectronics was a hobby with him, he could locate them fairly easily. He found several during the normal course of house maintenance and repair. He painted two rooms and painted over the tiny cameras. They were probably connected to a transmitter left in the attic. He didn't bother with that, and left a microphone and a camera alone. He had nothing to hide except for the one room where he packed his suitcase.

It required weeks of outside yard work before he was satisfied that he had located the only camera covering the yard. He waited months until a big wind storm and approaching from behind, suddenly pointed it downward, hoping they would think it a casualty of the wind.

He knew that he was on a list, probably a short list.

♦

It was late in the fall when J snapped the latch on his suitcase. It was unpretentious; dirty, cheap — a tacky imitation of quality. He was in his 'safe' room. A piece of shirt was sticking out and he reopened the bag. The shirt was being used as wadding to separate bundles of money. These were scattered in with clothes, books, and sundries. This would be his first transfer of really big bucks.

The transfer of the money from his house to a bank had become necessary. He was confident that the yard was not under surveillance and used many gardening trips to slowly move the cash to the house. He had left one camera uncovered in his living room, hoping that would be enough to keep them from another visit to plant more. But this was a particularly nervous time, as big bucks sat barely concealed in the suitcase. He couldn't be certain that the gangsters wouldn't return to dig up his yard. Regardless, he planned to spend the money.

He had managed to spread several hundred thousand in his usual carry-on luggage and the clothes he wore for four trips so far. But several hundred thousand goes into his total stash about sixteen times and that adds up to a lot of exposure. It meant more trips, and each trip was a risk. So he decided that it was worth it to rely on the checked baggage for a big transfer or two. This was the most dangerous part of his plan.

Much time had been spent studying how to move the money out of his yard and into legitimate channels. The gray banking practices of Switzerland came in handy here. Several Swiss bankers had a reputation for being colleagues of the world's great criminals. All he had to do was smuggle the money there and deposit it. It was completely confidential. They probably just assumed that he was a drug dealer, crooked politician, or any one of dozens of occupations that kept the bank's equity the largest in the world.

Since J had been going to a couple of meetings a year in Europe for many years, it was reasonable to carry the money along. He had been in the customs computer as an international scientist with normal trips to foreign countries for most his life. He knew that his profile - neatly trimmed beard, casual clothes, professional demeanor- all marked him as benign.

For years he had passed through customs without anyone looking at his baggage. Long ago, after the dawn of international terrorism customs became unbearable. Airlines and tourist companies were going broke. Finally the USA had inaugurated a new system of identification, probably in an attempt to match the new ease of traveling within the EU. Frequent business travelers like J were allowed to get a thorough checkout, and a personal ID that currently included a scan of his iris. The commonsense procedure of profiling was thereby institutionalized. The best part was the shorter line at immigration stations that had the machines. The idea was that searches of personal luggage would go to near zero. He hadn't been subjected to a luggage search since he got this card a few years ago. Still, there were no guarantees. And there was a lot to lose.

He really didn't know what to do if by some quirk the content of his luggage was discovered. It was illegal to carry out of the country, of course. J was confident that he had a number of 'stories' for why the money was going to Europe and could get off with a hefty fine. The superrich class was moving money like this all the time. This wasn't the major problem. That would arise when the news item, 'Scientist carries huge stash of cash with him' hit the media. A certain list of suspects would be reduced to one. The gangsters watching him would pounce.

J became an expert on the scanners — studying them carefully before passing his first funds through. The operators were confronted with an astounding array of objects. J read their instruction manuals to see what they could recognize. Guns, igniters of bombs, parts which could be put together to make something dangerous, the inspectors were trained to recognize characteristic shapes. Their search relied heavily on the profiles and tools of terrorists and cranks. The key was that they were looking for specific images and ignored everything else. Money wasn't a target for them.

To terrorists, the intimidation factor was probably the largest deterrent, as all methods were likely ineffective in detecting modern plastics. Also, although it wasn't allowed to be obvious, the character profile of potential terrorists and drug runners was critical. If you didn't match any of the warning signs that included race, age, haircut, type clothing, nervous tics, impatience, even certain eye contact, the inspectors paid little attention to your luggage.

He was helped by the fact that the worry about well-heeled American passengers was small since the common market had become reality, and the USA conglomerate had broken up. The voodoo economics of the new century had emasculated the USA economy and the American dollar was worth much less than the EU that had replaced it as the world standard. The cold war of the eighties and the hot wars of the new century had submerged the USA economy with only a short respite when assets, from forests and parks to buildings were sold. All of this worked to J's advantage to produce an image of a harmless American. In fact, that's what he was.

Another factor that had to be considered was the threat of theft on the airline. He had found early that the risk of checked luggage being rifled by employees looking for valuables was huge, so this avenue wasn't even considered for years. Fortunately, one airline had initiated a sealing process for checked luggage that J planned to use. To counter pilferage, one could purchase plastic shrink-wrap for the luggage. Thus, a major effort would be required to break into the luggage, and it became obvious. Stealing was still possible but sufficiently less likely so J felt willing to risk a couple of million dollars. He was still amazed at his own cavalier attitude toward a couple of million dollars.

J's research for this trip had indicated that because of the new security system and robust advertising, the airline would be taking exceptional precautions for now. This was a window of opportunity. The thieves would likely lay low until laxity ruled again. At least this was his hypothesis. He reflected on how many of his hypotheses had proven wrong in his life.

His luggage had been carefully selected. The design, lining and packing had been tested so that even an X-ray didn't blatantly show the money. He had tested the system with toys that resembled contraband and with stashes of paper stock the size and shape of money. These never provoked inspection or burglary. So he was pretty confident as he set the drop-lock, keyed in the house alarm, and went outside to the waiting airport shuttle van.

At the airport, he wheeled the luggage to the check-in counter bypassing the ubiquitous porters. He obviously didn't need help physically to carry the bags, although the weight of the 'money bag' was considerable. And he didn't need the ego massage of another person at his service.

At the counter, he couldn't resist being exceptionally careful, checking the clerk's ticketing of the bag, and accepting the extra fee for wrapping it in security wrap. J knew that the clerk at the check-in counter placed the passenger identification tag on the luggage in a certain way if the traveler had a warning profile. The baggage handlers would then check this luggage. J didn't know how they would do this with the plastic around it. In any event he was confident that he didn't fit any of the warning signs.

The wrapping clerk was a bit surprised at its weight, and remarked, "Carrying your weight lifting equipment?"

"No," J answered, "just a lot of books." He suppressed the wild urge to educate the clerk, "A million dollars in twenties weighs a hundred and eighteen pounds. Even in hundreds it is thirty pounds, hundreds weigh more than twenties."

J had only the big bills. Still, his shipment weighed over fifty pounds. All together, including his plans to cash out his pension and sell his house, he had about eight million, or two hundred pounds of cash to move.

He wistfully watched the bag, like a mother watches her child entering kindergarten, as it moved away on the conveyer belt in its plastic embrace.

He got his window seat and the class upgrade for frequent-flyers — so necessary on a ten-hour flight — and moved quickly to the x-ray passage of his carry-on with its few hundred thousand dollars. This, as always before, was uneventful. A little smarts is all it takes. He would have preferred to take all of the money in carry-on.

When he disembarked at the London Heathrow airport he knew their procedure well. Unlike Gatwick, they almost never checked personal luggage. They had an eye print machine that verified his identity in moments, and probably measured respiration rates to identify nervous individuals. He was cool. Practice makes perfect, and he had practiced the art of relaxation. He didn't worry about this gate.

Nevertheless, when he got to the luggage carousal he found himself sweating so much that he made a detour to the restroom. Must be the big money. A little meditation in the loo was sufficient to block out overt anxiety over the arrival of his checked baggage stuffed with money. He got a luggage cart and distracted himself by ogling a Scandinavian blonde. Strangely enough, this lowered his pulse rate and calmed him.

When his bag had not arrived after well over half the people had left, he had time to remember the occasion that his luggage had vanished years ago. It was on a direct flight, and a companion's luggage arrived safely. Someone had evidently siphoned off some pieces for their own use. They got his favorite leather jacket. This was not unexpected. All had to accommodate to living in the urban jungle. Roulette was king; the lottery was omnipresent.

There was a flush of relief when he sighted his luggage cresting the belt and sliding down to the carousel. When he could see that the plastic was unbroken there was only one more hurdle. Customs in Europe was generally lax, but they would become thorough, even paranoiac, after a terrorist attack. J checked the media before traveling, but these days, such an event was not uncommon, and he could be caught in a security net at any time.

He went to a restroom and removed the plastic wrap. No need to put customs on to the fact that he had something that he highly valued, although they possibly already had notification.

There was an uncomfortably long line at customs. When it moved fast, J relaxed. Until he noticed the innocuous looking young woman a few places in front of him was being subjected to a luggage search. J considered bailing out of the line, but with a dozen people behind him, that was impossible.

Then he recognized his brain stem at work, fight or flight, and concentrated hard on suppressing the adrenaline flow that would be detectable by the numerous sharp-eyes at this barrier. He thought of work, a mathematical problem he couldn't solve, a budget he hated administering, and soon fell almost asleep, in the usual physiological state of his travels before the windfall. This successfully passed him through without event. He could finally really relax as he stood in a queue for a rental car.

He slept in the car while it was being ferried on the train through the Chunnel. Crossing borders in EC was much easier than crossing state lines in the USA these days. His meeting for this trip was in Paris. Driving through Paris, it was easy to assure that no one could follow him. Each intersection was a roundabout that was a free-for-all merge and meander game. J had reasonable experience at this and was confident that no one could possibly be on his tail after transecting Paris. This was necessary of course, because if the crooks saw his destination the jig would be up.

He drove late into the night before getting to a hotel in Geneva. He was careful about protecting his luggage, placing personal alarms on the hotel door, getting room service, and never leaving it alone. He had taken many precautions to appear of modest means. His clothes were off-the-shelf, his watch a step above Mickey Mouse; his impression was middle-class American tacky. Still, he was nervous until he entered the imposing portals of his bank.

Opening a bank account had been ridiculously easy. He was amazed that the account number was the key to withdrawal. If he lost it, he was in serious danger of losing the account. He had immediately written it in permanent ink on the bottom of his foot in binary, mirror image. It blended with several scars from a mistake in his youth.

J had been anxious to get the money to the Swiss bank. He wanted to get it away from his property. There had never been any danger of him spending it at home. He didn't have anything to spend it on. Still, simply having ten times more in his wallet than ever before had made life sweeter. Not that much sweeter, though, since he was already frustrated that there was nothing in the catalogs to tempt him anymore — he already had it all. At least he had a modest version of it all. The money might have sat there unused, but now it was nearly all committed.

No, if the previous owners of the stash had been monitoring him, and this now appeared certain, they would have to decide that this person wasn't spending beyond his means. This was provided they didn't follow him to Africa; provided they didn't know about the Tree.

A good name is better than riches.

Miguel de Cervantes
Don Quixote.

Ch 2.5 Peter

Snow was falling, as big flakes. Not densely, as each pancake flake had gathered mass from a large volume surrounding it. Not falling straight in the no-wind, but swinging side-to-side. They were like little white saucers, gently settling on those before. No breakage. Until J crunched millions of them into grainy waffled footprints with each step as he silently trod a street neighboring the University. He loved walking in the snow and he had quickly covered the miles from his house.

Like other college towns, there was an abundance of greenery, gables, dormers, leaded windows, fireplaces of rounded river rocks or sleek black cylinders, and tall trees — all now shrouded in white. At the end corner of the street he turned up the red brick stairs to a house and grounds that were a beautiful example of the local ambiance. The door had a small leaded glass window at eye level. The doorbell couldn't be heard but J knew that it was an electronic tune in the center of the house.

A man answered the door. In his fifties, wearing overalls, he looked like he would be more at home on the other side of the mountains in the wide, flat, farming regions. Except his hair was too long and unkempt. His light green eyes were too bright. His face seemed to hold a permanently amused expression, with a bushy eyebrow slightly cocked, a curve at one end of his mouth and three permanent creases across his forehead.

He looked directly through a person, into his inhibitions. And here there was understanding and acceptance. A beautiful bimbo or a thug with a gun would receive the same treatment. It was a peculiar world and he accepted it as so. This is Peter.

This place was originally the home of Peter and his family, when he had a family. They were gone now, his wife to the new flu, his several children to opportunities in far-away places. Peter seldom talked of them. He had done his job, launched them, and now they spent most of their energy surviving. Peter saw them once a year when there were celebrations at one of their Calzona, Midwest or Dixie houses. Peter financed these meetings, furnishing airplane tickets for all because he felt families should be together at least once a year.

Peter took excellent care of his house. It had been remodeled and now he shared it with several other men and women, most of them employees of the University. They were invariably scientists of some sort. At one time Peter had almost all students. Now many of the tenants were long-term. Those who didn't like the ambiance — and it was a decidedly different ambiance — usually moved on quickly. Those that liked it stayed, switching jobs, vocations, even spouses, to stay in this comfortable setting. Those who were comfortable here were often uncomfortable everywhere else.

The remodel had created one great room, three stories high, in the center of the house. The kitchen and a family/dining room were on one side of the first floor. On the other side stood a river stone fireplace that dominated the space. There was a conversation pit and reading area in the middle. This area was surrounded by suspended walkways serving the second and third floors. On the outside curve-- bedrooms, studies, libraries, and reading rooms were scattered. It was a big house. Peter bought it twenty years before for a tenth of its current value. Peter and J prospered from buying houses at a good time in the market. J regretted that he hadn't bought more. Peter never considered this aspect.

But then Peter never showed regret about anything. He was a contented man, a philosopher, in name and in fact. A physicist with increasingly spacey ideas, protected by tenure. He taught an introductory class, but mostly wandered the campus talking to anyone who wanted to talk. He was successful at this because he was one of the world's best listeners. He loved to listen to J.

J's wide-ranging critiques on society's problems fascinated Peter. He always acted amazed at J's grasp of complex issues, and salient solutions. He was more impressed by J's ability to get a letter published regularly in the local paper than he was by his colleagues' papers in learned journals. J was flattered. They had a very nice relationship based on similar circumstances, some similar philosophies, and very different styles --- Peter was a natural Panza.

J was very favorably impressed with Peter. Particularly since he had insights into Peter's thinking that no one else had discovered. One notable revelation came when they were discussing the unwitting contributions to warfare made by scientists. J recalled that Peter had sat on a committee that had sanctioned the use of extensive cloud seeding and other rainmaking efforts in Central America against insurgents. His initial comment was,

"Why did the committee vote to support this application of peaceful technology to warfare? Didn't you argue against it?"

Peter's response was the opposite of what J expected. "Why no, in fact I argued for it. I was glad to see it pass, in fact."

The size of J's eyes betrayed his dismay. "But even if you supported the applications of cloud seeding to muddy the trails, or give the insurgents colds, or whatever other silliness the military mind could dream up, you must have known that it was based on skimpy research and didn't have a snowflake's chance in Hell of succeeding."

"That's precisely why I supported it. It was a win-win situation. First, it pleased the military brass, they liked me, and I remained on the committee as long as I wished. Second, the results revealed the shoddy research done in establishing the theory and saved us from any large scale waste of money spent in the peaceful pursuit of this quixotic goal."

J recognized the method of Panza. He was being convinced. "Still, it sounds self-serving."

Peter smiled his friendly grin, "Of course. Nothing wrong with that. Particularly when you consider the added benefit to the people --- those planes dropping ice pellets weren't dropping bombs."

J didn't underestimate Peter's actions again.

He remembered their first encounter.

Despite his gentle nature, Peter was sometimes not a welcome visitor to faculty lectures. This was a result of one of Peter's more overt campaigns. He had arrived at the conclusion that most of scientific jargon originated not to facilitate understanding, but to inhibit it.

The reason that many professionals developed the complex terminology of their trade was that it allowed them to clothe simple thoughts and easy results in stylized garb that made it seem more profound. This inhibited questions, prevented anyone from seeing the real simplemindedness of the research or concept, and forestalled difficult questions. It certainly was the 'modus operandi' of the imitator professors, as Peter called them.

Thus, Peter had a well thought out rationale for making jargon the enemy. He had developed a technique for seeing through these linguistic facades. He would figure out the basic assumptions required for the lecturer's concepts to be valid and look for something in the results that violated the underlying hypotheses. He was surprised at how well this worked — how seldom scientists checked their theories back to the most fundamental assumptions. Many outside scholars had heard of him, and the wary often refused to give visitor lectures when they knew Peter would be there.

Since all science is built on layers of work reaching back years or generations, with some like brick outhouses and others like glass fairy castles; it was not irrational for a speaker to fear a question that could reveal a fatal flaw in their analysis. It was a characteristic of science that in the free marketplace of ideas, truth is the icon, and personal considerations must be ignored. This was why even a non-aggressive creature such as Peter had emerged as most adept at this kind of assassination. He rationalized that since truth was always the stated goal of a scientist, he was just doing them a favor, pointing out untruths. That was how J had been introduced to Peter.

That fine spring day, J had crossed over from earth sciences to the physics department to give a talk. He was feeling good, the sun was shining, and he was pleased to work in the beautiful campus environment. The physical journey from his office to the physics building was much like the scientific one. The simple, cheap, boxy structure of Earth Sciences was paid for by the Environmental Protection Agency, the government branch dedicated toward basic environmental studies. The Physics building, a famous architect's rendition in brick, glass, copper and imagination, was much larger in every respect, as befits the budget of its benefactor, the department of defense.

The physicists regarded study of the geophysical environment as almost a 'soft' science. Not because it was comparatively easy, but because it was relatively difficult, and therefore inexact. The keystone of physics, laboratory measurement, was not readily available in a laboratory that must encompass significant portions of the earth and often large segments of geological time. Hence, the precise hypotheses and building blocks of basic physics were replaced by tenuous assumptions. The nature of natural turbulence and other phenomena had no laboratory experiments to anchor their theory. Only astronomy, amongst the sciences, had as few observations to pin their theories to. This made earth scientists especially vulnerable to Peter's seminar hobby.

J was not forewarned of this landmine mouth. For two reasons, he was told later; first because they needed lecturers, and second because everyone loved to see Peter's act performed — on anyone else. It was sort of a miniature of mankind's insatiable curiosity at another person's gory accident. The physicists' NASCAR.

J's subject was atmospheric turbulence. It fit the criteria; difficult, little understood, not much data. Still, the talk had gone well — his jokes were tuned to the physicist's mind — and it seemed a friendly atmosphere. There were a few courteous questions, designed to show the questioner's knowledge. J gave his usual praise about the perceptiveness of the question.

Then, when Peter rose to point out the violation of a hallowed physical principal in one of his first assumptions, J's response was only subtly combative. "Yes, you're right, of course. My only excuse is that turbulence problems require tenuous guesses to launch any chance of practical results. So it's a far-out assumption. Give it a shot and throw it out if it doesn't work."

Peter was actually pleased with this response, as he said later, but he felt the impulse to push J a little further and made the mistake of commenting, "I've often wondered how you generate the audacity to make such assumptions."

J had learned from extensive reading of novels that featured Jewish mothers; when in an untenable position, counterattack. "Look, why are you attacking my tools of work? Do I come down here when you're working and kick away your broom?"

There was absolute silence. J wondered if he had overreacted and committed the cardinal sin in a science lecture; gotten up-tight. Peter jumped to his feet, apparently angry, and said. "You have a good point," he turned to the audience, "now this lecture is over and why don't you all go home so that I can clean up." The laughter mixed with sighs of relief at a tense situation diffused and the applause melted the tension in J's body.

Peter grabbed J's arm as he descended from the stage. "I have to buy you a beer. To apologize for my belligerence and so that I may have the pleasure of your company."

As they walked, Peter explained his campaign against 'scientificese', what he called the jargon designed to hide the actual simplicity of science from the prying eyes of the layman and to ward off simple salient comments. His method was to develop a talent for the latter.

J nodded his support and added, "This is not restricted to scientists. Lawyers have raised the use of semantic barriers to understanding to a fine art. Family doctors must hide the simple empirical nature of their cause-and-effect memorizations, lest we all realize that they are grossly rewarded for the simple facility of a good memory."

Peter liked the resonance with his pastime. "I'm not against rewarding a good memory; at least it is associated with intelligence."

Now J showed his passion: an earnest devotion to social criticism. "But there are larger issues to protest. Even simpler attributes with immense rewards exist in our society. Many are innate, like tallness in a basketball player, speed in a track star, beauty in actors or even the banal rote memorization skills of some supreme court appointees. So maybe we shouldn't pick on the poor scientist struggling to hide his insecurity in his hard-earned talent."

Peter looked closely at J's eyes. He had to be sure that this man was real. "I like you. Really like you. I need a friend like you. You must come to dinner after your beer."

J was attracted by this person's straightforward talk, especially when it included such flattering appreciation. That evening a firm friendship had been established.

♦

A few years later, J complicated Peter's life. He had carefully recorded his conversations with Peter. They were both curious about what their freewheeling banter would sound like in retrospection. Originally, J's motivation was to prove that Peter took the opposite side to the same topic on different occasions. It did show this, but only in the process of Peter reaching agreement with J each time. Peter's open-mindedness was confirmed. J's wasn't.

A surprise benefit came when, given the time to consider Peter's simple, direct approach to problems, J had compiled some of his wonderfully compact suggestions into a couple of short papers that had been published in a noted philosophy journal.

One of these papers had come about when J was ruminating on the difficulties of the expanding universe theory. Peter had noted, "It's almost like the concept of the red shift is getting in the way," and Peter had arrived at a far out version of a universe where the red shift didn't always dictate distance. It was surprising how the entire theoretical universe changed character with this alteration of a basic assumption. Hubbell's constant wasn't a constant, and the universe's age was a variable.

Arriving at alternative universes was Peter's forté. His other claim to fame was that he had been put up for the Noble prize in physics three times. Since there was always the threat that he would someday get it, his department was circumspect in dealing with him.

Some measure of fame had come to Peter from J's published notes. He accepted it naturally as an accidental reward for some magic concocted by J writing it up. His colleagues accepted it with trepidation. The net result was what J called the ionization of Peter, since he was less like a lion and more like a charged ion. He was like one of the unexploded blockbuster bombs that sat around London for many years after the second Great War, occupying valuable space, but untouched by anyone. He was granted a de facto status as philosopher resident in physics. His colleagues did listen a bit more carefully to what he had to say and some even benefited by it, although none so cited.

"Jesus, it's colder than a witch's tit", Peter slammed the door quickly. He loved clichés as much as J hated them. But J had to admit that 'Severe cold temperature' just did not carry the imagery. J could tolerate clichés only because they were sometimes terse truths. Most were trivial and easily ignored, but on occasions they were concise and precise.

Peter had such a good filter of fact versus myth that J sometimes used it to clear up situations. He would ramble a problem by Peter in scientific jargon and wait for a cliché that covered the situation in a simple metaphor.

For J, the pathway to intellectual enlightenment had stepping-stones with labels like evolution, ecology, esthetics, justice, agnosticism, science and common sense. He liked to think of these as large boulders that let one cross the river of ignorance from the cruel, crowded and chaotic world to an island of sensibility. They could be solid or slippery. The former were stones of reason, logic and mathematics. The latter were stones with labels like faith, love, trust and honor. One had to choose a panzaic path to a quixotic goal, sometimes resting on the solid stones, but needing to try some slippery ones. Peter had the firmest faculty for finding this path of anyone that J knew.

Now J was in need of council. "Can we talk in your room?" J knew that sometimes it was not visitable.

"Sure. It's the best place to watch the snowfall." Peter turned and started up the staircase that seemed to float over the floor, suspended from a heavy beam with steel rods to each runner.

As they made their way up to the top level, J nodded to two tenants. There were other good friends here.

Peter's room was on the south side. It was glass on three sides as was half the roof. One end was the personal library, with a very comfortable chair facing the view. The other end was Peter's 'bedroom', designated by the large bed backed to the rear wall. The master bath was behind that wall, and included a shower with a dozen small heads at various heights in all corners. J had stayed here on several occasions when Peter was traveling and he had enjoyed this feature.

Peter put two mugs in the microwave and waved J to the dining table against the windows. J took a minute to enjoy the view of snow falling in a solid curtain. It was a rare occurrence since the globe had warmed. Although he couldn't see beyond the next block, he knew that on a clear day, the 'mountain' — the huge volcano Mt. Rainier — was like the exclamation point on the right end of a sentence of Cascade Mountains.

"Have some Market orange spice tea." Peter set his favorite mug, a whale whose tail was the handle, deferentially in front of J. It was J's least favorite mug, uncomfortable to hold.

"Thanks. You know, I had a long talk with Deman yesterday. He sort of offered me a position, or rather a deal, or perhaps it was a threat. I suppose you could call it a golden parachute. It involved salary without work, anyway."

"All euphemisms for being fired." Peter was direct.

"I suppose so. But if being fired is made so comfortable that it is preferred to working, shouldn't it be chosen?"

"I suppose so. But is what you do really work? And what is this thing you will do next that is so comfortable?"

"The same research that I'm doing now, only with a slight raise in salary, and a large, maybe total, decrease in visibility around the University."

"There's no free lunch."

J smiled. That's what he wanted to hear. His gut feeling told him that; yet he still didn't know why the logic didn't lead to the same conclusion. But with the vote of two guts, he was ready to ignore Deman's offer if it was in earnest. One must always be prepared for such monumental decisions. He smiled at Peter, raising his glass in a toast, and reflected on how lucky he was to have this friend.

Let us make hay while the sun shines.

Miguel de Cervantes,
Don Quixote (1605)

Ch 2.6 A Cascades Hike

It was a clear day except for a few fair-weather cumuli. Yesterday's storm had swept the air clean and the mountain views were spectacular. Jagged peaks rose just across the valley. J moved quickly because he came with a group and he was trying to distance himself from the others. It wasn't that he was antisocial; he just derived maximum pleasure from being alone in the wilderness.

They were members of the Mountaineers club on the first spring climb. In the Northwest the rebirth season was marked by changeable weather. Storms came in regularly on the jet stream like gondola cars on a ski lift. There was always a cloud somewhere. But a beautiful day could be caught between stormy ones.

This was such a day. It was cold, with a snowflake or two, but lots of sun. In the winter months at forty-eight degrees latitude the sun rises at eight and sets at four. Daylight is cut shorter by mountain ranges to the west and east. Compensation comes during summer, when the sun rises at four and sets at ten. It's a wonderful variation if one can tune their activities to the change. The joy of a good spring day goes up with the latitude.

J liked to use the Mountaineer group to do the work of checking out the trail openings, arranging transportation, and for the occasional compatible comradeship. When he saw the web page announcement of a Sunday hike along a trail that was rarely open this early, he went for it.

It had turned out to be very nice. He arose early and arrived to grab a ride with the first departing car. It was a carload of four quiet people so J simply enjoyed looking out the window.

The trailhead was empty this early. Several more cars from their group arrived soon after, but J was out on the trail quickly. He got to an early lead; was passed after a couple of miles by two young machos that were so far ahead of him now that they were gone. After a few miles he was hiking essentially alone. The other hikers were behind him, some probably dropping off to early destinations.

It was a fairly steep trail, with old snow all around and a fresh inch on the trail. After three hours of upward trekking, J was getting tired. He had probably gone farther than he was initially planning to go, for two reasons — the two out front pulling and one who had been pushing from behind.

He reached a spur trail that he recalled. It climbed a short hundred meters to the ridge to gain a nice view. Glad to bail out of the race, he took this side trail and soon was comfortably sitting on a rock with a prime vista. He had earned the smooth dark chocolate pieces that he dug out of his pack. Only when he had just burned many calories did he allow such a high-fat luxury.

♦

Sitting on a rock in the Cascades inevitably sent his memories back to the money. With two children now in colleges, he had a significant draw on his income for another year or two. He had visited each of the colleges and paid a year's tuition in cash at each. This was not so unusual in the current culture, where banks were often suspect and the very rich had plenty of cash to play with. J was definitely not amongst the very rich, even with his secret windfall, however the colleges were not in a position to know that, or to care where it came from. It was confidential and therefore no big deal.

He was living within his income, even having difficulty spending his entire paycheck. He continued to contribute to a retirement program that got matching funds from the University. This had all grown to the point that he was a millionaire on his own right now. J had noted that this meant that all of his colleagues were also in this category. Probably a few million wasn't so much anymore.

Several years ago the observation that he earned less than most of his peers had helped him break from the cultural workaholic character. He even mentioned to his chairman that he had reduced his work to be commensurate with his compensation. The resulting lack of pressure to perform had done great things for his contentment with life.

Thinking about his secretive millionaire colleagues suggested to him that it would probably not be ostentatious if he overtly spent some of this money. But there was the problem that there wasn't anything that he needed or wanted.

It reminded him of the time he walked through the elaborate residences of the French kings at Versailles. He kept thinking; here they had essentially infinite resources. They built immense palaces with hundreds of rooms, large-scale gardens, and famous paintings everywhere. The increase from one to two rooms or two paintings must be a significant increase in the quality of life. An increase of four, eight or sixteen would be a recognizable increase in comfort, then luxury. But at some point there must surely be a law of diminishing returns. Just more friends or parasites — they must become indistinguishable — to surround you, and more parties to appreciate them and for them to appreciate you.

It sounded boring to J. He wouldn't trade his house for most of the castles he had visited. Money spent on personal comforts provides little beyond a point, and he must be living in the neighborhood of that point. For these reasons he had almost forgotten his hidden hoard.

Now he had dug up and transferred most of the money to the Swiss bank and arranged to spend it. It was this covert operation, and of course the burglary, that kept him glancing over his shoulder these days. Last week when he looked he found himself face to face with an enforcer type.

He was in the exclusive downtown men's store where he found the ultra comfortable Pendleton look-alikes for price tags that only the very rich could look at without nausea. The Guy smiled at him like he knew him. "How's it going, Dude?"

J was used to being addressed by strangers downtown. But not by dark suited, beeper ornamented, adrenaline stuffed bouncers with bulges where their guns were stashed. He answered. "Depressed, actually. The price tags are giving me indigestion."

"You look like you can afford this stuff." The guy was being provocative.

"Good. That's nearly as nice as being able to afford it." J moved around the table hoping to outdistance the conversation.

"Looks like your pants came from here." This was aggressive.

"Guess you'd have to take a closer look. They really came from Costco." True.

The Guy laughed. "Then what are you doing in here?"

That was the question that J didn't want to hear. Before he could think of an answer the guy walked past J and entered the door marked 'Private'.

J had been thinking about this encounter for a week now. They were letting him know that they knew something about him and were watching him. He hadn't the faintest idea what it meant or what to do about it. But he would find out.

♦

The crunch of boots alerted him that someone was joining him. In line with his reverie he felt a burst of fear. But the intruder was intent on the uneven rocks and apparently hadn't noticed him. When finally they looked up from below the rock, there were familiar eyes, jumping out green even from here, framed in the parka hood. But he didn't place them right away.

Now a familiar voice was speaking. "You're in my favorite spot. Would you mind if I joined you?"

"Certainly not, come on up." J was above rudeness to preserve his solitude.

When the Mountaineer sat down a few feet away, J still couldn't see a face, but felt some kind of kinship. He offered some chocolate.

When the parka hood was pushed back he recognized his new student. She looked at him as if she was surprised to see who he was. "Well, hello. I didn't realize that it was you ahead of me. You set a fast pace."

"You didn't realize because it was a fast pace?" J spoke before he recognized the defensiveness of it and felt obliged to go deeper, "For a middle-aged man, it was good, but you were closing on me fast."

"Lessee, I'm a bit over twenty, you're around forty. I'm called old by my ten year old nephew. So I'll buy twenty-years as a lot: you are indeed a middle-aged man." J could tell that she was watching him closely to see his reaction to this. It was studiously nothing, except perhaps for that involuntary twitch that revealed his disappointment in this assessment.

She continued, responding to his sensitivity. "Actually, I was just hurrying to get to this spot." And apparently she had already thought about this age difference.

J wanted to change the subject and naturally fell into his provocative-jesting, testing, modus operandi. "You're sure that you didn't just follow my footprints to get some of my chocolate?"

"If I didn't know about this spot, would I take the chance of interrupting you relieving yourself?"

J was glad she was going to be easy to talk to, "Touché. I'm sorry I occupied your spot."

"That's OK. I'm used to it. There aren't many unoccupied places in the mountains anymore. And I only found this one last fall; you probably have prior claim. I was hoping that the Cascades were less explored than the Rockies, where we usually vacationed."

It was a familiar lament to J, he parlayed the bond. "Even in March, five miles in, on an obscure spur."

"Right. I found this spot when I was looking for the place where Honest Ceed was struck by lightning." Ceed was a liberal politician in the 1990s who never lied or even exaggerated. He was respected, even revered by the population. Probably headed toward the presidency. Then on a hike up this trail he disappeared. The media reported that he was struck dead by lightning."

J was sympathetic. "Yes, I was curious about that fortuitous death, for conservatives, myself. I looked for the alleged spot. But it is farther up and off a difficult spur. Ceed must have been in good shape."

"Yeah. When I finally found it I was impressed, and pooped."

Kay was happy to slide into this easy banter. She wasn't ready to reveal any of her serious attitudes toward life to a relative stranger. Of course she had calculated their age difference. Unlike J, she thought often about the interpersonal relationships of everyone around her. She had early been fascinated by the strength of the hormonally driven responses that dominated the species. She had always hoped that there was something more to a person. Precious little showed up from preschool through undergraduate school. Now she was finally confronting the occasional triumph of the analytically driven personality. She loved the world of science for creating a mix of abilities and personalities. She had yet to determine whether the hormone or intellect driven persona was superior. She loved them both.

They talked about the mountains, favorite trails, bears and other adventures. They talked until they realized that they were quite late and would have to move quickly to get back to the parking lot in a reasonable approximation of the meeting time.

They jogged and slid down the trail. At one point J pretended to fall off the trail, sliding down a snow chute that made a nice shortcut across the switchbacks. She saw his method and followed him at the next small chute with somewhat less control, unless she had planned to end up headfirst on her back. J had stopped to wait; he didn't want to lose her.

Despite their fast pace, or what J thought was a fast pace, they were passed by the young men about a mile from the trailhead. Since they would not be far behind them and everyone would now know they were coming, they could slow up a bit. Still, by the time they were near the bottom it was late so J decided to make a last grand gesture and take a shortcut on a long snow chute that he had checked out on the way up.

He could tell that she had decided to take the slide too, hearing her worried "Oh" on the steep upper part. When he stopped at the bottom, he rose and turned just in time to have her slide under him. His feet were knocked out from under him, and they ended together in the missionary position. It lasted but a fraction of a second, then a playful smile before she twisted quickly out from under him and apologized. "I'm sorry, I was out of control." First time he had seen her nonplussed.

He was somewhat flustered himself and just managed a compliant response. "That's OK. Takes a lot of practice to glissade down one of those chutes in control."

Kay smiled, mostly to herself. She wasn't naïve or embarrassed. But it wasn't appropriate to reveal the depth of her sophistication to a professor just yet, maybe never.

They quickly walked up a gentle slope and promptly encountered several other hikers who apparently had watched the slide, or maybe just the end of it judging by their demeanor. J nodded to them, smiled and said "Better than sledding." Enough ambiguity for them; they returned the smile and nod and quickly moved on.

J answered Kay's question, "What did that mean?" with a shrug since his ride was honking. They separated to their respective carriers and he carpooled home in a quiet car.

That evening, J relived the day. He was in front of a robust fire. It was spewing out carcinogens. His wife would not allow fires after she discovered this, but after her death he had yielded to several life-shortening vices. But today he was feeling that life was good. Not the cynical intellectual life that he and Deman talked about. It was the intellectually stimulated brainstem life. Maybe he would get back into it. It would be a matter of reawakening feelings that had been sleeping. He closed the glass fire doors, curled up and went to sleep.

♦

Kay had an appointment with J a week later. She had some good ideas for her thesis topic and J appreciated the scientific interchange. A competent student was the most valuable asset a professor could have.

At one point J said, "I think that I'm going to enjoy your getting your thesis under me." This was a common expression, innocently said, but it had obvious overtones as a sexual innuendo and was instantly recognized as such by both.

Kay blushed a bit, but J was mistaken if he thought it was from the double entendre. It was more likely from the chastisement that she was going to deliver. "I don't want sexual related baggage to interfere with my smooth progress to a degree."

J felt obliged to explain. "I don't want to be burdened worrying about the political correctness of my every action and utterance. Discourse censored is not communication. Truth is the victim. Even I do not know whether my innuendo is Freudian, hormonal or innocently ignorant. But in any case I'll accept it and not let it interfere with the pursuit of truth."

She flashed the radiant smile. "I think maybe we said the same thing. I've got to go now. I'll manage to get my degree even if you turn out to be a Don Juan." Her smile managed to remove any offense that might be implied.

"You might find it difficult because you've got the wrong Don." J enjoyed the enigma and he wasn't about to explain it now. He smiled, nodded and turned back to his desk. It was evident that his scientific objectivity was being tested. She was pushing buttons that he had forgotten were there.

Ch 2.7 A trip with Deman.

It's raining in the Northwest. Ubiquitous parkas, a sea of rain hats and khaki pants are making their way from the parking garage to the airport terminal. J is traveling with Deman. He is making a final big money transfer. He has a little more than a million dollars in his luggage and on his person.

They arrive at the airport in an 'Airport Express' van that has advertisements for bulletproof glass, self-sealing tires, and instant backup. 'Your safest way to the airport' is their motto. Deman pays for the van with a card bearing his fingerprint.

Deman is confident, enjoying the occasion. "It revitalizes me to travel and experience the risk, fear, adventure. You would be surprised at how many people at the university never leave their home or work compound. Even you, who seem to manage to escape regularly, probably don't do anything more adventurous than indulge in a high cholesterol dinner."

J just smiled, shifted his wheeled carry-on to the other hand, looked at the ceiling and resisted the temptation to give Deman a peek at the piles of money nestled inside. If his luggage got inspected this trip at least Deman would have to reevaluate.

They proceeded to the Business-class check-in. J often received frequent-flyer upgrades, but this was the first time that he had a paid ticket for this section. Those who traveled with the administrators got to assume their prerogatives.

The carry-on luggage was put through the scanners and they walked through the metal detectors. J assumed that they were subjected to a final scrutiny through the mirrors that lined the corridor to the airplane gate. They both had retina scan cards so the time through security was short.

To J, travel in general is getting in a box at one place, shaken about, deposited at another. Like dice in a cup. The box, the shakes, the duration, all varied, from trip to trip, from generation to generation. Currently it is being put in a cubic box of airspace that is called an airplane seat and subjected to atmospheric turbulence at irregular intervals.

Their airplane was the latest effort of the local manufacturer, a new era jet. It was big, with spacious interior, and at last, almost comfortable seats for all. The simultaneous advent of an oil crisis with the development of advanced teleconferencing using multiple large flat screens and holograms, instant high fidelity connections gave the business community freedom to initiate a boycott of airlines because of their callous treatment of passengers. Immediate support from leisure travelers who were tired of long lines and cramped seating had forced a quick turn-around by the airline industry. Security became more efficient, employing high tech advances. An automatic anti-missile flare system was routine. There was reasonable space for seating. They went from cattle-car to living room comfort in a few years. Of course the cost went up but it was worth it. Still, a long trip like this would still be tedious and at times physically painful.

There was the inevitable walk past the first-class seats in the front of the plane. They were first to board so all could see them. It was no strain for the rich to pay the hundred percent premium for first class. The exposure must be a big part of it since the general upgrades in economy class seats and meals left little else to be gained. These were some of the people who had helped destroy his culture yet kept their own privileged perks. They weren't the main players, however. Those flew in their own planes.

Deman was inspecting the schedule for his individual TV, "Just sports, TV shows and boring movies. I miss the free press. Now we have so many taboos --- anything not mainstream, even criticism of politics. Politics was my main entertainment. Think of the first presidential resignation; that was a high point in human drama. Of course you were barely born; I was a slightly aware tot. But I remember my parents discussing it as the high point of their political experience. Forcing out a president was a turning point in our democracy. The media, having tasted blood, subsequently became ravenous. They made the evening news a soap opera."

J said, "It also woke up the powerful, super-rich power brokers. They realized that they needed to get organized. And they did. They decided the Republican Party was ripe for takeover. They began buying the press and the legislatures."

"A brilliant strategy." Deman appreciated it.

"But they used the combination to effectively bring down many powerful politicians whose only crime was an open mind, an honest opinion, or the extracurricular infidelity. Even you might be vulnerable."

"Let's hope so."

J looked closely at Deman. He knew that Deman was liable on the first two items but had no idea about the third. He stepped away from the implication. "Then at the same time they launched the era of debauchery of the free press, the trivialization of meaningful news and the glorification of banal news and programming." J learned this at his mother's knee. "The question became how to survive in politics while encumbered with the normal transgressions of Homo Sap. The natural result of this filter to our politicians is that we proceeded to elect accomplished hypocrites, liars, or just nudniks."

"The more easy to manipulate."

"Maybe. But they didn't do very well in holding the union together once they had trampled the constitution."

Deman shook his head, adding almost proudly, "But always in the background is a cadre of knowledgeable cynics handling the politician's strings in response to the pubescent public pulse. 'Manipulate the media and manage the masses' was their mantra."

"Yes. They played them both; in a duet which signaled the demise of laissez-faire capitalistic democracy as certainly as the privileged oligarchy doomed communism. It just took longer."

"Maybe they did us a favor by postponing the inevitable."

"But the inevitable rumbles on." J was looking out the window. "I remember when the first surveillance cameras were put in banks to film robbers. People cheered when the crooks were nailed. They accepted the cameras at most intersections nailing the red-light violators, sending an automatic ticket with a picture in the mail. Instant money for the city. Then, when the cameras were put on school buses to record rowdy behavior students behaved because they were going to get caught, and everyone was pleased. Crimes recorded on ubiquitous video cameras showed the power of television in court."

"Sounds good. Then malls 'protected' the people by keeping watch on every corner of the facility. Not incidentally, shoplifters were picked up. Cameras were placed on streets and drug dealers were caught. Another nice thing was the decrease in personal assault, the scourge of the nineties. All these benefits — what was there to complain about?"

J smiled, "I thought about protesting once or twice but it was futile."

Deman pointed his martini olive at J. "And then, as the violence attending the terrorist attacks reached into every corner of the public domain, so too the cameras were not far behind. Presto, in a shorter time than Orwell could have imagined, omnipresent public surveillance was approved, even demanded, by the public. My only refuge from appearing on TV is my home."

J had to smile thinking of his own home. "That would be nice. When anyone could buy a cheap camera no bigger than my thumb, hide it anywhere and watch the action on a wireless connection to their computer monitor, we were soon monitoring each other. Soon millions of videos were available on the internet, provided by those to whom privacy was inconsequential. Sapiens' surveillance ubiquitous.

"Mistakes were made. I think that lack of foresight in just a few areas marked the difference between success and failure of our economy, our system, our culture. How close we came, maybe even a few votes in a key election. We had the lesson of the sixties where we followed lies into an unwinnable war. Yet we did it again just forty years later. We had the lesson of the eighties where we woke the sleeping extreme right wing. Yet we did it again just thirty years later by taxing the bejabbers out of beloved bullets. Isn't there some saying about not knowing history and doomed to repeat it?"

The two of them were always on the same brain wavelengths so J got the expected result. Deman suspected that J knew Santayana's exact quote. It was Deman's favorite.

"Maybe a fatal flaw of capitalism can be encapsulated in its lack of foresight. Markets respond to short-term gains. In business, absolute dominance absolutely numbs foresight."

"Is this some law of economics?"

"No. But it should be. We all decried the stupidity of the leaders of the big three automakers in the USA when Japan overwhelmed them in the markets of the seventies with reliable, efficient automobiles. They finally forged back with the help of government money and controls and the atrophy at the top of the Japanese companies."

"That took over twenty years, a generation."

"Yes, and they don't read history. Then comes the mind numbing lack of foresight. You got it nearly right, 'Those who cannot remember the past, are condemned to repeat it'. On top in the nineties, they circumvented the modest fuel efficiency requirements, built huge, gas guzzling cars called trucks and marketed as SUVs and actually decreased average fuel efficiency. GM got so committed to big oil that they killed their own potential savior, a reasonably good electric car.

"Of course history repeats; the '74 oil crisis was reborn from the

Middle East wars. The Japanese fuel-efficient cars and hybrids morphing into electrics again overwhelmed the USA automakers and this time they were down for the count. Even revived by the government, they still didn't get it. They deserved to be extinct." Deman shook his head.

He went on without enthusiasm, "Democracy. We certainly proved that this concept doesn't work. But leaders through the ages have known that democracy, as ruled by the majority, didn't work very well. Shaw knew, 'Democracy is the substitution of election by the incompetent many for appointment of the corrupt few.'

"I know. You don't expect much and are pleased by anything short of total catastrophe." J sounded detached, perhaps envious.

Deman took another sip of his martini. It was evidently vitalizing his vocal chords, as he continued, "There's blame for everybody. There were those Quixotic intellectuals who satirized the fops for the rich and didn't even realize that they themselves had become irrelevant to the war in which their icons, rationality and logic, were being slain. This was you, wasn't it?"

"Some truth to it. The manipulators of the US democracy had discovered the secret to winning and it had nothing to do with intelligence, everything to do with charisma. That was you, wasn't it?"

But the martini in front of Deman was nearly consumed and had placed him in a mellow mood already. He just said, "Yep. It's been nice and profitable." Deman was comfortable with being a part of it.

J was just discouraged. "That ability to use power to your own ends consecrates the chosen. Your puppeteers can elect almost anyone they like for their front man by pandering to the lowest instincts of the electorate. No new taxes for them, and of course not for the super-rich either."

"Yes, thank you. I have to give credit to the minds that manipulated the demise of quixotic democracy. It was not without logic that they first attacked the educational system, deleting its funding base and infecting the electorate with the primary virus of ignorance."

"At least it was less messy than their alternate method of control, assassination."

"I don't know about that. I suppose statistics support that most victims were liberals."

"So we have to appreciate the humanitarian way." The sarcasm was heavy.

The facets of his own party served to remind Deman of his deal with the devil. "Yes, it was a brilliant military-like maneuver, the manipulation of our morés. Within a couple of decades came the impeachment, the fraudulent election, three constitutional amendments; right-to-life, guns for all and the faith-based demise of the separation of church and state."

J frowned. "It was too much. We almost turned it around. But your forces were too strong. Just who are these brilliant people controlling our destiny? They articulated brilliantly, with big words, ivy league degrees, and computer models. They reminded me of the winners of our annual forecast contest in the meteorology department. A statistician observed that forecasting 'more of the same' --- tomorrow is like today with a small perturbation --- won most often. The wall-street economists simply did this and claimed it was brilliant. They had to hope some big perturbation that they hadn't allowed for didn't come along. Of course when one did, the house of cards fell in on them, and they were as dumbfounded as anyone."

Now Deman frowned. "They were simply as dumb as anyone. You don't get more Quixotic than being an Ayn Rand disciple. These simpletons were warned, then kicked in the seat, yet they persisted in their faith until a total economic crash."

"My feeling is that they totally lacked any scientific understanding of anything. They did buy mathematicians to create a model, but it was clueless, a house of false assumptions."

"Boy, did it fail. Math isn't always the answer."

"It can dress up a vacuous model or solidify a brilliant one. In this case, they forgot to factor in the variables that fatally crashed their simple minded models."

"You know, even I have no idea how they managed to fool so many of us for so long."

J was surprised that Deman didn't have a better explanation for the crash of 08. Who were these clay kingpins? J didn't know that he was already on a track to find out for himself.

♦

The Copenhagen airport is an extended shopping mall. To attract the maximum number of customers the custom procedures here were minimized. Fair-skinned persons such as Deman and J were almost never asked more than 'staying long?'

Deman was having an extended conversation with the woman at the desk. She seemed agitated, but waved him on with a motion suggesting sweeping something out of her sight. J was sorry that he would be seen as an associate of Deman. However, J was likewise swept on with a stamp that fell right on top of a recent elegant Cambodian stamp.

"What did you do to irritate her?" J tried not to sound irritated himself.

"I made a comment that I smuggled in some tea and scones. I forgot how sensitive Denmark is to its sad state of food rationing. The escalating price of grains, fruits and whatever else China had money to buy has really laid waste to their economy. I guess they're sensitive about it."

"Not smart to use the word 'smuggle' at a customs station."

"True. They're suffering from their lack of an economist who could calculate the food requirements of a billion Chinese who were developing an increasing ability to bid on the world market."

J nodded. "Our economists didn't do very well in predicting the world dislocation in food prices either. The USA diet simply became more meager, and therefore healthier. A good result from the leap in world food prices."

Deman was chagrined at his example of inexperience in international diplomacy. "The Danes were lucky to have ties to the EU agricultural regions. They would have been in trouble if they had to buy food on the world market. Anyway, we won't have any more inspections for the rest of the trip." Deman did not know about J's plans to go on to Africa.

Later, the two had passed on the underground rail from the International terminal to the domestic and were now boarding the flight to Germany. The conference was in Garmish, in the Alps, and most of the delegates, including Deman, were packing skis. J was planning a visit to other 'colleagues' and would not be staying on to vacation afterward.

In fact he would rent a car and drive to Switzerland the first day, skipping meetings to deposit his cash. It was not a good idea to have valuables in your hotel room anywhere in the world these days. Terrorism and petty crime were impacting cultures in similar ways over wide ranges of basic mores. The terrorist acts got the news but the everyday mayhem to simple moralities was taking a bigger toll on humanity, stressing the fabric of civilized life. It was very uncomfortable that most people in Europe blamed the US. First we had polarized our own electorate and then we almost singlehandedly created the immense world polarization with a sequence of ill-chosen wars.

J and Deman went directly from the Munich airport to an underground station of the S-bahn, a decades-old rapid transit system that helped make this section of the world quite livable. J knew that the train now ran on electric power from wind and solar generation. Germany had taken a dominant lead in alternate-to-oil energies during the USA energy dark ages.

In Munich, they rode a few escalators to the transfer to the Garmish train. At five hundred kilometers per hour they were in the heart of the mountains in half an hour. Then there was a short trip in an electric car rental to the base of the cable car, which finally deposited them in a hotel that was carved into the mountain. Looking out into a huge bowl of snow, J could make out tiny chair lifts which he knew from experience stretch a mile up the sides of the immense bowl.

He checked his door lock and began to unpack. The parka was laid on the bed and J's pocketknife cut several seams. A similar process extracted money from inside his shirt, his pants, his hat and his shoes.

He emptied the luggage; gathering together the money and discarding the camouflage that made it appear as books and papers in the X-ray. He unfolded a tightly bound ski bag. Cutting up the cardboard that lined the suitcase he firmed up the ski bag so that when stuffed with the money it looked as if it carried skis. He took a break to go down to the hotel store and buy a ski outfit. He needed something to wear.

When he exited the elevator in the lobby he noticed a 'suit' seated in a lounge chair facing the elevator. He was disturbed that the suit also noticed him. He knew the gangsters were often monitoring him in Seattle but this was the first time he had noticed any one tailing him abroad. He had been puzzled by their restraint. He couldn't know they were preoccupied with other suspects higher on their list. If he had known, he would have expected them to eventually get to him. After all, he knew that everyone else was innocent.

He bought clothes, made his way back to the elevator without looking over again. J returned to his room with a deep sigh. He called Deman, pleaded jet lag, ordered a room-service meal and curled up with a book by the window. His eye mostly stayed on the spectacular view of snow-capped mountains.

J was up early. This was the sticky part. He had to get the money down to his car without tipping off the surveillance guy. He carried the 'skis' down one floor and summoned an elevator. He experienced tense moments as the elevator proceeded directly down to the train level below the main lobby. His timing was precise, and the train left seconds after he got on. He praised his own caution when one of the men lounging around the station looked sharply at him and moved in the direction of the train, too late to catch it. He felt his heart rate elevate, grateful for European timetables. J quelled the suicidal impulse to wave.

The drop was uncomplicated. J simply walked into the Geneva office of his bank, stated that he had a deposit to make, and was escorted to a room where the money was counted. They didn't even ask why he chose such a strange bag for the cash. They were probably used to it all. He was given a receipt with the number of the account, the amount deposited and the total. The last number was now several million dollars. He had already spent as much again and would spend more on this trip. He shred the telltale paper before he left the bank.

J was given a kind of surreal feeling by the Swiss banking industry. So much money, so many wealthy people. Corrupt leaders of small countries, huge crooks, industrial tycoons, and trust funded jet setters. He looked at himself inside the lobby of the bank, and at the few other clients he could see. Everyone seemed so well behaved, so quiet, so ordinary in a way.

The immorality of maintaining this outlet for the outrageous excesses of the world was disturbing. And J was astounded by the amount of money involved. His cache was apparently nothing out of the ordinary. He made a small interest — the bankers didn't need to offer good interest rates-- they had a service that people relied on too much to shop elsewhere. Maybe they also knew most their clients had compromised their integrity so they had no need to offer a fair rate. He didn't think they really considered the ethics too deeply. When the old USA reformist president had tried to end these tax shelters, huge amounts of it were transferred to successfully stop him. It was the citadel of Lassaise faire capitalism. The benchmark of greed. J would be happy when he was relieved of the necessity of attending this sad milieu. He would spend most of the money as soon as possible.

When he left the bank he bought some skis and boots to fill the bag and stopped at a ski area to have lunch. He bought an area badge and skied just a run. It made him reflect on the difference with his first ski experience. He'd come a long way. Up or down, he wasn't sure.

Then he slowly made his way back to his room. He went to the meeting reception that evening. He was genial and friendly, catching up with all the scientists he hadn't seen in a while. He took part in a few conversations about the lectures he had missed without making anyone aware that he missed them.

A few days later anyone tailing him would hopefully be frustrated. J had no need for his suitcase or extra clothes and they were easily disposed of in another room. In the evening he checked out on the television connection to the desk and joined several friends on a dinner trip to the valley. He didn't see any sign of a tail all evening, and after he dropped his friends off near the train station, saying he had forgotten an errand, he simply drove out of town. He took several hours to lose himself in small towns along the way, to go to markets, to stop at tea shops. It seemed to him no one was watching him, but there was no way he could be sure. They would be upset at losing him. His pulse rate was fluctuating as he decided to go on with his plans anyway. He remembered Junior.

He headed for the airport in Italy, easily unloading the anonymous car at the check in. He flew to Africa to spend a few days in Kenya and Tanzania. Europe was the most advanced and free country these days; the African states were still in disarray. It was easy to arrange a relatively secretive trip. He went for several reasons. It was nostalgic to choose here since he and his wife had first visited the area more than ten years before. It was an exploratory trip, for he was thinking of the future. And most of all, it was an inspection trip for this was where his money was ending up.

◆

J scanned the horizon with binoculars in every direction, carefully noting any animal life. There was always some. Today there were lions to the south, awakened early from their afternoon slumber by the cooling effect of the rain. Lions in the south meant he would hike to the north. The north pool looked quiet and he resolved to head there. He focused briefly on Kilimanjaro, looming high above in the northeast less than a hundred miles away. It was over nineteen thousand feet high, fifteen thousand feet above him.

After a last close scrutiny of a clump of rocks and brush about twenty yards to the west, J went down to pick up his equipment. Carrying his gear, he walked down a very long corridor to stone stairs heading a short distance upward. A switch opened a horizontal panel at the top of the stairs. J emerged in a room that was the interior of one of the rocks that he had checked from above. From here, he looked at a video monitor that covered his exit area. The camera was fixed high in the tree. Only then did he touch an unobtrusive switch that opened the door in front of him. He stepped out into a niche in the rocks where he paused to close the unique front door to his home. He moved with caution over the stone and out to the north. He relaxed as he progressed out on to the plain, confident in his preparation and his competence with the rifle in his hands.

At about a hundred yards J paused to look back at his home. It was an oasis with a pond and about ten trees. There was a huge central baobab tree with its tremendously wide trunk — it would take twenty men to circle the tree's girth with their outstretched arms. The tree maintained its huge diameter to sixty feet above the ground. Numerous branches shot out in every direction above thirty feet. It looked like a tree turned upside down, with roots projecting upward. In fact, there were three trunks, two smaller ones beside the main one. The upper branches sheltered the other plants from the noonday heat. There were always some small animals sheltering in his clump of trees.

The central Tree was not a living thing, however the two periphery trunks were real baobabs, carefully preserved, and now growing against the fake trunk. The baobab tree could live to a thousand years, possibly longer than J's steel one.

It was a deciduous tree with a very odoriferous aroma when the flowers bloomed at night. Euphemistically called 'musky' in his research books, it actually resembled the smell of rotting meat. The bats required for pollination loved the distinctive odor.

The baobab produces seedpods called monkey bread. Few animals can break these open to get to the contents that taste strongly of cream of tartar. One group that could get into the pods was the baboons. Their visit was an event that always thrilled J. He harvested seedpods at another tree and tied them up on this one to supplement the production of the real trees. It was never dull around the tree.

"Persons living in this modern world who do not know the basic facts that determine their very existence, functioning, and surrounding, are living in a dream world. Such persons are, in a very real sense, not sane."

—Gerald Holton,
science historian

Ch 2.8 The New USA

It was the occasion of the May high pressure. These few days in May brought welcome clear weather and warmer temperatures to the Northwest. The storm track had moved north into Canada. It was the real end of winter and the contrast made it one of nature's splendid offerings. J was at work. He hadn't managed to figure a way to take off — so he was lecturing to a class while part of his mind was scheming how to leave campus for home and a place in the sun.

This was a science class with a twist — it discussed the place of science in the culture. J felt that scientists were too narrowly educated, so he tried to introduce philosophy whenever he could get away with it. The format was a free expression exchange as J dubbed the give and take. A dog-eat-dog verbal slugfest was the way the students put it. The students were all graduate students and by their own evaluation full of knowledge. Today the class had taken an engaging turn.

J had introduced a topic on environmental degradation. Then it was necessary to mention the steady decline in research money to explain the lack of data, "Of course the private sector wasn't inclined to support the expensive research into ozone holes in the stratosphere, breathing problems from air pollution, or global changes in climate for the 'distant' future. This, despite the fact that 'distant' had moved from a hundred years to ten. And it became obvious that air pollution is a big factor in all of these disasters.

He could put the whole scenario in a nutshell. "With the new millennium the voter's distrust of taxes, politicians and government led to the decay of infrastructure and national enterprise. For projects from potholes to satellites, responsibility blurred, and funding for basic infrastructure became moribund. The R2-B2 reactionary conservative reigns-- redistribution of wealth ever upward- an entrenched class structure in our society- the terrorist attacks bringing an incredible political crunch with patriotic fervor to limit citizen rights as a result, then the expensive quixotic wars to protect our oil under their sand, poor fiscal policy rewarding the rich and greedy while neglecting development of alternate energies leading to economic decay, the collapse of the separation of church and state and finally the Revolution to the reconstituted states. This was the coup d'état. Two hundred years of good effort essentially down the drain."

One of J's graduate students, Teton, had a penchant for organization and detail and had a request for more background. "It would help to recall our history in a little more detail to establish the current situation. It might help us see a solution. I suppose that it is probably impossible within the bounds of political correctness."

Baker, an intellectual who was beautiful even though she had no hair, even eye lashes, due to some pernicious perturbation of her genetic soup, entered aggressively, "We can start with the flood of legislation that emanated from the Neanderthal government at the dawn of the new millennium. They shifted the burden of 'government mandate' to the states." A Deman student, she agreed with looking at history.

Aaron tried to maintain a low profile usually but he did reveal something about himself every time he spoke. "Not a bad idea."

"Yes, Aaron, get the government off our backs and into our bodies. These same legislators imposed fundamentalist backed federal restrictions on a woman's control over her own body and even condemned evolution teaching in general. Instead of 'new millennia' it was 'old milieu'." She had an agenda with a powerful love of history. J liked imagining the conversations with her advisor.

Christopher was one of J's grad students, another aggressive observer. He agreed the changes were sudden but added, "That was just the social part; economically they gave the national treasury to the super-rich."

"The sad part was this is a Democracy. It's what the people voted for." Teton seemed to see things from a more detached overview.

Baker reminded Teton, "Not a majority. The electorate was split down the middle. The purloined election exposed the soft underbelly of our political system. Raise a hundred million dollars and it's difficult not to get elected. Then a simple pay back with a tax break. At all levels, strident, single-issue true believers can overwhelm a busy majority with broad interests."

Christopher weighed in, "Yes, but if you have broad interests you're bound to be wrong on some of them. Soft is the right word though. I suggest it applied higher than the belly, try the cerebrum." Christopher spoke from a Lincolnesque visage at six and a half feet. He always remained erect and felt an obligation to aim somewhere in the vicinity of the profound.

J stayed in the game. "Tuned to these weaknesses in the electorate the politicians had learned they could ignore majority opinions in deference to moneyed special interest groups."

Christopher rode that wave as well. "Very successfully since candidates with the money for media manipulation invariably won elections. We know that in 1972 a group of very rich members of the energy elite sat down at a table and plotted the future with brilliant success. They designed the takeover of the media, installed the talking heads and most important, the pied-piper talk show hosts for the fearful under-educated public. The key attributes of these front men were being glib, shot through with material greed and a disdain for education."

Aaron was ever the conservative cynic. "Just like we 'know' that sixty-six million years ago a panel of dinosaurs sat down and plotted their future with great success. They saw that the ongoing demise of most of their species opened the way to mammal dominance so they planned their evolution to occupy one niche, the air, and evolved into birds."

Christopher laughed. "Makes sense. The big ones even prey on small mammals. They're probably biding their time until conditions are ripe for a re-emergence as the dominant force."

Teton needed to get back to his summery, "Hey, we agree. It's obvious in retrospect. The soft-brained voters supported the takeover by the super-rich 'cause they love their commercials, their sports, their hang-the-cost, sex-sells-all and the other brain-stem appeals. They did wake up a bit and tried to stop the downfall of the US, but it was too little, too late. This left the frustrated majority with revolution as an only recourse. It came and went. There were new political arenas but it all smells the same."

J had his favorite point to make. "It was to be expected. You can't run a successful modern democracy when the average voter thinks that evolution is an esoteric scientific theory."

"And thinks the processes of calculus — differentiation and integration — are racial segregation and affirmative action," Teton said, grinning, they were having a love fest. Baker chimed in with a smile for Teton, "And that both are 'unnatural'."

Christopher looked at Baker with friendly solidarity. "Worse yet, a lot of them believe the arrangement of stars affects their destiny."

Teton opted for practical application. "OK. Let's get back on track. The lack of USA trained math and technology workers led to an immigration-based work force in the new technology domain. As they rose to better pay and status we got a schism. The newcomer was the elite, the native-born the effete." Baker and Christopher giggled and chortled at this and the conversation deteriorated into humor and mayhem for a little while. Christopher checked whether J was into it. "Do you think that an earlier start toward better curriculum could have saved us? Could we have had a lifesaver with improved education? Better teachers, better pay, smaller classes and a general emphasis on intellectual attainment might have saved the old Union?"

J hedged, "We'll never know, will we? Since these basic improvements to the culture were tried, but the financial meltdown meant they never came. If they couldn't manage to teach algebra how could they educate every student in anthropology, biology, botany and geophysics?"

"You begged the question again." Baker frowned.

"Right. The answer is no."

"Did any one try?" Christopher was understandably plaintive.

"A lot of people did. But not enough people. It wasn't easy, believe me. I recall making an effort toward teaching a course in the philosophy department. They did actually consider a curriculum I suggested. This class would have advanced the hypothesis that a fatal flaw in cultural design was that it didn't emphasize the supreme accomplishments of human thought, especially the body of thought known as science.

"It discussed problems such as 'why did the voters choose to give the wealth and power to a few families' and how it became understandable in the context of evolution's dictates. The human animal inherited programming for expected status in the hierarchy just like other predators. There were a few 'alphas' but many 'betas'. The latter are content, even pleased, to give the power to the "alpha" and accept their lower-class position. Less responsibility for one thing. Power has been handed over to the supposedly natural born leaders.

"Well, this concept was not well received by the philosophy professors. I suspect the reason arose in my syllabus where the label 'half-educated' was applied to those who lacked the science background that I considered essential." He shook his head, "Should have realized that this included most of the department."

Baker, always polite along the surface conventions, raised a hand. "Probably because professors are mostly frustrated 'alphas'."

Teton could join in this topic based on his life experience. "Why is

there a tendency in our species to resent the clever, witty, knowledgeable
— calling them 'smart-alec' and 'nerdy'? They are usually excluded from
leadership positions. It surely has something to do with our evolutionary
disposition. Something in our genetic disposition must wire us to recoil
from the intelligent person and love the trite talk-show twit. It has always
been dangerous to exhibit intelligence in the youthful culture."

Christopher also empathized with this. "Right. It was a sure passport to
nerddom. It follows along an evolutionary perspective that the downward
spiral in intellectual capability was reinforced. Those who controlled the
power and wealth of the nation wouldn't have anything to do with a smart
woman. She would cause trouble and she just naturally scared the guys
anyway. Not something they were used to. Scared the pants on them."

Baker winced but knew where Christopher was coming from. She
continued with her analysis. "So the intelligent individual who does not
hide her brilliance well is excluded from cultural perks and maybe even
marriage. Since most intellectuals don't seem to be able to hide it, that
leaves the intellectually challenged in charge. They accrue the huge salaries,
commensurate power and occupy the highest offices."

"What the heck, they are 'nice people' who appear harmless."
Christopher was commenting on their successful camouflage, the majority
of corporate and administrative staff who conformed so well.

"But that façade is frail," Baker objected, "their understanding of the
human dilemma is shallow. They are shiny as a brass doorknob and just as
astute. This trend cumulated in the legislators who didn't have a clue why
they became known as the troglodyte congress."

"And an executive branch that started deceptive, expensive, quixotic
wars."

"And dummies in charge of economics."

J listened with interest. "Perhaps the genes don't like the brain
development that goes off doing its own thing above and beyond
propagation. Intelligence de-selected."

Baker's hobby was history. "Interesting theory. But from a short-term
point of view the institutional structure of our Republic was not strong
enough to withstand the assault of the combination of the corporate
self-interest with the fundamentalist religious. Elections were easily
manipulated and when enough of their ilk got into the Supreme Court
they had control of all three branches of government. We had at least five
on the court who had little or even no science classes beyond high school.
The pope dictated abortion policy. We became a theocracy.

"There were brief respites. But enough people voted emotionally that the manipulators were able to carry the day. Power went again to a functionary with knowledge deep as rust."

J smiled as he turned the analogy on itself, "A thin layer of rust can find a crack in steel and break it."

Aaron liked that. "Ah yes. We elected the dynasty president who got the country as a gift and proceeded to play with it until it broke, as was his wont." Looking at Baker he continued: "Elected with the swing vote of a woman!"

Christopher was working on establishing himself as a Renaissance man. "Religious idealisms were another flaw. Sancho Panzas or agnostics don't strap bombs to themselves, fly planes into buildings or dedicate their lives to the local preacher's heaven. Jefferson's great contribution to the constitution —separation of church and state —should have remained intact. The founding fathers knew that they had to keep the true believers out of government."

Baker raised an invisible eyebrow. "But another kind of true believer, in greed and power, won. Then their overreach finally inspired a reaction and those who could be were thrown out."

Teton, although he loves Baker's intellectual virtuosity, wants to get back on track to finish this historic summary. "OK. But it was too late for the Republic. The Revolution was hastened by the matter of the second "Crusades", amazingly, a word used by our president to describe that expensive fiasco. Not to mention how many enemies it bred anew. We were a nation of followers and the alpha dogs in control were rabid."

Baker wanted to return to history. "We designed our own destruction; the undermining of our system produced the collapse. We got back on track, but too late."

Teton yielded to their two-part harmony. He didn't want to offend Baker. It was pretty obvious he was captivated with the mind under that bald pate. "The end, like the beginning, was precipitated by decades of fatally flawed economics, then a tax revolt when the errors were pointed out."

Aaron had to criticize, "That seems too simple."

Teton was grateful. "Right, the roots could probably be traced directly to a deeper quixotic perspective; the belief by a significant sector of the population and politicians that they had a divine pipeline to the morality pool." Teton figured that should hit home with Aaron.

J said, "So I ask you: is this sad supercilious condition simply a result of a lack of scientific understanding of what Homo sapiens really is?"

Baker tolerantly smiled a partial agreement. "Probably. But the mechanism of the descent of the old states to revolution was a slippery slope. We had democratically put the wolves in charge of the henhouse. Then the terrorist attack was a strong perturbation. As terrorism spread with random snipers, bombs and mayhem to the Internet, the fragility of the US concepts of freedom were exposed. The idea that people were innocent until proven guilty, trust in some basic safety, and equality amongst the people --- each was compromised to save the culture; and yet the culture still decayed."

Christopher said, "Yeah. I mean, it was so obvious. Everybody needed to say 'Whoa, now. What are you doin'? I don't support that.' The split between the true believers in the Middle East and the true believers in the White House blazed with self-righteous rhetoric. Moderate voices questioned the wisdom of both; and were silenced in both camps.

"It was amazing when we elected the first president who was," here a pause, "an intellectual. Even when we got back on the right track, it was late. Just like we were too late with combating global warming."

J had memories. "Talk about screeching feedback. Science and education was misused and unsupported. The result was the substitution of faith for observations, preaching for research, obtuseness for logic and fear for freedom. It was too late to save the initial Republic and the new states were born out of the chaos."

Christopher was more succinct. "The old USA perished from the terminal stupidity of half the electorate."

"And one political party." Teton looked at the token conservative.

Aaron was a little pugnacious about re-interpreting. "At least there was a peaceful realignment of states. Up in this godforsaken corner the merger of the northwestern region and Northern California to become the state of Cascadia was natural. The natives shared strong return-to-nature movements with a spectrum of kooky communal, nearly communistic aims."

"Probably true." Teton's naturally friendly face lit up a bit as he discussed his state. "We had to fight for it though. There was the battle with the most militant elements. Took a while to build strong borders to protect the people and the environment --- keep the economy stable up here. It makes sense to call the Colombia River the Divider, separating us, the moderate northwest, from the biggest state on the other side."

Aaron sat up a little taller. He was proud of his home state. "Midwest is our strongest state militarily, politically and spiritually; America's heartland from the Cascades to the Mississippi." It may have been salutary to remind the class that they were in a pocket of quiet. But the noise outside seeped in. J looked thoughtfully at his errant student. Needed to pay more attention there. It was like having your own devil at your back, but right in front of you. He wondered how the hell he could moderate his teaching technique for somebody like that. It wasn't really something he could do.

"Jesus Christ, it is also the right-wing, religious, militia state." Teton looked at Aaron as if asking, 'Why aren't you there?'

J winced. Well, Teton could do it. He had his converts, obviously. He might be glad of that. He wondered if he had taught them all to put their necks on the line. He supposed so. Was that a good thing? In theory, maybe. To hold back that deluge. But it was, perhaps, like sending children into a hopeless war. Gallipolis.

Aaron was jumping on Teton for jumping on him.

"For a secularist, you invoke the name of Jesus often enough."

"I do. Don't know why. My second favorite expression is 'Holy shit'. I suppose they're related." Teton was willing to think about it.

Baker felt the need to interject as she was aware of the antagonism between these two, both interested in getting to know her better. She preferred Teton, the intellectual- but appreciated Aaron's interest. He was a handsome hulk. "Ok Aaron, your state is the biggest and strongest militarily, but it is also the have-not state since global warming and depleted water have destroyed the agricultural base."

Teton happily returned to their two-part harmony of historical wrap-up. "So we have the eco-state Cascadia and the religious state Midwest representing the two sides of the divide established by the politics of the new century. The materialistic states formed the logical state of Calzona with an iron curtain on their southern border with Mexico."

"And on their eastern border with Texas, now in New Dixie." Baker refined the details.

Teton was happy to finish their review. "Right. The Confederacy was reborn in the New Dixie and the Union was resurrected and expanded westward to absorb the northeast corner of the Midwest and create the state of New England. Many went back to the good old days. The borders are a bit beefed up but we're still one nation."

Baker nodded. "Only Alaska remained Alaska. We had the Islands left over to make a state and round out our seven United States of America." They were still proud, despite their criticism.

J appreciated their summary. "I guess we were lucky that the creation of the new States was not as violent a dissolution as happened in the Soviet Union, Yugoslavia, Iraq, Pakistan and India. But it produced a similar result; there is a much looser federation with a lot less punch. "

Baker was ready to move ahead. "The result was really a formalization of the ideological schisms along state boundaries. And that is where we are now. Mired in the past. — Dark Ages II. What do we do about it?"

Christopher liked the question. "OK. The current situation is that the new conglomerate states are even less interested than the old in cooperating to study a huge problem like global climate change. They can't afford to chip in to fund satellites to sense the pulse of the planet or even cooperate with the privatized weather service. They were unable to save forests on federal lands. Cascadia could never get together with its neighbors to measure or mitigate interstate air and water pollution."

J seemed to be serving as the optimist this session. "We do seem to have lost our way. The USA went in the opposite direction to Europe. Their unification worked better than our fragmentation. Everyone needs a clan structure, a resource to turn to. The controlled capitalism of Europe and China worked better than our total commitment to greed. But we have survived. Clambering out of the political abyss was like restoring a cherished piece of broken crystal. It isn't pretty, but it still resembles the original a bit.

"So once again," and this was the quantum conjecture that J embraced, "the cultural vice was poor education — ignorance of science, evolution- and consequently any understanding of the existence, nature or limitations of Homo Sap. But no one could convince those in charge to accept this hypothesis."

The buzzer sounded, frustrating the students as they had just worked themselves to the current state, the current dilemma. It would have to wait.

"All of us are in the gutter. Some are looking at the stars."

Oscar Wilde.

"Some are looking at the clouds for the next rainstorm."

Sancho Panza (RAB)

Ch 2.9 A Class, A Date

It was twenty-four hours after the last session of the 'Science and Society' class. The history review had fired frustration, but that appeared forgotten this morning.

J surveyed his students. At the graduate level they were dedicated individuals. They were in this class because they had concern for the environment and most realized the government had failed to address the issue. He knew they had probably discussed the situation. He always hoped that some had thought of an innovative way to help get the society and culture back on track. But none was forthcoming when he asked.

Aaron finally broke the silence. He had been silently upset the previous day. He provided a provocative question. "So, what do you think, professor? Where do we stand now? Are there any answers to prevent the deterioration of the environment? Or is it hopeless? How about a frank, honest answer."

J paused a moment. J had not gotten to know Aaron. He knew of Aaron's conservative politics and that probably turned off his interest. Basically his question was like the one that J had addressed at the Regents' Friends lecture. The answer had to be the same. J briefly wondered, was this student really interested in what J thought? Or was it just a prescription question to bolster his class participation? Another student tipped the balance by adding a further 'What do you really think?' And another.

"OK. I really think the reasons for the deterioration are obvious. The scientific solution is simple. There are no scientific barriers to reversing the current trend and creating a beautiful, nurturing environment for Homo sapiens. The barriers are nearly all sociological. But since they are having a difficult time addressing them in the science-challenged sociology department, we'll spend a few minutes here." Part of his brain said, 'Oh boy, here we go.'

"The situation is a bit like that facing Galileo in the 1600s. For two thousand years the litany that the earth was the center of the universe, fixed and constant, held sway. This was because the principal thinker of the 400 BC era was Aristotle and he did a lot right, but he also made a few errors. In the hundreds of intervening years several people had noticed the abundant evidence to the contrary. Copernicus had deduced the correct arrangement based solely on common sense and simple observation a hundred years before Galileo employed the telescope to actually see the truth. But Copernicus' theory was contrary to the politically correct dogma.

"This was possibly one of the first examples of the familiar dichotomy between scientists, in particular the theoretician and the experimenter."

K knew of this from her father. "I've heard that it is more of a tradition of competitive criticism, at times purely intellectual, at times unconscious."

"That's the rosy picture. It goes by several names: between theory and experiment, analytic analysis and curve fitting, thinkers and doers."

"I've heard it's civil yet grating."

"Well we try to make it civil. It is grating because there is an assumed superiority of and by the first named in each pair. There is always an aura to doing theory, but there are great rewards to doing experiments with a little creative curve-fitting. I always suggest to my students that they try to be on the strong side of each pairing."

"But Galileo was on both sides. When he performed the experiment of looking at Jupiter and saw moons going around that planet, he embraced Copernicus's theory. But in general, since the barriers to an open minded approach to new ideas are buried deep in our cultural sociology, I expect that about half of you will innately reject my diagnosis. The other half will agree but many will realize that the solution will never be implemented. You have heard it before, but it has become unlawful, if not plain dangerous, to state it publicly. Under the banner of 'political correctness' truth has been the victim.

"The obvious underlying problem is overpopulation. Capitalism's mantra, 'growth' just isn't good in a long run. The planet is like a rose bush with a serious aphid problem. My parents' generation was like the aphids that were born just as the rose budded. They lived the charmed life occupying every niche, every bud, every tender shoot- and eventually every toughened branch. My generation inherited the fruits of their harvest, the flowers were still in bloom, and the juices still flowed sufficient for everyone. Let me tell you it was delicious.

"Now we're all over the bush sucking up the sap. The plant is in trouble. I worry that the gardener, the God of the garden, will come by and spray the rose bush to save it."

The metaphor seemed to have grabbed their attention. "I suppose aphids go to aphid heaven where roses are vassals to be homes for aphids."

"I suppose there are no aphids in rose heaven. Or in gardener's heaven?"

J shrugged. "As usual, more questions arise than answers. Heaven is a hopelessly complicated construction."

He inspected their faces. Was there anyone violently opposed to this line of talk? Most religious students were simply fatalistic in their set position on population control. They placed their anti-abortion, big-family training into a compartment and attempted to weave their science education around it. In a graduate science class they would be rare. They learned to be very circumspect.

They would also be aware of politically correct rules against teaching religion, or anti-religion, and all the other rules of sexual, racial, economic or intellectual harassment. He knew that the number of the righteous religious had increased rapidly after they had come out of the intellectual closet during the R2-B2 dark ages. Their numbers had brought the intellectual community to its knees, impaired the education system, and then severely wounded the democracy. They survived the resulting chaos. They were quixotic true believers flexible enough to be panzaic survivors. An irony to be sure.

J was influenced by his conversation with Deman. He considered backing off. Unfortunately, Kay wasn't concerned with politics and had gotten interested in the problem. "But aren't you begging the question?"

Against his better judgment he decided to answer her. After all, they were in the 'Ecology State'. He would be out of a job in any other state. "All right. You want some direct solutions. All likely agendas would start with controlling the population. If you read it as controlling copulation, it is impossible. But if you look upon it as using economic and intellectual incentives, then it is doable.

"The evidence is in. We know that in overpopulated communities many children, and then adults, become aimless and parasitic. We have already discovered that intelligent, educated and prosperous beings do not have a lot of children. They have too many other things to do. So this suggests the need for, and the avenue to, a solution — we simply make everyone educated and prosperous."

There were a few snorts of derision at this Quixote fantasy.

"Would you buy 'educated and working'? But wait. Before you accuse me of being glib, I say that is not as impossible as it sounds. With population control and planning we're on the way to making people — employees — a valuable commodity. First, take away the incentive for employers to pay double overtime rather than hire more. Then mandate the thirty-hour workweek. This takes care of unemployment and creates leisure. Europe exploited this fact long ago. Their people enjoy a six-week vacation while we average two.

"Leisure is used for fun and mischief, creating new business. You see, I can think like an economist. I find it fun. It takes less effort than it does to think like a physicist. Most important, this leisure time can be used to improve the mind. We just have to create the incentive.

"Of course to mandate a work week requires other mandates — like national health care and social security such that twice as many workers don't cost twice as many benefits. But the model for this too has existed for a generation in European society. They have universal health care, few guns, emasculation of church influence on state business, great public transportation, humongous vacations, decreasing ratio of rich to poor people and strong federal direction. The USA got out to an early start on these things but we reversed the trend in the 'eighties.

"Change was necessary. A new way had to be found; the old one wasn't working. Unfortunately, by the time we found a leader with common sense, it was too late."

This was certainly, by definition, politically incorrect. As Deman pointed out, he was driven by an unknown genetic impulse. Not content with only one provocation he continued, "Second, let's finally phase out the internal combustion engine. Start by imposing a large tax on a gallon of gas. The benefits from this simple move are so numerous that the failure to do this decades ago stands out as the political gaff of the century. Instead, we put the purveyors of this misdirected economy in charge of the country. The dependence on oil ran us into territory we couldn't know. Fighting wars in obscure Middle East deserts brought us up against religious attitudes we couldn't understand. Not just why they hated us but why they loved their own sorry state. Particularly the less enfranchised women." Said with a glance and raised eyebrow at Kay.

She was nonplussed. "Overpopulation and under education zonks all ability to think about anything but survival."

J accepted that. "For starters, ending our dependence on oil would save the environment from global warming, air and water pollution, ubiquitous stress from unremitting noise and a dangerous omnipresent fluid runoff. Taxes needn't offend the rich directly, only in their corporate role. Incentives to provide public services and amenities could be tied to wealth building projects and enterprise.

"Tax cars by size and horsepower. Do the same to lawnmowers, snowmobiles and boats.

"Use the money to educate, but also to fertilize the study of alternate means of transportation and power. This has been suppressed by the automobile and oil industries since the 1930s. Of course the social repercussions of man's association of his ego with his auto must be managed in the process. But advertising and politicians have shown that people are easily manipulated. Individual energy independence via solar energy, passive and active, has been available for decades."

Baker asked, "Why don't we hear about these things?"

Kay suggested, "Maybe the media doesn't think we're interested?

"Maybe the sponsors of the news would object to a lot of airtime undercutting their way of life."

J got back on theme. "Anyway, once you realize that the system isn't working and must be changed, it isn't too difficult to fix. Jacking up the education system is the best solution, but that is probably too slow. It first needs motivation towards getting an education. Let's consider some more controversial possibilities." J was looking out the window, gathering his thoughts from the blue sky. Otherwise he might have noted the wary expressions in front of him.

He felt that these were the things which needed to be said, but never were, anywhere in the University. When J finally looked back into the faces of the class he could tell that the best students were being provoked and considering his words. He saw eyes that were a little wider around them, a silence that was complete. He let it rip, though; they need to know.

"OK. I'll give you a little test to see how receptive you are to new ideas. Currently, the only criterion to vote is to be alive for a certain number of years. Let's make small additional requirements. Give one vote to those who breathe. Then establish a certification program to reward accomplishments- like educational degrees, developing a business, election to office, environmental projects, civic projects and learning the Cha Cha Cha. Maybe give two votes to those who attain some certification of education. Give three, four or more to people at your level." He let that sink in; they would see the merit. "I would probably get ten." This sense of humor was definitely not self-effacing, rather, self-defeating. But again it seemed to be congenital, and the student's groans only reminded him of his cultural defect.

"OK, more direct routes to a manageable society. Ban guns. Undemocratic, even Draconian, you say. But their single-mindedness has led to the cultural anarchy we have now. With the purest of intentions they are unfortunately the naïve foils of the militant, having created a fertile environment for the terrorist. It's too easy for the criminal and the crazy to be armed. And we have an ample supply of both.

"Then there's the faith-based anti-abortion group. They could be taxed for the worldwide tragedies from overpopulation. If they really believe in it, they should be willing to pay for it."

Baker was following closely. "Of course this must all be democratically installed. This ballot sounds like it would have to be a sworn statement or people would just check the boxes for maximum votes. We would need a lot more lawyers."

J laughed.

"Whoa. You are absolutely correct. Sounds like we've come full-circle? I agree there would be a lot of problems to be worked out. Records and voting could be all in the computer. Except we've seen how that can be corrupted. In fact, the problems are probably insurmountable. Homo Sap is the problem. He might also be the solution, but that is going to take a lot of new ideas.

"Can one convince the whole congress that they need to be aware of the scientific as well as political basis for relevant decisions? Of course not. It seems we are mired in ignorance with little chance of breaking loose. Democracy actually works against change. Got to reach that consensus after all."

This soliloquy ought to flush out the true believers. J looked closely. Everyone looked a bit shocked. At least half were smiling. But there were nervous smiles.

"Well, you asked. That's all the time I have for solutions right now. You can see that they are readily forthcoming. They are easily available. But they do butt up against some of our cherished notions of individual rights and innate privacy. They are certainly quixotic. They fly in the face of most of our cultural heritage. It would require another revolution, another, less vindictive, Enlightenment.

"Plato recommended it. Alexander, Napoleon, Lenin and Obama tried it. It never worked. But you asked me for solutions, not practical solutions.

In which case I would probably have said 'there are none'. Still, we could try. If you're drowning it's worth a try to learn to swim."

♦

After class, Kay ran to catch up with J, "You know, Aaron is a shill."

"A what?" J really didn't know the current interpretation of this word.

"You know, a snitch, an ad-rat, an informer for the administration." J looked questionably at Aaron, who was walking fifty feet away. He was laughing and talking with two other students. He was immaculately dressed. J knew he was very proper in class. The last class had made it obvious that he had dissenting views. Still, Aaron tried to be even handed with other students. J was dubious about the actual fact of being paid to report on classes. He tested his interpretation, "Such a nice guy."

Kay was watching him, thinking, 'Is he really that naive, or just politically dumb?'

J looked at her, wondering if she was politically dumb or simply really that naïve. "So why did you ask me that question in class?"

This stopped her. She looked truly pained. "I didn't think. I mean I didn't think you would give such an unrestrained answer. I expected you to be circumspect."

"Why no, I'm not. My parents felt that was a primitive ritual." Thus proving he was rarely 'circumspect'.

She had a puzzled look that turned into a striking smile.

"I wouldn't know about that. But you are awfully circumcised around me. Ever since I chastised you over your latent come-ons you've been very careful. It's like you're afraid to talk friendly — the current salvo excepted."

J was impressed with the way she accepted the pun with aplomb, tossed it back, and got serious all in one breath. "I suppose that I'm inhibited by the administrative threats about student-professor relations. And I have become aware that you are very attractive which means everyone is expecting you to be hit upon. I hate to do the expected."

"That's nice. Well, I always feel that if I'm going to be assumed to be guilty of something that I'd like to do then I might as well do it."

"The crime fits the punishment?"

"Yes. Besides, after today's lecture, what have you got to lose?"

"OK, let me buy you a cappuccino."

"Yes, I'll let you buy me a cappuccino."

The cappuccinos were tall and frothy at the student hub. The conversation was also frothy. As J's laughter quieted, he said, "Of course it is perfectly understandable for us to sit here and discuss your thesis prospects. But I'm afraid that merriment is not a common ingredient of fluid dynamics theses. There are at least three people I can see, their minds clicking over about all this laughter and joy. It's obvious to them I'm a professor hitting on a student."

"So," she shook her head, "why don't we discuss fluid dynamics."

Damn, is she a vamp, or a tease, or maybe she is just interested in him as a confrere. J shook his head, "When my testosterone is flowing my cerebrum shuts down. Everything is brainstem. It sometimes takes an hour to purge."

"Sheesh, glad I don't have that handicap."

"But we can have a serious discussion on other, simpler, topics, where I have a set library of responses that I can refer to. How about what to do with Aaron, what I could do to facilitate your thesis, and whether you're going to have dinner with me this Friday."

"Well, I have other classes with Aaron. I'll try and feel him out. I hope that you have noticed that I'm a good scientist and now that I've got your attention I hope my thesis is in the bag. Dinner is probably inevitable, but Friday is too soon."

Damn again. How's she going to handle Aaron? Of course she's a very good scientist. Friday is too soon but who in the hell is in charge here? "I can live with that," was all that came out of J.

I drink when I have occasion, and sometimes when I have no occasion.

Miguel de Cervantes (1547–1616),
Spanish novelist and dramatist.
Don Quixote (1605).

Ch 2.10 A Party

The baobab grows soft & pulpy, and elephants love the tree. They visit at regular intervals, swallowing the whole fruit pods that fall to the floor under the tree. The tree relied upon them to disperse the hard, black, indigestible seeds. Transported afar, the elephant dung would then often be rolled in a ball by dung beetles, which then planted the seeds in the ground as they used the partially digested dung for food in their dens. J's library of the area was extensive, and by now he was an expert on the regional ecology, from climate to dung.

The elephants also like to gouge out strips of the moist bark of the baobab tree during the dry season. Fortunately, the baobab tree had a remarkable healing process for this assault, generating new bark, and that served to produce a rough, gnarled and deeply ridged irregular trunk. The gerbil, gray mouse, barn owl, bats and bush babies used these and other indentations as homes.

Sometimes the elephants would undermine a young tree just as it was getting mature, and trample it down to eat the bark, pulp & branches. When they started in on the trees encircling J's home, he protected them with appropriate sounds that made the elephants wary of his central trees. During his absences these trees had been attacked, but by then they were large enough to regenerate. The elephants didn't seem to bother J's fortress Tree. They may have tried and bent a tusk. Perhaps they could sense the stainless steel not far beneath the bark cover.

Birds appreciate the tree for its many hollow niches. The combination of the real and the perpetually dormant tree seemed to make J's place particularly attractive. High above, an eagle made its nest. And nearby, flirting with the eagle, weaverbirds hung their ingenious structures. The tree was a grand central station in the local ecosystem.

♦

J's student Christopher, a really bright guy, took J's fluid dynamics course when he entered graduate school eight years ago. The average stay for a Ph.D. was six years. This student had been distracted during his thesis work when he found that he was in love with the mathematics grad student who consulted with him. It was a traumatic realization for him, since the other student was also male.

J recalled their conversation about it. Christopher had stopped at his office late one afternoon and revealed his predilection, asking J, "What do you think about it?"

J had honestly answered, "I don't think much about it."

This upset Christopher.

"So, if you're not supportive of this kind of lifestyle, maybe I need to find another guidance professor."

"No, you misunderstand. I don't think about it very much. About the same as I think about how I love my mother or the lint in everyone's navel."

"How can you not think about it, when it is so important to so many people?"

"I'll think about their lint if they thrust their belly in my face, or if they tell me the lint is clogging their ability to think. But basically, I prefer the management of this trait to be personally handled." J just didn't think it was his business. A judgment call destined to be called Quixotic.

"Well, what about all the prejudice and outright violence that is directed at gays?" Christopher knew that this was a sure thing.

"Of course I deplore that. It is illogical. Born of an ignorance of genetics. But our genes were primarily programmed for a million years to prefer procreation; that is, they're straight. Perhaps there was a fitness feedback associated with overpopulation problems and value to non-reproducing individuals. But this was more recent. There is still an innate Homo Sap animosity toward different sexual preferences. As with other tendencies toward violence, it takes a bit of education to overcome. It is folly to parade any sexual peccadilloes before an untutored public. In fact, I have never liked to hear locker-room stories about macho sexual conquests of any kind." This wasn't going to do it, J knew.

"OK, I agree. But do I have to hide?"

"Have you any idea of how many ideas, thoughts, and sexual fantasies of mine have to be hidden?" J reflected that he was on soft ground here. The national inhibitions toward frank talk of sexual predilections and hormonal impulses had disappeared in the last decade. The new generation had decided that hypocrisy was the enemy, and frank sexual talk became common. But it was mostly talk, as the general sexual mores were still fairly conservative. They did talk a good game though, and J wasn't certain why the gays shouldn't be able to join in.

Christopher went on, not realizing that J was coming around in his thoughts, "Yes, but you don't have to confront those feelings in daily conversations, or in dating rituals. You don't get questions about them, like a young person has to constantly deal with their sexuality. I can't tell you how many people have tried to 'get me a girl'. They don't take subtle hints. They can't empathize. So I have to consider that it should be announced and celebrated."

J shook his head, "Your sexual preferences should be public domain?"

This gave Christopher pause. J knew that his 'deviation from the norm' must have re-trained him to consider carefully every statement. His experience had produced this rule at no little expense. And the very newness had taught him that breaking the rule was hard to avoid. Finally Christopher replied, "No, but sex is just a biochemical glue that bonds you to another person. Nothing to be ashamed about. It is this bonding that I don't want to deny."

"Damn, if you just made as much sense in explaining your thesis topic, you'd be done by now."

"Well, if I can get the question of what to do about this behind me, I will be able to finish."

Christopher must have made some decision; with a year of concentrated hard work he finished his last draft. This night, J was having a celebration party at his house.

◆

J's parties were singular. He had put out an e-mail inviting everyone to Christopher's celebration. All the students were there; and half the faculty. There was good food, drink, and audacious conversation.

June weather was a gamble in the Northwest. Rains were most common, but for the past two decades increasingly strong rainstorms alternated with warm, dry spells. Luckily, a perfect day between storms arrived on this Saturday. J finished cleaning with the help of Christopher and another of his students while he defrosted a feast for the crowd — flash freezing and microwaves greatly simplified party giving. His hunter-gatherer instincts were amply satisfied in the long aisles of frozen food at the local market.

Now a cook's talent was mainly in the judgment of 'time to process'. Seconds made the difference.

He presided over tapping the keg of local brew. The amber beer was modeled after English bitters, perfected in the Northwest. The Chardonnay was a home grown variety, too, as good as could be found, and for a moderate price. Cascadia State had prospered economically under the new-states revolution.

Not that price deterred J these days, but he avoided anything ostentatious. However, small things could be perfect. Of the three bottles of red wine on the counter, one was a French burgundy that tasted as good as red wine gets. It cost twenty times as much as the other bottles. To varying degree this had become a common touch at his parties and dinners. No one had ever exposed this little escapade, and the comments amused him. They ranged from appreciation of the taste — and requests for where to get a bottle --- 'It was a gift' — to the usual casual acceptance.

Later, his imported Italian espresso machine would use the world famous Seattle coffee. They'd have delicious chocolate decadence pie. It was life at its best. J always paused to appreciate it, and reflect on his good fortune in timing — born at the right time. No Pharaoh, no king of the Middle Ages, ever ate such palate pleasing cuisine. He landed in a great place, temporally and geographically. Of course, the downside of living in such a beautiful region was the influx of hoards of immigrants, from the entire world as islands and coastal regions vanished under the swelling sea. They increased the population to the point where many of the original attractions of the area were now gone.

J's house sat on a hill overlooking Lake Washington- a thirty-mile long, three-mile wide stretch of water filling an ancient glaciated valley. The landscape was redolent with Douglas fir, the tall evergreen that grew like a mega-weed in the Northwest. Originally it was a blanket on the state, but now it occurred amidst farms and suburbs like dark green veins in granite. There were also a few pockets of cedar left over, but being a prettier building wood and slow growing, they were few and far apart. In some areas there were stands of Sequoia, planted by Homo sapiens over a hundred years ago. They were the young trees on the block.

The original forests were all gone now. The new forests were planted after people realized what they had lost. If only they could also plant the species that were lost. Many swaths of trees had been planted to hide the houses, business, and parking lots of this densely populated region. It gave J a nice view of woods and water. It was more panoramic than Peter's view;

J had three-quarters of a circle. Along the horizon, the Cascade Mountains provided a ragged edge, where J could tell the week of the year by the peak or valley where the sun rose — whenever he could see it rise unclouded.

To the south, Mt. Rainier's mass outshone any other Cascade mountain. Upstairs, J had a telescope trained on its flank. The southern neighbors several houses away always assumed it was trained on their bedroom window and consequently lived with their blinds closed. J always wondered what they could possibly be doing that they thought remotely interested him.

◆

J and two of his students were sitting on the deck relaxing now, waiting for arrivals. They enjoyed testing the brew and admiring the patchwork of sunlight that brightened parts of the lake and selected piles of cumulus. They were discussing the final thesis presentation that afternoon.

"If I didn't know your quixotic soul, I might think your acknowledgments of gratitude at the beginning of your talk were designed to shock the fragile minds into numbness so they couldn't concentrate on your material." J wondered if Peter had advised his student.

Christopher thought about this, smiled and shook his head, "It wasn't pure Quixotic. I do have the inclination toward revealing the truth. But I also considered their reactions."

Another student of J's easily empathized. She was a vivacious blond named Juliet who was close to finishing her Ph.D. She had experienced all the interactions associated with her biological characteristics that were rare for a science degree. "I understand. In my presentation, I think I'll say thanks to every faculty member who has hit on me, revealing that I am a sexual target; perhaps even insinuating that one was successful. That should distract their minds for awhile."

"But they'll think it's me," J demurred seriously.

"Is that so bad?" As she developed her thesis, a nice piece of work, she became confident in her ability to handle anything. J's students all had developed a comfortable banter in their conversations. It was difficult to tell when anyone was serious.

J was serious. "Well, if it had happened and no one thought it had, that would be great. If it happened and they knew, that would be OK. If it didn't happen and they didn't know, that would be zero. But when, as in this case, it didn't happen and they think it did, that's just annoying."

"I see. Well, maybe you'll be able to convince me to move it up a case or two." She is a charming girl, definitely more capable than J at the sexual bantering game. Christopher must have swallowed a piece of ice judging from the noises he made.

"Not to number one?" J was still more comfortable being anonymous.

"No. I think that we would both consider that if we didn't fear the ramifications. If we did become involved, I would prefer everyone knew. This is because I have an agenda to become known as a scientist. I can, and will, make it on my own merits, but publicity helps. Of the kind, 'I don't care what you say about me, just get my name right'. We all know that many scientific stars are not that far from those in the entertainment industry. And my conquest of you would be something I would have to brag about."

Christopher added in J's direction, "It's your own fault, you know. All of your students have been exposed to your opinion that the sexual drive is the engine of Homo sapiens' industry, and to survive and be successful we must harness it toward our own goals. It is, as you would inevitably say, Panzaic reality."

J smiled pensively.

"I've got to be careful what I say. I hope you haven't forgotten the part about the restraints to this harnessing process, facing such actions with the constraints of your culture."

Juliet tossed her head and the flow of her golden hair dazzled J, and even Christopher. They got to see the extent of it only at parties. It was tightly controlled at school. "I did forget that. Of course I always expect you to cover your ass from administrative wrath. But don't worry. I do abide by restraints, tho occasionally it is fun to let it all hang out. We're all friends in enlightenment here, and I'm talking in the spirit set this afternoon by Christopher." She raised her glass with a nod to Christopher.

"Yes, Christopher has just publicly emerged from the closet by thanking his close 'companion', and doesn't have any interest in our contemplated sexual indiscretions; I hope." J aimed a questioning eyebrow toward Christopher.

"You're right. You can talk in front of me like I'm a post. My hormones do not direct me to get any prurient interest in your conversation, or proposition." He cocked his eyebrow critically at Juliet.

The doorbell announced the first guest's arrival. Christopher and Juliet went to put up the volleyball net and J walked to the open door and greeted

Kay and Teton behind her. Teton made a beeline for the poolroom, where his party job had become to level the pool table. It wasn't the best table and liked to adopt a gentle incline --- which changed the whole nature of the game. J liked this, as he could use it as a balance against better players.

Kay presented J with a bottle of wine — identical to J's Chardonnay — and as they walked toward the kitchen noted the other students through the large picture windows. "I was going to come early to help, but you didn't pay attention to my hints. I see Christopher and sexbomb were able to help out." Kay had picked up on this nickname for Juliet. When she found that the term didn't faze Juliet and in fact was her e-mail address, a fast, firm friendship developed.

J was a little apologetic, "You're all equal, but some are more equal than others. I don't know you as well as those two, who have been with me for years."

"Yes, of course, sorry to be so sensitive. My time will come." Kay played the Game. She liked to use flirting as a technique to keep the rest of the world guessing.

"Quicker than most is my guess. But since you're a volunteer, let me get you something to do." J did not pick up on the leading suggestion. The administrative restraints inhibited him. Also he had a penchant for moving slowly until his mind was made up.

J led her to the sideboard where the drinks were, "Here, why don't you open and check the wines to be sure none are bad, might even check the keg. Then you might go out to the lawn and help put up the badminton."

J had turned to answer the doorbell when he heard Kay exclaim, "Wow, I know which bottle I'm going to test first. I thought you said everything was from Costless. This is from a large bankroll." J's journey to the door was abruptly redirected back to the appreciative Kay,

"How do you know this?" was all he could manage, since he had to concentrate on maintaining a nonplused manner.

"Because this is one of my father's favorites. Even he complains about the price."

J picked up on the "even he" but merely said, "It's a gift to me, but I'd rather not lord it over folk about how high it flies. Let it ride, okay?"

"No problem."

J sighed, only slightly relieved. He turned to get the second ringing of the bell.

"Say, is it OK if I have a glass?"

"That's what it's for." At least she was primed to appreciate it for its full worth. He registered in himself a slight aversion to Kay now. He knew where it came from. He had always resented the heirs of the rich. He felt they had an unfair advantage that actually worked to their disadvantage — producing personalities that were narrow. He wondered how he had missed this in Kay's background, since his students all fit a mold that included lower to middle-class origins. He guessed that her work record had misled him. Ah well, maybe it was an irrational bias built into his brain.

Later, J was chastising himself over the red flag of the over expensive wine. As Deman said, he tended to try and shoot himself in the foot just standing there. He had gotten careless, as is inevitable in any procedure done many times with success. He tried unsuccessfully to remember what his explanation was going to be when he first pulled this trick two years ago.

He was distracted as Christopher called out for J to come pick up the tune on the piano. Someone had requested music from Christopher, knowing he was a whiz on the trumpet. He coyly agreed, if he could have backup from J or Teton. The three of them had rehearsed several times for just this occasion. If no one asked, they would have offered.

They played a hybrid of Jazz and rock and roll, enough of a classic to be a certain hit. When alone they might experiment, but with an audience this tune had proven charisma. They started with the trumpet, since that was the request, but they could go on and on from any point with this beat. It was the seventy-two a minute throb of Homo sapiens' pleasure pattern. Brahms knew this, and it was the secret of rock and roll success. J made sure that they exploited this insight.

J picked up the measure, absorbing the music into his body like a blotter. It was a treat for the nerves like chocolate decadence for the taste buds, or a kiss for the pituitary gland. The fact that he knew the biological antecedents for the brain stem reaction actually helped. He was primed and knew how to focus.

J had a fair voice, and could keep it in control so its limitations weren't evident. His singing part was smooth and mellow, and he was so lost in it that he didn't realize that Kay was sitting on the bench beside him until his part was up. "You aren't a normal professor."

"That's what the administration keeps telling me."

"How did you find time to learn mathematics, physics, statistics, and the piano?"

"Well, I didn't discover sex until I was twenty one." J smiled at the truth of it.

"I know what you mean. I learned to play piano when I was ten. But I'm classical, and a reader." J improvised with his jazz.

"We'll have to play a duet some time." He hoped that the double entendre was allowed at parties. He had no intention or even inclination to any duets on either side of the entendre. But it was vitalizing to coexist with vibrant creatures like Kay and Juliet. Both were rare occurrences in academia. J enjoyed flirting for the sake of the exercise alone.

The trio exhausted their slim repertoire quickly. After two cycles, the second with most of the party joining, J was ready to move on. He knew enough just to establish that he could do it. Teton could continue on the guitar forever, and Christopher was willing to improvise for what seemed an eternity.

J retired to the outside deck, considering whether to join the night time badminton. He was collared by a colleague, Quincy, a man who possessed all the apparent characteristics of a college president. Some flaw prevented him from reaching those lofty heights, however. Perhaps it involved the observation that he was a self-confessed pedantic bore, although J had not observed this to be a deterrent to administrative success. He was the best example of knowledge alone not being enough. He was formally courteous to a fault. But somehow, his presentation always inspired opposition, even when in accordance. One irritating feature was his certainty, even when his knowledge of a subject wasn't up to his usual standard.

J had just made the mistake of finding one of these subjects, wine. In his usual fashion, Quincy had stated that the quality didn't vary much, so that it was pure folly to spend more than thirty on a bottle. J, whose feelings were very similar, had returned the harmonious observation that he had never been able to determine the difference between a ten and fifty dollar bottle. Whereupon Quincy pounced, and loudly stated that he certainly could at least do that. Often he had to work to be contrary, since everyone was now wary of his conversational style.

Before J could think about this, Kay appeared at his elbow proffering a bottle to refill Quincy's empty glass, "Perhaps you can tell us which one this is?" J winced when he saw the bottle in her hand.

Quincy actually took his time. He swirled it around, sipped and chewed on it, contemplated considerably before declaring it the high priced end around thirty. "But it is probably too full-bodied." J just nodded his head, said "congratulations" instead of "how is that possible?" and excused himself to play badminton.

As always, it got to be very late. Another visit to the still bountiful fare and the cappuccino machine left most his guests satiated. In the warm, friendly environment, no one wanted to leave. But those with chores the morrow made their excuses, until the small cadre of his students were all that remained- exercising their camaraderie with the host. They helped him clean a little bit, declared the party a success, and finally wound their way home.

J was exhausted from the preparations and the responsibility as catalyst for the fun. He went to the sideboard looking for the good bottle of wine, but couldn't see it. A voice from the deck called out, "Looking for this?" and there was the bottle waving gently in Kay's hand.

He sat in the chair beside her, "Is there any left?"

"Yes, although probably only because I hid it."

J smiled appreciatively. "Since nearly everyone brought a bottle of wine tonight I hoped that some might survive." He recalled that was rarely true. Someone always liked 'that little wine' better than the rest.

"Well, Quincy was there looking for that 'French or German bottle of wine'. The message from his taste buds must have reached his brain. You probably didn't want him to see the label, and I felt guilty for teasing him."

"You do good work. But dangerous work."

"I'm a woman. I aim to please. I'm only after a PhD, money, love, fame, and happiness." There was a pause between items as though each was an afterthought.

"In that order, I presume. I guess when your goals are so lofty even one out of five isn't bad".

"Which one do you have in mind?"

"Well, I can't see you giving up your PhD for love nor money."

She laughed, "Absolutely right. That's my immediate goal in life. I haven't even thought about what comes next." She changed the subject. "Why do you have such a huge house all to yourself?"

"I had a wife and two children here at one time. Now it's just inertia I guess. And then there's the view." J decided not to mention the spectacular view from his bedroom-study on the floor above.

She could see that a melancholy nerve had been touched. She was always thinking, evaluating, weighing possibilities. She lost several friends who couldn't stand this process.

She evaluated J coolly. At school he was a part of the University, a fixture almost. The position on the lectern drew respect as did being the author of published papers and books. Then there was the envy of a travel schedule that covered the globe. It all created an image that was remote. He was a means to an end – the doctorate. Certainly his controversial nature made him more interesting than the usual. Here in J's home, partying and relaxing, he became a potential friend, an ordinary person.

Except she couldn't avoid an abundance of hormonal feelings that swirled through the clinical evaluation that she had had of him as a mentor. A guy who could play music, who had sharp wit and an alert twinkle. She noted how her interest was piqued. Physically she would respond to whether he was clever, humorous, good looking, or intellectual. But she realized the illogical nature of most of those feelings; this was chemistry talking. She had the discipline to exorcise such thoughts from her brainstem. She spent another hour probing the depths of this man, hoping to find reasons to support the exorcism.

That night, when J checked his electronic mail, message number two was a rather terse summons to Deman's office again, Monday morning. This time at nine.

Skepticism, like chastity, should not be relinquished too readily.

George Santayana

Ch 2.11 Making Contact

Around the Tree oasis there are several granite rock outcrops that shelter numerous animals. J sometimes felt that the whole complex was a small city. Today for his walk, the sun was warm, the grass and ground smelled wet and fresh. To walk, breathe, smell and listen felt good.

It took an hour to carefully traverse the plain between J's home and the large watering place. The pool occupied several acres in an elongated path. The hippopotamus reigned here.

The hippos were a surprise to J. They could run as fast as he on the plain. The huge toothy mouth threatened a bite that J never wanted to experience. He knew that they were vegetarians, but they occasionally took a bite out of an unlucky mammal. This would usually be fatal to humans. An aquatic agility sealed their power. He learned to avoid them.

The water was usually less than six feet deep, and the hippos ran around the bottom, keeping it smooth and stirred. They ate the lush water lily pads and just about all other foliage surrounding the pool. The water was fairly murky, not crystal clear as it was at his pool, or the much larger Mzima Springs.

There were many trees around the water. J had a favorite blind he had built in a tree overlooking the action. He climbed without much noise into place. He looked down at the beach, which was a magnet for the local fauna— and a battlefield. The many animals' hooves made the beach and surroundings a muddy mess. It wasn't beautiful; but it was fascinating.

Within an hour a small herd of impala had stopped to drink. J watched riveted as he spied a crocodile lying in wait ten feet beyond the drinking animals. Finally, a youngster was jostled to the edge, where it momentarily stumbled. That was all the croc needed, and the young animal was grabbed by a leg and quickly dragged to the depths. The herd bolted, retreating twenty yards, waited two minutes, and returned to their drinking business. Not even a sign of a grieving mother.

He spent the afternoon checking the area. Like a warden, he knew every plant, den, and path of the animals that frequented here. His survey complete, he turned toward home so that he could reach the Tree by sunset. The evening sounds were intensifying. Some of the carnivores had continued their afternoon naps after the storm and were only now moving to hunt. The night belonged to them.

J moved uneventfully to his home oasis. When he approached the entrance door in the rocks, a guttural sound emanated from behind him. J simply smiled from satisfaction that the infrared sensor had picked up his body heat and sent a message to the recorder that was now playing the lion's hunting grunt from a hidden speaker. This little device was sufficient to keep most animals away from his rock entrance. He entered the shelter between the rocks, moved a magnetic key to the right spot, and was quickly inside, safe and secure from a dangerous world.

◆

It was four in the afternoon, pitch black and raining outside. J sat at his desk writing a proposal to the remnant NASA for support to analyze data from a four hundred million dollar satellite. He didn't figure the chances to get the money were very good since the analysis branch of NASA had lost its funding in the reorganization years ago. The only reason the satellite went up last year was because it was approved ten years ago. Still, this is what he did for a living. It was roulette. If he submitted enough appeals for money one of them would often succeed.

A soft knock on his nearly closed door produced Kay. "Sorry to bother you but I've got to give you some bad news."

"Please take a number."

"Aaron is definitely a shill, and reports to a top gun, probably a regent."

"He seemed normal to me. A little against the stream, but a regular student. But maybe that's his appeal. You're certain?"

"Yes, he told me. Worse yet, he's not just doing it for the money, which is significant, but he is a classic true believer. Or in your case, unbeliever of your unbeliefs. I'm so sorry I didn't find out sooner."

J contemplated several questions on just how she found out, and if she was sorry because it had been difficult to do. Instead, "It's raining too hard to ride home." He knew she also commuted by bike.

"If I could only take back my teasing you into your soliloquy." She seemed genuinely anguished at her simple question in the lecture that led to J's philosophizing, so politically incorrect.

J was cheered that this upset her so. "Good choice of word. Methinks a soliloquy is like an extended sneeze. It takes a small tickle to release a torrent which lies waiting for the slightest excuse."

He was doubly cheered when her reaction told him this was just what she wanted to hear. "I'm grateful that you feel that way. I wouldn't want to get you in trouble. I love your course. I love the material. I love what you said. It doesn't happen to me often, but I feel so naive — I mean dumb — for asking a leading question when I had heard the rumor about Aaron. I didn't think, and I honestly apologize."

J was struck by her choice of words: 'love' three times, 'Dumb', and 'apology'. Strong emotions were revealed there. This came from a source that he had come to think of as coolly practical.

"Come on, you can buy me a cappuccino to make up for it." J got up and grabbed his coat.

"Let off cheap." Her eyebrows rose nicely.

"And a cinnamon roll." He held the door open for her.

"I can do that."

"Then there's the penance." They were in the hall with parkas and rain hats on. Why not push his luck.

"Is there an end?"

"Of course. It is yours to select. I, on the other hand, have endless ideas."

Wisely, Kay just laughed and fell in beside him as they sloshed through the rain puddles the short distance to the campus cafe. The place was nearly deserted and they found a choice seat by the window. A river of rain cascaded above them on the skylights.

After a while Kay decided that J was not going to initiate any conversation. He just contentedly drank his drink and divided his gaze between the coffee, her and the water. She asked, "How was the European Geophysics Society meeting?"

"It was sadly stimulating. Exciting, but frustrating. I didn't understand so much. They have moved beyond me in many areas."

"Even in our field where you started it?"

"They're riding in a Mercedes Benz hybrid with great gas mileage and a big tank. We're in a Chevy SUV — terrible mileage."

"Funding again." Kay kept abreast of the politics, for she would be competing for one of the shrinking number of jobs.

"I'll ask my friends about a job for you in Paris. Or maybe Garmish? Better yet, how about the Serengeti?" This was an impulsive disclosure. But he had to talk about what he'd seen.

"What's in Africa?"

"Well, it's not something I've mentioned to anyone. No one here knows, but I took a brief vacation in Africa for a few days after the conference. Most would think it harebrained during these terrorist-trying times. But it was worth the risk. I've seen it a hundred times on video, but being there is singular. Millions of large animals still run free somewhere in this world. Lots of space, golden grass, sparse elegant trees, spectacular sun rising and setting." He shook his head remembering his plane ride.

"Where were you, what did you do?" She was quite interested.

J decided this short burst had relieved his impulse to talk about it, now he had to diffuse it. "It was just a quick, mostly flying safari over the parks and reserves in Tanzania. Over the Serengeti, Tsavo, and other parks near the flank of Kilimanjaro, out of a small town called Tomgo. I had always dreamed of visiting this place. So I snuck in a quick trip."

Kay was beaming. "Strangely enough, I know that area. My father took our family there on safari when I was in high school. I loved seeing the animals. I remember the trees. The baobab trees stood alone or in small clumps in the plain like giant saguaro in the southwest deserts. They are huge and each was surrounded by a bunch of smaller trees and bushes. It was an oasis in a desert of grass. We camped under one, I remember, and I felt so secure in its shelter."

J was transfixed. Their paths were intertwined. More than she could guess. "Yes, they are amazing trees. Either they make it big or they perish — botanical laissez-faire Capitalism. We too, landed near one and camped under it." To say the least, thought J.

K said, "It must have been amazing. Too bad there isn't any science done in Africa so that there would be a conference there."

"Speaking of conferences, I have found the funds for you to go to the Oceanography Society meeting in Hawaii next winter — hopefully to explore your thesis topic." J figured that this should successfully change the subject.

"Wonderful. Is this my penance?"

J smiled, "Haven't given it any thought yet, maybe I can work something out- like a written report."

"Oh boy, a week away from rainy winter gloom into surf and sun. Whatever it is, I can bear it."

She couldn't know that changes, only partly initiated by her naive class question, would make the Hawaiian trip a no-go. J took his last bite and rose, "Rain stopped. Out into the wonder of the elements."

Life is just one damned thing after another.

Elbert Hubbard

Ch 2.12 The Way it Is

J strolled across campus the next morning at five past nine. He felt uneasy about this meeting. The timing was wrong. He and Deman could only stand their high-octane interaction about once a month. They had already had two encounters this month. Deman didn't want conversation with J right now, and being hauled into the office like this certainly said something.

It seemed late for reaction to the Friends of Faculty lecture. There had been one or two notably volatile subjects raised in turbulence class. The possibility of Aaron's 'report' on him came to mind.

As he walked, his mood turned from resolve to continue his present existence regardless of threats, to wondering whether Deman was considering end-runs around tenure. He knew there were exceptions to the job-for-life contract. Moral lack of caution was one lack of caution, but he had avoided that one so far. Maybe being irreligious was morally irresponsible. By the time he entered Deman's inner sanctum J was apprehensive.

"Good morning, J. In fact, in case you were wondering; anti-religious fomenting is regarded as moral imprudence in the book." Deman started out with this, anticipating J's analysis. J was again reminded that Deman was faster than he was, quicker on his feet. He had barely got there before Deman was ahead of him.

Deman was obviously unhappy with his role this morning. There was no smile of any category and his chiseled features were frozen, in not a hard, but a sad countenance. "Let me remind you of your own teachings. We both know that the university is a fortress of careful thought with respect to what is truly known. It's less conservative than the general population in some topics such as the hard sciences, where new observations can force revolutionary change.

"However, in some disciplines it is often driven by a doctrinal witch doctor dressed in academic robes. Psychological barriers inhibit change. Genes are a conservative bunch. I grant your contention that the main virtue of academia is the sheltering of the few who do the wonderful things to enlighten our species. This required job protection, called tenure."

"I'm glad you are aware of tenure."

"Yes. I'm more versed on it than you are. You and I have often discussed how it is such a good deal to have safe harbor, guaranteed employment --- that it attracts the wheeler-dealers, the bureaucrats; the persevering charlatans. They know how to jump through the hoops. It's correct that they make small distinction on what has gone before. I'm well aware that for every unique contribution offering insight, there are a dozen mimics offering regurgitated pap. Sometimes it takes a genius to tell the difference. Unfortunately, they now comprise the majority."

Deman wanted to get through this. "We both know that the doctorate is a certificate of persistence. Tenure, that intended protection for the abrasive innovators, has become the safe haven for mimic scholars.

"Knowing all this, you must realize you're at risk when you criticize the status quo because it is the mainstay for these people. It doesn't leave you much support.

"You know that I enjoy our interactions. And you know that I agree with you on just about all of your opinions. What we don't agree on is that detail, the modus operandi of life."

"That's a detail?"

"You are a foolish Don Q and I have taken Sancho Panza's lead. You are hell-bent to dump the truth on the innocent while I am driven by survival instincts. That's fine, as long as the two don't come in contact.

"Yesterday, they did. I have been assigned responsibility to do something about a long list of your transgressions. In aggregate, there wasn't much choice. The bottom line is, from a list of offences any one of which would be adequate justification, you're fired."

J was startled, despite his anticipation. "That's pretty strong. I thought that no one with tenure had been fired in decades."

"That's a fallacy. The myth of sanctified tenure is necessary to massage the tender egos of the faculty, but in reality, several people have been fired for political reasons."

"That's a surprise."

"The reason that you don't hear about it is the good news, the golden parachute offered as you leave, without rancor, to go on to bigger and better — or at least different things.

"But make no mistake about it; this is an arbitrary and final decision. The 'without rancor' qualification is firm. If you don't take the parachute and the conditions with it, you fall free. The sound of your landing will disturb us all, but not as much as it will you."

J was facing the issue, "Losing my job in the prime of life is a big price to pay for speaking one's mind. I'm willing to pay it. Yet I do have to survive. I suspect the same prejudiced Mafia will also jeopardize my future employment. How do they handle my protests that this is religious persecution?"

"You are naïve. You would be an anti-Christ. Publicity, media, lawyers, and hence, public opinion, are the big interests fighting you. Haven't you followed the major trials? Few people believed those rich defendants were innocent. Yet they were found innocent. Few people might believe you are guilty. Yet you will be found guilty."

"Why is that?"

"It is actually easier to defend the guilty than it is the innocent. The latter think that justice is on their side, that the system is there to protect them. Their errors in such judgments set them up for a huge blind spot. It's too easy to manipulate the outcome with the tools at hand.

"There's more, of course. The administration operatives know your history in detail. For instance, they know that you were a well-documented agitator in the Revolution, just seeking 'truth' as you would say it. There's a record that you attended a revolutionary meeting."

"Is that a crime?"

"You need to read the Patriot Act. I know you did it out of curiosity, but remember this: the lawyer will ask you one question only, 'Were you at this meeting, yes or no?' There is no room for explanation. The answer is 'yes', not 'yes, but I was just curious and looked in for only a moment'. You say yes, or perjure yourself, and the lawyer moves on, having writ your guilt."

J knew this to be true. It was common knowledge as millions of citizens had watched high-priced lawyers make a mockery of the intent of the law in showcase trials. He didn't have much to say. He knew that if there were a way out, Deman would have offered it. He regarded him as a friend. "Where did this come from?"

"From way above me, a regent dictates this decision. You've put yourself in such fire that I wondered about my own survival because of my known association with you. This, incidentally, is another facet of the threat. Go easy, and you go alone. Thrash out, and all of your friends go too."

"Jesus. What a hatchet man you are." J shook his head, grinning a little. He brought this on, subconsciously. It was obvious. He must be ready to move. It was still wrenching, though.

"That's the way this is breaking. Heavy guns up there. I'm not advising you to be quiet for my sake. I can take care of myself. But you do have other friends, like Peter, and your graduate students."

"You're convincing me. But you're taking a lot. Not just my familiar life and professional security, but a reasonable salary for life."

"Yes, a lot. University salaries are perfectly adequate, partly to keep the faculty more circumspect than you have been. Fortunately for you, those who are banishing you consider this comfortable level of salary — small potatoes. They're happy to pay this pittance to you, forever."

"Why does that scare me?"

"Shouldn't. However, it is a two-edged sword. The wealth of those who run our culture works to your advantage — you get a nice salary for life, in retirement, for doing nothing except being quiet about the process. It will all be legal and on paper. That's the way it is. Could be worse."

J understood. "I will have a difficult time not biting the hand that feeds me. But I have enough Panza in me to know where survival lies. I presume that I will still have free speech. I just won't have the bully pulpit of the University professor. It hurts my gut that they can dispatch me so easily."

"We well know that the great wealthy are an obscenity, a damming testament to the failure of mankind to establish a viable culture. Some of the top echelon may suspect it themselves. I doubt they're going to volunteer to redistribute the wealth and power in time, though."

"Would you?"

"No"

The sympathetic distraction provided by Deman was working, amazingly enough. J's mind could not help processing the idea. "I'm getting numb to the power structure. But it's a shame. The U.S. got a start on avoiding this, as long as there were new domains to develop, the west to settle."

"We ran out of space." Deman shrugged.

J took a few steps and finally sat down. "I wonder if I can melt into the media-manipulated masses." Not a serious proposal, but he mused on the society he was supposed to join. "I can eat cake in the form of prime time TV, sports games and music. I'll be easily persuaded to vote for a dream platform, to buy lies like 'no new taxes', 'this war is your war' and generally to think simplistically about any issue offered." J sat up, abandoning his place in that group. "The kind of lazy thinking that pimps the popularity of astrology and fundamentalist religions."

Deman tried to sound positive, "Yes, they're having a blissful time.

Just think; you will be removed from tilting the windmills of all these hopeless human foibles."

"All right, I have helped convince myself, why don't you draw up the package, guarantees, procedures, and send it to me. Right now, I've got to get away from the stink of it." J moved to the door.

Deman knew exactly what J was feeling. "It might help you to read Kafka. This administration was frighteningly described by him."

J knew the story, and reflected on the similarities. Tossed about by unknown powers. He walked slowly back toward his office. Already he was getting the feeling that the cocoon that sheltered him was being withdrawn. The number of walks remaining to him through this lovely environment was finite. The open spaces, the fine old buildings, even the hurrying students seemed like a fine old garment that had to be discarded. Maybe he just hadn't noticed how flimsy the material was, in actuality.

◆

A feminine form appeared in his path. J was so deep in thought that he was barely aware of what was around him. But Kay emerged in his vision like a home quay to a fogbound ship.

Kay spoke softly, "I found out that you were speaking with Deman this morning. I'm sorry that I'm such a snoop, but I seem to have a compulsion to inject myself into the fabric of your life."

"A short tapestry. Retired at forty. I think I'll have a mid-life crisis today."

"How can they do that??"

"Let's first think about who 'they' are. 'They' control the universities, the governments, even the way the electorate thinks. 'They' seldom have to exercise their power; the threat is enough. But that threat is the levee that directs the flow of our culture."

It gave some comfort to demonize his persecutors.

"How do 'they' manipulate people to eschew graduation for gratification, and even to respect and defend 'their' power-obsessed control of mankind's destiny? How do 'they' elect simpleton presidents and destroy intelligent ones? Since 'they' can do that, controlling the university is a piece of cake, and I, a crumb." His pace punctuated his words. Kay hustled to keep up.

She was startled at the vehemence in his words. "Wow, you seem to have mounted your steed and taken up your sword. I wonder how these people become so all powerful."

"Good question. They inherit automobile factories and design ugly and fuel inefficient behemoths that became white elephants in periodic, predictable fuel crises. They're the oil dynasty. How do the same people stay in power despite stupid mistake after idiotic oversight? I wish I knew. They always emerge unscathed, though. They appear to make a lot of blunders, but they're obviously cleverer than I."

Kay had to restrain herself from grabbing J's hand. "Well, at least I'm glad to see that you're still lecturing. I'm only concerned with one of 'their' capabilities here, control of the university faculty. What can I do?"

"Thanks, but nothing need be done for me. At least some improvement has been made since the guillotine. When the dissenters are few, they can be well taken care of, in a 'civilized' manner. I guess the bigger question is what can be done for you? You need a new guidance professor. It will be a bit of a problem, particularly since you are so independent."

"Perhaps I'll resign."

"They'll accept."

There was a noteworthy pause before, "OK." Kay is thinking about the all-consuming goal of getting that passport to academia, the PhD. She did say that she wouldn't give that up for love or money.

"Isn't that a quixotic display? You know such gestures are futile."

"As Deman points out, that's what got me where I am not. It's the martyr myth. You're doing a good job of reactionary support but it would be an emotionally based decision. It won't wash in the plain light of logic." J slowed to an ordinary stroll. The first flush of shock had begun to fade. He was even beginning to consider his options. His wide-open future.

"I know."

"Still, I appreciate the diversion. The fact is I'm not in a great deal of pain over this. More like irksome indigestion. Of course, that's usually enough to keep me awake."

"What are your options?"

"I have everything I had before, including my salary, except I no longer have my job."

"That's not so bad."

"It would seem so. This makes it bad."

"Now I'm not with it."

"I'm being silenced. Bought. Intimidated. Discarded. These are intolerable terms to an egotist. I prefer: respected, feared --- even ignored. These are the environs of the sage, the prophet, all those who just might be right. I worry now that I've been wrong. If survival is right, then I have been wrong. Deman warned me of the futility of falling on a quixotic sword. I fear most being stupid."

Kay could not comment on this state of mind, but she rallied to his side.

They were walking slowly past the building where they worked. J wanted to think outside, with a good supply of oxygen. "I've always said when things fall apart there is always Opportunity. Growth is change. Got to change in order to grow. This pile of manure that surrounds me should nurture growth."

Kay was sympathetic, but beginning to worry about her future. "I feel outrage at your situation. But you're right about my single minded goal — the degree."

"Thanks. My ego may not accept sympathy when it wants respect, but right now I'm in a position vulnerable to sympathy." He looked at her face. "I know that's not the only sentiment you're offering. But it's my problem just now. The uncertainty won't last long. Why don't we talk more about this in a day or two, when I've sorted my thoughts, and maybe my future? And yours."

Kay scowled, but she nodded. She grabbed his arm and they walked.

◆

That evening, after a day where J scarcely registered his surroundings, he took the therapeutic bike ride home. He unwound with a simple soup dinner and played the piano — revealing to him that he must be depressed.

At this point, he had to reflect that he had really screwed up his life. He had gotten himself involved with a serious level of violent criminals, for no reason beyond impulse. It was clear that he was on a list of suspects.

Now his professional career was permanently jeopardized. He had an impulse to push quixotic goals --- to reveal the truth even when he knew no one wanted to hear it. He simply hadn't shown the caution for self-preservation that an intelligent being must --- to survive in the existing culture. He felt pretty stupid as he climbed the stairs, and punched the answering machine play button on the way to bed.

Kay's message was "This too will soon be history. Good night." Peter called to ask about his meeting, and the third message was from a young male voice, "This is Gad. I attended your lecture to the Friends of the Faculty last fall. I've been thinking a lot about it, done some research.

Would you be able to meet with me tomorrow to discuss some ideas that I have? If so, call my secretary at 4BB and we'll meet for lunch."

J recognized the name. The local hero. Richest man in the city, the country, the whole gob of dirt. That was the guy in thick glasses. He thought about his call to the secretary, "Will I call? Is a ten pound robin fat?" What else did he have to do?

Thomas Hardy (1840–1928),
British novelist and poet.
Book title.

Ch 2.13 A Talk in Time

J got into his old car to make the trip across the lake to the software 'campus' that was Gad's workplace. The early hybrid car was old because that was his attitude toward cars; and he took into consideration the gangsters who were watching his lifestyle. His beater was out of place amongst the shiny new BMWs in the parking lot that he found tucked under a central plaza of the Megasoft campus. A disregard for the price of gasoline even at seven dollars a gallon. As he emerged from the disguised elevator terminal, he was struck by the green surrounding him. Emerald lawns formed a backdrop for yellow, lime and olive green colored bushes and trees. Photosynthesis abounding. The air must be really clean here. He smiled to himself. The rest of the world was becoming soiled, but now he walked in rarefied airs. Deman would be satisfied.

There was much more open space than on the University campus. It was an artful mixture of small lakes surrounded by grass and trees with two-story buildings of concrete and glass. J still thought of it as an 'Industrial park' although it was pretentiously called a 'University'.

Gad's office building was central, but otherwise scarcely distinguishable from the other buildings. He had heard that Gad did not wear the usual trappings of the super-rich and he was glad to see evidence of that.

He had not really considered what this conversation was going to be. For him, Deman's proclamation had occupied his thoughts. He was still looking backward, and that wouldn't do.

J was casual and unassuming as he entered Gad's sanctum. The secretary was probably not used to this attitude, but treated him with a respect that impressed him even more. Right away, Gad came out to greet him. It felt like an ordinary business meeting, and that was promising. Gad waved to the secretary as he motioned to J, "I think we'll go out to lunch at Harry's today, please make a reservation. We'll be back in an hour and a half."

J was hoping that Harry's was a high-class place; one doesn't get lunch bought by 'the richest' very often. This hope faded as he heard the secretary speak into her audio phone, 'Harry's Pizza House'. He followed Gad into the elevator and wondered how to make small talk. They were courteous with one another. J admired the landscaping.

He wasn't very impressed with Gad's car, though. It was an early electric that was half batteries. J did enjoy the quiet ride once they got going, however, and he began to envy the ability to buy early; to support the eco engine when it first came out. That was quite a talisman, actually. He concentrated on the polite questions he was fielding. Gad seemed to be feeling him out, in much the same manner J usually employed with others.

Since J was experienced at this game and tuned in to Gad's intentions he exercised his customary bluntness, "Why don't I give you a quick oral biography to get us over this hill. I have several: one for people who need to justify giving me money — degrees, publications and honors; one for job applications — degrees, publications and bright ideas; and one for establishing potential friendships — bright ideas and basic thoughts on manner and meaning of life."

Gad didn't smile much, just nodded, "Good. How about all three. You can give the first to my secretary, the second to my colleague, Harry, after lunch, and the third to me for lunch hour."

"No problem. A half hour ought to do it."

"Haven't you an hour's worth?"

"Yes, but if we've only an hour, the second half is for you to reciprocate."

Gad looked closely at J. "Good point. Maybe I'm a little unfamiliar with the two-way street these days. I'm afraid that in my position, people haven't been demanding that of me lately. I'm pleased that you do."

Harry's was a pizza joint, but with a difference. First, the pizza was fancy French and there was an amply diverse menu. The multi-level terrace had abundant space, with tables set widely apart. Each had a view over the lake, and most had surrounding flora that made for privacy.

It was an extravagant use of prime real estate — the property tax must be huge. Harry came to say hello and seat them in a choice table, perquisites that J expected. He was surprised at the easy regard between Gad and Harry.

He was even more surprised to find that this was the 'Harry' who would look at his resume'. He found the restaurant owner had been a colleague of Gad's in the development years. He had made the choice to quit the business several years ago to found, and devote his time to running the comfortable restaurant. He was only the fifth or sixth richest man in America. This was his Siddhartha's choice.

J ordered his favorite beer, and then regretted it when Gad had a glass of the 'house' red wine. When Gad asked what the wine was today, J recognized it to be a close relative of his recent choice for the party teaser. It looked like it was being served at several tables, having been decanted to a carafe on a central table. J felt some intimidation- with Buddha for a waiter, a house wine that few could afford, and complete casualness from the capitalist elite class. He decided to launch into his spiel before it became passé.

"I can best give you an understanding of me by telling you about my interests. Don Quixote is my martyr; Sancho Panza my hero. Harvard I reluctantly respect but Berkeley is my passion. Blind faith is the enemy, socio-biology the religion, evolution the truth — all relatively speaking, of course, and subject to change.

"My icons are natural selection, honesty, chocolate, consideration and individual freedom. I have fun at cards and tennis, skiing and scuba, reading and trying to understand nature and the world around me. I have all the foibles that flesh is heir to, and an abiding desire to accommodate them to an orderly life, culture and philosophy. I've been blessed with an intellect I can use- but mostly the opportunity to hone it in the educational system for an inordinately long time. There's so much to do in life that interests me greatly that I must pick and choose carefully. That's it in a nutshell."

Reaching down into his portfolio, he withdrew a thin sheaf of papers. "And here are all of the details in my conventional resume'. What will we do with the remaining twenty-five minutes?"

Gad finally did smile. "You seem to have covered most of the important points in a few declarative sentences. Marks you as an outsider to my normal business interactions. This kind of introduction normally can take more than an hour. I guess that you have the advantage in that you don't have to worry about my sensibilities and hang-ups since there is no expectation of future interaction. And with a comfortable professorship, you're not concerned about my support."

J reflected on this. Apparently Gad was not in the hierarchy of power that had recently dispatched him. He just nodded.

Gad continued, "That is what takes the time. Normal conversation circles around the central issues and closes in on the basics gradually. On my part, I probably need the half-hour, because I anticipate considerable future interaction, and recognize some of my limitations in education are likely to clash with some of your limitations in tolerance for my position. So I will confuse our interaction with discretion and reticence."

A good start, J surprised himself by smiling. Honesty and frankness merged with perception. He relaxed, and only then realized that he hadn't been relaxed up to this point.

Gad continued with his biography. "My parents were both Liberals, even as they accumulated wealth. They gave me the best of prep schools and college so that I had a good practical knowledge before I learned how to think. I missed the social life because I discovered the wonderful world of computers early on and it has consumed me since. I was in the right place at the right time — I don't deny it. Of course it has led me to a great fortune, but that is only an addendum. I never sought money, it just accumulates as I pursue my passion — propagation of the computer into the fabric of the future."

The food arrived; apparently it wasn't necessary to order. Gad continued, "In fact, the money was a problem. I got distracted from my central goals by the weight of that albatross, a huge golden one around my neck. I have to spend valuable time figuring out how to spend it, to keep it from growing to obscene proportions. I suppose you don't think that I'm very successful at this. And it's true. So I feel tremendous pressure to do something with this money, partly because it is a real challenge, and partly just to keep it from growing out of hand.

"I've always supported higher taxes for higher incomes — a graduated tax is very sensible to me. But not everybody wants that. Some insist that I've earned the money and get legislation passed that simply increases wealth. If it sounds like I'm complaining, I am.

"I don't have the interest or talent to successfully organize my philanthropy. At first, it was heady. We saved a million lives. Then I realized that we saved them from disease only to let them die of starvation. As you would quickly say, we were quixotic, just like the early missionaries. Fundamental changes in culture, theirs and ours, are needed.

"Too many of the suggestions from my colleagues would bend me down that dusty path to megalomania. Maybe absolute power does absolutely corrupt, and I'm leaning toward removing that burden from my reach."

They ate for a while. J wasn't certain what it was, but it was delicious. He hoped it was healthy, too. Gad continued to give him an insight into the quandary that success had caused for him. They talked about the weather and the warming trend- in the process they finished the meal. Before the dessert course, Gad excused himself to 'go have a word with Harry'. Probably looking at the resume', figured J. He wondered why they were even looking at him, since his history indicated minimal talents for computer interests.

Gad, Harry and a fantastic desert arrived at the table together. Harry took a seat and Gad continued his casual conversation. "I believe that you can be of great help to me in this problem. I've figured how to get rid of a chunk of this monster money. I'm going to give it to a quixotic quest, as you would say. I'm going to give it to you, to build a University to do exactly what you suggested in your talk."

J's reaction was singular. His mind rapidly pursued the potential new course in his life to several ends, almost like a drowning person's life flashes before them. "I just tossed that out as a hopeless quixotic ideal. It will take some adjustment to consider it seriously. I have to think about what this is going to do to my current lifestyle. Do you believe that an idealist, admittedly with a ruthless practical streak, but an idiot idealist in the driver's seat, can manage an enterprise like that, and not have a nervous breakdown? I had a hell of a time simply making the many decisions in the remodel of my kitchen — ruined my life for months."

Harry smiled, "This will probably do it for years."

J nodded, paused and then murmured, "I figure only about two or three."

Gad raised his eyebrows, like he was surprised at a so-soon decision, "Then you'll do it? Have you thought enough about it?"

Good question, J decided he had better do a little more of just that. As he considered that Gad was able to do something about the hitherto impossible task of changing the University concept, he blinked a few times. But he had long ago realized that huge tasks were as easily resolved as small ones. Here was a thinking man with big bucks. He liked the big idea that J had tossed out as a straw man. Well, J could elaborate from there.

"I think that I'll have a glass of that wine, while I muse on it." Harry was happy to fetch the carafe and pour a glass. J paused to admire the deep red color. He experienced a surreal moment. As if that bottle of wine on his table at home had brought this on. Good wine, superlative opportunity. It felt unreal. J tested the waters around him.

"So we build a new University. People it with cerebral seekers. Not of the Holy Grail, but of an equally ephemeral quantity: the answer to the questions, how does this Universe work? What's it all for? Is there a reason for existence? Where does Homo Sap fit in? Really seek the truths. Whoa, this is probably the real 'Holy Grail'."

Harry smiled. "Just another religious nut?"

J actually nodded. "No matter. On the Panzaic side, we try to halt the death spiral of the kindred species. Or at least make it amount to something — a tiny step along the long path from cosmetic to cosmosic knowledge. Perhaps like a chrysalis stage for the computer/machine dynasty. That should grab you."

Harry really enjoyed that remark, looking at Gad intently. This was evidently a familiar topic of conversation.

J continued. "Or the evolutionary infant of a better breed. Maybe just food for a greater life form. Develop the humility to relax unto it. Push the pre-frontal lobe's control over several million years of cerebral conditioning to merely survive and propagate. Work on the solutions with a sound scientific grounding.

"Then there is my friend Deman's possibility, 'As long as it rewards this brief interval.'"

Gad was pleased. "Sounds like you already have a plan."

"The odds don't favor success. Plato tried it. Marx, too. Cervantes made an icy comment on it. I use his metaphor as a tool possibly too much. Maybe he was just a nay sayer, 'Idealists always fail'. But he did suggest Panzas could succeed at their modest goal, with motivation obtained from Don Quixote. Is this unrefined hypothesis anti-intellectual? How is this going to be reconciled with a bias toward cranial cultivation? After all, that's the only talent that we have that's not better developed by other species.

"To get to the point, do we need a University training just to harness impulses? Quixote accurately perceives the problems that arise from our complex genetic heritage plunked into our rapidly mutating milieu. It's the solution that escapes him. We can't just joust at symptoms."

"Is the goal to look at simple things very deeply?" Gad undoubtedly did this.

"I think that more progress comes from looking at complicated things very shallowly." J had done both.

"The first method often doesn't seem to work well, and the second requires a lot of measurements to get curve fits. Can we just learn to implement Quixote's goals using Panza's methods?" Harry showed that he understood J, and obviously liked Cervantes.

"Would that be wise? Panzaic reality may dictate that only a select group will matter. Elitism is a panzaic solution. There's no rule that says panzaic solutions are always fair, or even right.

"That said, we know that much of the time quixotic solutions are irrational, erratic, imprecise, shortsighted, simplistic, misinformed, and misguided. And often disasters. While often Panza's solutions are rational, simple and commonsensical. And sometimes unfair.

"But Quixote transcends while Panza simply prevails. I invoke these names as adjectives to describe complex ideas. Everything can be phrased in their dichotomy. Saves time."

Gad contributed, "Stop me if I'm wrong, but I really liked your stating that the solutions to most of our problems were already available. I believe that the basic propositions for a successful species evolution have already appeared often in books — all kinds of books — science, science fiction, social commentary, historical, biographical and comic."

Harry interjected, "Along with every possible failure."

Gad grinned. "OK. Maybe we can chart a safe course for mankind by simply avoiding every direction shown in the popular media. I may be overly sensitive because I've had so much attention from the media. People are very interested in huge success. But they also seem to be fascinated by failure. Other people's failure. I guess it makes them feel good just to be surviving.

"The media feeds on this interest; this fascination with peoples' failures. This is a problem because most people get their information, their education, from the media. Watch the news and you'd think that all we do is suffer one failing after another.

"But failure is defined with respect to mores, and the media is the last to know of changing mores. Their reporting fosters fear and failure. They seem to lack ideals, responding only to feedback through polls and circulation. There has to be something better to guide mankind." Gad stopped abruptly. "Am I sounding like your Quixote?"

Harry had also thought about it. "Yes, you are. But I happen to think that is your best side. Most of us never worry about meaning of existence seriously. There are a lot of people out there who have their head screwed on right, but with their mores a little out of step. Usually they live quiet lives trying to offend a minimum number of the people around them. Be a farmer, drive a ferry or run a restaurant. It's sort of like the advice to drivers to avoid the aggressive drivers afflicted with 'road rage'. Keep a constant, average speed, don't do anything aggressive and avoid the psychos. There's balm in a stress-free environment. I've found great contentment in just surviving from sunrise to sunset."

J had his second glass of that spectacular wine while spinning his equally spectacular plan. "Great, you've put your finger on it. But there is a danger of succumbing to this safe environment. Absolute comfort absolutely corrupts the imagination. We want to get those beleaguered people together into an environment where they can think and speak freely without offending the hang-ups of someone listening with a gun in their pocket. Try it at a university, not because it is the best place, but because it is the least bad. It would be a helluva experiment."

Harry asks, "Is there going to be an agenda at this school, just like any religious college, just another set of 'truths'?"

J looked appreciatively at Harry. He would ask the right questions to keep the project honest. "Yes, it sounds like there will be an agenda. But there can be a difference if it contains only an ephemeral goal, a logical path, and absolutely no arbitrary edicts or constraints. Certainly there would be no pressure to join in collective thinking. The 'joining' must be done only because one individually decides that it is the logical set of attitudes compatible with educated thinking."

Harry started to interject, but J held his hand up and smiled, "You're going to call it faith. OK, there is faith in the scientific method: entertain all ideas; but subject all to skepticism and observation. 'Truths' are dependent on observations. Revisit concepts as time and boundary conditions change. No absolutes. This is education as it was meant to be; simply learning how to think."

Harry got a word in. "Do you believe that knowing how to think, with a good scientific education, is enough to solve our immense societal problems?"

"It does sound too simple. But a good understanding of science shapes attitudes and personality. It just might be the key to global understanding. When one understands evolution, then one doesn't buy the ethereal promises of religions. You could never convince an open mind to hijack and fly a plane into a building. In fact you could never convince an evolutionist to blindly hate 'the infidel' or the 'nigger', the Jew, the Arab or any other arbitrary class of Homo sapiens."

Gad was smiling, apparently convinced that he had the right man, and a decent idea. "Critical thinking as God. At least we seem to be reaching a consensus in a base set of knowledge, call it the college axioms. It still leaves room for uncertainty and disagreement. All of that must be there. I agree that the chances of success might be slim. But I think that I'm going to enjoy this project as a hobby." He looked to see if this offended J.

J just nodded, "Me, too. At the least it will be a Meteora-like place preserving science based liberal ideas during the chaotic dark ages of Neocon control."

Gad liked that. "So, getting a faculty will be your first and most difficult job. There's an unknown filter out there in society that lets through some glorious singular personalities. We can't know what it is. But we need to identify the prodigal products. I can help with that, since that's the primary challenge of building a good business.

"But even more than that, we need to cultivate them. That's your challenge. Are you sure that you want to tackle this titanic task?"

"It happens that you got me at a good time. I don't have anything better to do. In fact, at the moment I don't have anything else to do." They wouldn't understand this, and J wasn't going to explain it. "There are no guarantees that Homo Sap is the right building material for what we have in mind. In fact, there's a lot of evidence to the contrary. But there's no knowing without doing the experiment. Can you tell me exactly why you want to do this, beyond the economics?"

Gad raised his eyebrows as if the answer was obvious. "The why was given by you. You asked, is it possible to produce, educate, and create Renaissance people at and below the graduate school level? Is science education the missing ingredient in previous attempts at Utopia? Do Homo sapiens have the right stuff? These are the right questions in my opinion." Gad had thought about it.

"Fine. Exactly how, where and when?"

"The 'how' will be in the hands of my staff, at your beck and call. A small percent of my assets will fuel the project- so that's no problem. The 'where' is a large block of land that I have over on the Olympic Peninsula. The 'when' is now. Do we have a deal?"

J, without hesitation, extended his hand, "Piece of cake."

All three of them were exhilarated. They raised their glasses of the dark red elixir, "To a noble experiment."

He's a muddle-headed fool, with frequent lucid intervals.

Miguel de Cervantes (1547–1616)

Ch 2.14 New Directions

J was never one to suppress an exuberant mood. For one thing they were so rare they had to be savored. For another, the good-mood chemicals were favorable to the cardiovascular system. This walk between his office and the administration building, made in gloom a scant three days ago, was now a gambol in the light rain. It was a mixture of nostalgia that it might be his last walk along this path and pleasure that it was the last. Oh, he would miss the flora especially in the fall and the fauna in the first warm days of spring when the short skirts replaced the jeans. But he was confident that other equally interesting walks would replace it.

He had called this morning. "Hey Deman, life takes another of its strange twists. I've got some interesting news and a proposition. Got time to talk?"

Deman was inclined to avoid any more uncomfortable conversations, but there was a note in J's tone that persuaded him that something was strangely affecting his friend. Curiosity aroused, he changed tune. "Fine, let's get together. But I've just a few minutes; have to go to another onerous meeting."

◆

Returning from his meeting with Gad, J had relaxed at home and savored the moment that extended until dawn. Deman would not be the first person he had talked to. When he finally awoke late the next day and rode into campus, he called Kay to make a date for dinner. She had other plans, but when he said, "I've news. Nothing's changed at the University from when we last talked. But I can still be your guidance professor, so don't fret about it."

"And you're only going to tell me how this could be over dinner."

"Yes, unless your other thing is really big, this takes precedence."

"What time and where?"

"Early, say six. I'll pick you up in my car. We'll go to Harry's pizza." J was determined to get his fill of the house wine at Harry's.

"I didn't know you had a car. Also didn't know that you liked pizza. Are there more revelations coming?"

"That's just a preview of coming attractions. See you."

♦

Deman's secretary was standing by his door. If she had a metal detector, she would have used it on J. J graced her with his gentlest smile. "Don't worry; I've come to offer your boss a gold plated olive branch."

He walked into Deman's office, sat down in the comfortable settee by the window looking out on campus, stretched out and gave a sigh, "Life is sweet." Deman was alarmed, but said nothing, just moved warily to a position close to the door.

"In our talks, we often set up fantasy situations where Homo Sap had a chance to escape from the vortex that sucks the best to oblivion. If we could just escape from the bonds of working for a daily living, or from the uncontrollable brain stem impulses, or from our limited existence in space and time, what dreams must come."

Deman looked impatiently at J. He wasn't in the mood for philosophy, figuring that those days were behind them.

J just relaxed into the reversed roles of a day ago. "But even under these optimal conditions we always have had a difficult time hypothesizing situations where humanity will triumph to the next millennium. Yes, many times we have theorized over what we would do if we were in charge, unfettered."

J was taking his time. It was clear that Deman was like a fish out of water. "Well I've got a new one. Let's assume that there is given us, say you and me, complete control over a university, from the beginning. Whatever we suggest, it will be done. For instance, I believe that both of us would insist that the only administration people are those who work for the faculty doing the grunt work.

"There is no fund raising hierarchy. Hence we're beholden to no directors and we will have no perfunctory duties. Just one fat cat adventure capitalist. We decide the curriculum; make the faculty and the student selections. Science is in the driver's seat.

"We have this autonomy because money is not a problem. We teach whatever we deem necessary to produce people capable of — ah; there's the problem. What do we teach them, to know, to be, to do? I'm not sure that I'm up to this. Any ideas? I need your help. I'm offering you a job. Did I mention that money was not a problem?"

Deman was oscillating between being concerned with his friend's state of mind and wonder. "If you're sane, which may be a marginal hypothesis, there are a few problems to be resolved in your hypothetical situation before I would accept." Actually, Deman judged that his friend was one of the sanest persons he had ever met. Could there be something to this?

He knew J well enough to realize that his question wasn't just banter. In any case, he'd play along. "I think we're up to it. We've discussed it philosophically many times. The only missing ingredient was money." He had gotten the message. He sat down back at his desk and waited for J to continue.

J was toying with this new problem. "I wonder if Don Quixote had access to infinite resources would his enterprises still have led to havoc in the lives he touched."

"You probably aren't going to like my opinion — the disruption would have been even worse, more effectively disastrous."

"Yes, I knew you were going to say that. More effective mayhem. Maybe I've bit off more problems than I can eschew." J seemed genuinely worried, and Deman couldn't know what he was worried about. He asked, "What is it that has liberated you, yet panicked you in two minutes?"

"Infinite resources. I've accepted a new job since you fired me. My partner and I are building a University across the sound. I'm not worried about the mechanics, since my partner is Gad. I am getting worried now about my ability to give it a fair shake. I really need your help. I'll give you a fifty per cent raise or ten per cent more than anyone else on the new campus, whichever is less."

Now it was Deman's turn to be pensive. He had no reason to doubt J. In his fund raising activities he learned the enormous resources of the super-rich. So it wasn't really as surprising to him as J expected.

"I think that you've fallen, in your usual stumble-bum way, into a perfect project for us both to manage our mid-life crises. My firing you depressed us both. Now we get an opportunity to escape this lock-step environment for a better one. You may worry about its success. To me, if everything is as you say, the only important thing is that it's going to be an interesting and comfortable ride. You on your white horse and me at your side in my BMW imparting reality."

J knew that Deman would join him. If nothing else, it would answer a lot of questions they had been floating these past years. "Your salary starts next week when we start recruiting a faculty and simultaneously a student body. The Olympic College building program is underway today and we need to get started. There are lots of decisions to make. For instance, I wonder if we should include the graduate students and even the undergrads in all decisions."

Deman frowned, "That's been tried often, usually with bad results. Because the student, almost by definition, is lacking in education. Furthermore, they're mostly quixotic. Hence they're naively conservative. All this helps them get a decent education through the hormonal intensive years. But, like our evolutionary predilection toward violence and territorial imperative, conservative idealism is pure liability for the next step into open-minded skepticism."

They would find a middle ground for student participation. "Yes, you're right. You're going to be worth your huge salary. And we've already attacked this problem, remember? The proof of 'right' can be in the observation of what comes to be. A meritocracy."

Deman was ambivalent. "There's a big difference between theorizing and actually putting into operation these ideas. There are going to be mistakes. Who gets final assessment?"

J had thought about this. "We will at first. The benevolent dictator mode is risky, but often successful. It has to be designed to phase itself out as it becomes unnecessary."

Deman raised an eyebrow. "Didn't the communists have that plan?"

"Good point. We may need to write it in. We'll give it another try with better leaders maybe. Limited domain might work; the Athens example, without the slaves."

"They might be essential. Graduate students might serve this purpose."

"Ah yes, we exploit their quixotic mien. Mitigate it by making the daily decisions in common. Usually, this would be the purview of the faculty."

"It probably has to be the faculty at first. But most traditional college faculty has never been on the less trodden road. We will have to broaden our search domain. If we don't get a critical number of percipient teachers, failure is certain."

J paused and took a deep breath. "As I think about it, it seems an impossible task."

Deman was convinced from J's concern that this was a going enterprise. He gave an optimistic assessment, "Well, I'm not worried. I've seen several good prospects apply at the University. They were all rejected, of course.

I guess the saving grace is that there are many places for conventional thinkers, but only Olympic College will be for the quixotic dreamers who function as Panzaic Liberals. Anyway, it's the journey that's important, not the goal."

♦

Last night, in preparing for dinner with Kay, J had put on his best slacks, a designer silk and cotton mix that looked like jeans until one got close or touched the fabric. A Northwest shirt that Pendleton had designed to look like the popular hundred dollar one but felt like the thousand dollars that it cost. It had super-soft material from a rare Himalayan goat. The demand from the rich had created some products that J had yielded to, not without some guilt. And not without stealth, paying cash, with no one looking. His encounter in the store suggested they had their inside information. Robert Burns knew long ago that "The best laid schemes o' mice an' men gang aft a-gley." No doubt if a Mafia guy saw him *buy* these clothes the gig would be up.

The clothes were designed to be luxurious without being ostentatious. The rich had discovered that they couldn't safely flaunt it. There was widespread resentment at the large schism in society. At least J's riches had not come from greed, but from chance. He had honestly stolen them, like Robin Hood. It gave him a nice sense of camaraderie with Gad. Both were in the right place at the right time. Circumstances were not so different, except in magnitude.

When he stopped to think, he had to marvel at his fortune. If J had believed in a higher power he would have felt that it was giving him special attention at this juncture.

He felt that the accident of his wanton wealth was a large mistake. The gangsters were evidently zeroing in on him. He felt that he was under constant surveillance. First the crooks, then the upheaval of the new university. He felt culpable, for a minute. What if his risk in the mountains sacrificed this chance for a great university? He would have to be extraordinarily careful, at least until the school was safely under way. He felt the burden of having the idea, and needing to see it to fruition.

J's orderly life was not just threatened, it was shattered. It was history. One benefit he saw — his new environment would be protected. Out on the Olympic coast any intruder would be obvious. He was ready to begin Gad's project immediately.

When Kay greeted J at her apartment door, she had on similar garb, but the real, off-the-shelf things. He had guessed by now she had a source of wealth from her family, but he registered that she presented a false façade. Kay made no real secret of it; she just blended in with her fellow students and colleagues with protective coloring. It was practical to do so. And she had wit, and allure. J reflected that he chose to be here rather than at Peter's or Deman's place. Tonight it was no contest.

Kay had also taken thought in dressing for this dinner. J's tone was so exhilarated on the phone, and she wasn't sure how she felt about all the assumptions he seemed to make. He was so confident. He wasn't talking to her just as a preferred student, or even a flirtation. For the first time in her life she was in a situation where she didn't know what was going to happen next. Or how she was going to react to it.

She was glad that at this point J couldn't know that his insistence was overkill. Her other date didn't stand a chance against his invitation, in any case. She had tried to analyze this interest in someone that her friends would all consider 'much older'. It was evident that her affection had something to do with the close relationship with her father. She had been his only child. It was a big adjustment when her staunch support and dear friend died a few years ago. She had relied on his sage advice, bolstered by his knowledge of science, to lead her to become the independent loner she was now. Measured against this standard, suitors of her age were sorely insufficient. She realized that her logical analysis was a damper on romantic thoughts. The whole thing was kind of confusing.

She had begun to think of this attitude as a bad handicap, so that she was missing out in the chemical celebrations that her friends were drinking of, profoundly and usually serially, that they labeled love. She noted that also missing were the hangovers. Still, the date she cancelled had been an attempt to join in with her peers.

Now, she was considering these chemicals in her own stew as she answered the door. It was not like a shot of whisky, more like a sip of fine wine. Her father often said the best wine needed to have time and room to breath before it could be tasted with an informed palate.

She was amazed at Harry's Pizza. Not the kind of Pizza parlor that she had dressed for. She was impressed when Harry appeared and greeted J, who had called Harry and surprised him by asking for nothing more than a dinner reservation.

J was succinct, "We'll have dinner, as you choose, and two glasses of the excellent house red, please." Harry beamed. He was actually happy when people recognized the quality of the house red. He lost money on every glass, but pleasing his customers was more important. It was J's party red wine done large.

"Do you come here often?" Kay was getting a little worried about J's secret life.

"Haven't been here since yesterday." J had come to the conclusion — perhaps he read it somewhere — that a little mystery was good for relationships.

"Who were you with yesterday?"

"Well, you may have heard of him, he owns Megasoft."

Kay nodded as she pondered this fact. Time to walk carefully. She knew that the Megasoft conglomerate often demanded total commitment from their chosen people --- in return for the wonderful opportunities they offered. She figured this was what had happened. It would be easy to lose track of J to this competition.

Exercising her usual subtlety, she asked, "For God's sake, tell me what he said."

J recognized her consternation at the new twist, "He offered to buy me a University."

"Buy you a University. What University is for sale?"

"A brand new University. Never driven. No strings. I suggested it flippantly in my talk to the Friends of the University."

Kay was not unlike Deman in her lack of complete surprise. "My father always remarked on how Leland Stanford bought himself immortality for a few million bucks — best investment a person could make, he used to say. I guess Gad knows this."

"Maybe, but I doubt that has much to do with the concept of the school. More like Jefferson wanting to start education on the high road. Gad suggested the generic Olympic College as a name. He has another problem that is worrying a lot of the super-rich — too much money. He has to get rid of it in philanthropic projects, and this seemed like a good money hole."

Dinner arrived just in time for Kay. She needed time to readjust her perspective on the evening. The food was an easy distraction; she recognized the wine as being extraordinary, and marveled at the savoir-faire of her dinner partner. They would spend the rest of the evening planning a University, with completion of her Ph.D. as a factor in the design of the place. Several times during the evening she made the comment, "I can't believe it. We are designing a University. A cool University." Never had this overused adjective been more extended. It was going to be a University like no other.

◆

The Rhesus monkey chattered from his favorite high branch to his mate about the streaks of red, pointing to the emerging sun. J woke and rolled over to look at the clock, trying to decide whether he had had enough sleep.

Since the time indicated that he could breakfast to the sunrise and morning visits of the animals to the pool, he rolled out of bed. Today was washday, so he gathered the clothes strewn around the room and opened the door to the laundry chute. This was a slick metal slide that delivered laundry from the bedroom to the basement. It was designed to corkscrew around the inside of the Tree, so that it could also function as a slide to deliver J to the basement. He had used it occasionally for fun and to save time.

This morning he stripped off his pajamas tossed them into the chute and put on one of the several rugby shirts and Levi outfits in the small closet. There were shorts and safari shirts for the slightly warmer months of summer. He moved to the stairway and climbed down to the kitchen.

He laid out fresh fruit gathered from trees in the vicinity. Then breakfast bread of the month and the ritual of cappuccino. Now, before he ate breakfast, he would do a half-hour of aerobics. This combined with a run or walk outside, comprised his daily exercise regime. On some days it was too dangerous to go out. He then had the gym equipment with a huge selection of videotapes to pass his exercise time.

Back to breakfast of cereal and fruit — a banana like product from trees over ten miles away. Once or twice a week, he had an egg, often one the size of a melon, sans most of the yolk of course. He looked forward to this cholesterol adventure, adding vegetables and cheese that was cryogenically preserved for years. All in all, the morning ritual was exactly the same as it had been in Seattle. Occasionally, during the dry season, he would even add a bike ride. It all served to keep him from remembering the god-awful reasons he was here.

Part III
Experiment in the Woods

We were young. We were arrogant. We were ridiculous. There were excesses.
We were brash, foolish. We had factional fights. But we were right.

Abbey Hoffman, on Berkeley, 1960s

Ch 3.1 The Olympic Campus

The Olympic Peninsula of Cascadia, in the old Washington State, is remote from the rest of the state, which is remote from the rest of the country. It has young mountains, ancient groves of tall trees, impenetrable rain forests, and miles of beach with no road access.

The Olympic Range wrings moisture from the clouds as the weather wends its way from the west. On the upslope seaside, trees are immense, undergrowth impenetrable, with four hundred inches of rainfall a year. On the downslope side, winds descend to warm the air and evaporate the remaining moisture. It is dry and warm.

After the parched winds leave the peninsula they will gather moisture from Puget Sound in the next few miles of their eastward journey. Then as they rise over the Cascade Range the wringing-out process is repeated, serving Seattle its renowned rainfall.

Once more the process is repeated over the Rocky Mountains before heading for the uniform prairies beyond. The mountains and the climate are inseparable.

There are many large regions in the West that are impossible for human survival. Sometimes there isn't enough water for hundreds of miles. Sometimes there is too much, on vast flood plains or in valleys subject to huge floods and landslides. Yet within these regions are niches of ample bounty and abundant beauty to please all the needs of the human palate. Climate, fashioned from topology, has dictated the march of Homo sapiens' infiltration of nearly every one of these livable crannies. The developed area of the northwest corner of the contiguous U.S.A. is centered on the flat, fertile, fecund shores of the huge estuary called Puget Sound. The inhabitants are surrounded by large lakes that are all hundreds of miles from the Pacific Ocean.

The intervening Olympic peninsula is larger than many old states with a population less than many towns. At the eastern side of the peninsula, in the rain shadow of Mt. Olympus, within an old growth forest there is a new campus. The campus still looks like ancient woods. The modest buildings are small additions to the scene. Five years have passed since J left UW.

The new campus on the Olympic Peninsula has remained pristine by virtue of its isolation — a long drive, a narrow bridge, and a sporadic ferry service lay between the population mass in Puget Sound and the privately owned tract of trees. Before the campus benefactor stepped in they had been destined for clear cutting.

The campus was built into the age-old forest with care. Cedar bark defines the pathways; asphalt is absent. The forests are mixed fir, cedar and some pine. It is a shorter, thinner forest than found on the western side of the mountain range. On this side one can random walk without a machete.

It's true that the omnipresent auto can be found in the periphery garage. But it's underground and out of sight. So too are the ubiquitous requisites of civilization, the electrical, water and sewage lines.

The campus is energy independent. At the birth of Cascadia, the ties that bonded the energy economy to oil were severed. Once the oil barons' mythology was revealed, the nation found that it was remarkably simple to generate energy, and nearly every building got reasonably priced power from solar, wind or local hydroelectric sources.

On OC campus, power dribbled in from several sources. Solar contributed significantly, since there had been huge gains in photovoltaic generation by Europe and China. The US had been taken out of the race by the successful conspiracy of oil and auto moguls. The dangers to the globe of continued burning of hydrocarbons in large cars had been suppressed until it was too late to prevent severe warming effects; for everyone on the planet. There were winners and losers. Russia and Canada gained better climates; and the retirees in New England state didn't need to move to Florida --- the climate of Florida had moved to them.

It was good that less heating was needed, but at 48° latitude the sun shone less than a third of the day in winter and its celestial path was merely a squashed arc over the mountains. Only the German solar system worked well here. They had become to solar voltaics what Saudi Arabia had been to oil while the US slept.

Back-up electricity flowed from a wind farm on a nearby ridge where winds were persistent. There was a small hydroelectric facility a kilometer to the south. In an emergency, there was a wood-fired steam generator. Oil was too expensive, coal polluted the air and large hydroelectric dams punched the salmon.

The students and faculty live on the campus. The road in is narrow with a steep cliff or two so the campus is not a tourist destination. In fact it is very much a closed community.

There is a hub with a cafeteria, lounge and space for large functions. The main teaching rooms are long, low wood and brown-brick mixtures, scattered in small units about the campus. They have a room for instructional meetings at each end, amenities in the center with a lounge to each side. The last were very comfortable sunken 'conversation pits' often entirely enclosed in glass. Greenhouses for heat and ideas. On a worldly scale, it is an oasis in an intellectual desert. Like the Greek monks' retreats on the natural towers in Meteora where books were preserved through the dark ages, the isolated campus is trying to shelter liberal ideas through the anti-intellectual, anti-environmental culture that prevails outside.

The milieu is similar to that of the UW campus, or what that campus was like before the last six building programs. Moving down a winding path of bark the smell of cedar is heavy, an elixir to some primitive pleasure center in the olfactory nerves. It serves as a constant reminder to the students that their campus is in the center of a forest. The smell of a primal home. Good aromas that foster good health that promotes good minds.

The cedars are everywhere; from seedlings to giants. Sunlight is the main casualty. The ground is green; but it is moss rather than grass. There are a few meadows to let the sunshine in, and the dispersed log buildings are situated on their northern edges. At this latitude, a southern exposure is quintessential.

The sides of the buildings are the gold of fresh cedar planks. It would be another twenty years before they attained the dark hues of the UW faculty club. The windows are double-paned, and in some cases sectioned into diamonds with leaded joints.

◆

J and Gad are walking along a path. J is happily conducting a tour. "I know that you are up on the campus culture, but I'm going to give you my VIP guest spiel anyway." Gad had sent several people to tour the campus over the past few years and served as a recruiter of students.

"We decided very soon that five years were needed to get the breadth of education that was the school's goal. After all, it took me ten."

Gad smiled his riposte, "Took me three."

J was not intimidated by his benefactor, "Yeah, but you are undereducated."

"True. But I'm catching up --- winging our net courses."

J knew that Gad had a good record under his Internet alias, Mr. Good. Still playing with God. "We're now seeing the first group of fifth-year seniors. The fifth year is going to be special. After spending two years in what we consider remedial education in science and two years in a broad range of hard and soft science, we are ready to approach the more broad-spectrum realms. We'll look at biology and geophysics where they merge with history and philosophy. Couldn't do that in only four years."

"That bothered me. I could barely sit still for two years."

J looked at Gad, trying to read just how much it bothered him. Then he looked at the cedar path, the surrounding forest and the rustic log classroom buildings. "I understand. We're trying to make it a comfortable environment while developing the passion for knowledge that you had for industry."

Gad slowed his pace, since he tended to walk twice as fast as J. "Changing the curriculum helped. The liberal arts were always taught from historical standpoints, mostly by regurgitation. Now that we have put them off until after a complete basic science education it will be more thought-provoking. I really love putting the nation state in its evolutionary context."

J was nodding to himself. He was excited about this experiment. "We had to discard the term 'humanities' since it had lost its meaning. This year we can intelligently explore these human endeavors from brain-stem appreciation of art to the boundaries of cerebral philosophy and science. It's going to be stimulating to see what comes of it. You'll just get a smorgasbord of introductory lectures today."

Gad held the classroom door open for J. "With the curriculum all on the net I can keep up with the lectures to a degree that would surprise you. The future is there; a way to break out of our cedar curtain." He was an optimist as only great success can breed. They found seats along the wall and were scarcely noticed.

In this building sunlight streamed through the windows onto the long central table surrounded by chairs. The chairs were cushioned and imposing yet uncomfortable enough to keep the occupant awake. The professor was nattily dressed, stately, and quite old. There was an alpine fir growing in a box in every corner of the room; botany was a natural hobby for this man.

Nearly every seat was taken, probably because of a President's Prize in Biology and in Literature. And the fact that he had jumped the prestigious eastern college ship for this backwoods dinghy, as the Washington Post had put it.

Because of this honored life, he started off the year with his own personal history. He rightly assumed that it would serve as inspiration. Students called him 'None'. In the convoluted terminology of the campus, this was short for Number One, in deference to his position in the field of biology.

The lecture began a second after the bell chimed. "When I was five, my father called me out to a serious talk on the beach. The wide sandy strip between the surf and the scrub forest was where I lived from sunup to sundown. My family home on the ridge above had a spectacular view of this South Atlantic beach. Our house consisted of a single fairly large room made of mud bricks and some highly prized wood rafters that my father had hauled up the steep hillside with great effort in the middle of the night.

"He built the entire structure one weekend before I was born. The laws said that once built and lived in, it could not be destroyed. There were rights for squatters in Rio in those days. We had a view equal to that of the homes of the super-rich on the next ridge over. It was a wonderful place to live. The place was always full, with my two brothers, three sisters and two aunts.

"This sunny day like any other my father handed me a soccer ball and said, 'You're a clever fellow. That's good, because brains are important in soccer. Let me tell you there is only one way out of the Favella for you, and that is with this ball. Live with it. Make it a part of you. I know that you can do it, because my father and I very nearly did. You shall have the benefit of our experience.'

"So that was the story of my next fifteen years. I made the national team, played in the World Cup, collected lots of money, then quit to get a high school degree and eventually went to a University in the U.S.A."

It was apparent that this revelation was new to many of the students. It impressed many of them more than his academic honors. He knew this and used it. "I hit the U.S.A. at its peak. Science funding was strong, and we worked hard and published naturally like the world was our playpen. At the top, the challenges were so exciting that there was nothing we'd rather do. Not even be a rock star, or a movie idol. There was a more profound glamour in being an internationally known scientist. Even the general public as represented by the net generation admired us." His eyes had a far-off look as he was reliving those times.

"We had discovered the golden key to knowledge. Or rather, somehow we were able to borrow this key and use it to unlock the mysteries of life. Of course, Darwin had forged the key a century before, but few knew how to use it. We felt like King Arthur when he pulled the sword of power from the stone. It was there just for the grasping; but like King Arthur, one must be conditioned to possess it.

"With an understanding of the myriad applications of evolution's premises — survival of the fittest, statistical promulgation of an optimized solution, and the humble underpinnings of Darwin's seminal concept — we were on our way to understanding just about everything.

"From geophysics to genetics, from cosmic interactions to molecular biology, we saw the 'truth'. When we looked with the clarity of evolution's vision, unfettered by anthropomorphic blinders, without the mind binding cobwebs of blind faith, we could see things as they are."

A muffled "Hallelujah" was heard, and reminded the professor that this was a student body selected for skeptical scrutiny.

"We still might not know why they are; but we actually enjoy this mystery. The harsh hubris of natural selection isn't uplifting or ennobling to us as a species. It provides a valuable dose of humility. We are reconciled to that. I view it as our challenge at this school to provide you with this golden key."

He looked around intently at each face, trying to fathom which of the students had this cognizance and which were still unaware. He knew from experience that despite the careful selection of students, less than half had made significant progress toward this breakthrough in the ability to think along an original path. By the fifth year he hoped the percentage was nearing ninety per cent.

"But eventually, some of us who worked with biological evolution for decades got frustrated when challenged to predict the future evolution of Homo sapiens. Our rules said that the time scale was thousands of years even for evolutionary changes that were occasionally punched hard by environmental changes. There doesn't seem to be that kind of time available to us now. We could see that to last another hundred years we will need a lot of changes.

"I was not content to just do my job, make esoteric discoveries, and publish them as an end. It was apparent to me that if the species wants to survive, it needs to evolve. Now. And I was curious about whether it was even possible, and incidentally if it was, toward what end?

Baker had eagerly moved from UW to OC. She was the Teaching Assistant for this course. Here she injected a cautious question, "But isn't Homo sapiens different in that it has the current ultimate weapon, the cerebral brain? We might be in a new era where evolution of cultural bits via the human language, internet and library has freed our species to manage its own evolution, and on a time scale much shorter than that of the gene."

He appreciated her questions. They kept him in touch with what many of the students were thinking. This had to be dealt with. "That would be nice. But perhaps it's a 'weapon of mass destruction' given the number of extinctions it has caused. The brain is a marvelous instrument. We need to beware, to look that gift horse in the mouth. We accept that natural selection favored body processes that facilitated procreation. Therefore it must also have created the cerebrum to help the body to survive and do its procreative work. Is the brain ever really liberated from this assignment? Has the gene simply designed the brain to guide the culture to benefit the gene?"

"We're just patsies for the gene? There's no free will?" Baker didn't like that.

"Of course! But it's too complicated to be absolute. So relax, you've got a touch of free will." And I'll grant that the brain seems to have the ability to produce ideals and functions that seem independent of the gene's clumsy criterion. But it also seems to be ready and able to create 'faith' and religion, which in general do the gene's bidding, fostering cultural environments that favor procreation."

The old man spoke rapidly; it seemed like he had a lot to say and little time left in which to say it. "Let's pursue this question and look on the light side. We know that the brain is foremost a tool for survival. That in this function it sometimes hallucinates, often capriciously forgets or blocks from recall, and goes on strike at crisis times, all dictated by the brain stem in the interest of survival.

"But we can hypothesize that the gene sitting in the driver's seat tinkered with Homo sapiens' biology to help it propagate itself — and accidentally created a monster, the cerebrum, which breaks free of the propagation dictate.

"Of course these days we have the tools via biogenetics to alter our physiology. We have chosen the sex of the child, bred for height, hair, pleasant looks, and disease resistance. We can alter DNA to change the program for just about any physical development. As these capabilities developed at the turn of the millennium: structural biology, chemistry and socio-biology freed Homo sapiens design from many survival imperatives. We can engineer the genes to shut out the Aids virus, welcome in the cancer killing organic molecule, or select whichever cell development we desire. We could live to 1000."

Baker is on it, "Picture the population explosion in that case."

"OK. We won't do it. Especially since we can't even select a criterion for the process beyond the simplistic dictate, survival - and its handmaiden, procreation. We must avoid the trap of believing, by virtue of our accomplishments and local dominance, that we are uniquely chosen. We're at the top of the local food chain by chance. On the other hand, we should probably try to make the most of it.

"But let's assume that there is a meaning to life. We can't determine anything specific yet by logic alone. Except perhaps, the overwhelming truth in Darwin's evolutionary definition of fitness as the ability to persist. Evidently whatever created life by chance or even design, if that's your predilection, chooses or plans on its ability to survive. So we can assume that this is important to the assumption that life has meaning. The inescapable conclusion is that if we want to contribute to finding the meaning of life, we should do anything we can to enhance the ability of life to continue.

"Actually, the design, or evolutionary path, has evidently reached a critical branch point. It seems that it has produced an intelligent, able to interact with evolution, life form. It's like the gene says to its creation, 'OK. I've taken you to this point on the path to meaning, now it's up to you. Are you intelligent enough to design the next step, by tweaking evolutionary dictate to produce a more intelligent, longer lasting life form? Or do you take the path to failure --- we've reached perfection, we're going to heaven, a fantasy place we envision, so let's stop here.'

"It would seem that we should do the obvious things that enhance human survival and intellectual enhancement. I'm assuming it is also obvious that the 'continue like always' dictum of evolution, enhance beauty and athletic ability, is not getting us to the 'next level'."

"So we are tempted to go comfortably with that obvious motivator, survival. Look a little more closely at the cerebrum, Homo sapiens' greatest achievement, as a possible vehicle to ride to the next step in subsistence. Even when inspired only by that venerable, simple-minded criterion ---

persistence, there still is incentive to provide the capability to carry on to the obvious next arena --- space. This is a big step and first the cerebrum has to achieve dominance over the instinctive functions of the medulla oblongata."

A young woman who was used to being the top student in class raised her hand, turned to look with camaraderie at the tall student in the back of the room and asked: "The new brain would have to replicate more efficiently. To evolve, it would have to have an advantage at some stage of existence. How can that come about?"

When the professor smiled as he did now, the myriad lines and creases on his face betrayed his eighty years. It was the same smile he gave much younger people on the tennis court before proceeding to beat them with lobs and drop shots. "I like that question. To help I'll throw out a few possibilities for you to work with. Like, the cerebrum achieves dominance, and imposes a breeding requirement on the population that reinforces creatures that demonstrate cerebral dominance.

"Or, perhaps we pursue simple genetic manipulation of the design of the medulla oblongata. Or, we surrender sexual reproduction and all its baggage to cloning and genetic manipulation to keep the evolving parasites in check — think of what freedom that would give us."

The tall fellow in the back of class interjected, "How boring."

There was another smile, or grimace, it wasn't clear. "Let's explore the optimistic hypothesis brought up by my questioner here in the front row." He gave a nod of appreciation in her direction.

"Let's consider the tantalizing possibilities of the cultural component analogous to the gene. It has been called the meme, and is comprised of a unit of brain memory that has been passed on sensually. In its best form it is an idea.

"You've learned that Homo sapiens' strong suit is the ability to be a time-binder. We do not have to reinvent the wheel because the knowledge is implanted in our brain either by a teacher, a picture, a book, or observation of the real thing. From the ancient's story-telling to computer instruction, every act of teaching attempts to implant cultural memes in the brain." There was a stir at the far side of the table.

"But the DNA contains only genetic material." The tall guy stood up to ask this question, perhaps to get a better look at his colleague in the front row.

"Correct. The meme must be culturally implanted. It has been shown that there can be a genetic conditioning for receptivity to certain memes.

Some are coated in the mystique of brainstem wiring for greed, fear or piety. If the gene with this characteristic then has survival value, then the meme will have the endurance of the gene."

"If only by encouraging the genes that favor development of the meme?"

"True. And unfortunately, as with the gene, there is optimization by survival of the fittest. There are a hundred bad ideas for each good one. There appears to be no requirement for accuracy."

Baker looked at None with almost reverent respect. "That explains why dishonest advertising is so successful. They could persuade the average man to routinely vote to make the richest and most powerful elements of society even stronger. Brainstem weaknesses like religious faith and love of that ultimate survival tool, the gun, were expertly exploited."

"Sounds reasonable. The schism we have today wasn't imposed by force; the people bought it. So, just as bad genes can be inherited, bad memes can be ingrained. "

"We have met the enemy, and it is us?" Teton looked at Baker with a smile.

None cocked a bushy gray eyebrow. He wasn't sure that he liked Teton distracting his teaching assistant. "True. But enemy of what? Perhaps an egalitarian society? But who's to say that should be the goal? We know that class division in a society, a persistent cultural characteristic, a meme, was a prelude to revolution– even before meme manipulation conditioned the populace to propagate cultural divisions into the democratic processes. The people don't necessarily vote their own interests, but to perpetrate the status quo. When we accept our lot, and grant power and wealth to a privileged elite, we have an oligarchy in equilibrium even in a democracy." The last words were accompanied by a sad shaking of the head, reflecting personal experience.

The students were thinking — this was going to be a tough course. But they were engaging their cerebrums, suppressing their medulla oblongata distractions, and listening with concentration. It was, after all, the environment.

The two observers eased out of the room. It was time to look at another class.

Enlightenment is the emancipation of man from a state of self-imposed tutelage. This state is due to his incapacity to use his own intelligence without external guidance.... Dare to use your own Intelligence! This is the battle-cry of the Enlightenment.

Immanuel Kant 1785

The USA experienced enlightenment from the founding fathers design until the limbo of the world wars and recovery; then we lurched into the dark ages as the twentieth century closed. We can only hope that a second enlightenment will come.

Anon.

Ch 3.2 Two Classes

A look around this obscure corner of the Olympic Peninsula revealed what bright ideas and a liberal amount of Liberal money could bring about. J discovered two amazing things in these years. One was that immense feats could be accomplished when money was not a problem. The campus opened after less than a year of construction. Another two and it was essentially finished. Each student population was double the last one.

The second amazement was that the student body and the faculty were both fairly easy to find. There was a latent hunger for intellectualism that had lain dormant since the eighties. It had gone underground during the right-wing assaults at the turn of the century. Then it emerged as the excesses of the rich and greedy broke the old USA and an intellectual administration was elected. But once again, the idealisms proposed as policy scared the heck out of the power brokers, religious conservatives and anti-tax and anti-gun control factions, providing a moneyed unprincipled force with enough power to bring down don Quixote. Once again the tide shifted, and as the venerated separation of church and state vanished, intellectual thinking became as dangerous as in Galileo's day. The revolution was inevitable.

In Cascadia, there had been a raucous political battle and eventually the doctrinaire groups fled east. The result was a fairly loose state government that was still carefully conservative but fiercely independent minded. The new-generation of super-rich still contained enough closet liberals with sufficient power to allow an experiment like Olympic College to exist.

The classroom design at OC was perfect for the campus philosophy. When knowledge is king- pretension is plebian, informality is ubiquitous. Inside the classroom, the rough-hewn womb of the walls provided security. The warm wood of the floor, ceiling and the central table promoted beauty and informality. There was no need for cashmere sweaters or designer jeans to mark status. This was measured by one's conversation. Just looking around a classroom there was no way to determine by appearance the merely capable from the stellar talent. Even the professors tended to blend in to the students, all wearing informal college clothes.

Continuing their tour, J and Gad walked to the center of the building where the conversation areas offered espresso machines. They meticulously ground their coffee, filled, tapped and wrenched tight the coffee holder, steamed an inch of milk into three of foam, and blasted the super hot water through the funnel, the coffee into special cups. It took time, but both enjoyed talking about their little experiment.

As the second classes of the morning were ready to begin, they took seats in the classroom at the other end of this building from the first class. On the notebook screen is, 'Biology and Sociology', and underneath in smaller, italic font, 'or Biology's Role in Enjoying Life', and smaller yet; 'That's right — Sex Education'. Another famous freethinker taught this class. Nicole was a striking woman, vibrant in her fifties.

She has a strong, low-pitched voice. "There are great pleasures in knowledge. Even within the humiliatingly humbling aspects of evolution's cognition. Hey, if you're going to be a species on this planet, what better than the dominant one? What a tool, the brain. Sexual reproduction, hallelujah. We have a variety of positive feedback genes and memes, or pleasure buttons. And we know how to push them all." Nicole is evidently 'with-it'.

"What Homo sapiens frequently doesn't know is how to stop pushing these buttons. Some of the feedback is beneficial to the individual in small doses, deleterious in large amounts. Examples are too many delicious calories converted to fat, sexual gratification taken to fetishes, love to obsession, masturbation to preoccupation, alcohol taste and buzz to addiction — likewise any other of a myriad of mind altering drugs.

"The Greeks knew --- they had a rule; nothing in excess. They knew the theory, but lacked the discipline. They didn't follow their rule very well. They ate well. They grew taller than we do today. They had very tolerant ideas toward sex. They drank a lot. It's sounding good, isn't it?" This was said to a youth in the front row, who was just thinking that he would have made a great Greek.

"It must have been good, and frenetic. Their average life span was twenty-two years. You're already there." Most of her class thought she would have been entertaining at the Saturday night comedy hour at the Den. Some already knew she could occasionally be found on stage.

"In this class you get what could be called the Panzaic side of biology and evolution. You get the highfalutin theory from None. Here, we'll concentrate on the practical applications that make for a real cool thinker, an intellectual force for existence, a smooth party chatterer and a nice satisfactory life."

J was carried along with her train of thought. The two of them verbally jousted many times. Before he thought, he sotto voiced, "Is that all?"

She rolled with the laughter, "Of course not, I forgot — and a contribution toward saving the world.

"We'll look at simple things, like the positive effects of laughter to good health. There are the benefits of relaxation — from meditation to martinis. The sense-of-accomplishment rush. In balance, they create great contentment in life. Out of balance, you can be buried in the rat race or a couch potato. Given time, rush and relaxation can work together. With insufficient time, they can work against one another.

"With the proper knowledge, we can use the physiological buttons to our advantage to get the pleasure feedback. During this course, I'm going to reveal these buttons to you buried in the context of basic biology. You will have to listen-up if you want to hear them. Don't pass them around, the final exam will ask for them. It's all in the mind here, and individual homework and practice will help."

This professor had it easy; the students were universally interested in the topic. There would be lively dialog throughout the quarter. She looked on this course as fun and games. Much later, at the senior or graduate level, the successful amongst them would take her famous course on religion. It was one of the climax courses at OC.

She walked around the table as she continued. "Where do we begin? With some dry biological facts and stats. About why the genes evolved a reward system for whenever you do something that enhances reproduction."

Juliet was here, and she had the confidence to contribute, "Or sometimes merely to allow survival."

"In order to reproduce of course," was the quick reply. "Perhaps we can then gain some control over which chemicals we want released, and when. As you probably suspect, it involves considerable effort to understand the myriad complexities of the mind-body pleasure components of the ethos. Just remember; anything worthwhile requires work.

"Work takes many forms, all dictated by biological drives. The simplest drive is hunger. A more complex one is sex. I like to concentrate on the latter." Several quiet "amens" were heard from the class.

"The drive of sex is so fundamental that it probably underlies all of our historical evolution, not just of physiology, but the culture of every civilization. It has not been popular to discuss since it is not merely politically incorrect, but culturally taboo to take a good look at sex, out loud.

"If a more frank attitude had been prevalent in the first century of the U.S.A. experiment, for instance, we could have taught that the practice of slavery was driven not just by a need for cheap labor, but also by the desire to have concubines to propagate the owner's genes. Subservient human beings as beasts of burden and increased opportunity for sex. The evidence is in the record — of the high prices of females, particularly virgins, and the practice of denied access to other males. They weren't looking for just any old source of more slaves. The work done by slaves freed the owner to accumulate and copulate." There was something magical in this professor's ability to look in the eyes of a male student when delivering this line.

"The experiments of evolution in the development of culture are logical while being blind to their fatal flaws. We'll look at previous developments and then see if we can spot the current flaws." She was back at the front, standing on the small platform to gain some height.

"For instance, there was a common trend in early civilizations, starting with Babylon and including China's and India's emperors, the Egyptian pharaohs, and the sun kings of the Aztec and Inca right up to the fifteenth century. Each totalitarian regime dominated for hundreds of years. What's striking is that evolution had produced this efficient breeding machine, the despot, in so many places at once. Remember, a despot is one who has the wealth, and hence power, to arbitrarily dispatch any of his subjects, in particular, any competition to his breeding activities. Hence all of these leaders had thousands of mates, as many as they could accommodate, with the singular purpose of propagating their genes."

"Not bad, if you're the Man." This came from the hunk in the front row.

Nicole loved this kind of straight man. "Turns out: 'Is bad'. Apparently too much of anything can be boring, even tedious. Biology determines the social system. Biology makes mistakes. Evolution didn't design the sex distribution for this type of culture. Ten thousand women for one man leaves a lot of men wanting. The mistake here was the act of frustrating — sexually frustrating — the huge majority of men. It didn't seem like survival of the fittest, since there was no contest, just inheritance. Whence comes revolution."

"They could have dispatched nine of every ten male babies."

She looked appreciatively at the latent potentate sitting in the first row. "Good points for thinking. They probably thought about it. But they needed armies.

"Democracy got its impulse from the fact that most men didn't like this system. In fact, neither did the emperors, describing the chore of 'distributing their semen' as onerous. Perhaps they had an inkling that they were just doing the gene's work."

She loved to work this observation into her lectures somewhere. The men students invariably found it impossible to empathize with the emperors' attitude. The women students accepted it as logical. She still didn't know the complete reasons for these different reactions. But the resulting conversation was always fascinating.

"The practical aspects of a good education in Darwin's abecedarian contribution are endless. I call them the Gifts from Evolution. First, there's the humility it brings. For years my grandson, impressed from dinnertime conversations, thought that our species was the 'human bean'. Just a special version of what was on our plate."

It was clear to the two observers that several of the male students were still reeling under the revelation that this professor was a grandmother.

Gorgeous granny gave the students a warm sexy smile, to further confuse them. "The foremost thing is: there is no 'right' choice beyond 'survival of the fittest'. Natural selection chooses by not choosing. It just tries everything; some of its choices survive to propagate its heritage. On the short term there are lots of free lunches. It says nothing about loftier goals; survival is the only criteria. That's good. It leaves us to invent the right and wrong. That's bad, we haven't a clue.

"In this context our discussions of sexual aspects of our species are greatly facilitated and de-titillated. There is less puzzlement over the place of men and women. Designed for different functions, the hormonal balance is the evolutionary formula for survival of the species. From 'Viva le difference' to the simplistic 'Men are from Mars, women from Venus', the differences and similarities are simply related to the mix of hormones. A man is simply a bag of hormones. Woman is similar, but the choice of hormones is more benign."

In this class Nicole enjoyed longer soliloquies than were allowed by the students in other classes. This was undoubtedly because the students still harbored inhibitions from their childhood education that made it difficult to ask questions. They all feared their question would reflect their own sexual frame of reference. Correctly in fact.

"For one thing, the male is led to frequent, polygamous sex; the female seems to find a monogamist relation satisfactory. The male's predilection toward infidelity is evident, hypothesized by the genetic theory that males are uncertain of parentage and must sow the seed widely. It is substantiated by an abundance of empirical evidence.

"Not so evident is the proclivity of the female towards dalliance. She is always looking for the best genes. The law of the scrotum — female promiscuity is proportional to the volume of the male scrotum — was empirically established amongst all of the great apes. It was later found to apply to all species. And there is ample empirical evidence that it holds true for the moderately large size scrotum of Homo sapiens.

"This is just knowledge based on science. But it is also a tool for understanding social sciences, fascinating trivia for the layman, and dangerous fuel for the rationalizations of charlatans. Try the scrotum-promiscuity law at your next party. You'll be a hit."

"Particularly if you let them think that it works on an individual basis." This came from a thoughtful woman believer.

This comment please Nicole, and she looked at this student and continued as though talking to her only. "Both sexes have hormones choosing either approach to sexual fidelity. Both paths have been selected by the gene's experimentally derived drive toward propagation. Knowing this, all of us should use our brains to tailor our lives to accommodate the directives from the hormones- within the confines of the logical choices for survival and a pleasant life."

A young student who looked like she might doubt her own ability asked, "But if it is all hard-wired into the brain then we have no choice."

"Yes, that's a frightening thought. But I'll suggest that we have input; a cultural, environmental tweak on the gene's program. It may be enough. A little biological knowledge can resolve gigantic cultural dilemmas. It can also furnish little practical tips; knowledge that smoothes your sex life. Although sometimes I suspect that the biological decree is so great that we'd best just relax and attempt to survive, perhaps even enjoy the dictated course of our genes. Then, when we get past the mating, procreation, propagating the species, what's left over is ours to enjoy — considerable time for our species."

"What's left to enjoy?" The hunk in front strikes again. Nicole positioned herself in front of him.

"For one thing — sex. The imperative may be diminished, but the capability and experience are there. With knowledge you can relax and enjoy."

"What if society doesn't want you to enjoy?" This came from a feminine young male.

"OK. Let's pursue this hormone thing a bit farther. The distribution of the mix is a continuum; some ratio of male and female hormones resides in every person. Pity those on the extremes, with only the one hormonal directive. Zero empathy, singular purposes, closed minds are de rigueur. Fortunately the majority has a mix and can rationalize, and wend their way, looking for a similar chemical stew with which to mingle their genes. Understanding of bisexuality and homosexuality becomes a breeze, no cause for alarm or anxiety. Those with the extreme or balanced mixes can only strive to find acceptance and understanding of their fears by the mainliners."

Hunk says, "I think that I'm a mainliner."

"So you are." She turned to encompass the room. "If you are aware of your own duality, you can choose when to use it and when to lose it. If you have been dealt a hormonal mix that is more than a standard deviation away from the norm- you have to engage the cranium to enhance your chances of survival. The dual purposes are there because they have a survival benefit for the species, as a whole. But perhaps not for you. Adjust. Biological science can give you hormonal adjustment; the brain can give you innovation and enterprise. Relax."

She acknowledged a question from a soft-voiced male. "Can you give us a specific example right now of one of these practical tips that smooth our lives, please?" He couldn't bring himself to say 'sex lives'.

She knew what he wanted. "Certainly. We know that a female's preference in choice of male is influenced by her monthly cycle. When she is ovulating, biology dictates that she prefers men with strong masculine features. When menstruating or less likely to get pregnant, she prefers more feminine looks. This is evidently rooted in evolutionary trends that correlated masculine characteristics with healthy offspring. It's probably irrelevant to survival now. But if you know your type features and the woman's cycle, you can tailor and time your approach for maximum success. Maybe later in the course I'll give you some tips on how to judge where a woman is in her cycle. It isn't easy — some of them don't know."

She did have an agenda. Her goal was no less lofty than that of None. She wanted to know the meaning of life, and pursue the 'Grail'. But she also wanted to enjoy the trip. "When we learn and believe that we are a chemical stew wrought by evolution, it makes many culturally explosive problems become obvious. It doesn't mean the solution to the problem is obvious, just that we understand the problem and can work in the right direction.

"For instance, the crime of rape is grossly misunderstood because of the role of hormones. The myth that it is mainly an act of violence, or a sickness, or even contemplated by only the criminal, are concepts of those ignorant of evolution's simple rules. The realities are different. What some call the 'absurd' condemnation of the victim for dressing provocatively or just being in the wrong place at the wrong time, can be logical criticisms in a Panzaic sense." Some frowns appear at this point. She approves of this; thought often flourishes behind a frown.

"What do men want? That's easy. They want women. Right?"

Every male nodded agreement, smiling. So did every female, shaking their head.

"They want women to impregnate. Deposit their seed. You know.

"What do women want? That's a little more difficult, but with the same drivers. They want a particular kind of man, one with good seeds and a disposition to protect the product of that emission. Women think a little ahead. But mainly, depositing and receiving that little seed is what our dominant hormones are designed to do." After all, she is a woman giving this lecture.

"On a more practical level, you know that the female approach is quite different to that of the male. Evolution dictates that the goal of the sexual act is to procreate, --- just like the bible says. Hence she is interested in prolonging the interaction to make certain of getting the sperm. And she is interested in relating the act to a durable relationship, also known as love, as this is most efficient for raising the little buggers. "The male is interested in climaxing, delivering the sperm, and then quickly loses interest and wants to depart. He is susceptible to 'love' but that is on another plane. Males who dallied in the vulnerable position sometimes ended up with clubs or spears from behind in the constant competition with the other males. Those who fled survived to breed again.

Students had been attempting to raise their hands for questions, but the lecture was laying out the parameters. Justification for these positions would come later. Finally, she paused and nodded to a shyly raised feminine hand.

"What about basic human ethics?"

Nicole had spent hours discussing the place of ethics in evolution. Often she could answer simply, 'You can find the answer in a paper written by a student of mine.' But in class she worked with the leading question. "Understanding that Homo sapiens is the local example of the fittest survivor satisfies many ethical problems of seemingly huge pretense with simple truisms.

"For instance, abortion is the disposal of a human fetus before it emerges from the mother's womb. The life form, Homo sapiens, is a successful animal species by virtue of its ability to develop into a thinking entity. Each fetus has this potential. It is nothing but potential at birth and for perhaps even years after birth. Given the immense danger to the species from overpopulation, the odds that its net contribution will be negative are better than ten to one."

"So we should abort nearly everyone." This came from a young man whose spirituality had been offended several times already.

"Just most males." Contributed by a savvy woman.

Nicole pursued the point. "The culture has long ago decided that the mass-murderer should be killed, since they obviously cause more harm than good. The intelligent culture also decides, for the good of the species, that too many progeny destroy the environment and trash the society. Hence, inhibiting fertilization and terminating some fetuses are logical actions. Simply based on statistics we should be very selective in who and how many we allow to be born."

The spiritual one revealed inherent reservations. "Then logical is ethical?"

The teacher showed a strained smile, threw a terse "Yes," as an aside to the questioner, and continued, "Only the belief that Homo sapiens is sacred, based on some irrational faith, counsels against this procedure. Taken to the extreme, some have even considered that the decision not to have children, to not admit a 'waiting soul', is murder the same as execution. This reduces us all to the level of a soul-bearing container, and deprecates any intellectual advancement. This group, encompassing many religions, is successful because it is a positive feedback procedure — not allowing abortion produces more protoplasm with little or no education, little education produces more no-abortions. It is a subtle little process evolved in the gene to manipulate Homo sapiens through the brain memes."

"Then illogical is unethical?"

"Not always. But I can think of nothing more unethical than overpopulating the environment." She paused here. In some parts of the world or timeline she would be burned at the stake or stoned for this kind of statement. So she still cautiously peered at each student. The campus was a sanctuary, an intellectual oasis, but it was an open one. She knew that word of her explosive lectures had been written of 'outside'.

But except for the reserved young man everyone seemed happy, accepting her comments as some novel new facts. She continued, "One can channel many manual functions into automatic, so that several deeds can be done simultaneously. Ride a bike, prepare a talk, and hum a tune. But to maximize input to the pleasure sensation one should concentrate.

"To savor life, enjoyable procedures should be done singly with awareness. Never eat chocolate while reading a book, or conversing, watching the tube, or for God's sake while making love. The last was for the Hunk. Perhaps even while listening to music, because I suspect the attention must be shuttled back and forth. It takes effort to get the most out of life's pleasures.

"Clouds must be concentrated on, rain must be listened to, beautiful faces must be scrutinized, some flowers smelled, some just gazed upon, and sex must be singularly savored. Knowledge is essential. It helps the enjoyment of chocolate to know that the sweet-sensing taste buds are at the sides of the tongue. It helps sex to know what the hormones want."

This is what the curriculum is about. This professor has an exciting, survey-type course. To be sure, the students have all taken classes in mathematics, physics, botany, biology and chemistry that embody the tedium that forge the fences that too often kept out the majority of people. Teaching these preliminary classes requires technique and diligence --- this class must be handled with a certain flair. Few would deny that it was so done.

◆

After lunch, J and Gad continue their tour of the campus curriculum. J turns through a clump of trees. "We'll finish the day with a visit to a first-year introductory class. It should be relatively restful."

They headed for the western edge of campus, hiking up a ridge that would be called a mountain in half of the old-states. The zone is alpine, and a few short, contorted firs dot the red dirt and granite slopes. A well-worn path leads a quarter of a mile to an inconspicuous door. Inside is the most conventional of lecture rooms, a small amphitheater in a semi-circle surrounding a lectern.

The room is buried in the crest, so that behind the podium, a wall of windows yields a grand view of the Strait of Juan de Fuca to the northwest. The Strait receives the Pacific twice daily as tide rises to flush the hundreds of kilometers of channels and bays that make up the Puget Sound. If it weren't for the view, this would be a classroom like any other around the world. It is the only such classroom on the OC campus.

The lecturer is also singular. A young man, dressed conservatively in slacks, a pastel blue shirt covered by a forest green sweater and a tweed jacket. One had to look carefully to check that there was no tie in the two inches between the sweater and the throat. This was evidently a serious class, a disciplined class, and apparently the traditional classroom mode was in order here. The freshman class settled comfortably into the environment of their expectations. This was by design. Too much change too fast is traumatic for the psyche.

"Welcome to Science I, Physics and Astronomy- the first class in a three-year sequence of basic physical science that is required of all students. This philosophy emerged from the initial brainstorming done by the entire faculty when the curriculum was set. The idea is that one, and possibly the major, flaw in our cultural fabric is the shallow level of science in the general public's grasp. It is an extraordinary generalization. We know that pockets of enlightenment have existed during the past few hundred years, but they lacked something critical to survive. It's possible that thing was science. Our founding fathers all embraced the enlightenment; and all had a serious interest in science. It is possible that is why we have been so successful.

"In the past few decades there has been little or no communication between the scientist and the nonscientist in our culture. The blame lies with both, but the burden falls on the scientist. The burden is by default. It is possible for the scientist to acquire a decent liberal arts education after the science is obtained, and quite a few have done this. It seems to be nearly impossible for the liberal arts graduate to step into a science program. It is done, but very rarely. The result is that the majority of our educated populace is only half educated.

"Herein lays the biggest problem for the scientist trying to relate to the nonscientists. He sounds arrogant. He *is* arrogant to the nonscientist. You all will have enough science to be called scientists. But the same skeptical attitude and respect for verification that stands you well with your fellow scientist will make you seem arrogant to the layperson."

This was all acceptable to the freshmen. They still listened to the professor as if he was God. They would learn to do otherwise at OC.

"One of the goals of this college is to remedy this unfortunate situation that makes the scientist antisocial. The reality is that you're going to end up as a member of an educated minority in a hostile culture. We'll try to give you the tools to deal with that too. But first, let us begin with your ascendancy to incompatibility.

"As you've probably heard several times already, evolution is the first step. It is true even here in physics. This is because learning is like planting a garden. The soil must be carefully prepared and full of nutrients before the seed is placed. Your understanding of philosophy and the so-called Arts will be smooth and fruitful when it is planted in the soil of science knowledge.

"When a person realizes that ninety-nine per cent of their genetic make-up is identical to that of a chimp, their perspective on the relative place of the species in the scheme of things should change. You'll hear in biology that their discipline, with a half dozen modifiers, is the nitty-gritty of evolution. But the other end, the big picture, can best be addressed with geophysics and astronomy.

"I don't include the mathematics that you're learning in another core course. I consider it a tool for all of science. The approach called Statistics has to be employed, and the myriad pitfalls of the application must be understood. Great and gross deeds have been promulgated through fair and foul statistics — not necessarily exclusively correlated. I know that you will understand these obtuse references because your math professor and I communicate regularly.

"Nor do I include philosophy, which is simply speculation. When it is done within scientific constraints, it can be valuable and entertaining. When done arbitrarily, it can be bunk. Now, not everyone on the faculty will agree with me in these statements, but enough do that I can teach my educated opinion. There is no 'truth' and that is all right with me."

This young man had an engaging manner. He could be a talking head

— a newsreader on a major network for a lot more money. Indeed, he was doing that when J contacted him about this job. J knew about his first job at a major university, where he was assigned to teach an introductory class in astronomy. His style got him through most of the year. But soon enough, some of the students realized that what he was saying was not from the books.

Students were trained to accept their professors' word, and expected them to have all the answers. When even fundamentals were questioned, and many questions were left dangling, frustration festered. His student ratings were always dragged down by several very low ratings from true believers. Tenure denied, he tried another school, with similar results. Cynicism firmly established; he got a good paying honest job where substance in what he was saying was never even a pretension. However, he was terribly frustrated, a burden borne by intellectuals since the species began to think.

This job, to him, was heaven. "We will study the hard evidence that welds astronomy and physics. And we will note that even under the most conservative of statistical chances there could be ten to a hundred million planets in just this galaxy that are nearly identical to earth. So that even if one takes the viewpoint that only one in a thousand such planets will develop life forms, there still might be a million of them out there in the neighborhood."

A young woman has a salient observation. "If there're only ten billion planets that have evolved an advanced life form like us in the about thirteen billion years that the universe has existed, and it appears that an advanced civilization has a good chance of lasting only about several thousand years," she paused as though calculating the numbers in her head, "then at any specific time, there's likely only a few others in the whole galaxy."

This Professor appreciated the special ability of these students to keep him honest. But he knew the equation, and was ready with an answer. "We can pursue many scenarios, since few facts get in the way. So we might assume that sun, planet and civilization develop at similar rates in a given galaxy, so that a good percentage of these planets mature at about the same time, at least enough to increase the odds to an expectation of hundreds of other civilizations at this moment in time.

"And of course that's only in this galaxy. It appears that there are at last count several hundred billion galaxies, going up every time we get a more powerful telescope. So I hope you are more comfortable with trillions of possibilities.

"In addition, many scientists, noting that life exists on earth in every niche with or without sunlight, oxygen, or photosynthesis, would say life development is certain on any planet that is even near to earth's temperature range. This ups the number of possible life forms again.

"There will be other factors that change these statistics up or down. To evaluate them, you're going to want to be able to understand the physics behind the knowledge of these stars, galaxies, black holes, planets and strings. When I get done with this motivational lecture, we'll start learning how this information is borne to us at the speed of light.

"There's another factor to all of these life forms. As the young lady suggested, some might be considerably ahead of us on the evolutionary ladder, maybe by a billion years. Now we were about at the worm state a billion years ago, and simply microbes three billion years ago. What will we be a billion years from now? What are these alien civilizations like with a billion-year head start? That's food for thought. More to the point, what will Physics be like? Is it constant? We had better get to work."

♦

Gad was stimulated as they walked back. "These were all interesting courses. Something's happening. The concept is clear. The brain is being tweaked."

"Hopefully, the traditional cobwebs that have fettered the minds of Homo sapiens for centuries are being swept away. The broom is scientific knowledge. Get the facts, then address the crucial questions."

"Seems sensible, yet we still don't know toward what end." Gad raised his eyebrows as high as they would go, J pointed a finger upward along with them. "Higher and higher, wherever that leads."

The laughter and warmth of the conversation of the two men expressed their enjoyment, digging into the adventure before them.

Ch. 3.3 Mt. Olympus

In the center of the mountain range that crowns the Olympic Peninsula is the highest mountain on the peninsula. Snaking down its slopes is a river of blue ice. The Blue Glacier is the largest glacier in the state. It wends its way off Mt. Olympus in several stages. The best views were available when the local charter plane delivered scientists to the high altitude cabin. This was their base for studying the glacier. The plane landed on the upper level of the glacier, just below the cirque that was the base of the peak massif- and the umbilical cord of the glacier. From a commercial jet high above the mountain, the light plane looked like a fly settling on a huge white bedspread. The part of the glacier that formed the runway was gently sloping upward and relatively flat with few crevasses. The landing was fairly simple, as the upward slope slowed the plane quickly.

On the other hand, the take-off was spectacular. The plane did not really have to lift off; rather the glacier just dropped off beneath the plane to its next gently flowing domain a thousand feet below. The commitment to take-off was total.

Several years before, the whole program was in limbo when engine failure on take-off ended the first pilot's business. At last another pilot was found, who embraced the philosophy 'Life is a great adventure or nothing'. J was thinking the either-or option was probably pertinent this day as he and Kay placed their lives in the pilot's hands.

The small two-engine plane climbed with the curve of the mountain. They flew up the glacier as a pelican flies up an ocean swell. When it leveled out, they were only a few feet above the surface, looking for a smooth area. As the steepening cliff at the head of the glacier loomed ahead, still two thousand feet below the towering summit, it occurred to J that landing here was also a total commitment. If something went wrong, the only response could be a heart wrenching turn to the right- over the low ridge and the geophysics cabin.

For a hundred years the upper glacier had been smooth up to ten meters below the bergschrund, where a series of deep crevasses developed. There was usually one wide horizontal fissure a few hundred meters below the cliff. And so it was today.

The plane touched the snow gently and moved up the incline wearing out the forward momentum, stopping short of the crevasse. The pilot taxied quickly toward the rocky ridge where the cabin was perched. Kay, J, and Henri, an earnest young geophysicist who held project leadership, got out of the plane and headed for the cabin. Henri's job was to maintain the station. He was a former student of J's.

The students who worked here were unloading supplies. They had all walked and climbed the thirty miles in. J had done this prerequisite trek many years ago, and Kay had accomplished it just last year. So they felt justified in taking this easy way to the cabin for an extended weekend this fall. It was a choice of either hours of perspiration or a quick flood of adrenaline.

As in a play's opening moments, there was little or no conversation for the extended time they took to survey their surroundings, admire the mixture of black rock and hard white ice that formed the western face of the peak and a ridge southward across the glacier. To the north, the mountain dropped steeply beyond the cabin.

They helped unload the plane and watched with resolute support as the pilot took off into the void. The plane dropped out of sight like a ship disappears into the curve of the sea. It was seconds that seemed like minutes before the plane finally appeared far below, heading down the valley toward home.

After some tidying and unpacking, Henri brought out schnapps and they each found a comfortable stone seat to view the sunset. J commented to Henri, "Sometimes I think that it just isn't fair, that some people's work takes them to wonderful environments all the time, while most are confined to factories and florescent tubes."

Henri sighed, "That's why I am what I am. Don't ever believe anyone in our profession who says they're too busy to notice their natural surroundings. The ambiance is why we're here as much as the curiosity about what makes it tick. Of course the entry ticket, a PhD in an earth science is not exactly free admission. It keeps the ranks small."

Kay laughed, intimately familiar with the labor involved in getting the ticket. "I'm happy that you invite your colleagues to share in your banquet."

J was looking across a mile of ice, "I suspect the bureaucrats know. That is why they can pay you half what you could earn selling something useful."

"Don't ever tell them; but it's worth it. We now have another banquet, with pasta as the featured performer."

The meal was three-star, considering the location. The conversation was lively, and the revelry drifted out over the icy surroundings, echoed off the steep massif, and bothered not a solitary animal. The only clinker in the evening was when Henri, full of wine, stumbled on the single stair to the cabin and sprained his ankle.

"My ankle needs a rest. I fear that this means you will have to take the lead tomorrow when you climb the peak," addressed to J. "You have climbed it before."

"But I've never led."

"It is easy. Just follow the tracks of our climb last week. You've two neophytes going with you, Kay and a new graduate student, Steven, who arrived only today. It is your chance to be a real leader. And from what I've heard of Kay, she is prepared to take over if you falter." Henri hobbled to his room at the end of the cabin and bid them goodnight.

J looked at Kay. "Are you sure that you want to go?"

"It may be my one chance. And you know what life is." Said with a Mona Lisa smile that revealed the concern under the bravado.

◆

The next day was bright, windless and cold. There wasn't a reason not to make the climb. They started out, crampons strapped to their boots, a nylon rope linked to each of the three waists with fifty feet between them, and each with an ice ax. It was such a powerful 'Thing-To-Do', that none of them questioned the logic of it. The awesome spectacle before them sucked them in like an orchid does an insect.

Kay questioned J once as they walked the upper edge of the long, deep crevasse, "Are you sure this is the way?"

"Well I don't know if they came this way because it is stable ice, educational, or just exciting, but they came this way," J's frank comment.

When they reached the bergschrund marking the boundary between the glacier and the rock, J stopped and looked at the crumbling mixture of crevasses and ice serracs at the rock wall juncture. There was an ice crest rising from thirty-foot depths leading to the rock shelf that was evidently used in the last climb. Under the effect of days of bright sun, it was now only a foot wide at the top, with four feet to cross and an upward step to the rock on the other side. J spent no time deciding to seek another route.

Now, off the 'beaten' track, and near the irregularity of the flowing ice along its meeting point with the solid mountain, he probed each step with his ice ax. It was slow going, but his caution was vindicated when the thrust of the ice ax pushed it unresisting to the metal asp in his hand on two occasions. Each time new routes were hastily selected. They eventually found a gentle meeting of ice and rock, crossed easily, sat and rested. They removed the cramp-on spikes, and started the climb up the cold granite ridge.

An hour later, the ridge became too steep, and the trail moved out over the Western glacier. Back in spikes and ropes, after an hour they were within sight of the summit. At this point they came to a large solid-looking wide ice bridge. On both sides, the cold blue of glacial ice merged to depths that couldn't be seen without moving closer to the edge than they were inclined to do. The right side was separated from the ridge rock by twenty feet and on the left side the crevasse continued into the distance. It was clearly cross here or turn back.

J turned to Kay with a confident look. "Why don't you plant your ax in the ice as firmly as you can, wind the rope a couple of loops around it, sit down and get comfortable. Your job is to 'arrest' me in the odd chance that the bridge collapses."

She nodded soberly, as though she actually thought that she would stop his plunge, rather than follow J, the ax, and the rope into the depths. "Yes sir."

She felt a little more confident when Steven did the same fifty feet below her.

J crossed uneventfully, anchored himself securely beyond, and smiled at Kay with a come-hither wave. "Next."

When she settled next to him she simply muttered, "piece of cake." J wondered how many of his favorite expressions were going to be in her thesis.

They had lunch on the peak. Nothing was higher for hundreds of miles, but many comparable peaks were visible. These were part of the huge folds in the continental rock pushed upward as the Juan de Fuca plate dived under the continental plate. Occasional volcanic peaks dotted the Cascade Range, but here the shear fault-block folds produced a range of towering granite peaks. From an airplane, this line of snow-covered peaks loomed as white pimples on the green earth. The immensity of the surroundings, while sitting on one particular pimple, provided them with a sense of individual insignificance.

The talk had naturally turned to beautiful places. J had to mention the Kalahari in Africa. A visit there for a conference that included a safari in this southern Africa desert had evidently deeply affected him.

"The animals are awesome. The Spring Bok is a beautiful antelope, brown, black and white markings; it is exciting to watch it run, bounce and turn. I suppose it is fascinating to watch this done when pursued by a lion or hyena, since they are favorite prey.

"The indigenous brown hyena is extraordinary, with a beautiful long coat like a huge vicuna, in stark contrast to the spotted, ugly hyena that evolved to the north. Since the ugly one is more successful, I see that beauty is not worshipped in all species."

"Maybe it's the definition of beauty that varies."

"Possibly. Another beautiful thing was the huge smooth dunes providing vistas and updrafts for the eagle and hawk. Small flowers, aromatic and edible, attempt to hold the dunes vertical with deep taproots reaching an amazing hundred meters down. Only these roots survive the droughts. A limited number of animals are knowledgeable enough to dig them to survive on their water. A balance is struck, and the flower propagates just enough to slake the thirst of its clientele.

"Given thousands of years, most things have come to some sort of equilibrium that we can recognize." J was talking to himself as much as to Kay.

"Why did you go to Africa?"

"It is the crucible of life, the fountain and the cesspool of civilization. Nature runs amok, from termites to tin pot human dictators. There was equilibrium between Homo Sap and the environment for thousands of years.

"Then the missionaries came and told them of the sacredness of each life, helped them cure many diseases, and lectured them to forbid their methods of family planning that ranged from natural forms of birth control to infanticide. The capitalist companies came to 'help' them into the twenty-first century — read consumerism — and sacrificed the long term environment for short term profit every time. We also sold them arms."

Kay looked out at the mountains. "I know. I worried about the animals. The 'civilized' world demanded ivory, so the elephants were gone in decades, except for those in the Parks. The religious quirks of Eastern macho males needing rhino horns for daggers and aphrodisiacs; and the rhino disappeared. Even the Parks couldn't save them."

"The West satisfies their military-industrial complex by selling exotic weapons to primitive cultures. Sophisticated weapons in an unsophisticated culture are a formula for disaster." J had experience from his travels.

Kay reflected, "Look what it did to the USA."

J laughed at the offbeat application. "But Africa is a big place. There are still regions that remain as they were a million years ago. There is something ethereal about existing at a moment in time in a spot where you know that you are just an instant in an immense continuum. True humility is a comfortable coat."

She nodded, but laughed in turn, "You wear it rarely. But then, humility is relative. You don't feel humble when talking to or about God, but you do when talking about a Spring Bok."

He added, "Or climate prediction, Darwin's contributions, earthquake prophecy, the universe, woman's intuition, understanding turbulence —this list can get long."

Kay was not to be brought to shoptalk. "Back in Africa; when I visited with my father, we safaried in the Serengeti. The night I spent there was unforgettable. Could I ever get used to the roar of a lion in the background? Then things got quieter after the lion roared.

"They also breathe loudly. One walked around my tent in the night and I could hear every pant, it was disconcerting. Protected by only the thin cotton tent, I wasn't frightened, but a little on edge, and exhilarated."

J could understand this. "I've felt that too in the Serengeti. It is a timeless place. Despite the sense of lowliness from realizing what a little blip in time our species has spent here, it is comforting, too. Can't explain it."

Kay felt simpatico, "No need to. That's what I felt. I certainly never have the time to feel that in the work-ethic society."

J just nodded. By now he expected Kay to be in tune with his feelings. "One thing I noticed concerned the value of space, of vistas, of loneliness to a person. I believe that there must be a strong internal yearning of a Homo Sapiens to be in a spot with vistas, green or yellow expanses, and small sounds from a distance, that feed his psyche and nourish contentment. It's undoubtedly a chemical reaction, a neuron connection that releases endorphins. But it is an important ingredient of happiness."

"We are lucky to be able to come someplace like this to get a taste of it.

Luckier still to work in our new environment." Kay sighed; like everyone else who gets to sit on top of a mountain, she was moved to philosophy. "We're such a small perturbation on the fabric of earth, let alone the cosmos. I sometimes have the same ambivalence as Deman about idealistic, ascetic commitments to long range projects. I, and you, have proven that we can sublimate our base desires to enterprises of what we think are great pith and motion."

J nodded. "You have to admit, developing a thesis, and a University, are great stimulations."

Kay had watched J in his passionate pursuit of 'truth' as the new university developed. She was just as committed to her thesis work, and recognized it imparted an escape from dominance by basal drives. "Yes, of course we love the mental stimulation, but sometimes I long to relax and let the lower levels of my brain engage. We should compromise occasionally with the primary, animalistic rewards of our basic drives?"

J looked out over several gleaming white glaciers at a few sharp peaks of dark granite. "Like what, our basic desire to fly? There's a cliff on the other side of the peak that will provide you ten seconds of exhilarating free flight."

She glanced down to a valley five thousand feet below. "No thanks, the landing costs are too great for me. I was thinking of something more primordial, like wanton dancing, primal screaming or even mating."

Hearing only the last possibility, J answered, "Leave it to you to suggest such a thing while hanging on a cliff of ice, covered in four layers of clothing, and tied to two men." He was half kidding, half complaining. "Our next trip will be to a more accommodating environment and I'll call your bluff."

Kay smiled, "I suppose that it is a bluff, and I'm sure that the altitude, cold and fatigue have blurred my logic."

"Logic is not a necessary, or even friendly, tool for the mating ritual," J smiled at Kay's smile.

"Yes. This is one of the first times in years that we have been in a setting where logic wasn't king and there was room for the biochemical interactions to take place." She was reflecting on the fact that the challenge of her thesis, which had dominated her life for years now, was finishing within a year. Thoughts were turning to other things. Life could begin again. She mused that the seduction of J would be as challenging as her thesis. But she was up to it.

Fortunately J was on a similar track. The University had been an all-consuming task, but it was time to disengage a bit. "The college is rolling smoothly now. Maybe we should look into opportunities for future primal settings." They nodded agreement that something singular had taken place. A new topic had been sanctioned.

This was all lost on Steven, who was in his own young unsophisticated world, moving around the peak and peering into the depths below.

"We'll yield to the primordial drive to satisfy hunger with peanut butter sandwiches." J smiled at the cold white surroundings.

♦

On the descent, J was still feeling euphoric about their conversation and enjoying the scenery as they crossed the glacier when the student, third in line, slipped on the ice above the big crevasse. Steven hollered, and proceeded to slide in. J turned in time to see that Kay was simply watching the slithering rope as it disappeared into the hole. He rapidly but methodically planted his ax, anchored the rope, threw his weight onto the ax, and was ready to arrest her fall by the time she had had been tugged into the crevasse by her fallen companion.

It was clear that they weren't both dangling below, because his anchor would not have stopped the weight of both of them. The student, or both, must have reached bottom. J hollered to the edge of the crevasse, "How are you?"

The answer was quick, floating up from the cavern, "Fine. How are you?"

J laughed, a wonderful attribute, keeping cool in time of peril, "Now all I have to do is haul you both out. What is Steven's position?"

"He is wedged at the bottom. The crevasse narrows about fifty feet down. He says that he's fine, lying on his back."

"OK. So I just have to lift you." J carefully unwound the rope, anchored it around his waist and moved to a point that he judged was directly above Kay's position. He moved in an arc keeping tension on the lifeline between them. After resting a moment, he jammed his ice ax once again into the snow and the ice underneath. He slid around the anchor to test it, and when it seemed to hold, he slowly circled it, winding the rope around for a secure hold. He then moved to a position nearer the edge, seated himself securely, and began hauling on the rope.

After ten minutes of hauling Kay's voice sounded close. "We're at the end of the line between Steven and me. I'm about two feet below the edge. This isn't going to work. You can't possibly lift both of us."

J was good at these decisions. 'There is always a way' was simply one of his guiding principles. On the practical side, ideas had been sloshing around in his head during the long haul up. "I'm going to tie you off, then toss you the other end of the rope. Hang on for awhile." He moved back to the embedded ice ax. The sharp edge of the crevasse made it relatively simple to hold the line steady and he was able to hold Kay's line with one hand while unwinding his previous turns. He then secured the shortened line to the ax, untied the line from his waist, shucked his pack and foraged for his knife. He tied it to the loose end and moved down toward the edge. "How is Steven?"

"He's still talking to me. Says he is tired and very cold."

"You're going to have to tie the most important knot of your life. Did you ever study knots?"

"Yes. But I can't remember a thing."

"I'll talk you through it. We have to tie the loose end of the rope to the rope below you, so that you can cut yourself loose. The knot is designed so that tension will tighten the knot. Most knots would just let it slip through. We don't want to lose the link with Steven."

He slid the rope end with the knife over the edge. Kay grabbed the rope, retrieved the knife, and tucked it into a pocket. She pivoted to tie the knot, carefully following J's instructions. After a long minute Kay's voice came, sounding firm and confidant. "It's done. I now know how to tie a knot when I'm upside down. I'm ready to cut."

"Hold on to the loose end so that you can secure the knot. It will have to hold Steven's weight."

Another minute passed. "OK. I've done it, and secured the top end to the new rope with a couple of half hitches."

J pulled on the new rope until it was taut. It was now secured to Steven.

Kay's voice rose from the abyss. "Now haul me up the last two feet, please."

J was ready, and in a couple of minutes Kay appeared over the edge. She squirmed up to him, placed him in a bear hug, and they rested for several minutes without a word. The task of getting Steven out was on their minds. Now every effort would be made to rescue him. It wasn't going to be easy. J had barely enough strength to lift Kay, and Steven weighed half again as much. Realizing the difficulty for the two of them, he finally remembered the satellite cell phone in his pack. He set the gear up as quickly as possible, with safety ropes anchored to their ice axes. The cold in a crevasse would soon lead to hypothermia. He used five minutes to call the camp and tell them of the situation. Then he and Kay set themselves on the rope to Steven like preparing for a tug-of-war.

The hardest part was the initial jerk. Steven must have been wedged rather tightly. J hollered down to him to try to get loose, shed his pack, and try to help using the sides. Steven's lethargic voice came back saying something like he was trying. After another minute, Steven said he was ready and J hollered to prepare for a jerk. Counting to three, he and Kay put all their weight into the rope — and lifted Steven three or four inches.

J was happy, "Piece of cake, as you would say. Only forty-nine and a half feet to go."

They rose to their feet, counted to three, and leaned back with the effort. This time Steven rose twice as far. "We'll be out of here by morning."

Two hours later, with Steven somewhat less than half way out, they spotted the lights of the search party from the cabin. They were ecstatic to hand the hauling chores over to fresh muscles, and Steven was out of the crevasse in another thirty minutes. He was barely conscious, recovering slowly. The motley group slowly made its way back to the cabin, and Kay and J crashed into their bunks with another shared experience.

♦

They were up early the last morning, packed and ready for the flight out. The sun was just cresting the Cascade Peaks a hundred miles to the east. They had taken a short walk up the ridge to get a better view of the peak as it slowly shed the nightly dark. J took his eye off that soul-lifting view for a moment to look at Kay. She was looking at him and they were in danger of missing the event of sunrise and the possibility of a green flash. "This is a good biochemical production environment." J couldn't help the prosaic language.

Kay slowly nodded. "There must be some interest between us for me to miss the moment of sunrise."

They turned to watch the spectacle as the warmth of morning washed over the nearby peaks. They were standing close together since the view was best where the ridge got narrow. The peaks emerged from the dark one by one as the sun crested the Cascade Range to illuminate the Olympic Range. J was inspired to discuss the tectonic forces behind these relatively young mountains, describing the peaks. Kay was looking at his face, as if she had to read his lips to hear him over the sound of the mountain wind on the ridge.

In the wanderings of his gaze, it chanced by her face, caught her eyes, and stopped his conversation cold. She had leaned forward imperceptibly. That is, imperceptibly to anyone but J, to whom it seemed to provoke a cerebral Armageddon. He sputtered quickly, "What do you think about that?" referring to whatever it was he had been talking about.

She drew back, perceptibly. "Why do you suppose that you change the venue when I introduce a new variable? By ignoring you or merely leaning toward you I can unleash a torrent of philosophy or turn it off like a faucet."

"I talk a lot because silence sometimes scares me. Some stupid programming in my psyche makes me perceive your lean as a soccer goalie sees a charging player with the ball, about to shoot; I'm pressured by the fear of making a mistake."

"But doesn't a successful soccer goalie turn off the brain and rely on instinct at a time like that?"

He had to think about that for a moment. "Yes, but before that, hours of training and practice in the basics have assured him that his instincts will do the right thing."

"And you're telling me that you haven't had training in these basics?"

"Only at the very amateur level."

"No wonder they call you 'metaphor man'. If this metaphor is correct, we need to practice." She looked at him fully and smiled again. She had a great arsenal of smiles — the tolerant smile, one of rapport, anger, sympathy, boredom- and the provocative smile. The last one was present. Memory of it stayed with J all the way home, through the elevator-drop take-off, the hour drive to campus, across the central plaza to the dorms and graduate apartments where Kay stayed, and finally back to his office. Only when he got into working a neat mathematical problem did it fade into the background.

◆

J couldn't tell you why he had the tree house constructed. He had always been concerned with the state of the world: the politics, the environment and his species' poignant and paltry attempts at finding its place in the scheme of things. He had been introspective for as long as he could remember. It did battle with his hormonal tendencies during his teen-age years. He felt lucky to survive the pubescent period while his pre-frontal cortex developed. Then with this tool for deliberation he chose to fight the tendency of his species toward self-destruction, and just naturally used the questioning of existence and meaning-of-life as a necessary addendum to whetting his intellectual powers. Eventually, it dictated his vocation.

Anyone who followed these subjects knew that Homo sapiens were not making it. Possibly he considered the Tree as a refuge from all of this if he got burned out. When he was fed up with the sorry short-sighted societies the tree was a place where he could leave it all behind. Always in reserve he had the Panzaic Plea. This rationalization was one means of escape from the inevitable frustration due any broadly educated person who looked serious topics in the face. So occasionally he had been able to bag thoughts of the future and live in the moment. At these times he had climbed the local snow cones that ran down the spine of the West Coast, jumping crevasses with the knowledge that it wouldn't be a gnat's eyelash in the cosmos if he fell to the depths.

The myopic omnipotent attitude went into abeyance during the family years. But with his partner gone early to life's lottery, his children raised and self-sufficient, it had returned. This fatalism led him into hobbies like hang-gliding, white-water kayaking and flying ultra-lights. There were still mountains to climb and flying devices to try. Since once again there would be no large ripples with his passing, even in the local pond, it made him feel free.

And then suddenly he had a lot of extra cash lying around, with no place to spend it. With it came a threat from the previous owners that seemed to wax and wane over the years in a cycle that responded to forces outside his ken. The reasons for hiding the money were obvious, and events had shown that it was essential. Poor Junior was killed, after all, merely for being in the vicinity.

Circumstances dictate. It just seemed like a good idea to build a tree fort in Africa. It might have simply been a tree house. But he had so much money to spend it became a technological marvel.

Then as Kay entered the scene, J fantasized about a get-away cottage for two. Except the two were heavily involved in mainstream science, requiring university meetings, satellites, huge computers, and the other paraphernalia of their micro-culture. They were economically enslaved to the University as securely as a coal miner being kept in his company town. They were entranced by the quixotic vision of Homo sapiens' attempt to escape the fate that human fanaticism foretold for this dinky planet. In that contented life, between his infrequent visits to the site and transfers of money to pay the carefully selected crew, J sometimes nearly forgot about the Tree.

Tell me what company thou keepest, and I'll tell thee what thou art.

Cervantes

Ch 3.4 In Town with Peter.

The sun was shining; but each day was less bright as the sun began to follow an increasingly flattened arc across the southern sky. The bright crimsons and cinnamons of fall were fast fading.

A class was ending in one of the rustic classroom buildings. The professor emerged trailing two students who were animatedly questioning him. This particular class required the entire science curriculum and J's philosophy course as pre-requisites. It was called Physics and the Cosmos. At least that's what it said on the course outline.

The Professor was known as 'Prof Peculiar', in the sense of 'unusual', sometimes with frustration, sometimes with affection. His looks were normal, yet consensus was that he was a homely guy. He had the old-world poverty look of a Welsh miner that labeled him poor and simple. The first part described his background well; the last was far from the mark. He got all of his clothes from rummage sales. There was no good way of describing him. Yet Peter was thriving at OC.

Students in his class had to work to get him to say anything definitive, everything was qualified. When he did get serious, they had to work hard to understand the often complex concepts. He seemed a shy, nice guy, not likely a professor, and certainly at the far end of the spectrum from Deman, who was teaching at the other end of the building.

They did know that his bank account was probably not average. He got a million bucks when they gave him his Nobel Prize three years ago. Very few knew exactly what he got the prize for. They might know that it was something about the averageness of the universe. Others thought it was for Peter's Anthropomorphic Exclusion Principle, that any process that required home sapiens participation was not fundamental. They knew that the quantum mechanics professors were frequently questioning Peter, since this principle challenged their concepts. Or it might be the dark matter hypothesis --- it's not what they think it is --- that required an unknown alteration in gravitational theory.

Peter's peers, if you could call any of the faculty that, even in the selective cabbage patch of OC, were equally at odds about how to feel about him. He never offended. Yet those who didn't know him well felt there was never a commitment. Even his wife had felt this way right up to a proposal out of the blue. But when it got down to his physics philosophy, most of them agreed that his accomplishment was likely the supreme application of the Panzaic Principle. The reality, the fundamental rule, the saving grace of the universe was its mediocrity.

Peter had a couple of graduate students who aspired to be like him. Once a month they would get together with Peter and J and a few other students at the campus tavern. Usually Teton, Christopher and Juliet were there. To J's disappointment, Kay hadn't joined this group. She had a conflict with a thespian club meeting.

The students walking with Peter met J at a juncture of the pathways and all continued to the tavern. They got one of the side rooms with a view of forests and mountains. A couple of pitchers of microbrew were on the table and the meeting was called to order with a raised mug, a nod and a solemn 'cheers'. After a round of beer and banter, Peter opened the meeting, "Anything new?"

Baker, who had made the transition to OC with Deman, remained an active student as she neared completion of her degree. "One of my thesis committee, Prof. None, reviewed a paper by someone in England who successfully cloned a chimp. He was upset because his proposal to clone a graduate student had gotten turned down flat. The reviewers all knew that he was completely capable of cloning a human. But he had law-abiding fealty, and would never dream of not following the correct channels, or even of disguising his research. Of course, human cloning is banned by our government."

Teton gave support. "It's well known that around the world, and even in the USA, there is ample funding from super-rich individuals so that research can proceed. There is no impossible difficulty in the process, and everyone expects an announcement any day from some far-eastern country that a cloned Homo sapiens was breathing the polluted air."

J commented, "Yes, well I understand his feelings, but I can't get behind him completely. I know the argument of a couple of you — since Homo Sap can't control or anticipate the consequences of scientific discoveries, might as well just let the chips fall. Like without the atomic bomb we likely would have had more of the miserable world wars and never had stability to discover that various economic systems can fail relatively peacefully on their own.

"However, our last long brainstorming session on the future of cloning led to the unanimous conclusion that cloning would primarily be used to reproduce athletes, or the rich and beautiful people. And a clone would just be another individual with half the personality determined by their environment. We're not in need of another method of making more Homo Sap. I move we table this subject."

"Second," from Peter, and that was enough for all to agree.

Peter addressed Cecile, "How is the spiking program?"

Cecile had notes to present her data. "Since we decided that this was a proper crusade over two years ago, the campaign has expanded considerably. Per our initial motivation, we have spiked about one tenth of the vulnerable trees on campus. Since it took several months to get campus approval for the project, it was slow going at first. But there has been a lot of volunteer help. It became public knowledge when we put up notices at the entrance to campus.

"And we all know the right-wing agony as they wrestle with their consciences over 'Trees are there for Homo sapiens to make houses and a profit,' versus their icon, 'Property rights'."

"That alone made it worthwhile," injected Peter.

"Yes, and now the project is finished, since we decided at the last meeting that we didn't need to spike very many of the trees, just let them think we might have."

J asked, "What about off-campus?"

Proudly, Cecile answered, "By now, we've nearly perfected the technique. We can make it obvious or undetectable. Mostly, we set one obvious nail with a logo in brass and then add several invisible ones. We sell the spikes at cost to anyone who has trees that they legally want to disable from logging. The operation is expanding. There are a number of campus organizations around the country that serve as distribution points. Our web site is very popular. It's all above board.

"We haven't touched anything without permission except the few in Calzona and Cascadia on public land that were approved at our meetings. We attached a tag similar to ours but different. The shiny copper head of our signature spike was made to look like a poor copy in these cases. Inconsistency, confusion and the panzaic are the usual guides. We want the idea to spread without making us notorious."

Teton was particularly enjoying the volunteer project because he liked to be with Baker, his significant other. "We received a report just last week from a student whose father is a manager in a logging mill. Like most mills, they had been accepting logs from anyone, even though they likely came from a national park. They have decided to reject all logs without a heritage because of the inherent risks, now. We have put the logging pirates out of business there." A toast to success led to a call for another pitcher. Celebrations in environmental protection were too rare to pass up, even a small triumph.

Peter was pleased. It was his idea, and the project was perfect for the purposes of this group, which was to devise strategies for protecting the environment outside of the normal channels. It set the standard for other campaigns of the group, such as the widely publicized report that marlin were unsafe to eat because of mercury poisoning — that saved a lot of marlin. It was rumored that a couple of the more militant members found it necessary to spike a couple of marlin to give this story impetus. There was strong debate over this, which degenerated into a Panzaic, 'ends justifies the means', versus quixotic, the "truth and nothing but the truth", discussion.

They addressed only issues that had failed in the normal channels. They followed accepted general practice, which meant that they enjoyed wide latitude in what was permissible. It was laissez-faire environmentalism.

♦

Later, as Peter and J walked the path toward home, J asked, "How is your project to infiltrate the local community?"

"It's not to 'infiltrate' the community. It's more like joining the community, being accepted and living the simple life."

"Sorry, wrong choice of words."

"It is going very well, and I look upon it as a vacation from the rigors and depressing world realities that we face every day here on campus. Oh, they face problems too, but on a much less pervasive level. Besides, I'm now accepted there better than here."

"That's nice." J thought that 'big deal' would have been more appropriate. "So the incompatibility with your peer group has finally gotten to you? I think of this as your 'badge of truth', your contribution to individuality."

"Whatever. It's just a comfortable escape."

J was the only one to know of Peter's project to establish an identity in the local logging town of Port Angeles. It helped that his plain rugged features made him look more like a farmer than a professor. Peter had bought a house and set up a little business selling specialty toys, mechanical ones with intricate movements that physicists, engineers, and blue-collar workers could appreciate. He was supposedly constantly on shopping trips to get the toys from Europe and other exotic places, so the locals accepted his long absences. In reality, he got the toys from his collection in his campus basement. He got to invent and build some classic designs. It was therapeutic.

Port Angeles had a reputation of being very conservative and even dangerous for liberal ideas. The students and faculty of OC generally avoided it, preferring to make the ferry trip to Seattle or to visit another local town, Port Townsend, where tourism had created a friendly environment. In general, the campus was a self-contained village with most extra-curricular attractions so the students were content to stay in their safe cocoon.

Peter's project to establish a second identity was not uncommon amongst those who desired their privacy in the modern culture. The standard identity of virtually everyone in society was common knowledge in a myriad of data banks. Big brother was an amorphous social contract that allowed anyone with a modicum of computer savvy to access the vitals of anyone's life.

One popular way to gain privacy was to begin again with a new persona, one with no credit history, no organizational belongings or contributions, no subscriptions or filled out product registrations. Peter had made his private identity a hobby.

"Why don't you come in with me tomorrow? Take a weekend off, enjoy the simple life, and listen to Siddhartha. Meet me at my house in the morning."

♦

"It is not going to be easy." Peter was warning J, as they sat at his 'make-up' table in his home. "I learned early, the animosity toward our campus is even greater than I anticipated. Hence, you will be amused at the precautions that I take. But that is part of it, deception, intrigue, danger — so far no violence or sex, but they are clearly readily available."

Peter had accomplished a subtle transformation. It was surprising how little it took to make him more distinctive. His usual features lent themselves to simple emphasis. He had slightly darkened his eyebrows in place of the normal invisible blond ones. Brushed hair was a revolution, including a neat part. That alone would probably make him unrecognizable on campus. He then added a nice shirt, replacing his usual baggy rugby jersey. J shook his head over the transformation. He didn't look anything like 'Prof Peculiar'. Peter liked to think that it brought out the average man, even handsome. He didn't quickly answer J's question, "Your new persona looks good. Why don't you employ some make-up in your campus image?" Peter just shrugged, with his trademark, "I don't know."

J was a bit more difficult, but Peter had a good time experimenting. Soon J was Peter's cousin from Germany, visiting for the weekend. "You can even assume the persona of an unreformed Nazi. You will not be exactly liked, but tolerated much more than the real you."

They had to sneak out under their parkas, wide brimmed Western hats and sunglasses to Peter's car in the underground garage. There were few people on the road this Friday morning; the three-day weekend was pretty standard these days.

At the main highway, Peter took a turn in the opposite direction of town. "I don't suppose they are still monitoring every car on campus, but I'm cautious. When the old states were consolidated into the new seven, the militias were supposedly sent packing to Midwest; however, I detect quite a few of those types in town. Nice, fun-loving, quasi-Sancho Panza types — they don't trust any concepts of government since they believe they're all corruptible. They're quite right, of course.

"Except, most of them trust the Bible for the big answers, that's word-of-God. I'm skeptical but I can live with that, and I think that it would be good for you to assume the role of a true believer, and I don't mean Buddha."

"OK. I've often wondered what it would be like to answer all questions from a simple book. Say, are you going to Seattle?" Peter had driven half an hour toward the ferry terminal.

"There's a place near the ferry parking lot that is perfect for me to store my cars, this one and the one I use in town."

A half-hour later, they were heading back in a perfectly average old American car. They pulled into a rickety wood plank garage that was attached to the back of a two-story building that fronted on Main street, nestled between two similar buildings. Peter's flat was on the second floor, above his store.

As they emerged, a classic lumberjack loomed over them. J instinctively flinched, and breathed easier only when he saw that the big man was pumping Peter's hand and had a glad-to-see-you smile.

Peter said, "Otto, it is good to see you. Here is my first cousin from

Germany, Adolph." This was J's first introduction to his name. He could see that he'd better remain alert this weekend.

"From Germany, eh. My grandfather was from there --- Bavaria."

J had spent time there, so he answered affirmatively, heeding Peter's advice that to really experience the culture, he should join in at every chance. "Ja. And what name has he?"

"Augstein. He was a very active man with the ladies; we could easily be related without the name."

J smiled, he expected to be assaulted with bawdy humor, and tried empathizing with the man, "Could be. My grandmother had twelve children."

"There you are, the chances are getting better. We shall have to explore it further at Bennies'." And he was off, to do his own important thing, or just to leave them alone.

Peter was happy to explain. "Bennies', with the apostrophe in the wrong place — there's only one Bennie — is the local bar, a doppelganger from the Middle Ages. It's delightful. We'll be sure to hit it tonight." Peter made his way up the back stairs with his suitcase of toys. The flat was meager, dismissed by Peter with the comment, "When in town, a flat is just a place to sleep."

The downstairs toy store was another matter. It had the ambiance that is the secret of successful shopkeepers. Maybe not those who sell the most, but those who love their merchandise, their environment, their store. The displays were arranged in shifting motifs, the light streamed through the big storefront barred window where the choice selection of goods was displayed. In the back, behind the wooden counter with the huge old cash register, a comfortable stool provided a secure podium for the shopkeeper's platform.

When Peter descended the stairs, he found J experimenting with a mechanical bank, a copy of an original that was hundreds of years old. A coin performed a small miracle before disappearing into its maw. Peter smiled at J's efforts, "I could play with those for hours. There is something more satisfying about it than even my most deluxe computer game."

J was impressed. "You have a wonderful home away from home here. I have sometimes looked with envy at the shopkeeper; sole proprietor, king of their domain, as they exist in the center of their shop like a spider in a web. Particularly when I realized that some don't care whether a customer is snared. Some of them are just pleased to share their merchandise. I have even had an Asian carpet salesman decline to sell me a beautiful rug after he finished extolling its virtues. He realized that he didn't want to part with it."

Peter nodded, "That happens to me, of course. Particularly as I don't need the income, I sell only to someone who will love it as much as I do."

He opened a piece of luggage that looked like a businessman's attaché case. Inside was a train set, winding through a village and mountains. As Peter activated it, J saw a ski-lift operating up the mountain, a boat moving on the lake, and the centerpiece train, precise in every detail, slowly chugging through town. "I have always loved train layouts. I had one as a child that I played with every week. Then I had one in the attic for years. Put away in boxes for decades. I always wanted to recapture that enjoyment, but was always too busy. Now I find the time and pleasure here."

They played in the toyshop until dinner, which was an Indian palak paneer resurrected by the microwave with Western Washington premier cabernet sauvignon. A mellow evening and J was ready to retire when Peter announced that it was time to hit the town. They walked out the back door and two blocks down the turn-of-century main street to Bennies'.

◆

J was an otter in a crocodile pond at Bennies'. While he was more than a match at any intellectual gathering, he was mortal at slapstick and bawdy. His had done a stint at the Comedy Club that had tuned his senses so that he could avoid overt faux pas and get back into the banter. He discovered a latent talent for the bawdy joke, and entertained a few patrons with his English wit dressed in a German accent.

Things were going rather well until he was approached by the Beautiful Broad. In the realm of barroom social interaction, she was a faster crocodile. He switched to being the foil for her humor. He had a minimal but sufficient talent for that, which unfortunately endeared him to the Beautiful Broad. She seemed to be a Port Angeles darling. A local favorite.

Now in the past J would have been very interested in this talented woman. If he had another life to live in this environment he would dive right in. She had all the attributes that he desired in a woman, except she had absolutely no education. Timid forays into religion, woman's rights, or patriotism all yielded the conventional brainwashing. It would take twenty years of education to bring this diamond in the rough to a compatible level of learning. What a shame that Homo Sap wasted its talents so much.

The sadness that gripped J with this realization made him excuse himself and retreat to becoming a listener at Peter's gathering. He was just getting interested in Peter's grass roots persona when Otto appeared, addressing him from beneath an imposing scowl.

"You're not into women? My sister got mixed signals from you, buddy." Otto was taking it personally.

"Yes," Peter laid it on, "I thought you were the ladies' man."

J was going to get out of this. "I forgot to tell you, my dear friend, I have a wife." Augstein's heir raised his brows. These guys were cousins?

"And two children." This time Peter's eyebrows rose, why would he bring such a stranger home with him?

J was enjoying the pressure on Peter. "They are twins, born a little over a year ago. I married your old sweetheart, Inge. I didn't want to tell you in case you would be angry." He was glad to see Peter laughing at him.

"Why should I be angry? She was sleeping with half the town. But she is the most beautiful woman in Garmish." Peter had injected enough interest in this new twist of conversation that the spurned damsel too had joined in listening to the two cousins' verbal sparring.

J wondered if verbal sparring was enough for these folk- would he find it necessary to punch Peter in the mouth? It was a wild and not completely unattractive thought. He expected that Peter entertained the idea more readily than he did, and J increased his guard.

The crowd around them had a finely tuned sense for such skirmishes, and recognized quickly when they were getting out of hand. Strong arms guided both J and Peter to the bar with ameliorating talk, "Remember, blood is thicker than water." Whatever that meant, J figured that it was the right thing for people to say here. Calm was restored. Peter and J chortled at the bar, enjoying their own subtext to the events. They caroused well into the next day.

It wasn't until breakfast that Peter and J could reflect on how thin was the veneer of intellectualism they wore.

♦

J was very interested in privacy these days. He had received an ominous package last week. Two thousand dollars wrapped in oiled paper. Even in this protected environment the gangsters were pressing him. He didn't know where he was on their suspect list, but he knew that it was two thousand dollars worth of interest.

*The individual appears for an instant, joins the community
of thought, modifies it and dies; but the species, that dies
not, reaps the fruit of his ephemeral existence.*

Randolph Henry Ash (M. Britt)

Ch 3.5 A Class in Alternative Ideas

*The camouflage of the Tree was state-of-the-art. When building a fortress it
helps to think like an attacker. It is done with the knowledge that just about
every defensive 'line' devised by Homo sapiens has been conquered. It is easier
to design an offence to a known defense. The old states' 'star wars' anti-missile
defense floundered when it was shown the multi-billion-dollar defense could
be overwhelmed by ten offensive missiles at ten thousand-dollars each.*

*There was a panel on each floor of the Tree with buttons, lights, switches,
speakers and a TV monitor. These could bring inside the sights and sounds
from outdoors. There were infrared motion detectors with artfully disguised
sensing heads all around the tree. The system was meant to inform of nearby
animal activity and would function as a perfect intruder alarm. Several video
cameras were carefully mounted high in the surroundings. Micro-technology
had produced cheap cameras that were the size of a thumb. At the Tree, a
resident could be a peeping Tom on the primordial earth. Designed like a
Middle Ages fortress to be self-sufficient for extended periods of time. Every
new twenty-first century technological advance could be found, since this was
J's hobby.*

*The project had gained momentum on its own. It had become a labor of
love for Wylie and his workers. Early in the process J had enjoyed the planning,
the design, and every step of the building. There was a time when he considered
simply joining the work crew and then staying on. This happened during the
third oil crisis as the fractured nation considered war in the Middle East once
more when USA oil supplies were restricted. But as his work and personal
life got intense, the financing became his main job. That made the project less
interesting to him.*

*The oil rich nations, united under an Islamic version of democracy with
total integration of church and state had decided once again to apply pressure
on the gas-guzzling giants. They were worried over global warming. Decades of
warm weather records, strengthening storms and rising ocean levels made the
dichotomy over whether this was 'natural' or manmade moot. It was difficult*

for the New States to mobilize world opinion against the oil baronies since the world largely agreed with them. The USA, now often called the New States, always known as the great consumer nation, was alone, as it had been since 2004. There was only a weak international voice. And no one could get the seven states to agree on anything.

J had spent much of that summer at the tree construction to avoid the agony of that national trauma. But the great adventure of building Olympic Campus became prominent, and the lure of romance with Kay became dominant. J went back to the Homo Sap-race. He managed only occasional visits as the Tree became a reality.

◆

Rain was pouring off the needles of the firs filling the creek beds that ran through Olympic campus. The path was still porous and puddle-free, designed for just such storms. Two students were walking leisurely to class, engaged in conversation.

"I wonder what he is going to do today. This is definitely the weirdest class I have ever taken. A whole quarter devoted to 'Alternate Ways of Thinking'."

"Yeah, until I got here there wasn't much competition for weird. The classes here are never boring. But this class is really different. He puts you into a situation where you have to be able to think on your feet."

"That's probably 'cause he was a pretty famous film director before he decided to move here. Going to his classes is a bit like going to the movies."

They drifted into a classroom lodge, into their class, and sat down at the long heavy table. Everyone always remarked about how these tables should be in a tavern and this time there actually were pitchers of beer and glasses on the table. It was a fourth year class, but fresh juice was provided for the underage prodigies and any abstainers. There was a sign on the table that said "I'll be a little late, so bide time with beverages."

Ten minutes later, a student who was pouring his second glass missed it entirely when a loud crack, simultaneous with a flash of light, hit the room.

Most assumed that the building had been struck by lightning. The storm even made this likely. Comments flew, "I've never been that close to lightning," "Where did it strike?" "Anybody hurt?" and "Why did it strike this building with all those trees around?"

Laughter silenced them all, and they all turned to the source. A man in woodsman clothes stood at the end of the room, farthest from the door. He stopped laughing and spoke, "At least one of you is thinking. Why would it strike this building? It wouldn't. Unless something powerful arranged it. That would be me. I am your speaker for the day. The theatrics were presented not just to get your attention, but to help convince you of my claims."

He had a radiant smile, and it went searing through those in the room to touch every person individually. There were too white teeth, too red lips, and eyebrows too sharply carved. All combined to project a unique identity. He continued in a commanding baritone, "To wit: I am an alien. Call me Al. I'm living here on your planet partly as a vacation, and partly as a field study for my profession. The vacation part cost me ten of your years' salary. That's a lot, even though my lifetime as a Homo sapiens is merely a short vacation relative to the natural span of my existence. I even paid the premium for a guaranteed life here until I terminate it. It lets me stop the continuum up to three times to rework any disasters — like a fatal car wreck or the happenstance encounter with a violent mugger or terrorist. Life is a gamble in the jungle.

"Matter of fact, I've only used one so far and I'm over half way through my vacation, which ends when I get bored and decide to terminate. Maybe I could use one to prove my credibility here. But no, backing up the time line in the program, even sixty seconds, causes large disruptions in myriad other random events in the nearby universe. There are other caveats. Any questions?"

The man, although it wasn't clear that it was a man, was evidently not the professor in disguise. He was too tall, too slim, his face too handsome to be even a major makeover. There was also the fact that he seemed to be standing about three inches above the floor. This was done so subtly that only a few students noticed.

One who didn't notice, because he didn't notice much outside his books, jovially asked, "I want a demonstration. Do something which proves you're an alien and not some hack actor hired by the professor."

"I take it you don't have any problems with how I managed to arrive here without your noticing, and I don't think that your professor has a big enough budget for the sound and light show. But, I am happy to oblige, since I certainly understand your desire.

"I'll pick something that you respect; I'll demonstrate that I have cosmic knowledge. For instance, I can sense a few things about you. You arose at six this morning, had a breakfast drink of maize and rice since your mother has indoctrinated you into the health mode. However, you cheat your mother by preparing a cappuccino with the machine you bought this quarter and have used daily in your newfound addiction.

"It was probably because of your guilt that you dropped your favorite coffee cup and broke off the handle today. In your mind, you said, 'No problem, I'll get another, I can afford it.' Mother's rich."

The student was frowning. Most students were looking at him with amusement. He said, "You're guessing," without much confidence.

Al moved closer, zeroing in on him. "Then there was last night — I can do up to a day, beyond that the picture gets fuzzy — you went to the closet in the bedroom where you hide yet another vice. This is getting a little personal, do I need to continue?"

Now everyone was staring at the student trying to pick up his reaction. From his expression and color, it appeared that every comment was on target. As he looked around the room, he realized his center-stage position, and struggled to regain composure. He considered briefly, but feared further revelations, so evidently decided to cut his losses.

"No, you don't need to continue." Whether he was convinced or not, he was going to stop these uncanny revelations. But the figure was no longer in front of the class.

"A wise decision." This came from the opposite end of the room, where the speaker had apparently translated in the blink of an eye. Now, everyone's eyes were on him. Yet he sort of slowly dissolved and immediately the class found him where he was a moment ago. "That is all the time I have for demonstrations. If you still doubt, it doesn't matter a bit. Let's get on with the lecture. I'm going to offer an opinion on 'Man's Place in the Universe'. No trifling topics for me.

"I consented to come here, break my cover, because what's going on here is the best chance I've seen for survival of your species on this spinning blue ball. And you're not a bad species development. Admittedly, you're only the second or third brainy experiment. It does raise you to a significantly higher plateau. The bad news is you still have dominant brainstem dictates. But that's also the good news, and why it is an enjoyable vacation.

"But I digress. Let me tell it like it is. You have all heard of the petty role of earth in the cosmos, that there are billions of stars in your galaxy and you observe billions of galaxies, and counting — there are really a lot more. Then there is the possibility of more universes...Sheesh! It always gets me that members of your species think the earth is the center of the whole shebang.

"Anyway, if you know the teeniest about statistics, a small shred about bias and the dangers of self-disillusionment - if you have a modicum of modesty- then you know your life form isn't likely to be unique. In fact it isn't likely to be significant, confined as it is to such an infinitesimal domain. This is in fact the case, of course."

A mesmerized woman sitting a meter away had the confidence to say, "You sound like all of my professors."

He moved to within her space, fixed her with a piercing gaze, and replied, "You're absolutely right. That's why I'm here. The founders of this college have done most of the preliminary work. So, let's hear from you the obvious questions that must come from such an opportunity. What's it all for? And what's my place in it? Right?"

She very slowly nodded, overwhelmed by his close presence.

"Well — I certainly don't know. I'm a hell of a lot closer to the answer than any of you are. My domain is gargantuan compared to yours. But there's still a lot more beyond me. Evidently answering that question isn't a requisite for an enjoyable and productive life.

"My personal solution is to work toward answering these questions as an avocation. Maybe make a little headway during my lifetime. Enjoy the stay. And I won't continue indefinitely."

He turned suddenly to confront a student who was about to speak. "I know; these are what you would call Panzaic thoughts.

"So let's get to the essence, or is it the ephemeral, the quixotic? My analysis of how it is going on this hunk of dirt. Maybe I'll give a suggestion or two.

"First, there is the race to survive. Evolution is a harsh taskmaster. Muck up too much of the cosmos, and you're history. The Gaia theory of cosmic self regulating is not all wrong, only maybe a matter of scale. Homo sapiens have done well to survive to this level. But the principle that you're operating on is infinite expansion. You know that isn't going to work for long.

"As far as you can see, evolution's only imperative is survival. Laughingly associated with the fittest. Ah well, relatively speaking, maybe. Good enough. But it's time to think. The brain has to team up with the gene to explore new frontiers. The gene is too dumb. But it isn't about to take orders from its prodigal son.

"Homo sapiens have to hoodwink the gene to contain its creative impulses until expansion room is found. In this regard, Homo sapiens can be viewed as a significant evolutionary step."

Ideas were coming at a furious clip, but no one had thought to take notes. Al really had their attention. "Maybe the best way to do this is to squelch the gene's imperatives. Another way is to bestow ascendancy on the machine. Carbon to silicon based society. Why not? You don't even know which I am.

"Either way, the problem now, the only little hurdle that I'm going to address here, is how to get out of the current dead-end."

The students were rapt. Everyone was listening riveted to every word. It was not clear how many were convinced of the speaker's authenticity or how many were looking for test questions. One of the more lively and analytic students raised her hand, rather tentatively for her.

"You have a question?" He fixed her with that intense gaze.

She shuddered, but continued, "Yes I have. Your ability to transport suggests that we are not in a finite domain. This is supported by the equations of quantum mechanics."

Al nodded and leaned even closer. "Ah, I love those little cerebrums you people have. Particularly when they are housed in such attractive packages." Apparently Al wasn't bound by political correctness.

"That's the kind of critical thinking that will get you there. Your deduction is correct. Just don't get sidetracked by worrying about veracity of cherished beliefs. Like your faith in physics — for those of you who thought that you were unencumbered with dogma."

"If we can't trust physics, what can we trust?" This from the physics whiz in the class.

"Well, how about some flexible philosophy, we could call it evolutionary physics? That is, let physical 'laws' evolve. They do, you know. It's pretty obvious now that laws are scale dependent. But they're also time dependent. Yes, the rules change not just with scale but also with time. No need for universal law, they actually change, mutate. Like a new species evolves.

"What happens to the mathematical description of a species when it evolves into another? And you might be ready for another set of physics to explain things like the relation of the red shift of light from galaxies to their speed, for Pete's sake, and the singularities such as black holes and the need for ten dimensions to put all this stuff in."

The students had accepted this 'professor'. Another asked, "So you don't think that science has the answer to our basic questions?"

The alien professor made himself comfortable on top of the end table. "I ask you, what good is science?

"Think of it. In general, science trivializes sex, beauty, Homo sapiens, athletics, perhaps even music. A list of everything that you love." Said directly to the face of a tall, athletic looking young man.

"And there's a second list — science exalts observation, nature, evolution, Homo sapiens, uncertainty, ethos and detail. Things that you must be dragged kicking and screaming into studying."

A student notes, "You put Homo sapiens in both lists."

Al, "Yes, to see if anyone is awake. However in this case, Homo sapiens belong in both places. They are the most talented animal species on this planet, the third hunk of rock from a mediocre star in an average galaxy in just another universe. There, I've put Homo sapiens in both lists in one sentence."

Another student says, "Perhaps beauty and music could also be in both lists. And where is Truth?"

"Right on for beauty. Music is another thing, another lecture. It is much more fundamental than you could imagine. Truth? It's in the trivial list. Surprised? Science has stumbled every time it relied on truth, often in the form of laws. Ptolemy's laws, Kepler's laws, Newton's laws, laws of Nature, physics and good grief, economics and sociology. Plank's, Von Karman's, Kirchoff's, Einstein's speed-of-light ... constants. Constants! For Darwin's sake, how does anyone on this piece of fluff have the audacity to assume something's universally constant?"

They all did, but none had enough audacity to defend their position. Al was a preacher; they were believers. He continued his tirade. "Those constants — they all depend on scale, on perspective, and on time. There's another thing. Time is a dimension? What balderdash! Time isn't even time as you see it.

"The more we learn, the more we don't know. The farther we get from 'the truth'. Until we decide that absolute truth is not important. Good thing, because it probably doesn't exist.

"On the other hand, truth, like speed, is relativistic, and relative truth is very important, a second list item. We have to be precise in the definition."

Al paused here, with a faraway look in his cavernous eyes, as though he was contemplating the truth in his own statements.

"Let's get back to the main line. Where to begin to correct the downward spiral that you Homo sapiens are currently in? You are fouling the nest, losing your ideals instead of upgrading them, creating a mediocrity.

"Do you need a revolutionary approach, changing almost every aspect of political enterprise? Or, can you begin at some corner — e.g. a mundane scheme for planned parenthood and family structure, parlayed into respect for education, science over faith, the brain over the body, altruism for the species and its persistence, respect for intellectualism, adventure of the human spirit and exploration, a political party and...?" It looked like he could hardly keep from laughing at some hidden joke. "Forget it. You recently actually tried it. I was impressed. But dark forces prevail." Said directly to the prettily packaged intellect.

Flustered, she asks, "Haven't we accomplished anything?"

"Well sure. There are Homo sapiens thinkers — not necessarily an oxymoron. The future of Homo sapiens depends on getting everyone up to speed using his or her brains. But the future of the planet does not. You should accept that Homo sapiens might be just a passing fluke. Yeah, the brain might be failing here. The stem functions, so necessary for survival early on, appear to be too strong. This may be a fatal flaw to higher development and long-term survival.

"The sexual drive, just enough in the beginning, has a too powerful grip on Homo sapiens' character now. You've controlled it only with "behave and get rewarded in heaven" myths. Most of your species haven't embraced the truths of evolution; therefore don't even understand their own motivations. A higher motivation to explore the wonders possible with the brain functions is unfortunately not evident."

A thoughtful student asks, "If we're such a miserable species, why did you choose to be one of us for your 'vacation?' "

"I'm supposed to say 'good question', right? Well, you've put your finger on an interesting fact. It can be boring, all the time successfully suppressing the instincts. I could have come here as a tiger and experienced the thrill of the hunt and kill — the total power over my microenvironment.

"But Homo sapiens have more base pleasures. You've yielded dominion to all these brainstem functions and the cerebrum is an excellent tool for exploring them. You are having a shortsighted good time. I'll grant you that, and that's why I'm here. It's a nice place to visit, but I wouldn't want to live here."

He picked the lectern up, twirled it around over his head, and gently replaced it, smiling at the student's expressions. "And that brings us back to the higher position on the meaning of existence. The bulk of your species receive too much simple gratification from just responding to these elementary brainstem drives. The result is a mass media focus on mating ritual — sexual interaction and power positioning. Or is it power interaction and sexual positioning?" The last was said leeringly to the vivacious awestruck fan.

"Are you saying we're doomed? Another Armageddon preacher?" This comes from a well-trained skeptic. "It seems that we have controlled our sexual urges relatively well compared to most species."

"Yes, you do give lip-service to many intellectual topics. But you haven't controlled it well. All you've done is introduce a little modesty and a lot of guilt. Other species have limited periods when the female is in heat. Their rutting season is short. Yours is every day of the year. I observe, and participate, gladly." Said pointedly to Vivacious.

"The exploitation of sexual power, manifested in charisma, wielded by religious leaders of all stripes, and politicians in most instances, thrives at the expense of intellectual development. The sexual emphasis on youth has produced a too-quick maturation to power so that the genetically favored attain power sometimes before their pre-frontal lobe develops.

"It is way too much work to develop the analytic powers of reasoning with the brain when there are such quick rewards of a sensuous smile, a suggestive hair style, or a seductive voice. Not to mention the rewards for the physical talents like being able to manipulate a sphere with a hand or stick.

"But the problem is not in the aberrational talents, which must be produced in any mutational based gene pool. It is in the mass's inability to sort out truth or worth. You, your species — you poor suckers have no long-term goal.

"So what's left? Let's talk about your short-term goal. Let's talk about sex."

Glasses were raised. They were enjoying this lecture, whatever it was.

"Hence, Homo sapiens arrive at the following dilemma that consumes the culture's energy.

"You are all tempted toward coquetry. Her genes want the stability of the monogamous partner, but are still tempted toward the virile gene. His genes want the stability of a strong partner, but feel drawn to improve his numbers to ensure progeny. Hence, a façade is set up of fidelity to monogamy, and the inevitable infidelity is pushed under the carpet. This is a superficial, but effective solution for your stupid dichotomy.

"Unfortunately, it falls under scrutiny from the simple-minded idealist and the self-serving media minions. This nearly universal hypocrisy serves these forces well. That these societal critics almost always fail themselves doesn't seem to inhibit them from destroying the fabric of their culture by exposing the hypocrisy of others. Frail democracies fall to fools posturing. How are you going to avoid this pitfall?"

This was all familiar territory to the students. But they never had gotten it as 'Truth,' from a 'Higher' authority. There were no more interruptions. No one even bothered to finish the beer.

Al held them like a deer in headlights. "Let me give it a shot. There should be a goal, probably arising from the environment. Contemplation of the universe and one's place in it could provide a goal. But this requires understanding derived from a well-nurtured intellectual development. You're not heading that way yet.

"In fact, the process of attaining this intellectual development is constantly under attack. You all know that a democracy is bound to fail since the media-maneuvered majority cannot be persuaded by reason — they overwhelmingly respond to brainstem stimulation. In this case, success comes only if a combination of intellectualism with charismatic forces is established. You saw it happen briefly before it succumbed to the revolution. It was tried in the French Enlightenment, but failed as the people couldn't handle such freedom. It made great strides in your country's beginnings, embracing enlightenment. Lasted quite a while. Then a final attempt at enlightenment, but fear, greed and lust had gained too much ground, all it did was precipitate the revolution."

"Does enlightenment always fail?"

"No. I know of one example just around the corner from you in Alpha Centuri. On a few ideal planets about six billion years old that have an intelligent life form development. We'll call it Homo sapiens — a wise man. They've devised some simple rules that allow them to rise above the ooze.

"Their first priority — develop the Intellect. This is the first requirement for the long-term goal of understanding what it is all about, this universe. There are as many schools as necessary to have full time schooling for all the population for the first half of their lives. There is one teacher for a few students. This, imparting and receiving knowledge, is the main occupation and preoccupation.

"Their second, and last priority --- they don't like too many rules --- there exists a maximum population for a manageable world and they established formulas and rules to maintain levels. This was easy after the first priority was accomplished. Each life is valuable. They've an advantage since in their species the female is seldom in heat. There is centralized government, with ample checks and balances. You once had a handle on that."

A student who was still thinking asks, "What level of population would this be for us?"

"A rough value would be about two or three billion." Said with an ironic arched smile.

"There are a limited number of political laws. There's a constitution based on scientific understanding of Homo sapiens and its place in the scheme of things, subject to change periodically with new knowledge. It evaluates Homo sapiens, sets up general goals and rights like life, liberty and pursuit of happiness. Of course all candidates have equal time, equal money.

"Violence, weapons, defense are studied to be controlled, understood, and available if necessary under checks and balances. A 'someone has to do it' occupation, rotated like selective service.

"Civilization is a thick veneer. Crime is rare; music and math are very advanced, and nearby space is well known. They had a good break in developing electricity as the primary power source generated by wind and waves, with renewable localized energy sources, reserving the combustible fuels for limited big things. I think they will make it to the next step.

"This would seem to be a more successful operation than on this hunk of mud." Al issued the challenge.

"A lot of that sounds familiar." This came from the same coolly skeptical student.

"Certainly. This isn't the worst place in this corner of the cosmos — you've got a lot of the ingredients that are necessary. Sometimes I think there is a critical mass of knowledge pushed ahead by grass roots solutions that is necessary to assure the success of a global species. You might be close."

"What can we do?" It was a good-tempered question.

"First of all, I think I mentioned your out-of-control population. The extraordinary thing is that controlling it would take you a long way toward solving nearly every one of Homo sapiens' problems. I know it from statistical observation of many planets. But it is also an obvious theoretical deduction.

"I'm here to tell you, a world where everyone has what we all want, space, beauty, living convenience, health — it's possible with a minimally planned economy. Manage population, land and wealth distribution.

"But you don't get it.

"Get this. I could tell you where to look for a natural substance, how to deal it, what to do with it --- to make you nearly immortal. But I can't do it to you. Why? Because you're just a bunch of fuckers. If people stopped dying, in the many miserable ways you embrace, then you'd overpopulate this lovely planet posthaste.

"If you want to evolve --- to get to the next level --- you're going to have to learn the lessons of evolution, embrace the humility of being just another animal, get rid of all the fairy tales and move on. That's what the four years of science can do for you. Do it for yourself. Because you're just a drop in the bucket, a magnificent minority, the longest of shots. But you've got to go with what you've got.

"Still, you don't get it.... why?

"Well, you're so egotistical; most of your curriculum deals with studying yourself and your deeds. Most of the education on this snippet planet is still concerned with primordial, precultural drives...the brainstem preoccupations. Objective analysis and scientific understanding are an appendix rather than a primer.

"Have I got that right?" Said to a teenager near the back of the table, but now close enough to Al that he grasped his arm as he thrust the question into his face.

He was a precocious teenager, confident and sober. "Yes, I'm cool. But what else is new?"

"Right. This should be old hat to you. But most of you, yes even you at this oasis, do not have sufficient knowledge of science to even begin addressing the problems.

"I admit that there always have been some with an adequate scope, feeling, and perspective of Homo sapiens the species. Unfortunately that's not enough. In fact these specimens are often so narrowly educated in their science that they are worse off than the liberally educated sociologists. The process of learning so much science is so inefficient that it takes all of their time. All work and no play make your humanity rather dull."

Cheers greeted this. Al continued to put-down the scientists. "The number-crunchers often have marginal knowledge beyond their narrow perspectives. These computer nursemaids have goals that are career and security oriented. Science can be all consuming, of interest and energy. So, the educational revolution must account not just for the scientifically illiterate general public, but also for the majority of sociologically illiterate scientists. That's a truly big task."

Al was back in front of the class. "It is just like your princes of knowledge at this card-house are all the time giving the endowment to some squat squire of the idealistic Don who at least has the insight to pose a few pertinent questions.

"So I say, give it a shot. Pledge not to live only in the private solitude of your personal accomplishments. Do not live your life so your only end is survival or staying ahead of the peaks and valleys of the NASDAQ. I wish you luck."

With that, there was another sonic bang, the lights went out for a half-minute, and when restored, the visiting 'professor' was gone. So was the beer. Many were impressed.

As the students filed out, they appeared dazed, they didn't talk in the usual way, they didn't look around in a normal way. They might have noticed the opposite end classroom door was still closed. In fact it was blocked, and behind it, two persons were drinking yet another, unlaced pitcher of beer and enjoying themselves immensely. One was the individual who was bouncing around the classroom that usually belonged to the other person, the professor for the course.

"You are good. I knew from our previous work with your magic act that you could pull it off. But you are also a worthy actor. If I weren't so busy with the stage props, I'd believe you myself. By the way, you were right about my barely being able to afford the thunder and lightning, plus building modifications, flawless plastics, and bribery to fund mild hallucinogens in the beer."

Al smiled, with a wistful overtone that revealed that he too had been affected by the speech he delivered, mostly courtesy of the professor. He was wired so that they had been constantly in contact during the play. "Aren't you fortunate that you could convince me to donate my time. But it was worth it. It was such a highly intelligent, critically thinking audience.

"Particularly that young lad who called it right in the beginning. A hack actor indeed, gave me a bit of a scare. But your anticipation of this question, and preparation for me, did the trick. I'm glad you were able to transmit those personal notes to me. You must have a sublime network to furnish this information on your students."

"Much information is available to any hacker such as me in the computer cache of student chat room visits. It's amazing how few of them know how to erase their electronic trail. So with some research — boring research I might add — I could anticipate the question, and the likely asker. Unfortunately, there were three. I had to do a lot of preparatory work for this show. Some of it is just projection — I was a student once."

Al nodded, understanding, "You do stuff that I might consider immoral; that would get you in deep trouble in most places. I suppose you feel that the end justifies the means. Anyway, I enjoyed it. That I could fool them — it was the ultimate challenge. Will you be able to tell how many entertained even the possibility that I'm Don Quixote of Vega2? Do you need me for the test?"

"No. And I'll not be able to tell. After all, this is a course on 'Alternative Thought'. They have scientific skepticism mixed with a mind open to new possibilities. They may not know themselves. They'll not get the truth out of me, either. Anyway, the serious questions you broached are independent of whether or not you're an alien or an actor. They got it from a new perspective. I'll let you know how they do."

Ch. 3.6 Stopover in Paris

The two baobab trees with their multiple trunks now wound almost entirely around the steel tree. In the last few years the real trees had used the central pillar as support like a huge garden stake. These trees were probably the only baobab trees to receive the benefits of the potent fertilizer that J had stocked for garden needs. They were now grand in their own right, occupying the south and west quadrants of the central tree, providing the foliage to make the camouflage complete. J had exercised judicious pruning to keep lines of sight open.

When covered, the windows were invisible. One would have to climb to within a meter of the shutters and carefully inspect to see the seams, and the first windows were at five meters height. A leopard that had used some of the lower branches of the Tree for storing kills one season hadn't noticed anything. That was great fun. He felt a cousinship with the surrounding wildlife.

In the first few years, natives occasionally visited the waterhole without seeing anything out of the ordinary. As long as J didn't make a stupid strategic error, like leaving the windows uncovered at the wrong time or listening to his gonads instead of his gray matter, the disguise would remain complete. J had instructions and spares for everything, although he hadn't needed to use his handy skills for repair more than a time or two in over four years. The place was an engineering work of art.

The look-out-deck was open to the sky. All around were branches of the real trees taking advantage of the steel crutch to soar above the deck. They provided shade from the hot sun. But not too dense an umbrella as J kept the overhead trimmed. This was also his observatory, and he loved to survey the skies with a telescope. Looking at a multitude of stars reminded him that there were probably countless other attempts at intelligent life forms; this was a source of pleasure to him. J had slept out here often. The clarity of the stars, without a strong glow from a big city nearby, was a source of wonder almost every evening.

Even when he was inside, the control panels on each floor kept him intimately in touch with the outdoors. J kept the sound sensors turned on most of the time. In the first week, a lion passing by, probably returning to a quiet sleeping spot, interrupted his early breakfast. There was a loud roar of contentment with a long trailer of huffing before a profound silence returned. The rush of adrenaline that this gave J put it number one on his hit parade of outside sounds. The brainstem activities had become primary.

◆

J had been immersed in the building of the campus, the faculty, and the student body of the Olympic Campus for the past four years. He easily delegated authority, and with money not a problem it hadn't been too much work. Still, he longed for leisure; time for a simple backpack into the mountains, a two-day walk on an isolated beach, or just reading a good novel. Time to explore a relationship with Kay.

From her side, she had her contribution to the 'birth of OC' too, and the added layer of intensity of focus required for writing a Ph.D. thesis. They saw each other frequently, but like ferries passing each other at regular intervals on the Sound, always docking at different ports.

Her thesis was developing well, pushing frontiers beyond his expertise. He felt objective in giving it a grade of excellent. They both submitted a paper to an international conference in Paris in April. An accepted paper was necessary to justify the travel allotment from his grant money.

He asked a friend on the review committee about her paper and his friend informed him that the committee was impressed with her work and the only thing that he had to fear was that her paper would outshine his. J thought about this, and decided that would be fine.

Once they realized that they were going to have a week together in the world's most beautiful city, the atmosphere between them changed. They found they were feeling each other out much more, with a mission in mind. They even stopped to talk when they passed on campus, and in their weekly thesis discussions they finished off with a retreat to the Den for coffee and 'non-scientific' talk. The trip evoked a considered commitment from both of them.

◆

Now they were actually in a Paris hotel. They had sat together on the long flight and filled in just about all historical details of each other's lives. The metro to town and a short walk to their hotel placed them in the heart of Paris, twenty-four hours after their early morning departure from Seattle.

J knocked at the dark wood door of the old hotel room and when it opened he was greeted by Kay's exclamation, "Where have you been, I am so anxious to go walking!"

J decided not to mention his own exhaustion and a short nap, "I thought that you would want to rest after the long trip and short night on the plane."

She grabbed his arm and steered him down the stairwell. The polished wood floors seemed soft and yielding, squeaking from decades of stress. The banisters were intricately lathed. There were five flights of stairs. Elevators in Paris were addendum, sometimes fitting in nicely- patched to the outside of a centuries old building, sometimes just not feasible. Six flights of stairs were stoically accepted.

This was the case with their economical hotel loaded with charm. The reception area was compact, yet elegant in marble and mirrors. The red marble of the walls spanned the ten feet between the mosaic marble of the floor to the large wood beams of the ceiling. Nothing was simple. It was the opposite of J's home, yet strangely similar. Both were comfortable surroundings.

Just as every American visitor has been for two centuries, they were awed by the vistas down the wide streets lined with trees. Each intersection was an experience that often miraculously produced half a dozen streets like spokes. There often was a monument or statue in the distant center of a spoke, if not the Eiffel tower, or Napoleon's tomb capped with real gold.

It wasn't the perfect city, but it had the potential. Perhaps in a few years when the internal combustion engine had vanished into history it would become a quiet city of magic with clean air. And one wouldn't have to fight a car or scooter for a place on the sidewalk or the crosswalk. Was it nicer a hundred years ago, when there were no automobiles? Were horse feces as odious as car exhaust or just an irritant comparable to the current dog dung?

Kay and J chose the street with the Eiffel on the horizon, and walked to the tower beside the grassy spaces. Looking up from under the tower they reflected on how such a grand gesture a hundred and fifty years ago couldn't be considered today because the real estate would not be available nor would the tax money.

Across the river was the huge people's space, the Jardins du Trocadero, and its grand scale with many, many steps. It was alive with roller bladers, beggars, people with picnic lunches and tourists climbing to the top to look back at the magnificent view of public works. Invigorated, they walked the Avenue du President Wilson, with a solemn appreciation of the French acknowledgment of the American president. They headed up the Avenue Montaigne to the Avenue des Champs Elysees.

For a while, there were few people around. They paused at the corner to carefully watch a lonely mime dressed in unbroken white so that he was indistinguishable from the nearby statues. "Which of us can make him move to reveal himself? I'll give you thirty seconds then I'll take the same." J issued the challenge.

"OK." Kay moved slowly to a point directly in front of the human statue. She could see a flash of red as he blinked, so he must be looking at her through barely parted eyelids. After she produced her most dazzling smile, a sudden jump, and her best vamping pose without success, she was clearly desperate in her last five seconds. However, even the bump and grind that would have extracted a reaction from nearly all men failed. J smiled tolerantly at Kay as she returned defeated.

"Your turn. You're going to have to be good."

"You mean because bad didn't work?"

J walked to the mime, smiled and bowed to the statue, which didn't move a muscle. Then he reached in his pocket, found a Euro, and stepped to the statue's feet where a small pan stood. He again bowed low and dropped in the coin. The statue executed a portly bow of thanks, returning to its frozen position.

Kay was deferential, "Experience triumphs over naiveté again."

They continued their walk away from the Champs Elysees fashion shops and the Arc de Triomphe, deciding to leave that for another day. When they reached the broad park called Jardin des Tuileries, they quickly grabbed the first table they saw. Two exorbitantly priced coffees secured the table for as long as they wanted.

"We're as far from the equator here as we are in Seattle. How come everyone is outside eating, drinking and walking - but not at home?" Kay asked the northwest question.

"Uh, is it something about proximity to the sea, mountains, topology; and the resulting rain?" ventured J.

"I don't want that. I want 'because this is Paris, and people here want to be outside enjoying life and nature. They do it because they believe in it. They believe in it, because their lives are good.'"

J understood her mood. The atmosphere was conducive to shedding the burdens of scientific analysis. Relax and let the lower temporal drivers give the simple answers. "You are able to relax." J observed.

"I hope so. I have to work at it. It wasn't part of my education. You teach with a broad brush, but I don't remember you recommending relaxation to your students."

"I think you're right. I shall have to add that suggestion, somewhere between chaos and coherent structure. I like to think that it is implied, perhaps in my usual flippancy."

"Do you mean your planned fallibility, or just your congenital sloppiness?" This might have been a serious criticism, correct as it was, but it was tempered with a lovely smile and a demeanor suggesting an endearment rather than offense.

"One of my planned characteristics is to accept the barbs and bon mots of others with congenial aplomb. Part of this is because I don't think of my brilliant reply until about five minutes later. The other part is I'm willing to hear you condemn me or honor me, as long as you mention my name." J was thinking, 'I'm glad we're just verbal game playing; however there is too much truth in this.'

Tired and jet-lagged, after their extended café and a shared pastry they ducked down the next metro station and were soon on a train toward their hotel. In the center of the coach, an old man played excellent violin with a young accordionist. J was grateful for such talented background music to an otherwise hectic environment, and happily dropped a coin in the purse. He saw the raised eyebrow of the man and realized that the bimetal coin he chose was worth a ten-dollar bill in the USA, easily ten times the usual offering. But the pleasure in the man's smile washed away his miserly feelings. He winked back across the bridge of humanity built so simply between them.

Kay appraised this scene, and although she couldn't divine the reasons for the bond she saw, she provided her own interpretations.

After he said a weary, wary, 'bon nuit' to Kay at her hotel door, he walked the length of the corridor to his own room. J reflected on the fact that although they had had an engrossing conversation, and a satisfactory melding of personalities, this was one of the most awkward good nights he had managed since his first date. Nevertheless, he was asleep the instant his head touched the pillow.

♦

The next day they were still free as the meeting reception wasn't until the evening. The weather had gotten warmer, and millions of people flowed out of a hundred thousand flats to feel the spring sunshine.

J marveled that although they just missed a completely full metro train, another appeared within a minute, also equally filled, as were all the trains in both directions. The corridors to the surface twisted and turned and the scurrying mass of people tailgated each other at maximum walking speed. If one were to stop, several people collisions would ensue. Fortunately, once on the surface the avenues were broad and the crowds dispersed.

They looked for a place away from the omnipresent roar of les cars, and finally found it at the river. They were now walking along the Seine, and beginning to feel the imposition of the omnipresent lovers linked together at every corner and on every bench. Kay voiced the obvious thought, "What is it? The beautiful surroundings, the increased light on the pituitary after winter's deprivation, the warm evening, tradition, or is it just that the French are particularly beautiful and emotional people?"

"Yes. I think you got it somewhere in there." J didn't know where. "I read that immigration to France is huge, and the French cultural homogeneity is disappearing. We're here just in time."

"Well, it could simply be inertia. The French are raised looking at all these statues and paintings of lovers entwined, they simply position themselves similarly out of curiosity and that places the instincts in charge."

J thought that there was some truth to that. "Viva la Medulla Oblongata. It sounds like an interesting experiment."

She laughed. "I was thinking that. We should position ourselves and see if Paris works its magic on two jaded scientists." She looked at J to see if he would finally react.

He gave her his 'are you serious' look. "Aren't you too young to be jaded?"

"We'll see. So we're agreed. All we have to do is select a spot and a position?"

"You do the spot, I'll do the position." J was going to be fair about this.

They were in the sunshine on the left side of the bank. Kwazan cherries of Notre Dame's park were already in bloom; the river was flowing quickly and steely smooth. The sense of the grandeur of mankind's works surrounded them. Right in front of them, a couple got up to leave an entire bench to them. True science depends on luck as much as skill.

J and Kay sat primly apart, occupying the entire bench lest they become a ménage a trois. "Have you selected a position?" Kay spoke in a clinical tone. It was a noble and well-intentioned experiment.

"Yes, I was thinking of that prominent upstairs statue in Rodin's museum."

"But they are both women."

"I'll pretend. It shouldn't make any difference, should it?" J hadn't the faintest idea.

"You're introducing a subject that could occupy a long discussion and we'll get away from the primary mission. Let's get on with the experiment." She moved in close.

"I'm a little afraid that statues can maintain elegant postures easier than humans, so just use it as a guide." J was having second thoughts.

Kay placed her arms around J's neck. He put his arm behind her and swung her behind him to the stone of the bench. She brought her right leg up high encircling him, with a playful kick in the butt. He placed his hand to secure the position, with a pat in kind.

This was new for them in a gigantic way. They may have imagined it, but reality was very different. One must realize that Kay's habit was to look people directly in the eyes. She knew the color of everyone's eyes. Eye contact was part of her daily interactions.

On the other side, J almost never looked people directly in the eyes. He found that the impact was too disconcerting, as though the contact was a lance into his brain. When it occurred by chance, it often stopped his line of thought in mid-sentence. He made due with occasional glances at a person's face during most conversations. Now, he found himself forced to look into Kay's eyes from a very short distance. This eye contact was considerably more than they had ever had, and for J it even overwhelmed the bodily contact.

"Well, do you feel anything?" Kay had looked at J's eyes often, but she was finding the return gaze a different matter.

"Define 'feel'. Your eyes are green."

"And my name is Kay." She was puzzled by the shyness in J's demeanor. She decided to ask a question classically asked of students in oral exams, who apparently had lost it completely under the stress, "Can you tell me your address?"

"No."

She untangled her grip on him and pulled him to his feet. "Let's walk. I can't take advantage of your altered consciousness."

They silently walked along the Seine for quite a while, past the Ile de France, past the Louvre, the Left bank and the Musea d'Orsay. They walked up the stairs leaving the sanctuary of relative quiet to confront the people and traffic.

They were half way across one of mankind's better efforts at crossing a river, an elegant and romantic structure. Here, J touched Kay's hand, and they intertwined fingers for a few moments. Apparently this was enough, for when J stopped to turn to Kay and try the effect of looking into her eyes again, she was in synch as though they were in a well-rehearsed dance step. It started slowly, but the kiss involved them both totally, for a long time. People brushed around them, just another example of Parisian ambiance.

♦

The TGV train was maxed out at a hundred and eighty-six mph. Kay and J sat opposite each other looking at the whirring landscape. Kay was constantly in awe of the French ability to move people. "It took us only five minutes to get from my — our — hotel room to the train station. Now we'll be at Mont St. Michel long before any of those people in cars barreling down the freeway. I've lived my whole life and didn't know this was possible, except from blurbs in a newspaper or magazine, which is like a foggy view of actuality."

"You'll get a reality check when we rent a car for the last leg."

They picked up a car at the train station and were lost on the city streets within minutes. There is a charm to cities where the streets are never perpendicular. The intersections are complex; the houses have angles and views that couldn't occur in boring rectangles. This led the tourist to quick disorientation, but kept the uniformity of the endless apartment houses from monotony. That and the individuality that crept in to the details of every building built the ambiance. The fine details of the stonework on the average five-story apartment building would be art. Inlaid marble, a gargoyle, a statue, a hanging balcony, a cupola, turret or skylight broke nearly every facade into its own character. This aided the lost American motorists, as Kay recognized buildings they had passed during their rambling drive.

She took J's cue 'wish we had a map reader' and diverted her attention from the car twenty feet in front of them to the map drawer. Her comment was mildly plaintive, however. "You certainly assumed the French proclivity for driving bumper to bumper at high speed quickly."

"When in Rome, do it like they do, or words to that effect. I thought that was the modus operandi for this trip."

Kay thought that they were also practicing the mated rituals of familiar criticism, and so quickly in their relationship. She decided not to bring it up. "I see on the map why the dealer suggested heading south first to reach the periphery road that then takes us around the city to head north. Let's do it."

"No problem. Your assignment — which way's south?"

"It would be easier if we could see the sun. Can we tell from where the moss is on the buildings?" The weather had turned to showers and gusty winds. But signs soon led them to the exit from the city and the open road to the coast.

Their destination was Mont St. Michel, a church/fortification that stood on an island in a bay. The tide surged and retreated many miles in a rise and fall of over ten meters. The abbey built on the solid rock provided the ultimate picture of a safe haven.

J had to see this place, as it represented the nearest thing to a perfect defense that man had ever built. This had always been a particular interest of his. Especially with his fortress hidden away out of time and mind. This abbey and town had been under siege many times, particularly during the hundred years war. In over nine hundred years it had never been taken. The tide always came.

There was an added psychological complication; he mused, the threat of denial of entry into the hereafter, as St. Michel's job was to interview prospects for heaven in the dominant religion of the day. This undoubtedly assisted in the island's defense. He would remember that.

The first glimpse of the island was always magnificent, "That's awesome." Kay added depth to her generation's favorite word, meant to describe everything from sex to the taste of taco chips. "And we're going to stay there tonight. Ultimate romantic." Kay loved jargon.

"We'll give that a test soon." J was getting receptive to this jargon, and rapidly getting into romance.

They parked on the causeway a kilometer from the island. For the walk up, they stuffed overnight gear in a daypack; they didn't need much. Walking the narrow streets upward from the gate in the city wall, they glimpsed restaurants with fantastic views. "We're going to spend time eating here." Kay enthused.

"First things first." Said J as he turned into a hotel lobby.

They had a long dinner with a view of the bay and the pilgrims who were finishing their seven-kilometer journey over the sands immediately ahead of the tide. Kay and J headed over to leisurely walk the ramparts. The tide was nearing maximum flux and the inward flow was like a fast river, rapidly burying the sandbars and isolated rocks. "Everyone must stand here and imagine the attacking barbarians being swept away by the water." Kay voiced her thoughts.

"Yes, it is a comforting, deeply satisfying feeling." J knew of it.

"Like the enjoyment we feel at joining the crowd to watch this spectacular sunset?"

"Perhaps. But probably not up to the anticipation we feel at joining each other in bed." And J knew of it.

"Primordial feelings join national culture as the order of the day. Hooray," as she grabbed J's arm in a now familiar way, urging him to get along.

♦

Back at their hotel in Paris which conformed smoothly to the neighboring buildings on the block, on the entire street, and in the city. There were small half-meter by two-meter balconies outside tall French windows. The doors were always substantial and double paned. They gave the impression they locked out the cold, the sound and the burglar.

Kay's room was large and bright. Kay and J were in bed, at the moment engaged in conversation.

Kay was talking to the ten-foot ceiling. "Maybe it is just the environment, the tradition, the history, that makes Paris demand romance. Maybe it disappears when you leave. Maybe it disappears when you stay. There seems to be so much ritualization of love in Paris, but nearly an absence of affection. They seem to be passionately involved, intimately helpful, or rude.

"The real test of love comes when you leave Paris. When we return, maybe we should position ourselves just as we were before coming here and see if the Seattle environment reenforces platonic relations."

"Oh, the handicaps of dating a scientist. Ah, scratch 'dating', insert 'falling in love with.'" The term had been bantered about, and J was coming to terms with it.

Kay pounced, "You see, your first impulse is the French attitude, only when you reconsider do you do the American thing. The French are consumed by fashion. You can sell anything with the correct heavenly body draped over, around or on it. Romance is the ultimate French fashion. And, all that aside, I must say that I really groove on it." This said with a sultry smile in J's direction.

J rolled on his side and kissed Kay's ear, "I hope we can postpone that reality check until we reach Seattle. Africa, too, is a very romantic place."

She relaxed, shifted the active areas of her cranium south, and smiled, "All right. We need to give this new data a fair chance before tweaking it."

"Speaking of tweaking — you always reveal what you're thinking in your terminology...." There was no need to finish.

◆

The conference went smoothly. J's paper was good. No one questioned his conclusions and contentions. Several of his friends remarked on how well he looked, so that he even checked a mirror to see if he was radiating something. Maybe it was happiness.

Kay's paper was smooth. Her outfit and smiles encouraged an endless series of questions, all friendly, ending only after the next speaker vigorously signaled the chairman that it was past his time to begin.

They shared dinner at a sidewalk restaurant with a French couple J had met years ago. Dinner was comprised of dozens of oysters, langoustines, crab, clams, and countless sea snails and cockleshells all piled on a huge dish of ice. They had champagne from Champagne.

The French couple made several flimsily disguised references to the fact that their dinner partners were lovers. The tone was clear approval, like a welcoming. J still wondered how this fact was so obvious, when he could discern nothing they did differently than they had before they met in bed. He considered that the liaison was not likely to be hidden, even where it might matter, wherever that might be.

Pierre spoke to J, "So, my friend, you are going to vacation in Africa?"

"Yes. It is easy and economical to take a few days safari from here." This was true, and J had reason to want this to seem a natural thing to do.

"I trust that you read the state department reports on which government is relatively stable down there. They still seem to be playing musical chairs with camouflaged khaki clad despots one following another."

"I do. Kenya and Tanzania derive most of their income from the tourist dollar, which keeps them comfortable, even when political parties are shooting at each other." J was casual as he picked his after dinner drink from the tray in front of them.

Kay looked at Pierre, "But you're right. I'm hoping that the news is only sensationalizing violence, and peace can be found in between." Looking at J, "I'm relying on J's research."

"Me, too." J knew they would be amazed at how deep his research had been. "We're leaving tomorrow morning. Since we've now spent the usual three hours for dinner, I think we had better call it a night."

With one more veiled comment on their preoccupation, their friends said goodbye and they slowly walked the avenue toward their hotel. The streets were full at ten o'clock on a weekday night. This was a city that lived.

They did get to bed early. And they did get up early to catch a bus out to the airport for their flight south. They both slept the entire bus ride. They bid a fond and apprehensive farewell to Paris.

Ch 3.7 Africa

The tree sits in the center of the cradle of humanity if defined with respect to the first stirrings of what would become Homo sapiens. Some of the earliest known fossils of man and his precursors are found a hundred and fifty kilometers to the west in the Olduvai Gorge, bordering the Serengeti. To the North at Fort Ternan are the bones of a perfect 'missing link' between Homo sapiens and the other great apes.

Much of this land is harsh and crevassed — a million years of yellowing. But it is due for a change; since the Tree sits at the southern tip of a geological arrow pointing the path of destruction as the Great Rift rends its way to the south. In a million years the Tree site will either be on the coast of Africa or on an island in the Indian Ocean. On J's album of space photographs, the lakes were like blue-black leeches on the earth. They marked the dotted line where some day the Indian Ocean would flow from the Gulf of Aden to Madagascar.

This tortured land was just one aspect of the unhurried renting of the Horn of Africa that produced the great highlands, majestic volcanoes, and deep lakes. The result at J's moment is a huge array of ecological niches, all within a few hundred kilometers.

The faults and quakes whirled around Lake Victoria like winds around a low pressure, as though this was the spot that generated the energy to fling six thousand kilometers of land into the ocean. The two branches of the rift, like fronts spewing out from the storm center, headed north from Kilimanjaro and south from a symmetric point four hundred kilometers to the west of Lake Victoria.

J loved the dynamism of the region. He thanked Darwin for the gift of an excellent education in geophysics that made his brief moment so much more enjoyable. His lifetime was so short on this scale that he felt fortunate to experience one of the thousands of earthquakes that attended the change. The rift valleys produced the protective volcanic ash and later exposed the sediments that have yielded clues to four million years of hominid fossils.

◆

Kay and J sat in window seats in the fourth and fifth rows of the half empty plane. Scientists first, the view took precedence over sitting together. Both had remained epoxied to the window during the flight, watching the searing deserts up to the front lines of the Sahal, where the desert tendrils were clearly infiltrating deep into the scrubby tree and brush areas. One area showed clearly the effects of the indigenous populations and their livestock. A one-hundred-kilometer square of private pasture had been fenced off and protected from grazing and foraging. It appeared as a light green postage stamp on the white envelope of the desert. A wonderful part of Africa's immensity can be seen from a long distance flight over the northern sector. This region sits astride the equator providing a benign and persistent climate. It makes it easy to believe that it was the cradle of humanity, and a whole lot of other flora and fauna.

It was another two hundred kilometers before the natural forests began, revealing the retreating front line. Along the upper Nile there was jungle; dense, dehydrated jungle, with no trees higher than a few meters.

This continued for an hour before some savannas began appearing. Once the plains appeared, the incubative region of Africa was revealed. Even from thirty-six thousand feet, one could tell there were large herds of animals in some of these regions. Kay and J could put their heads together at the gap between their seats and the window, both able to see below. They spoke often during the flight, and missed each other's side by side company, but both cherished the view.

The plains had passed beneath them for nearly an hour now. Out the right window, Lake Victoria revealed its huge size, followed soon by Mt Kilimanjaro on the left side. J knew they were approaching their destination.

At one point they banked around tall cumulus clouds, and the plane shook from the turbulence. J was very happy that these disappeared before they began their approach to the Arusha international airport. It was probably the most meagerly equipped international airport in Africa. The plane was modern with state-of-the-art radar, but he didn't trust the people on the ground to keep the runway clear of elephants, let alone the elusive eagles.

When the plane neared the airport they pressed their cheeks to the window to see as steeply down as possible. Individual animals could be distinguished as they made their approach. The modern jet landed smoothly at the World War II runway with the small mid-nineteen-sixties terminal.

As they descended the ladder to the ground, they were barely a few paces from the plane when an official looking man spoke to J, "Passports, sir," extending his hand. J knew the system here. This was just a travel agent entrepreneur who had bribed the customs agents in order to get his talons inserted early on. This was Africa; graft, fraud, life and death were all around you, and the violent metaphors were natural.

He recalled how the first time he and his wife had traveled here and refused to be indentured to the travel agent that had ensnared them. They had spent three hours trying to get out of the airport. Even the giant, garishly uniformed man who summoned the taxies ignored them under some secret signal. They had finally succumbed; paid the agent a commission that had probably escalated in the intervening hour, and thereafter had a smooth trip.

J reflected on the cliché, 'Oh, that we could make this trip through life a second time, with the knowledge of the first,' as he gave the man their passports and several twenties, saying matter-of-factly, "I've been here before. All that I require is directions to a car rental agency and assistance in getting through customs, if you would be so kind." Baksheesh was the way on this continent. The man was disappointed, but a quick glance around revealed there were no other marks left for him to transfer his interests to, so he accompanied J.

They walked around the customs lines with a couple of others who had been selected as worthy by the entrepreneur vultures. They had a car and were heading for the hotel at the outskirts of town within fifteen minutes.

There was a fairly modern hotel in town, but this wasn't it. This hotel had character, even elegance. It was a hundred years old, made of wood, and miraculously hadn't burned to the ground yet. It was called the Safari Hotel, of course. Most of the plumbing had been replaced several times and worked well. It continued to prosper because of the Verandah, with its view of the Savanna. This was one of the two or three best places in the world to have tea or coffee in the late afternoon. The Verandah was supported on sturdy timber so that it projected out over the adjacent plain twelve feet high. Still, this only put the guests at eye level with some of the animals that approached as closely as the subtly disguised electric wire about thirty feet away. Their attraction was the waterhole plus the salt-laced soil.

First the new couple checked into their adjoining double rooms. After the bellboys left, they simultaneously opened the two connecting doors that converted the rooms to a suite. They met at the demarcation line and embraced in what was now a familiar position for them. "I'll meet you in the lobby in five minutes. I need a cup of coffee." J instructed as he backed toward his bathroom.

Kay didn't have time to ask the obvious question, 'Why do you need coffee after having it poured down you on the flight?' so she just shouted, "OK" as she made haste to get ready. Journeys with her father had made her a sophisticated traveler. Interaction with macho males in the long academic path had made her sensitive to the male psyche.

As the waiter led them to a balcony seat, J had the pleasure of being with the one you loved as they were first exposed to something extraordinary. Kay said "Oh," several times as they approached their seat, and "It's glorious." J felt the renewed pleasure, seeing the scene through new eyes. "It really gets good when the sun sets right out there."

"I can see why you couldn't wait to get out here. I'm less insulted now."

"I hope that I have my priorities right." J felt that it was marginal.

"I'll ask again at a more propitious time." This is good, thought Kay, but so am I. A second one followed this thought, I'm really getting into this hormonal thing.

"You're anticipating correctly. My priorities are periodic." J tucked Kay into the seat where she could see the nearby elephants.

♦

They were on a safari, sitting in Land Rovers, preceded by others and followed by a truck with their tent and meals. It was not authentic safari, but pure requires time. They saw the 'native species', even lions that were oblivious of their caravan. The camp was in the middle of a plain, with several large trees providing cover from the sun. The trek was essential to provide the nighttime experience.

Most of the animals could see much better than humans at night. Three-fourths of the animals had evolved to be most active in the cool darkness. The relief after the searing sun had set produced an audible sigh across the Serengeti. The noise was sometimes a murmur, sometimes a cacophony of whistles, chirps and roars. One could imagine the ballet of animals from the clicking horns of rutting impalas, the bellowing elephants, barking zebras and the shriek of the hyena. A hundred other sounds waxed and waned from sunset to dawn the first night.

On the second night, the sounds began again, but they fell into silence like the receding whistle from a moving train. Soon after, the wheezing, snorting, and finally roaring revealed the presence of lions as the main act of this night. These sounds acted on Homo Sap brainstems, and the tourists felt the same terror and fear that their ancestors felt thousands of years ago. When they went to sleep in their tents, only canvas separated them from a beast that could make short work of them. But for some reason, the lions were content to stalk through the camp, snorting and sniffing at the strange smells, and leaving their pungent scent behind.

Kay and J clung together and bathed in the emotions of an African night. They were a couple. No need to maintain appearances. Probably true even back in town. But J was permanently shell-shocked from his experience at UW. He knew how easily it would be to dispatch a professor sleeping with his student. Not that OC had any such rule; it just had no rule; and no rule leaves it open. In fact, in general, J didn't think that it was such a good idea for professor and student to become involved.

During the day they saw the impala, the wildebeests, and a dozen other herbivores. There were a few hungry lions that had been unsuccessful during the night. They saw the cheetah running and elephants dominating their domain.

The weather was hot, but still comfortable. Later it could get tedious. But this was an idyllic vacation. They felt that they had scarcely left the Verandah when they were back on it, talking about their week.

"How did you find this place?" Kay asked.

"I've always been fascinated with origins, right? And with animals, and Homo sapiens's place amongst them. This area has good weather, space, and no obvious overpopulation. There are large cities, but large areas exist that are preserved. The tourist money is the local god."

She sighed, "I don't know how to tell you how glad I am to be here. But you can tell that I'm trying. What is planned for tomorrow?"

"Just the local scene. Shopping here is an adventure. Bargain hard. The prices are so cheap that you tend to think that it isn't worthwhile to haggle. Why bargain to save money that's negligible to you but significant to them? Do it for the culture."

"Great. But first let's enjoy this sunset." They did it with style, in silence.

◆

In the morning, J lingered in bed, suggesting that he had something that felt like a mild case of food poisoning. He urged Kay to go out. He got out a map of the town, phoned the desk and hired a guide, and arranged for her to be busy for the next four hours. He assured her that his stomach troubles were familiar, and certain to be gone in a few hours. They would enjoy dinner on their last night here. Kay was reluctant, but acquiesced in the light of J's firm resolve.

Minutes after she had left, J donned traveling gear, went to a taxi around the corner from the hotel, and fifteen minutes later, he was at the other end of town from where he had directed Kay. A cowboy in Western array waved him to his side.

J had met Wylie playing soccer in the local men's league in Seattle. Then they met again when Wylie was working on UW campus projects. It was natural for J to recommend him for projects at OC. J liked to check the building projects at OC. He wasn't shy about recommending small changes, like elaborate automatic lights, built in weather stations in the conversation centers, and other state-of-the-art gadgets. Wylie was very receptive to these ideas, and the two got along well. This was despite the huge difference in background.

Wylie had apprenticed to a contractor directly out of high school. He was bright and a good athlete and was making a lot of money for a teenager. It was a great time to be young in North America. He had a good memory for those wonderful times and wouldn't change a thing. He experienced life to the fullest at an age when J was still struggling with puberty. He felt sorry for J, who didn't have any of these experiences until they were compromised by maturity.

Wylie had become a contractor with world connections, a wheeler-dealer who could be trusted by J. He was a rare individual, and he looked it. He wasn't large, but he had a big presence. This was accomplished with a lean, perfectly proportioned body held constantly in a rigid posture, chiseled features, laser eyes, and a sculpted leather cowboy hat that J envied every time he saw it.

When they met, it was a time when J was working on figuring out something to do with his life, and with the extra money. Destiny had dealt him a cruel blow taking his mate so early. It was a decree that he would lead an entirely different life from that set piece originally in the making.

And then by serendipity, as though to balance the loss, fate financed him. The idea for the Tree was born. Now that was a done deed, but to what end?

Wylie never questioned the meaning of life. He never even addressed this philosophical problem. Thus he avoided the curse of those who got frustrated and chose a fiction. In the blissfully unaware such as Wylie, it would take a wrench in the tranquility machine to provoke any scratching of the exotic itches. He ventured only to the edges of the cerebrum to enhance his brainstem impulses with the effects of imagination, faith, and some freethinking, designed by evolution to enhance the sex and power action. He didn't dally in this foggy ephemeral visit. This was the world of Wylie and his crew, the world of Sancho Panza. They found the same solution for their life style by default that Deman found intellectually via the Panzaic Plea. Personal comfort and pleasure reigns.

J was another entity, amongst the few who swim the deep waters of the cerebrum. To these people, the end is a search, a madcap ride, taking place in the now. Homo sapiens have no choice about time. He surfs on the crest of its expansion. But he exists in the midst of the other dimensions. With the tools of science and technology he can explore to their bounds. It was a lot of work, but the rewards were commensurate. If exhilaration, contentment, and awe were commodities with measure, the rewards were great. Don Quixote's rewards were in his own mind.

In the humdrum time at UW, J had conceived the ultimate escape. He had been inspired by his trip to the Serengeti. A home in this area where Homo sapiens did a whole lot of early evolving would be fitting. There were shards of modern civilization scattered about like flowers in a desert. The corruption in these states was on par with the worst in the world. But that made it even easier for a person with lots of money and offbeat plans.

J had been visiting Wylie's house and was impressed with the elaborate Treehouse that had been made for his kids — and probably a lot for himself. The thoughts came together in an idea that would occupy the two of them for several years.

It was not long 'til the issue of what to do with his millions of dollars had been decided. Soon after that J embarked on spending the billions of his college patron. He found it more interesting to help OC pursue its destiny than confront his own. The OC construction had delayed this project, but Wylie had managed much preliminary work during these years. When OC work tapered off, he accelerated the Tree project. He, and a small work force, had spent much of the last year here in Africa.

"Is everything going OK with your sight-seeing trip? I understand the soufflé fell flat on the second day." Wylie was announcing to J that his itinerary and everything else was an open book.

"It's been great. I couldn't resist some business since I happen to be in town. Do you have a status report for me?"

"You'll be pleased. Weather has been cooperative and construction smooth. The only things for you to do involve the usual permits with the bribes and red tape. Here's my list of things to do. They are the last ones, really, finishing touches. Sign on the dotted line. We should be done quickly and you can get back to your assignation." No criticism was meant, only helpful cooperation.

J looked at the construction plans that Wylie had put in front of him. Purchase orders and choices for several items were marked for signature. His original plans were on one side of the diagram, the other side showed a figure that looked the same, but had structural details labeled to the side. Both figures looked like a huge tree.

After an hour, the two parted with a friendly salute. J smiled, "I'll return when you expect to finish, in June, and we'll do the final inspection. I get the feeling that you're anxious to get back to experience the summer in Seattle."

"Me and all of my crew. A winter away from the rain is OK, but we hate to miss summer. It has to be an ancient drive, as you would say. I really feel the dryness. You're right; I can hardly wait. But I won't cut any corners."

"I know you won't. I was really lucky to find the perfect person for this job."

Wylie smiled and touched his hat with a nod.

◆

J was resting in his room when Kay returned from her shopping trip. She was pleased that he had completely recovered and sought to take advantage of it.

Kay sighed, "It seems to work in Africa too, the power of proximity, particularly when it is measured in centimeters."

"I've often wondered how two people could waste so much time simply gazing into each other's faces. Here I am, doing it. I don't want to analyze it; I just want to do it. This may be one of those things that is not improved by knowledge of scientific details."

She ran a finger from his cheek down his neck to his bare chest. "And the power of touch is extraordinary. I can understand why it is enough for some people to simply get a loving, sexual relationship and abandon all other pursuits in life."

"Yes, I can understand that. Even though a small voice is telling me that it is all secondary. It's just my genes trying to snare me into full-time procreation. My logic tells me 'so what as long as I'm enjoying it.' And I am truly enjoying it."

Kay was truly wondering, "This time two days hence, we'll be on the Olympic Peninsula in separate beds. I'll have a chapter to write, you'll have a class to prepare. We'll see how strong this attractive force is in the face of intellectual forces."

J tried a long kiss before saying, "I'll put my money on the brainstem."

Although it is not true that all conservatives are stupid people,
it is true that most stupid people are conservatives.

John Stuart Mill

Ch. 3.8 A New Factor

J was on a short hike on the weekend attached to a colloquium given at the old UW. He had a nice reunion with colleagues and afterward drove to the trailhead. Another car pulled up behind him in the otherwise vacant lot and two husky men had no trouble persuading him to accompany them. Hijacked. He was taken to a mansion in one of the exclusive guarded enclaves that had proliferated to shelter the super rich. There was no attempt to hide the destination and somehow J didn't feel that it would be at all productive to shout that he was being kidnapped to the guard at the enclave gate.

He was ushered into an elegant room of golden flagstone and mahogany. There was a massive desk to one side, a wall of windows on two sides looking on pools and fountains. J recognized a van Gogh and a Renoir on the wall. They were paintings he had seen in books only; he thought he could remember they were stolen from museums decades ago.

There was a small round table in the center of the room with some newspaper clippings. J glanced at the stories of hikers, hunters; ordinary people all missing somewhere, often in the vicinity of the Alpine Lakes region. The dates went back years. He felt a chill of foreboding, and a very unwelcome sense of responsibility. The world could turn very dark shortly. He wasn't ready for this. What had he been thinking not to prepare for this moment? Homo sap, indeed. He'd already failed to outsmart, by the very nature of his being here. Deep in the trap. Either luck, or wit, would be his only chance.

A door in the wood paneling behind the desk opened and a short, strikingly handsome man entered. Eyebrows, mustache, and lips seemed to be painted on they were so well defined. He was casually but elegantly dressed. He didn't mince words.

"OK, we know that you were in the vicinity of the heist. That's all we know about your connection, even though we know everything else there is to know about you and your petty life. I confess that we don't know if you're the thief. If we did, you wouldn't be here. Unfortunately for you, even if you are innocent, it is irrelevant at this point.

"There is another reason for this visit. I was there when you castigated the Friends of the Faculty in your pompous lecture. You think of yourself as an intellectual, an agnostic, and a know-it-all. I admire that. This is why we're having this conversation. I have this insatiable itch to enlighten you."

His attitude struck J as that of a parent scolding a child. For some reason, J felt like a child. He listened, hoping for an explanation.

"I live the life of a true intellectual. I have important and powerful friends around the globe. We get together and discuss philosophy much as you do . But we live and travel in luxury while you are consigned to steerage. To me, you are a wanna-be intellectual who just never has had the means to achieve the highest levels of thinking that man can currently attain.

"You are afraid to confront the logical conclusions of your own studies and observations. You are right that man is simply a most talented animal species. You're right that he is severely limited in his capacity to attain higher levels of thought, expansion to the universe or even contentment on earth. This leaves us only our brief period of existence to make what we can of it. We are doing just that. We're the true inheritors and users of the earth's wealth."

J shrugged. "We all know about the corporate elite."

The man smiled and shook his head. "You really don't understand. We are a level above the corporate CEOs and the nouveau riche; most of whom are intellectual pygmies. Actually, we have in our monthly meetings CEOs who are in charge of Oil, food, drugs, education, religions, military, entertainment and politics. My friends often call me the COE, which isn't far from the truth. Figure it out. We are the power behind the Mafias, the Tongs, the priests and everything else. We're the syndicate elite, the oligarchy that controls world commerce and governments. In this country we own the senate, we own the house, we own the Supreme Court , and most of the time we own the presidency. Hell, we own the electorate, and have for decades. What do you own? A few graduate students?"

"And the truth based on science, and maybe even a little better insight on the meaning of existence?" J was familiar, if not comfortable, with this quixotic attitude.

"There you go again. You really should pay more attention to your friend Deman. You're wasting your time on harebrained chimera. I've made the wager that Pascal should have made: I join your religion, but I bet that this life is all we have and I'm going to make the most of it. You disdain religion; we use it. Some even embrace it, with no influence on their ethics. We are able to address higher level questions, like when all your basic needs are satisfied to the best ability of the species, birth to death, inheritance and heredity, what thoughts should we have? Toward what ends?

"Do you have plans for occupying the thoughts and content of the masses that you would make literate and free from trivia? Banal data are their food and substance, their pleasures and passions, their trifling destiny. Do you just present them with the agony and ecstasy of day to day existence together with the humbling knowledge that this is all there is? Truth is powerful medicine with devastating side effects. It cures ignorance and causes chaos.

"Do you think that it is even remotely possible to educate them all to your level --- at least a dozen years of very expensive learning beyond their usual high school? What then? Will they patiently bear the burden of daily life in an imperfect world, raise children, pay taxes, flip hamburgers, clean sewers, and study philosophy if their destiny is manure no matter what they do?

"I think not. So we manipulate the great masses to produce and consume, creating a material world where they are content and we can skim the good life from the top. We encourage not ridicule their religions. This pap motivates them to toil and behave under placating illusions. Everyone's happy, and we are the happiest."

J voiced the usual question that sometimes gave Deman pause for thought. "You find hedonism and ephemeral gratification a worthy goal in life?"

"Yes, I do."

"OK, but you must spend a lot of time on manipulation and violence."

He just smiled his acceptance. "It is really quite simple to do once you have rationalized the doing of it. Other members of the species that get in the way, or even just bother us, we eliminate. Or arrange for them to eliminate each other. This can be done from peons to presidents. This is so easy to do that we must dream up ways to make it more interesting. Just about every assassination, every conspiracy theory that you have heard, we arranged. Of course, we don't personally get involved, anymore than you get involved in killing of the meat you eat. We are masters of organization."

There was no reason to not believe the man. The evidence was around him. The speaker seemed to look on him with pity. "To be sure, the bottom levels of the pyramid are rife with violence, misery and injustice. Life isn't fair. But we at the top tiers are completely isolated from the messy stuff. We have for generations now lived lives of ultimate privilege, global play, global control, ultimate health and medical care and maximum intellectual stimulation. We are probably the best that can be expected from our species.

"My intellectual stimulation is the only reason you're here. Your "reasoned" allegiance to the quixotic ideals that Homo sapiens just might have something meaningful in its future is as difficult for me to understand as it is for you to understand the religious apostle. Although I confess that I have gotten some insight from listening to your conversations with your slightly smarter friend."

J started to say something but was waved off. "Don't be so naïve. We listen to much of your personal life. It's challenging and sometimes more interesting than the average television. I have to admit that there hasn't been one iota of indication that you have the money.

"You are here because we have a message for you. Normally it is delivered at a much lower level. I brought you here only because I was titillated by the success of your effort to create a monastery for your little intellectual enterprise. And as a seeker of the truth, I couldn't resist giving it to one who has such a misguided sense of it. You know what I mean. You enjoy confronting the religious zealot with the banal contradictions of their failed philosophy. Your turn."

"I can't disagree so far."

The COE raised an eyebrow, nodded, and went on. "OK. Now here's the message. As you may or may not know, we lost a bit of money at a heist from our exchange point. An insignificant amount of money, but it had a special purpose. And there is a principal involved; and a challenge. Frankly, we don't know who took it, but we know it must have been one of a dozen. So we are systematically going down the list of suspects to pressure them. Our method is simply to give you notice. Enable us to recover the money within six months and you live. Otherwise, sometime soon thereafter you will die. That's all there is to it. You are the number six most likely suspect. You've seen the notices of the first five who didn't manage to help us. Good luck. I don't expect to see you again."

J raised his hand and nearly shouted as his protagonist was leaving the room. "Can I ask just a couple of questions — with very short answers?"

He paused, like yielding to a small child, "Well, all right."

"What is the integral of X-squared DX from zero to two?"

"I neither know nor care."

"OK. Thank you. I don't need the second question."

There was the slightest pause in the COE's demeanor. But J was on his way out the door. He may be the Chief of Everything, but the dork didn't even know calculus.

He was deposited back at his car as though nothing had happened. He was in shock, and headed for the most secure place he knew, catching the last ferry and arriving at home late at night. Even back in his house, he couldn't relax. The COE had challenged every vestige of quixotic idealism that he had remaining from Deman's assaults. Kafka squared. This time he had more information about the forces that controlled his life. The threat to his life was considered only as an afterthought.

If they knew his precise whereabouts, as they seemed to, he wasn't safe anywhere. Except for the next six months. Time to think. But it wasn't encouraging. If the COE's statements were true there was nowhere to hide. He felt sick in his stomach; his legs were weak at the idea of those uninvolved innocents who would have had no idea why they were being killed. Shit. It was the thoughtless nature of it, both on his part, letting all that time go by, and on the part of the sociopaths who thought so well of themselves.

But he knew that they weren't omnipotent. They didn't know about the Swiss bank account or the Tree. Otherwise the jig would be up. He was fairly certain that they generally didn't follow him to Switzerland. He was quite certain about the trips to Africa. There had been several of them. But he had always taken great caution, buying the tickets with cash at the airport under an assumed name. It had been very difficult to do for the last trip with Kay. Might have slipped up there. J didn't sleep much that weekend.

Knowledge of divine things for the most part, as
Heraclitus says, is lost to us by incredulity.

Plutarch (46–120),
Greek historian, biographer, and philosopher.

The natural course of the human mind is
certainly from credulity to skepticism.

Thomas Jefferson (1743–1826),
Scholar, U.S. president.

The supreme mystery of despotism, its prop and stay, is to keep
men in a state of deception, and with the specious title of religion
to cloak the fear by which they must be held in check, so that
they will fight for their servitude as if for salvation.

Baruch Spinoza
from 'Tractatus Theologico-Politicus', 1670

Ch. 3.9 A Spring lecture. Philosophy 400. Religion. Abortion. Summary.

It is the last day before Spring break. The seats at the table and around the walls are fully occupied. The lecture room is a cocoon of concentration. Everyone looks a bit like they have just played a full-court-press game of basketball. They probably have done the intellectual equivalent. Faces show anger, glee, amusement and animosity.

Nicole is seated on a stool in the front of the room. "Well, we have to sum it up, not just today's rambunctious session, but the entire quarter. You'll remember so little when you return from Spring break." She had an obvious French accent. She looked French, in the mode of that archetype that impressed Kay and J for the ability to produce beautiful people. As Peter would say, they had a leg up on attaining the universal average.

"The root of this course is found in conventional University courses. Courses with titles like 'The Bible, Koran or I Ching as Literature'. In those classes, most of the students are scientific illiterates, and much of the time so is the professor. Here, you have all had years of basic physics, math, biology, geophysics and more. And so have I.

"The result has been that our discussions were in no way related to those other courses on the other side of the Sound, or on the other side of the Pacific.

"We discussed the world's religions. Christianity, the force that controls our country, and extols a gentle individual. The I Ching is a numbers game that may be the least harmful of all. Perhaps more beneficial is the Buddhist aim of harmony with nature. Islam, which means surrender, is a forthright request to suspend your critical intellectualism. In India, we have the coexistence of Islam, the world's most monotheistic religion, with the world's most pantheistic religion, Hinduism. Wow, what a *mishmash!*" Like any good preacher, she put important words in focus.

"Then there's Communism, Capitalism, Nationalism and yea, even Science. I include the last for its provocative nature on this campus and just to provide balance."

This provoked a physics student, "Science doesn't have a God."

"Neither does Communism, and Buddha didn't want one. But I speak of god in the sense as do some physicists — an ephemeral entity behind existence. I think that you'll agree when I talk about Science's pseudo God, Empiricism.

"After all, in the beginning that's all there is, observation and speculation ---empiricism and theory. Empiricism rests on observation. Its shining success is noting a correlation between two variables. Theory generalizes the correlation. Sometimes, with mathematics, it extrapolates the results. Then it goes back to data to evaluate the predictions."

Baker, with her passion for history, was a natural as teaching assistant in this course. She also liked to say things simply. "So all we know is that when one thing happens, this other thing also happens in some proportion? Seems like there has always been a dichotomy between scientists over this."

" Yes. However I think it is more a tradition of competitive criticism, at times purely intellectual, at times unconscious."

Baker the critic was in form, "That's a rosy picture. It seems to separate different groups, theoreticians and experimenters, analytic analyzers and curve fitters, thinkers and doers." You could tell which group she felt she was in.

Nicole has been there, "Yet it seems to be generally civil; only occasionally grating. That seems to arise because there is an assumed superiority of and by the first named in each pair. Both have their points. Theory is exalting; but sometimes all there is, is a curve-fit. I suggest that you try to be on the strong side of each pairing. It can change with each issue."

Nicole smiled her acceptance of Baker's help. "And we may not have the faintest idea why two things correlate. The theory extrapolates based on some idea. Mathematics is the highest form of this idea. But theory itself must rest on empirical constants found in the correlations . The great constants of Newton, Plank, Hippocrates and Lord Acton are all empirical constants. Subject to change but overwhelmingly verified in our domain by observation and experiment. These two procedures are our truth-sayers."

This professor was a preacher befitting her topic. Her well-modulated voice would rise and fall, sometimes like a roller coaster on a single polysyllabic word, but most often on the words that sold the product. "Of course none of the major religions are unchanged by modern contingencies. Priests, ministers, lay people interpret the vague homilies of religion to meet the daily requirements. Their truth-sayers are too often the simple proclamations of the powerful and the persistent repetition by their ecclesiastics.

"As we examined history we found that the teachings of religion complain of the sins of violence, war and 'man's inhumanity to man'. Then they present a rationalization for doing these things justifiably to other people, usually unbelievers. First are the unsupported pronouncements that their religion is right, and that they have the patent on truth. Other people are 'heathens' or 'infidels'. This predisposed the 'members' to be fodder for wars, and to rationalize the most grievous of 'inhumanities to man and woman'. The clincher is a promise of eternal life in paradise. What simple mind wouldn't buy it? But consequently, at any moment in the past several hundred years one could march around the globe and identify a dozen regions where Man was in violent confrontation with religion as the measure of difference."

She tried to be objective. But she often raised the possibility that religions were the root of all evil. Yet she sympathized with them, like one would with errant children. "The simple Christian — despite the belief that Christ was the Son of God — could have led a moral life without imposing his cranial blemishes on others. The simple Muslim, even within the confines of true belief that the Koran was a product of Mohammad's direct pipeline to God, would not have nurtured extremists. But we observed the unifying thread of extremist rhetoric in diverse clerics. And we know that the Crusaders were devoted Christians and the twin tower terrorists were dutiful Muslims --- their faith provided their motivation with rewards of a promised heaven with bountiful perks."

"But you shouldn't indict all Muslims for the sins of a few." From a dark-skinned woman who had successfully compartmentalized her religion through many dichotomies in science and verbal skirmishes. This class finally forced her to confront the barriers in her own mind.

"That's correct, but quixotic. A panzaic attitude worries when someone who embraces your faith is capable of heinous acts. What about when they do it in your religion's name? When terrorists assume your mantle, you must accept some responsibility. You are after all in the best position to deny them this cloak of respectability. Instead, the Muslims formalize the taking of political power in the Jihad and label all non-Muslims as infidels."

Baker keeps it fair: "Of course many Christians are also told that they must convert the nonbeliever."

"And as a result it is fair to say that religions have been the major holding pond of terrorists. Their growth in a sense of self-righteousness and martyrdom nurtures the attitudes that produce the violence of terrorism. To be sure, most of the congregation does not support overt violence, but by providing the environment where the terrorist's hate is nurtured, they implicitly support it. Of course, some even find satisfaction in the terrorists being on their side."

"What is to prevent non-religious people from perpetrating these extremist crimes?" Baker is doing her part.

"Well, almost by definition, they are not true believers. It would be very hard to persuade someone whose faith is in sociobiology to die for some ephemeral cause. They wouldn't be receptive to promises of rewards in an afterlife. They would realize that the hormonally driven dictates of the religious leaders were scientifically vacuous. Without faith, the human cannon fodder for war and terrorism might be lacking."

Nicole had matured as the frank discussions about the power of blind faith to provide motivation and rationalization for terror slowly grew after the twin-tower attack. She moved from a 'live-and-let-live' attitude to 'The cancer in our cultures has been revealed, and should be removed.'

This course was considered essential at OC. It would be forbidden at every other college. It was part of the philosophy that the frank discussion of sex, politics and religion was grist for the understanding necessary to develop a successful culture.

The doomsday preaching continued, gently unrelentingly. "Primitive

Homo sapiens sacrificed people, usually children, generally female, to appease the gods. We've put that mainly behind us, but we still regularly sacrifice the intellect of our children, particularly our females, on the altar of religious faith and piety. The washing of the brain through thoughtless repetition of a myopic mantra is a form of circumcision, closing off paths of exploration and development. Clipping the wings of an eagle mind means it can never soar. Religion teaches people not to think skeptically but in unity. Undo science."

Christopher was there as an assistant. It was common at OC to have several professors involved in a class. To him, this was all old hat. "Isn't this all a rather obvious observation to anyone with a broad education?"

"We might hope so. But we're not certain yet. There are many people with high degrees who still possess a non-sequitur religion. I guess the key word is 'broad'.

"In fact all of this has been passé since the French revolution; totally forgotten by recent generations. At that time in France, the church was dismantled and houses of enlightenment were substituted. That this was a failure, and the churches reclaimed their edifices, is testimony to the fact that we don't face an easy problem — figuring out something to replace these houses of prostituted thought."

She had reminded them that for hundreds, even thousands of years, humanity had sought a means of government that was just. "Only in the juxtaposition of the United States revolution, with its pleas to every man to fight for a New World, and the free-thinking environment of the founding fathers, where the best aspects of the French Enlightenment were assumed, was the culture ripe for the document that was produced in a few months in Philadelphia and evolved in the next hundred years to a successful democracy."

She continued her summary, "To address this question, we had to return to the most basic of motivations. Mankind just naturally wonders about the meaning of life. There's no specific data beyond the dictate to survive and propagate, so we proceed to theory. I include the first efforts of the caveman, with his rudimentary theory for the stars, the astrophysicist with his concepts of black holes and a big bang, and the superstrings physicist trying to tie infinity to zero. These theories all emerge from assumptions that start with a little faith. Only when substantiated with observations and some measure of mathematical consistency does it survive long enough to be called a science.

"Unfortunately, the science regimen for weeding out false hypotheses by carefully examining data was often not understood and unsubstantiated theories were passed into public domain. When it is blind faith it is called religion. It then becomes encumbered with the trappings of mysticism and myopic preaching. It becomes absolutely *believed.* Those seduced by it have a great frustration with the attitude and critical nature of skeptical science when it addresses religion. There is an incompatibility that just isn't understood. One who did understand was Shakesphere,

'Tomorrow, and tomorrow, and tomorrow,
Creeps in this petty pace from day to day
To the last syllable of recorded time;
And all our yesterdays have lighted fools the way
to dusty death. Out, out, brief candle!
Life's but a walking shadow; a poor player,
That struts and frets his hour upon the stage,
and then is heard no more;
it is a tale told by an idiot, full of sound and fury,
signifying nothing.'

"We are all hiking the path to dusty death. But I know that just as the extraordinary concept of mathematical Chaos Theory tells us that the flap of a butterfly's wings in Boston can change a Pacific storm; my writing can affect the universe.

"When science rather than a religious faith is embraced, many of the sticky subjects become simple problems of making a logical choice, of selecting an optimum amongst several uncertain choices. We found it amazing how many of society's problems are solved by the simple realization that we are Homo sapiens, a talented mammal, but with serious limitations that need to be considered in most judgments."

Nicole turned as she walked back to the head of the classroom, "We then got back to reality and talked about a practical example, abortion. Because it is such a big factor in religious fiat, and became an instrument in the fatal weakening of American Democracy. The concept of life, with a soul at conception, is insufferably tied to religion. It is obviously a dictate of the gene that wants to propagate.

"We started off by agreeing to call the fetus a 'life' form that is extinguished at abortion. But we decided that calling it 'infanticide'" or 'murder' is to engage in myopic semantic distortion. From a scientific standpoint, we stepped back and examined the basic definitions and premises.

"'Life' is an indefinite term. The fetus is life. So too are all living organisms. If one protests the taking of life as a basic premise, one must assume a Buddhist' attitude toward all life—none must be destroyed, not even the malaria bearing mosquito.

"Now this isn't done in most religions, of course, so a judgment on the value of life must have been made. For instance, a man's life is worth more than a bug's, or that of a fish, or a spotted owl. Man finds this easy to do...even setting a small number of men's jobs worth more than the entire species of that owl. But we haven't the owl's opinion."

She was on a roll, and didn't want the mood broken, "How does one evaluate one Man's life, out of nine billion, versus the last pair of blue whales? Well, on the measure of intelligence, and value to the planetary ecosystem, many individual people might come in second, and certainly the human fetus would. The infants of our species have smaller brains, are less articulate, and are potentially more damaging to the planet than most other newborn animals. As an entity, they are really lacking.

"Oh, they do have promise. But the history of Homo sapiens is that most likely this is a promise of misery and degradation to the rest of the planet's creatures. In fact, it is often a threat to individual members of its own species, all in the name of procreation. The people who fear killing the fetus that might become the next Einstein don't understand statistics. The odds are immensely greater that it will become the next psychotic killer. We're taking a risk every time we allow another fetus to be born."

Christopher had a quick query. "Yes, but I wonder how many mass killers can we put up with in order to get another Einstein?"

She smiled her acceptance of a good point. "It would seem to be quite a few, but then we come up against the dangers of population explosion."

"We can't help but be receptive to anything that puts us, or our species, at the top of the value pinnacle. It naturally is very popular with people who never get to learn the marvelous intricacies of physics, biology, ecology, statistics, sociology, and science in general. They like the free ride. The knowledge they lack denies them the skeptical mien that comes with an understanding of evolution and natural selection.

"But if a person is fortunate and diligent enough, she learns that evolution teaches that her species is merely the biggest disturbance that we have on the planet at this time (say, the last few thousand years). Science shows us that the dinosaurs were in this position for over one thousand times as long, right?"

After four years, these sentences were clichés. She had them almost humming along. Here was the mob arousal sign. She wasn't above using it, "Right?" There was a uniform, "Yeah." Louder this time, and enthusiastic.

Her tone was a little higher now, and a little louder, a consummate expert in crowd arousal, "Man dominates because it has the ability to kill all life forms including its own, which it does regularly. Man breeds very rapidly and spreads to occupy all ecological niches, pushing out other life forms. This you know from your biology and sociology courses, and learned right here."

The 'yea' was louder and faster. There may have been an 'amen' or two.

"Thus the characteristic of being a benign influence on the environment, of not raping and razing fellow life forms is not a criterion for setting Man as the most exalted form of life." A pause. "One wonders what it is." They were quiet now, wondering.

"One must know the enemy. Is it simply our species? Is it religion? Uncritical faith? Why is it that so many blindly believe that our species is the ultimate, the end product, rather than a twinkling in space and time? And how do they have the audacity, the arrogance to say 'You've got to have faith that we're the reason for it all?' "

She looked out the window at the buds on the tree. A new cycle of life was beginning. She shook her head as she reminisced. "I'll never forget a picture I saw of a TV interview with a true believer. He had been tossed and trammeled by a tornado that had destroyed his house and family. He was lying in a hospital bed with an arm and a leg in traction. In response to the reporter's question about what he felt about being the only survivor, he said 'I thank God that I'm alive. He must have been looking over me this day.'

"Well I say he should be thankful that God wasn't looking after him every day."

Baker was quick: "I wonder why God didn't care about all the other people?"

There was a nod, a smile and another metered pause. "It requires a big leap of faith, a religious revelation that persuades an individual that he is the exalted species without the tedium of scientific justification. It is an easy step compared to learning by studying the knowledge parlayed by tens of thousands of other Homo sapiens.

"A single book is usually offered to the faithful as sufficient to know the meaning of life. Often they can muster the discipline to read and study this book, which depends on the geographical accident of one's birthplace.

"But for you who have worked hard to gather information into your brain, reading Darwin knows how many books, critically examining every one, the road was not so *easy!*" They actually cheered at this sentence.

"Now fundamental questions are answered just as easily by you as by the fiat of religion. With your knowledge, the choices are logically made at several levels. And your answers are better."

She pointed at Christopher anticipating his request. "For instance, to avoid the unpleasant procedure of abortion, we find many easy actions. The simplest one is to practice contraception. Prevention of conception is the logical mode of birth control. It's a natural mode too, that's why breast-feeding has a pretty good contraceptive effect on a woman."

She stood and walked to the front of the room, regretting the procedure that didn't allow her to have a pulpit. "But hey, we all understand that the damn hormones get out of control occasionally, accidents happen, and the choice gets a bit stickier; if only on a physical discomfiture level.

"The 'day after pill' is universally accepted except for a few primitive areas, but it can be called a form of abortion. Still, no problem if not encumbered with some arbitrary religious definition of life.

"For the freethinker these questions are straight-forward choices, difficult maybe, but logical." She was letting them come down gently from their mob high. The long lecture had been a smoothly accelerating psalm, slowly becoming faster and louder, with increasing pauses and accented words and phrases. Now it was like the foam of the broken wave washing over their feet. Her voice was calm and soothing. She loved to do this final appeal. For that was what she was doing, appealing to these youth to believe what she believed. She had faith that her scientifically sanctioned faith was 'right'. She had seen 'the light.'

"There is one last bulwark to this logical extrapolation of Darwin's dangerous idea to our pursuit of 'truth'. That is the immense reluctance of many of our species to accept that they are just a random product of a vast complexity of known design criteria, with unknown purpose and origin. We are reduced to a needlepoint in the vast tapestry of the cosmos. We spent a short time on creationism and intelligent design, dispatching them immediately with their burdens of illogical claims. The evolutionary change in many species' designs are evident in the fetus remnants of previous fins, tails, appendices and more."

She noted the concerned look on many faces, and the sad, satisfied smiles on others. "But we spent some time extolling the virtues of humility, the satisfaction of confidence in just the facts, and contentment with living a just and educated life — with just the right amount of sex and materialism.

"Then we had a particularly rancorous session when I suggested that a person's attitude toward the meaning of life should constitute a Mark. A Mark that is an asterisk on that individual's opinions and ability to evaluate what life is all about. It is a label that distinguishes when a particular person has chosen simple revelation over the difficult task of learning and developing their brainpower. This sounded barbaric to some of you. It reminded you of the scarlet letter for the adulteress, or the tattoo of the concentration camp internee.

"But we saw that culturally accepted Marks permeate our societies. Not just the nun's habit, the priest's frock, the elaborate headdress or the simple scarf, the robe or staff and the glorious military uniforms, but also the subtle collar, the shaved head or the skullcap and the symbol worn on a chain around the neck. These are all marks that the possessor has abandoned the path to true enlightenment and taken a side road toward blind faith and intellectual oblivion."

"Remember, as a Mark of limited cranial competence, it is only a strong suggestion. There are legions of people who haven't even addressed the questions. A Mark may indicate someone who has thought a great deal about meanings of existence, or simply made the use of a symbol for some exotic personal reason. But alas, it generally indicates they are like a musician who has devoted his life to playing 'Silent Night' on the tin drum because that was the instrument given to him by his parents.

"Our hypothesis here at OC, an optimistic one, is that these potential thinkers lack a fundamental capability embodied in science. We hope that you have been provided this ingredient necessary for efficient and critical thinking, and have been inoculated against these many boondoggles of the mind."

"Maybe we're the ones that need to develop a mark," a comment from Baker.

"Yes, a possibility. Like your sandals and sweatshirt. But in general the intellectual fears a mark. We are far from a homogeneous group. And it could be dangerous in our society.

"So we should learn to identify existing marks in society. It would save a lot of time in fruitless conversation. You should not find it difficult to search for a Mark for this purpose.

"You already do for many things. Much of it is subliminal. The advertisers and politicians analyze it to exploit it. It exists all around you in day-to-day interactions. Consider the power tie, the thousand-dollar suit, the first class seat, and the styled haircut. We recognize those with money and power almost instantly. We recognize those without as easily. You adjust your attitude toward the person correspondingly.

"There are marks in simple pronouncements. For instance from numerous political leaders at the turn of the century: 'A human fetus is physiologically a human individual — abortion of a fetus is therefore the equivalent of murder.' You can logically conclude that this person has mush for brains."

Christopher practices diplomacy, "Perhaps we should say, 'this person is motivated by blind faith and not a scientific understanding'."

She smiles, "Perhaps we should say."

A student offers, "How about the person who says 'I have to read my horoscope for today.'"

She loved these students. "Thank you. In fact, in a just society, we certainly wouldn't want to ban astrology. It might even have a modicum of happenstance truth, like babies born under summer constellations are happier than those of winter, having gotten off to a more comfortable start. But blind belief in astrology is a good delineator of ignorance of science. Marks like this help to identify the faithful without them knowing that we do.

"We can also recognize non-sequitur clichés like 'guns don't kill people, people do.' And hasty slurs like 'communism is evil,' or 'nigger' or 'infidel'. You must recognize these as Marks and perhaps abandon hope of reasoned conversation with individuals who spout this apocryphal pap. Cynical though it is, you must treat them as unable to converse on your plane, and apply psychology instead. It's a hard cruel world, and we're justified in making these assessments."

Baker has a simplification. "Don't use logic on a lion. It won't work."

Nicole beamed acceptance. "Look, I understand that sometimes an individual has invested much energy in higher learning, yet been frustrated by science's inability to answer meaning-of-life questions. Sometimes the need for an individual to answer these unanswerable questions is so great that they make the leap to faith-dictated reassurance. At least it is a stimulating story for an unanswerable question. This is understandable, a constant caution to any learning program."

A young man who had been struggling with the burden of a Dixie education injected, "I remember a noisy session when we discussed an example of scientifically irrational culture: racial prejudice."

She walked to the window, and continued as if she was addressing the gray squirrel scampering up a nearby tree, "Yes. It's a complicated world. But these genetic tendencies are easy ones to be made rational with education and discipline. Of course there is no scientific criterion for racial designation. When all humanity is viewed, it is clear that skin color differences are a continuum, not discrete. We decided that race, the distinctive definition, was a religious judgment."

Christopher adds, "I like the example that if a culture decided that big nosed people should be isolated then genetics would soon produce a class of distinctive people with large noses. They could be considered inferior or superior, probably depending on the nose of the local mullah."

She nodded, and moved on, "Finally, we discussed the best chance for an answer to our shortcomings. Some of it is relatively simple. Obvious remedies have been known for decades but are seldom enacted: teachers should become exalted members of the culture, intellect is rewarded, enlightened skepticism is esteemed; in short, education is the key species function. It was tried briefly in the first decade of this century, but the systematic decimation of science and our economy by the conservatives gave them a strong reactionary party, and we liberals were forced to revolution."

"Should scientists form a party?"

She smiled and shook her head. A glance at the small abstract clock told her that her hour was over. "No. It's like herding cats. And that brings me to one final caution. Beware of blindly respecting science or scientists. While most people do not have sufficient knowledge of science to even begin addressing the problems, many scientists also have an inadequate scope to their education, lacking the feelings and perspective to judge the foibles of humanity.

"Some are so narrowly educated that they can be worse off than the liberally educated sociologists. Some actually believe that any problem can be solved if it is only broken into small enough bits and put on a computer. But this doesn't even hold for that hub of scientific theory, the primitive mathematical equations for fluid flow. You know this from classes concerned with elementary physics, turbulence and chaos. So those true-believers probably shouldn't be called 'scientists' in our terminology.

"In this class, all we have done is to identify the problems that arise. Identification is half way to understanding. We were able to speculate on possibilities of a science-based culture. We saw how difficult it was. Still, we were shocked at how close it could be, at least in limited domains.

And then we were depressed at how impossible a universal enlightenment would be, given the immense numbers. We decided to work on a local fix, and that's where we are now. I hope it is a relatively happy state for you. It is for me. Good luck in your course papers. And then good luck in your culture."

She had picked up her notebook and was headed toward the door when she remembered. "Oh yes, a PS: Many of you will soon be leaving to spend the Spring break with your families. Some of you will discuss this course at home. Some won't. Remember, discretion and valor, reality versus idealism. Dare I say it, 'Panza, not Quixote'.

"Remember, this college is a refuge of knowledge in a sea of ignorance — sometimes of under-educated malice. Don't provoke or evangelize when you're outside the security of the campus; it is like stepping into a jungle. You are all smart enough, and have been taught the tools to survive the jungle. But there are still the random acts of violence and frustration, so be careful." She made the mistake of looking directly at Christopher as she asked, "Got that?"

Christopher nodded, "It's risky being smart in a world of dumb."

She paused, then smiled acceptance of the succinct summary. "You got it. I hope to see all of you in some courses next quarter."

Each male student vowed that it be so. So did most of the females unaided by their hormones. They liked her style. Same old stuff, but she was rocking. Got to fight fire with fire. She might be the 'Joan of Arc' of her cause.

I do not consider it an insult but rather a compliment to be called an agnostic. I do not pretend to know where many ignorant men are sure.

Clarence Seward Darrow (1857–1938),
U.S. lawyer.

Ch. 3.10 Biding Time

J was sitting at one end of a bleached gray log on an Olympic Park beach, Kay on the other end. They straddled the log so that they were facing each other. They were most comfortable and happiest when alone in the wilderness. The location of the new campus had greatly facilitated fulfilling this need. It was a short distance to some of the quietest, loneliest spots in the world.

The couple had reached a point where proprieties were damned. Kay was noting this fact, "I am much more relaxed now that I've realized it's impossible to prevent any person on campus from knowing that we are an item, no matter how elaborately and brilliantly we arrange our trysts."

He corrected her. "From preventing every person on campus from knowing."

J was planning another European trip. Kay had planned to come along, but had to cancel.

They were discussing serious matters. "OK, so you're about fifteen years older than I. I am sixty-five percent as old as you. When I'm in my fifties I'll be seventy-five percent as old as you — I'm catching up."

"You'll never make it."

"Close enough. Along about then and beyond there will possibly be a sexual interaction gap. But my physiology is such that my hormones are not as dominant as my brain cells. I can fantasize quite satisfactorily by myself, if need be. Presumably, you'll still be interacting with my brain cells well." Kay seemed to be a lawyer presenting her case.

J is tuned to that. "Already a lot of sex is in the brain. But I love those hormones— they're powerful drivers. But like everything else, they diminish without continuous exercise. I'm not certain what constitutes proper exercise or in just what shape my hormonal repertoire is languishing."

Kay's smile washed over J, as though she had just proven an important theorem, "That's where we're physiologically matched. Just about when you're passion-pooped, I'll undergo the great transmogrification of menopause, and we'll still be compatible. I'm just a reproductive creature from puberty to menopause. While you can keep at it until you're ninety."

Again, J is in his best scientific contemplative posture, "It's just those years before menopause that might be difficult. Perhaps in addition to HIV, HEPS, Ebola and whatever new tests they require for a marriage license today, I should have a long-term cardiovascular evaluation?"

Kay looked sharply at J. Was his satire just his normal sense of humor, or was he getting turned off? She saw a shimmer in his eyes that reassured her, "No, I checked out your cardiovascular just last night, don't you remember?"

"So that's what that was all about. And I thought it was the oysters. So I'm reassured."

♦

J was home, lounging on the floor in front of the fireplace. He had just returned from a solitary backpacking trip in the Cascades. It was something of a test, to see just how bold the gangsters were. He had even been tempted to return to the actual scene of what he thought of as an inheritance, just to titillate them since he assumed the six-month life sentence was guaranteed. But caution kept him away. Why be suicidal?

He knew that he was under surveillance, and was certain that much of his life was monitored. Not everything. He knew that the COE was exaggerating there. The isolation of Olympic campus made it difficult for them to be aggressive here. He assumed, as the man said, this money was small potatoes. It was just a diversion to them. If it were a big deal he would have been caught long ago.

He felt confident that they had found no sign of hidden wealth in his records. In fact, rather the reverse, since he had cashed out everything to pay for the Tree except a basic living allotment.

On this trip back to the Cascades, he visited another nearby alpine meadow with golden aspens, camped under the stars and dodged bullets. Gunfire was a hazard that was refined in the cities, but had recently spread to the backcountry. Rival gangs, racial or militia, designated areas for a rumble and approached it as a war zone. Woe to the poor campers who were caught in the wrong place. The uibiquitous guns were just another worsening of life in the weakened culture created by conservative fears.

Fortunately, the gang members were easily recognized, and J, who routinely surveyed his environment, picked them up in his binoculars as they approached his area in the afternoon. A quick pack-up and the only problem was to find a route that did not encounter this gang or their rivals, who must be somewhere around.

Since his valley was an obvious destination, J consulted his topo map and found an escape route that was too tedious for a gang to use. Still, it was a nervous climb. An hour into the climb, gunfire erupted in the valley. Sounded like M16 automatics, the ubiquitous tool of tough teenagers these days. Millions left over from the military. Lots of bullets had been cached by the army, appropriated by the state's guard and now a good source of income for the underpaid and unmotivated defense forces.

It was a poor weapon to have in the mountains. But the stupidity of the uneducated, unemployable city-bred youths in the wilderness was a given. It actually was a reliable factor of use to those trying to practice civilization around them. It allowed J to safely evade them. Although J didn't know it, it also inadvertently allowed him to evade another two who had been stealthily following him.

Later that afternoon safely settled back in his small house at OC, he was tired and beat from bushwhacking unimproved trail back to his car and then enduring the long ferry ride across the Sound. He considered that this was an appropriate anniversary theme, as he realized that this would probably be his last trip into the Cascade Mountains. The Olympic Mountains were just too convenient. And if he didn't figure something out soon, he might not be hiking anywhere. Time was going to run out on the criminal COE's ultimatum. Two weeks were gone already. At times, he had nearly forgotten it. It just was a fact of life, evidently bigger than his life. The simple solution was to ignore it, and enjoy life, however much might be remaining.

To relive the excitement of the big event a decade ago, he retrieved from a hiding spot in the forest near his house the last of the stash of money that moved here with him. It was spread about him on the carpet. He was getting ready for a trip, and these last few hundred thousand dollars were going with him.

In fact, the found money had already been spent. This was money he had accumulated by cashing out his retirement fund. It took a bit of maneuvering to convert it all to the large bills that he required to secretly transfer it to the Swiss bank. He would leave no paper trails. He had made money from the sale of his house in Seattle. There was enough deposited in a local bank for a down payment on a house if he and Kay were to set up housekeeping. His salary would support them, and Kay had a good potential earning ability.

In fact there was a chunk of money here that he planned to give away to a population control institute. Just to help these intelligent people survive a little longer --- not because there was any chance their goals would ever be reached.

The phone rang. He hesitated to answer as if the intruder could see the carpet of cash. Even after all of these years he was still leery, probably provoked by the sight of the money. He picked up the phone.

"Hi there. I'm surprised that you're home. I thought you said that you were returning tomorrow, or late today at the earliest." It was Kay.

"I was, but it was just too crowded."

"Wish I could have gone with you but my general exam has me up against the wall. Any way I got the feeling that you were on some kind of a nostalgia trip. Glad to be alone. The Alpine Lakes region sure seems to have a special attraction for you."

"Yes, I feel richer each time I return from there." J reflected on one more thing that he had lost by taking the money — he had never returned to that most beautiful place.

"I missed you. When did you get back?"

"About an hour ago," J shaved an hour.

"I'll help you unpack. See you in a few minutes?"

"Sure. But give me fifteen to clean up a bit?"

"OK, but not necessary. I love you for your mind and it's not dirty is it?"

"And it doesn't get smelly either. Better wait thirty minutes so I can shower." He was asking for time to stash the money and collect his thoughts. If she should see a carpet covered with money she would have more questions than he was prepared to answer right now.

"You go right ahead; maybe I'll join you. Help you clean up."

"And help me get messed up again." He hung up. She was like that. It was probably subliminal, but if she sensed that you didn't want something, her curiosity was aroused and the point was mercilessly pursued. For some reason he wanted time. She lived in a graduate student apartment complex just a few blocks away from his small house. She would be here in less than ten minutes.

Grabbing a grocery bag he quickly threw the money in until it was full. Damn stuff expands. He always thought it shrunk. He got a plastic garbage sack, filled it and tossed it in the wood storage closet just as the bell rang. Nice touch, ringing the bell. She had a key. Guess she was influenced by his requests.

♦

Survival is the primary instinct. J knew that when survival was at stake the other carefully processed wishes and goals would be subservient. In the middle of this summer his survival instincts got seriously tweaked. He was eating lunch alone at the faculty club, preparing his lecture for the once a week seminar. A tray was loudly plunked down on the table and when J looked up he recognized the COE, or chief crook as he thought of him.

"Good morning. I'm slumming. I presume that your quixotic cocoon includes providing healthy food." The COE had a friendly smile.

"No pesticides, no chemicals, nothing to threaten your long healthy rule."

"Good attitude. I just had an itch to see your place and increase your discomfiture level. You're down to three months of life."

"I'd forgotten."

"Didn't the cash present remind you?"

"So that's what that was all about."

"You're cool. I confess if circumstances were different I would welcome you into our elite circle. Brains are our most important quality. Maybe it could be arranged if you were able to come clean?"

"Even if possible I wonder if I would want to join your god council. I can't even join Deman in his hedonistic panzaic plea. You are a level above, the plea squared."

"I understand that. I give you credit, you got to me with your calculus test. Made me realize that I do lack equals in conversation. Nobody challenges me."

"It's a hard life I'm sure. Want to hear my latest theory about why we might be more than merely the local top dog?"

They actually had a decent conversation for the next twenty minutes. Then J left for class and the COE for more comfortable surroundings. They would never meet again.

In hope to merit Heaven by making earth a Hell.

Lord Byron

"The light at the end of the tunnel may be a train".

Anon. 3.9

Ch. 3.11 A Long Trip

A few days later J was in Africa again. He had stopped in Switzerland and withdrawn money to finish paying for work on the Tree. He was on the hotel verandah listening to Wylie.

"It's finished. We spent the last week restoring the environment to very nearly natural. After the rains and the growing season it will be a hidden retreat. I'll never understand why you wanted to put so much money into such an obscure place. But it's your money." Wylie was a true believer in capitalism and the power and privileges of money.

J was pleased, satisfied, but mostly amazed that it had finally come to completion. "By now I assume many natives and other locals have been told of the project." He knew that this was unavoidable and he didn't really know what they would think.

"It's really surprising how few. You know how it is when you live in a town; you never get out to see the sights. There were a few wandering tribesmen but no one got too close. The word that there was an elaborate observation blind for a big scientific study that we were doing is widely believed. And we helped rumors spreading that it wasn't a good place to visit. Or more practically they might get shot.

"The ways of the outside world are mysterious and accepted as incomprehensible by the people around here anyway. They've endured many military regimes, but the global economic meltdown mystifies them. The new viruses are their main concern. Some are even concerned about the warming planet. One nice thing though, we're not bothered by terrorism here.

"Of course my crew is fascinated. More than one would love to rent the place. I put the rent so high that they won't ask again. In a few days they'll all be back in Seattle, fifteen thousand kilometers from here, busy with their daily lives. I really believe that the place will sit there undisturbed forever."

They had flown out to the site and checked the building. J felt he could trust Wylie, and never found reason to think otherwise. He had the high standards of honesty and counsel that most Homo sapiens aspire to but often fall short of attaining.

Everything functioned perfectly, smelled like any new house, and exceeded J's expectations. He had certainly been a hands-off manager. But in several long soul-to-soul meetings with Wylie at the Safari bar he had conveyed what he wanted. From what he could see Wylie had projected his needs perfectly. They returned to the hotel and enjoyed a celebration that evening.

The next day J boarded the same plane as Wylie and the construction crew. Many of the men hadn't been back to Seattle in a year and the mood was upbeat with anticipation. In London, many of them transferred to a direct flight to Seattle while a few stayed on to see the London sights for a day or two.

J had a meeting at the venerable Royal Society of Scientists. The accommodations were what J termed opulent and he enjoyed them during the week of the meeting. He expected that the syndicate had him marked at this meeting since his name was on the agenda and the round-trip to London. But he had concocted an elaborate untraceable route to Africa and they were likely fuming over his whereabouts for the past week.

There was something about the tradition and ambiance of the Society meeting rooms, tearooms, after dinner sherry rooms and libraries that always made J feel that perhaps Homo Sapiens was making the grade in intellectual attainments at least in this small pocket of civilization. But he knew that Great Britain had proved otherwise. For the second week of informal meetings he chose to move to a small hotel in Chelsea and rode the tube in order to keep a proper perspective.

◆

Somewhere in fundamentalist Afghanistan, the old man in a long pointed white beard sat in an elaborate cave, looking at the clock. He had just finished another video which took credit for yet another act of faith conforming to the fatwa to which he had devoted his life and fortune. He expected to be busy the next few days.

◆

The two longshoremen, apparently WASPs from Dixie, were up early operating the container ship crane. They swung the huge big-as-a-bus container out over the Sound and cut it loose. It dropped into the water and slowly began sinking. The pressure sensitive fuse awakened and blinked.

The two men dropped to their knees, faced Mecca, and prayed. They had the faith that they would soon join their friends, family and allotted virgins in paradise.

◆

It had been an uneventful trip for J and despite the comfort and camaraderie at the meeting he had finally left to get back to Seattle a day early. He called Kay and she indicated that she might be able to meet him at the airport. The plane had flown through the night and J had a difficult time sleeping in coach seats. He had just eaten breakfast and was staring out the window at the approach of dawn. They were finally over the Cascades, when everything changed.

The night was bathed in blinding white light. The plane continued for seconds as the light dimmed. Then the airplane moved as though an unseen force hurled it sideways. The pilot had seen the flash and banked away from the epicenter so that the shock wave hit the underside of the plane. It was pure luck that after violent pitching, yawing and diving, the pilot was able to regain control, pulling out of the dive, heading south.

During all of this there was no noise except the protest of metal straining against stress limits and air turbulence buffeting the lifting surfaces as no engineer had ever dreamed. But the conservative safety factors built into the design kept the wings attached.

Even when the immediate danger seemed to be over the plane was deathly still. Most of them had recognized the flash as that of a nuclear explosion. The shock and turbulence had punctuated it. Now they were thinking about Seattle, the people waiting for them at the airport, their homes, and their lives.

Given the steady increase in terrorism and threats during the past decades no one doubted what had happened. A thermonuclear bomb had obliterated Seattle. The script had been presented in movies and magazines, the plutonium had become available and the instructions were on the net. The threats had been gathering from self-righteous religious groups to desperately harassed nations. The only question was where they would strike.

The answer appeared to be Seattle. Just a demonstration. On an unimportant, medium-populated, beautiful city. J assumed it was from a device in a basement or on a ship in the harbor.

When the plane landed in Portland J went directly to the TV lounge. The news established his worst fears; the device was probably on a ship docked in Seattle. The city was mostly obliterated along with towns bordering the Sound and the area between the Sound and the mountains on both sides. The Olympic peninsula was not spared the blast as J watched the local TV show views from satellites and planes circling twenty miles away. It looked bad for the OC campus; it was only fifty miles from the harbor. Worse, Kay might have been at the airport to meet him, and that was just two miles from the harbor. At least it would have been quick.

His impulse was to go and check. To be absolutely certain that Kay hadn't miraculously survived. But he knew well that radioactivity from the fallout and the radioactive rain that followed a water blast would be fatal to anyone venturing near Seattle for weeks. Still, his anguish told him to go anyway; if she survived the blast they might have a few weeks together. He was only a few hundred miles away.

J sat down in a corner paralyzed into inaction. Slowly he let the emotional imperatives ebb. His education was about this. What was the meaning of his life? What would Deman say? His vexing, challenging, entertaining arguments would be sorely missed. Dead now, he would have been pleased at the proof of his own meaningless — but enjoyable — existence. J knew there would be a huge gap without the counterpoints to his quixotic speculations provided by Deman. Left alone now with his idealistic conjectures would they lose their edge? He was inclined to yield this, their last contentious dichotomy, to Deman. Deprived in an instant of several channels to the future, at this moment he felt that life had no meaning.

What would Peter have said? Dead now, he would have said that for him, the quest for meaning was over, and that his far-out wager on an interested God would be resolved. J knew that Peter would also have provided him with a cliché, 'Where there's Life, there's Hope.' He extrapolated: 'Where there's no life, there's no hope'.

What would he do without Kay? This question J couldn't even begin to contemplate. He couldn't accept that she was dead. He would have difficulty saying that life without her had meaning. He couldn't know the answer but he did know that when he died the question became moot. The dead don't propagate, progeny or ideas.

He donned his stoic mantle. Once again fate had decreed that his life would take a violent turn. The quixotic dreams were over. There would be no Cultural Revolution emanating from OC. No house and family with Kay. No Kay.

His frivolous panzaic plans were pertinent. The Tree would be a refuge. But the pain of not anticipating and not moving in time to save Kay was draining his entire body. It was just yesterday that he had talked to her, too briefly, from London.

He thought of his son who lived in Seattle and his friends at OC. At least his daughter was away at a college in the east. He got up slowly. His instinct now was to flee. Only then did he think of the COE. Ah well, he thought, it's an ill Armageddon that bears no good.

He walked to the counter to get the fastest route to Arusha. There was nothing to buy, nothing to take, nothing to think. The clerk booked him with a blank disinterested attitude. Her thoughts, like those of many others, were on other things. The full one-way first-class fare to Europe was automatically charged to his credit card. It didn't bother him that he knew that he would never pay it.

The planes were loading as usual yet most people were relatively speechless. Everyone was silently relieved to be winging away from this horror visited on Seattle. J tried to get some sleep, but wasn't successful.

The airport in Frankfort was just as it always was. One couldn't tell from the look on any faces, from anyone's demeanor, from the clerk's litany of questions and ticketing, not even from the newspapers, that a major city in the USA had just disappeared. J wondered if this was going to become de rigueur for the society. Would the world go on as before just minus one large city? It reminded him of the casual doe-eyed innocence of the Canadian seal pups even as the sealers moved amongst them clubbing them to death. Perhaps civilization will just accept the new level of violence and write off a city here and there like it had done with tall buildings and stadiums --- the new equilibrium.

Right now J's pain was so great that he really didn't care. As the flight crossed the Mediterranean J thought about the preparations he had made even in the midst of living the greatest quixotic adventure. Cynicism wins again.

He wondered if there was a point where the downward spiral could have been stopped. It seemed like the deterioration of the American culture slowly accelerated with no obvious single event. There were the trials that revealed the country's cultural and racial schisms. Then the reaction from the whites produced even stronger right-wing victories in elections. There was the slow but certain extension of the power and excesses of the super-rich.

Then there was the intrusion of church into state. From the impeachment by the troglodytes, a hijacked election made secure by the terrorists' attack on New York, discarding the nuclear weapons treaty and safeguards of Russian bombs, the wars and economic debacle and then the States' revolution. There just wasn't a definitive point where people could stand up and scream 'enough'.

This terrorist bomb was a blind-side blow. Even though it was not totally unexpected — J had anticipated it for twenty years without it happening anywhere in the world. The likelihood had receded to the background of his mind with the emergence of other crises in USA cultural and political decay. Had he actually forgotten it? He cursed his carelessness. He lost Kay. He, and the world, also lost the OC dream, but at the moment that barely counted to him in comparison. He would miss his friends and family and future.

The tree was finished and secure. He reflected on the last minute remodeling for a second person who had just been vaporized. His intentions were to go there whenever the danger level grew high. But the danger level from a terrorist bomb had always been significant. Why did it have to be his city?

The television news in the European airport had just been reporting a 'major explosion' in the USA city of Seattle. No other reports. Just bad luck. Terrorists from a major religion had announced that it was a 'demonstration' and there followed a long list of demands for USA concessions to avoid the same fate for another city. It was claimed that a bomb lay hidden in a basement of every major city. At the same time several Arabic groups and a representative of Korea and even the newly belligerent China had hinted at the same process if their demands were not accommodated. Many groups apparently wanted 'credit'.

J wondered what the leaders who had built the 'impregnable' anti-missile shield were thinking now. It had always been a thinly disguised folly, a modern Maginot Line, a fop for the military-industrial complex. Now they were paying the price. J mused; they probably would never get elected or funded again.

Everything was routine on this flight. He looked down at Lake Victoria; saw huge flocks of birds flying low. Africa was the same. J thought that it was possible that most of the world would be the same. But he didn't want any more to do with it. At least on the grand scale. He would embrace the Panzaic Plea. Survive as comfortably as possible from day to day. Tend his garden. Probably Africa would be in the backwater of this latest Homo Sap convulsion whatever its extent.

J didn't know it, but his haste to get to Africa was necessary. In fact his plane was the last commercial airline flight into Arusha.

Part IV
At the Tree

Our revels now are ended. These our actors,
As I foretold you, were all spirits, and
Are melted into air, into thin air.
And, like the baseless fabric of this vision,
The cloud-capped towers, the gorgeous palaces,
The solemn temples, the great globe itself,
Yea, all which it inherit, shall dissolve
And like this insubstantial pageant faded,
Leave not a rack behind. We are such stuff
As dreams are made on, and our little life
Is rounded with a sleep....

Shakespeare, *The Tempest*

Ch 4.1 State of the world

J was in the top study, reading a log of his years in the Tree. The entries began barely a week after the annihilation of Seattle; a week before a similar fate took New York.

He had the best in high fidelity short-wave equipment, and listened to the news as the world unraveled. He listened non-stop at first, for it was like a play unfolding. Confusion was the only common theme.

Accusations could barely keep up with strident proclamations, claiming 'credit' for obliterating millions of people. The list of cities destroyed for 'demonstration' grew month by month. They were mainly in the Western world, a reverse Crusades. The USA's expensive 'Star Wars' defense was a non-factor. The 'shield' was totally irrelevant against the ship or basement bombs. As Deman would have said, they're fighting the last war; too bad they didn't read military history.

He listened to the news reports as one by one the world's great cities faltered and fell. It was the ultimate reality show. Retaliation was the byword. The infirmity of civilization was laid bare, as it became evident that a few individuals inspired by religious zeal could destroy the infrastructure and then the culture of the so-called 'advanced' societies. The basic struggle was set up over a thousand years of East-West conflict. The Middle East was fueled by an aggressive faith-based righteousness, similar to the USA fundamentalists, but even more dominant in the culture. The turn-of-the-century change in USA culture and policy lit the fuse to an accelerating breakdown. The true believers, branded terrorists in the West, started with bombs in cars and trucks, moved on to use hijacked airliners and private planes and finally to the implanted nuclear bombs. Their advantage was to use 'smart' bombs, controlled by an individual 'martyr' convinced his or her death would send them to a glorious heaven.

There were few nuclear weapons available to the terrorist societies, certainly compared to the thousands still in the West's arsenals. However other weapons were available to small groups with limited resources. A vial of anthrax could be deposited at a high-rise air-conditioning intake and kill everyone in the building. J heard reports that Tokyo, Baghdad and Jerusalem fell to germs distributed by a few cars driving around town, possibly from a deposit in their gas tank. Tight border controls had protected these cities from the bombs, but nothing could detect the germs that were being smuggled in. As the medical infrastructure broke down, the susceptibility to disease exploded. By the time Paris was abandoned to the products of several small dirty bombs placed by a group of well-funded Algerian fanatics, J was inured to the violence. It was the depressing realization of the failure of Homo Sap's attempt at civilization. Obviously, society was too fragile to shield against the fools fueled by fantasy religions and barbarian swords, germs and dangerous technology.

The dramatic events were the nuclear bombs. The frustrated West — the USA and Europe — apparently had no bombs on foreign soil, naively playing 'by the rules'. Finally they unleashed their military and their bombs to punish the many for the sins of the few. One rule, a spin-off of Mutually Assured Destruction was enacted when the fissionable material in the Seattle bomb was identified as produced in the North Korea reactor and the promised three nuclear bombs per city were sent. The "more civilized" West gave 24-hours notice to residents, reminding them that this was "the deal" since they decided to join the nuclear weapon 'club'. Middle East cities were obliterated, from Riyadh to Jakarta, as the western world blamed the region. Iran, with its in-your-face clandestine nuclear policy that truly 'Let the Genie out of the bottle" suffered hundreds of vindictive nuclear strikes. Simultaneously, kooks everywhere unleashed their petty but potent arsenals to vent their frustrations large and small, and often, just because they could.

It became apparent that one of the main frailties of modern civilization was its dependence on electricity. There was no food preservation, no communications, no computer dependent services — fundamental accoutrements of society didn't work. When this source of energy was

eliminated for a city or region, it soon succumbed to anarchy. The higher
the societal structure the harder it fell. The nuclear blasts killed a small
percentage of the people, but the decay from the destruction of the
infrastructure led to the deaths of a majority from starvation, disease,
accident, and violence.

The USA seemed to succumb within months, having gotten an early
start on infrastructural and cultural degeneracy. The USA had shot its wad
on high-tech armament and spurious wars and had been weakened as the
new century unraveled. This global agony was a largely low-tech, drawn
out affair. Nevertheless, it was pretty thorough. J thought about trying to
contact his daughter; he tried to call on the satellite phone. But there was
no answer, no answering machine even. He recalled the shock he felt when
he heard her city had been obliterated.

Later, 'fortress Europe', which had taken over the economic and
cultural leadership of the Western world, lost out during the last battle
between Eastern Islam and Western Christianity. The porous borders
of the expanded common market and the egalitarian philosophy made
it easy prey for the terrorists. At the same time, as though not to waste
them, their nuclear arsenal rained revenge on the assumed homelands of
the terrorists.

Around the world, religious zealot and militia often welcomed the
Armageddon they had predicted; and caused. It was as if human society
was a long, exciting play that peaked and then wound down slowly in
a series of anti-climaxes. Finally it went out not with a bang, but with
a whimper. There was no sudden extinction, but over a year or two,
civilization sort of winked out.

Those with generators, fuel, and some measure of security stayed on
the airwaves to report the sorry state. Although there were many of these,
the news was sad, repetitive, and depressing. Most of the time the news
wailed intermittently over the speakers in the workrooms at the Tree to
empty space. J never bothered to turn it off, but often retreated to the quiet
of a bedroom or study.

He listened closely for several days after a huge flash came from
the direction of the coastal city of Mombasa a few hundred kilometers
away. Apparently some African military regimes had been responsible
for a Western city or two, and retaliation by roaming submarines was
thorough.

After a few years, there was mostly silence, and J would stop to listen
if a human voice came on the air, since it would be a singular pocket of

survival. The one clear signal that continued the longest was from the space station. This group of people was doomed and they knew it after the first few months. They established an almost detached attitude, reporting to earth what they saw for any future civilization that might develop. This was the source of much of J's knowledge about the slow degeneration of the species around the globe.

They told how the belt of lights that circled the globe marking civilization soon dissolved into blackness. With their powerful telescopes they could see pockets of civilization but were forced to describe their catholic decay. They eventually got angry, and as their supplies gave out, could be heard to curse the mother civilization that had abandoned them.

There did not appear to be any organization to the chaos left on earth. The remaining pockets of civilization were besieged by biological demons, from man-enhanced anthrax to the natural diseases run amok. As the backup sources of electricity disappeared, the transmissions did too, and one day, as he walked by, J turned the silent set off.

Sitting in the Tree fort, watching Gaia perform a cleansing was in a strange way almost sadly satisfying. It was painful mainly for his species; but a form of catharsis for the rest of life on this planet. When people had said to J, Armageddon is coming, he had answered that he hoped that he would be around to see it. He was. But the numbing pain of his total losses in the first salvo had anesthetized him. He looked for signs of a nuclear winter, and the skies were full of soot for weeks, but then they cleared. Some agriculture would probably survive. There were some spectacular sunrises and sunsets.

He had never considered what was next. The desire to return to Seattle and search for Kay was strong and he considered it often. But the obstacles were overwhelming. World travel had been the first victim of the terrorist era. Now it was nonexistent. Although he felt he could manage it with his resources, he knew that logically the chances of finding Kay were nil. He felt a profound loneliness. All he could do was relax in his fortress, read and exist. Someday, when things settled down, he might return to Seattle. Years passed.

Life had become simple. No more family or friends. His credit and his creditors had vanished, along with the Swiss bank. There was nothing to fear from the mobster Czar. He had mixed feelings about the fact that the builders of the tree were all gone in the Seattle maelstrom. Some were good friends. But callous as the thought was, he realized that the secret of the tree was safe in a very dangerous world. Fate had decreed the Tree's security.

It was pointless to wonder about the cause. The greatest perturbations on human history were probably the assassinations. A simpleton can change history. This was a fact that all leaders worked to keep secret. So it came to be that a relatively small cadre of clever but woefully miss-educated Homo Sap with the aid of a small army of fools brought about civilization's demise.

Pockets of people persevered around the globe. As far as J could detect, much of Africa was the same as ever. The cities were the targets; where the germs proliferated.

The veneer of civilization was stripped and Don Quixotes were the first to vanish. The militant survivors, the sundry other paranoid groups, including the Sancho Panzas — truly a motley group — had hidden out. Those who survived, quietly, carefully emerged.

♦

As J finished dressing he looked like a hunter, in camouflaged Gore-Tex, leather broad brimmed hat, numerous instruments clipped to his belt with several more in the many pockets, and the essential high-powered rifle. He stacked the rifle and binoculars on the stairs and continued up to the top floor, dropping the wine off at the kitchen. Stairs pulled down from the ceiling of the observation room and a panel opened in the roof.

The lookout was a balcony, with a rampart that was about a meter and a half high. It wasn't a uniform circle, as tree branches emanated from all sides, subtly pruned so they didn't block the view. Some were real, some coated steel, and a few were substantial. From here, it appeared that J was definitely living in a tree house. The top level afforded a view in every direction.

He was in the perfect place. Homo sapiens wasn't the dominant player here. There were other mammals, the birds – which he saw as dinosaurs hiding out, biding their time, while enjoying their mastery of the third dimension; the insects, probably bacteria; hopefully not too many unfriendly viruses; and maybe more hidden life forms. These were the significant actors in this huge playhouse.

The corridor between the sea and Lake Victoria along the Kenya-Tanzania border was the archetypal Africa. It was always a fantastic place to visit, certainly if primordial pre-Homo sapiens milieu was your interest.

There was much more to see the farther out one traveled from the centrally located Tree. There were the forests and the possibility of a few remaining primates near Lake Tanganyika to the Southwest. Not the gorilla, of course — they had vanished forever a decade ago, soon followed by their executioners, the renegade Hutus. Tanzania was the home of the ivory mafia that was responsible for the near extinction of the elephants. They were on the brink for awhile, but the near extinction of mankind and thus the poachers changed the odds.

There were the geological wonders of the Great Rift Valley to the north where the Indian Ocean was invading the horn of Africa in a flanking maneuver. To the east the plains gently dropped five thousand feet in the four hundred kilometer distance to the coast. His location was in north central Tanzania. He thought of it as Gaia's Oasis, perhaps the cradle of humanity. A string of national parks and reserves had been established along the Tanzania-Kenya border for over a century. Within the seven hundred kilometer swath between the Indian Ocean and Lake Victoria, life still evolved, speciated, and disappeared. Here were the Ngorongoro Crater, the Serengeti, the Masai Mara Reserve, Amboseli Park, Tsavo Park, Mzima Springs and the centerpiece, Mt. Kilimanjaro.

J could explore the surrounds for hundreds of kilometers during 'vacations' to remote campsites. He had an ultralight aircraft and a hybrid Range Rover. It was his second car. The first had been stolen the first time he used it. He hadn't taken enough care selecting its hiding place on a sojourn to Arusha, the nearest town to the South. This misadventure had entailed a long walk home less a few valuable essentials. All except his gun. He was never without a gun. Times had changed.

He obtained the new Rover on a long hike to Mzima Springs, a magnet that attracted thousands of animals from the surrounding semi-arid bush country. It was sitting in the maintenance garage. He was pleased that it was a hybrid, but it wouldn't start when he put in a new battery. Probably why it was still there. He scrounged spare parts from another abandoned Rover nearby. When he replaced the starter it worked perfectly. J enjoyed an easy return home.

It was the best way to go great distances, and by far the safest. Gasoline was the main limitation. He had a supply that he was rationing. He could pump out an abandoned vehicle's tanks. But these were turning up empty more often than not these days.

By now he had trekked to all of the corridor parks. He had baked in the hot plains' sun, frozen in the snows of Kilimanjaro, and scuba-dived carefully with the hippos at Mzima Springs.

Before him there were plains, golden grass or scrub brush in nearly every direction. There were islands of rock and trees spotted randomly on the plain like a broken necklace of emeralds fallen on a beige carpet. To the east, the river continued on from his pond, at first underground in the gentle slope of the first kilometer then touching the surface, following the contour of the land south of the big mountain. Here, a line of trees, one or two as high as J's home, marked the river. It continued in a sinuous path toward the sea.

Streams fed the river from the flanks of Kilimanjaro before it curved northward to skirt the Southern border of the Tsavo national park. East of the mountain was Mzima Springs. On the coast was Mombasa, an ancient port surviving one of the retaliatory bombs.

The land to the west of the tree was full of history and life. Drought-prone areas were interspersed with productive Edens. Lake Manyara National Park – a watery paradise; Ngorongoro Crater – a ten mile bowl of fantastic wildlife; Olduvai Gorge – the fossil hunter's heaven; and across the fabulous Serengeti Plain was beautiful Lake Victoria. J's longest trek, six weeks last year, had taken him to the western edge of the Serengeti then north and back through Masai land and a reconnoiter of Nairobi.

Dear friend, theory is all gray,
And the golden tree of life is green.

Johann Wolfgang von Goethe (1749–1832)
German poet, playwright, and scientist.
Faust (1808).

Ch 4.2 J's World

Careful planning was necessary before sojourning from the Tree. On the first distant flight he had taken, planning to go to Mzima Springs, shots had rung out beneath him on the way out. He evasively turned and decided to abort that trip even before he noticed the hole in his fuel tank. The plane flew well and he put thirty kilometers between him and the source of the shots before he gently landed on a grassy slope. He plugged the leak with the cork from a wine bottle that he was forced to drink by his innate frugality and to calm his nerves.

A tense night was spent listening to roaming hyenas. The next day, he exhausted the fuel a few kilometers short of the home hanger. The baked plain made for a safe landing, and the Tree was walking distance. When he got time to look, there were two more holes in the wings. This kind of exploration had to wait.

Now, after a pause of over a year he was flying again, headed north. Beneath him the reliable sun baked the Serengeti. The seared thirsty grass of the plain merged yellow into brown as it gave way to the parched soil of the gorges that bordered the vast flatland. As the plane moved farther north, the colors moved too, to the greens of photosynthesis. The bowl below him looked to be full of pea soup with dark green broccoli clumps randomly scattered. This was fertile farmland, and the white settlers had brought farming and fences to the area. The wild animals had been pushed south. Now, the native fauna was busy reclaiming the productive niche below.

The people-dependent cattle had all fallen victim to the big cats and hyenas. This must have contributed to the explosion in predator population and now that the cattle were gone there were excess predators. It was not safe for a weak mammal to be walking or camping on this crowded bush land.

This morning a series of miscues provoked carelessness and he had gotten a late start. Now as the sky was turning red, he nervously looked for a safe area to land and spend the night. He was nearly to the Lake when looming darkness finally forced him to choose a barely qualified landing place. The herd animals scattered as he landed, and he taxied to a rock outcrop to seek a defensible position for the night.

After surrounding the aircraft with trigger wires, he cleared a platform against rock with an overhang forming some shelter. There was wood to gather and booby traps to place strategically. He saw several lions roaming the bush as it fell away from his camp. In his love-hate relationship with guns this moment saw him fondly cradling his 30-06 in his arms. He half sat, watching his aircraft — his only means to return to the tree without a formidable hike.

An hour after he dozed off, small rocks clattered to the ground just beyond his feet. When he looked up, he looked into the face of a lion, peering over the edge. J's reflexes ruled, and he blew the beast away just as it started to drop to his ledge. He hated killing the animals. But here, he had no choice. There were obviously too many of them anyway.

Lions apparently had more brains than sharks. There was no feeding frenzy with the bloody body spread out near his camp. They weren't interested in the aircraft as the trip wires and alarms were avoided. But he couldn't move to the plane — it was too flimsy a fort. So he sat in the vulnerable half-cave through the night, with no more temptations to sleep. He reflected on how his ancestors had done this and was sobered at the fear he would feel without the guns.

The first rays of light galvanized J into action. He would get out of here before the morning hunts. The motor started instantly befitting its immaculate maintenance schedule. The propeller noise barely kept the animals away enough for J to drive slowly around looking for a take-off strip. He regretted the strategy that had made the engine ultra-quiet for stealth.

He found a narrow runway that opened before him as he headed toward a zebra herd and never felt better at lifting off. He decided to cut this trip short and head back toward the relative wasteland to the southeast where the harsher land supported fewer animals. In the south, he was seldom challenged during his night's sleep.

◆

The tree's location: (**Colored map doesn't appear in the electronic version.**)

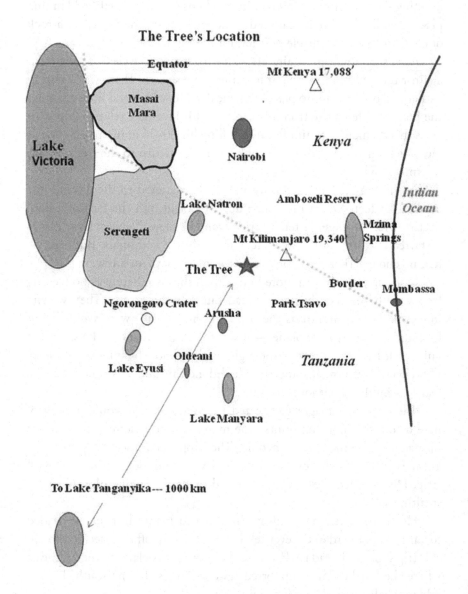

The Tree's Location

Ch 4.3 Events with Natives

J had occasional visitors to the Tree's oasis during the first few years. Mostly he just observed them. But there was some interaction.

One day J was working out in the gym when a proximity alarm sounded. He assumed that there were animal visitors to the pond, so he finished his workout before moving upstairs to investigate. When he finally looked through the lowest level porthole prior to moving upstairs to open the large window, he blinked fast. Only because he knew that he was looking through a wide angle viewer did he not panic at the face a meter in front of him.

The sound insulation was excellent, yet he tip-toed up the stairs to where he could open slits to get a better view. What he saw gave him chills. It was a real test of the defenses of the Tree.

About a dozen natives were milling about. This time they were evidently focused on the Tree, pointing upward and discussing branches. J wondered if there was someone already up on the Tree. The lookout deck was not hidden to anyone who managed to climb to that level, although the trapdoor to the interior was artfully disguised as part of the floor pattern.

His remote monitors showed no one on the Tree. He returned to look more closely at his visitors. He recognized them as Masai or closely related by their hair-do, the pierced ears, imposing stature, and general good looks. He carefully studied their dress and tattoos. They had visited the waterhole before, but never with a flicker of interest in the Tree.

For the next hour J watched the group as they explored his area. Fortunately the lion's grunt was deactivated — this would not fool this group for long. The Masai coming of age ritual was killing a lion.

Eventually one warrior climbed the Tree, discovering the lookout. Soon all were up there, and apparently very appreciative. J was worried that this would become a favorite picnic spot, as they dug out their lunch and settled in. He watched them over the surveillance monitor and was particularly alarmed when one of them climbed up a branch and exclaimed over the evidence of a year old pruning cut that J had made. He had not taken his usual procedure to disguise it up here. Finally, as late afternoon approached, they departed to the north. J was relieved, but knew that they would return.

He spent the next two days in his library, researching the local tribes. He located the specific group that had visited him, and read their tribal religion and customs with great interest. He learned all he needed to know about how these intruders thought. The Masai worshipped the lion. There was a formula for control of the Masai in the chronicle of their history and religion. J took note.

He worked for a week preparing for their return. He had to wire a backup generator into tandem with the main line. He had an electronic shop stocked with basic parts and many gadgets that he had yet to study. The technology for lasers and holograms was in his books. When they returned two weeks later, he was ready.

They appeared in the afternoon. He saw them approaching kilometers away. They apparently had no reason to fear the site, and possibly were intent on making it an away-station for hunting parties. They were carrying several large bundles.

When they reached the outer edge of the oasis, he switched the program into action. The natives stopped their festive chatter as one shouted something that J did not completely understand but he figured meant "The lion in the sky."

The native was pointing into a space between the central baobab and another tree. The hologram lion was focused here. It seemed to look at the dozen warriors, and snarled. Simultaneously, it said, in laboriously learned native Masai, "Do not flee. Look at me." In addition to their reverence for the lion, J had read that the natives assigned supernatural powers to the baobab tree. His intention was to elaborate on this religion.

The natives all obeyed. The leader was not afraid, even of a lion floating in the trees. He set the tone, and those who would flee, couldn't. They looked at the lion.

J watched for this reaction, and when they were all looking at the lion hologram, he pushed the button for the laser. A simple CO_2 coherent light, bright enough to blind anyone looking into it.

The natives were screaming at the effects of the bright red light. The lion voice said, "You have trespassed on my sanctuary. Go and warn others."

They were stunned. They weren't in much pain except for smarting eyes, and the inability to see imparted great fear. But the leader was sturdy, and after ascertaining that all were similarly stricken, gathered them together in an elephant parade, holding hands. Stumbling, they began the long difficult journey home.

J felt sadness at the violence he had done. The literature said that the blindness would be long lasting but possibly not permanent. He couldn't be certain. His survival was at stake and the Panzaic action was clear. The ruse was successful, and he never saw anyone from that region of Kenya again.

..

In the second year he had a close encounter with termination.

He had just returned from a morning hike, by now routine for him. He approached his entrance as usual, and only passively heard the recording of the hunting lion. As he fished in his pocket for the key, awareness flushed over him like a hot flash. The recording was not nearly this long. It was being supplemented, apparently by the real thing.

He barely had time to turn and raise the tranquilizing rifle to his shoulder when the lion leapt at him from meters away. Why, on this day of all others, had he elected to carry only the tranquilizing rifle? His shot was perfect; a little dart of serum entered the lion's mouth. But only the barrel of the rifle thrust between the lion's teeth kept him from a fatal bite. As they clashed, the lion was thrust to the side by the lever between J's shoulder and its tonsils. The lion violently shook its head and pawed at its mouth to flick out the annoying dart. They then eyed each other.

J had a claw rip in his shoulder, and felt dizzy as he faced his opponent. A long minute passed, the lion apparently puzzled at the strange injuries, small but aggravating. J was simply staring; he could not figure a thing to do. He passed out. Seconds later the lion did the same.

J awoke in a smoky, black enclosure. His shoulder was encased in leaves and bark. His only pain was local to the shoulder. As his eyes adjusted, he saw that there was light from a small slit in the side of the conical tent that surrounded him like a small cocoon. It revealed a native woman now looking at her awakened patient with alarm. She motioned for him to lie down, and brushed the doorway covering aside as she fled. He lay back, gathered his wits and was ready to meet the next visitor.

Very soon, a wizened native appeared in the doorway. He was tall, lacked the body piercing prevalent in these societies, but bore the leopard hood that J recognized as belonging to the Shaman. As he drew near, intently peering into J's eyes, his advanced age became apparent. Not many lived long enough to get the dominant gray in his evidently infrequently trimmed stubble of a beard. J was trying to figure what words he knew of the local languages that he had been studying when he was startled by the man's greeting.

"How you doing?"

Only raised eyebrows betrayed J's surprise. "I'm glad to be alive. But really puzzled."

"I'm Fleur, your local witch doctor. Who are you?"

"I'm J." And he couldn't add a descriptive term — what was he, the local recluse? "I really would like to know how I got here before we discuss anything else."

Fleur happily explained J's recent history. He had 'happened' on him and the lion, which he had been following hoping to scavenge some meat. He had dispatched the lion, still unconscious, with J's Bowie knife. He ministered to J, made him comfortable, covered them both with grass to hide them from the vultures, and then ran to summon aide from his tribe. That night they arrived and the next morning transported the live and dead carcasses to the village several dozen kilometers to the southwest.

As implausible as all of this sounded to J, he was in no position to argue. He went back to sleep.

Fleur's ministrations worked well and within two days J felt like walking around. He found that he was viewed with awe, since Fleur had simply told everyone that he found the lion dead and J wounded. To kill a lion in hand to hand combat definitely placed one in an elevated social standing in the tribe.

J found Fleur to be a lively and capable intellect. They got along well enough that after a few days, J felt confident enough to question Fleur frankly about how and why he was at the Tree so conveniently. Fleur was guileless and told J that when the lion he was following led him to the Tree, he was doubly interested.

He had heard rumors of the solitary white man, had observed him in his excursions more than once, and knew of the extensive activities years ago in this area. That was all he knew, and furthermore was extremely puzzled as to where J lived.

Reassured that Fleur was no threat, J asked to hear about him. He was astounded to learn that Fleur was educated at the University at Berkeley. His father had been the Shaman and he sent his heir to get the best knowledge available from the white man who dominated the earth, and more pertinently, their local world. Fleur had learned English at the Missionary school in Nairobi. Knowledge to a Shaman's son was probably more revered than it was to most sons in the West.

Fleur had chosen Berkeley for its reputation of liberal acceptance of diverse people, a trait bound to be important to a black foreigner with an offbeat education. Also, he got a scholarship.

"Two years of classes decades ago, including astronomy, meteorology, botany, biology and sex education was all I needed for a lifetime as the Shaman." Fleur spoke simply, with an expressionless stare at the recipient of his words. Only the disguised humor, irony and sarcasm revealed the intellect beneath the native appearance. "I was at the place of the birth of the Free Speech movement, the igniter of the wave of student activism that eventually toppled a president, then freed up students around the world.

"But my research showed a banal birth, involving the right to say 'shit' and 'fuck' in speeches on campus. The University administration, with several Peter Principled potentates, seemed to be quite reasonable in their requirements." Fleur loved the concept of bureaucrats who rise to their 'level of incompetence'. "OK, they said, preach your foul-mouthed sermons, just not on campus. A few meters away is fine. They even set up a speaker's stand just outside the gate to campus. But the movement's leader, a local charismatic power monger, knew the value of confrontation, and after maneuvering the bureaucrats into drawing a line, he immediately jumped over it. They had to react with an edict, and they created a martyr; made a movement. We know all about that procedure, here in the scrub. It's part of our education here, too.

"Fortunately, the less charismatic but more thoughtful group of students who were against the USA involvement in the Vietnam war used this vehicle to promulgate their message. It was the simple message born of the critical thinking atmosphere at Berkeley: 'We don't understand the culture, the land, or the reasons for the war. We do understand that whatever we do, win or lose, we'll end up broke and hated.' Too bad your country forgot these lessons in Iraq, Iran, Syria, South America, Somalia, Lebanon and Afghanistan."

J was astounded to find this pocket of intelligence in the scrub. "You must have found it frustrating."

"No. I loved it. I had no grand expectations. I watched with intensity, even contributed to the theory, based on my own understanding — or lack thereof — of the USA culture. I mean it works both ways — other cultures find it impossible to understand the USA way of life. My self-confidence was bolstered by an intense awareness of the total inability of my USA friends to understand my culture. That I was getting an education to go back to my jungle home and be a Shaman just blew their minds. But I didn't have to understand it. I just knew where I was happiest. I also knew that they weren't exactly happy with their culture. And my culture was doing fine in Africa. We had come to terms with our limitations and accommodated them well. Until your well-funded consumerism invaded us and it was all downhill afterwards."

J smiled, "It would have blown my mind, too, at that time. Now, I understand you. Your decision was intuitive Panza. You're lucky to be free of the Western devils, greed and power."

"You mean Sancho. I thought that he didn't think too much."

"Maybe too much credit is given to thinking."

"I know Shakesphere thought deeply, and he loved his Falstaff."

"And Cumus has his Sisyphus."

"Wow, he's everywhere --- I liked the Good Soldier Sweik!. Maybe you're right. I certainly don't entertain lofty goals for myself, or my species. I'm not free of the devils; just have them controlled. I sometimes think that I'm like Siddhartha. Look, we know from my experience with African culture developed over thousands, maybe millions of years, and US culture developed over 200 years plus borrowing another 200 from the Europeans; they are failures. Mankind seeks disaster. Why would anyone bet on survival? We can enjoy the moment, because there is no eternity. We're doing that here. It is the best that we, the limited species, can do. Once you understand that, you can relax and appreciate what you have. I've had a good 60-years and am hoping for another 10 or 20, even while the global species is self destructing."

J thought he saw Panza in Fleur's smile.

♦

As J got better, he appreciated the care of the woman assigned to this task more and more. She seemed to enjoy her job more and more. On one particularly cold day, J awoke to find her naked in bed with him, 'to provide warmth'. She was asleep, but not for long. J was well enough to appreciate this long lost function. Later, he asked Fleur if the woman's cohabitation with him would affect her status in the tribe. Would she be cast out as she would in many societies from the Greeks to the Geeks in the USA turn of the century dark ages?

Fluer's grimace suggested disgust. "Of course not. We don't hold anything against you unless you're hurting someone else. For Pete's sake, this is where much of human pleasure arises. We are moderate in our sexual activity so that it doesn't interfere with our contribution to society. But whatever two consenting people choose to do, we accept that as their choice. Even in our limited sample, some choose monogamy, some polygamy, several bounce between the two — we have bisexuals and gays too.

"The point is; we're all kind of schizophrenic on this. We recognize some of our actions arise from our instincts, some from our thought processes. By looking around at various cultures, notably yours, we know which instincts cause the most trouble in a society. We decided that instincts like territoriality and power are the really bad ones. They make some try to control the pleasurable ones in order to gain power. That's where the concepts of sin and race and class distinctions come from. These are the instincts that we really work to control. Of course the secret is simple: start by controlling your numbers. You see; I didn't sleep through all my classes."

A week later, J told Fleur that he was well enough to return home. He had established a firm friendship with Fleur. J realized a special pleasure in talking to another human after years of silence. He told Fleur that he would return to visit in the fall. He figured that a twice a year fix would be sufficient.

Also, a few of the native women were looking good to him, particularly his nurse, and he wasn't ready to go in that direction just now. Fleur had even hinted that J needed a woman, and he would be glad to help in the selection. There followed a discussion that revealed to J the truth in Fleur's assertions about the dichotomy in cultures.

"Here, in darkest Africa, the woman is lucky to be what she wants to be, what her genes tell her to be. Isn't it obvious that the man is designed by his genes to run, throw, hunt and protect his turf? The woman is designed by her genes to bear children, nurture, and work toward a stable environment. This I learned in one semester of biology.

"Oh, I know this is the solution designed by evolution to produce the best chance of survival, nothing more. We accept that there are variations in hormones that make some women great at men things and some men good at woman's things. Here, we don't force it. We 'go with the flow', and admit the occasional woman warrior or male nanny. No biggee.

"Now you just specify what balance of hormonal influence you feel comfortable with and I'll choose a woman." Fleur smiled seriously. Like J, he loved to provoke a person into thinking big thoughts.

J could not argue with this logic. It was essential Panza. He marveled at his good fortune in meeting another human like Peter with these gifts.

Nevertheless, J returned to the Tree alone. Maybe another time he would give it a chance. He was buffeted by his own cultural inhibitions. He would furnish Fleur with a satellite cell-phone and solar powered batteries. Space had been filled with competing satellites in their heyday so there were enough functioning to be useful. They would arrange to check with each other at the equinoxes and solstices.

Back at the Tree J had a medical clinic, and the details missed by Fleur's home remedies were cleared up. He was left only with a notable scar.

..

The next interaction with Fleur was traumatic.

It was a hot spring day when J heard someone shouting below the Tree. When he looked he saw Fleur wandering about the area, calling out occasionally, evidently looking for him. J was not ready to take any chances with his security and remained silent. After a short time Fleur walked off toward the north, still hollering occasionally.

J waited only an hour before following Fleur to his village. He found them in mourning. When he asked Fleur who they were mourning, the answer was, "Several persons. But that was in the past; this is for the future. We have suffered only one dead and two stolen over a year ago. Now, we are mourning what will come to be."

J asked no more, but sat down beside his friend and listened. He learned the sorry state of the region.

Most of the country's population had died in the years of bombs, guns and plagues, a lot from radiation poisoning since they didn't know to stay out of it; a lot more from disease. The Masai were deeply decimated due to their dependence on their cattle, which were early casualties. The increased lion population overwhelmed them. They had never been big on guns. Finally, famine was the big killer everywhere. Only a few groups were left in all of East Africa. The remaining tribes were generally peaceful, and they had only spears.

Except for the raiders. These were a small group of warrior/mercenaries who lived in the remains of the big city, Nairobi. They were all that was left of the people in the city. Now they went out on raiding forages once or twice a year. They were strong and vicious and killed with ease. There were guns available to those in the towns, but few bullets. When the warriors came with guns and ammunition they took what they wanted. At Fleur's tribe, one youth protested as they took his bride, and he was shot.

They had just heard that the warriors had need of women and were foraging again. The tribe was planning to move west. But they knew the warriors would follow, and with no women or children they were much more mobile. With flight not an option, Fleur had gone to tell J to warn him, and probably with some hope that J had a solution.

J had a solution. He had many solutions. But they were the solutions of the beast within. He returned to his home without any commitment or comment to Fleur beyond "I'll think about it. Turn on your cell-phone."

He had to think about it. What would Sancho Panza do? He would hide in the Tree, safe and removed. What would Don Quixote do? He would do battle. What does J do? Which of these two was his hero? Sometimes one, sometimes the other.

He had obtained the particulars from Fleur. There were only about two dozen warrior/terrorists. They apparently had a brewery, as drunken orgies were their trademark. But they had recently run out of material to brew. Their original supply of hops, grains and hay were gone, and they were getting even more beastly than before. J recognized the symptoms of alcohol withdrawal in some of the descriptions. Fleur's messenger had estimated that only a week would pass before they came to his vicinity.

J had done his thinking on the way back to the tree. He called Fleur and told him to send help. He moved down to his storage area, searching around deep in a seldom-used section behind his huge wine reserve. Here he found several crates of tequila, his lifetime supply. Ah well, he hadn't been drinking it much anyway. He doctored two cases of bottles. He had to break the seal of each bottle, but resealed it carefully.

It was a slow acting poison so it would be twenty-four hours before the danger would be known. That allowed plenty of time for them all to imbibe. He moved the cases out to the plains and waited for Fleur and his group. He was outside waiting for them when they arrived. He instructed them on how to hide it in the village, but not too well. They could then move west, leaving the baited trap.

After Fleur's band left with the doctored booze, J returned to his daily routine in the Tree. Two days later, he observed the warriors moving west. They stopped at his spot to rest and drink from the pond. Fortunately, they arrived in the evening, slept and moved on early in the morning so there was little time for them to scrutinize the Tree. From observing them and their savage behavior J felt less bad about the trap that lay ahead for them.

Months passed without hearing from Fleur. When he visited their new camp three months later, he found them just as they had always been. Fleur showed him the mass grave at the old site where they had buried what was left of the entire warrior band after the animals had visited. They had not had to dispose of any of the tainted liquor, since every drop had been drunk. Fleur simply related the facts. He was not elated, but sad in the same way that J was disappointed that he too was reduced to savagery. The fact was duly noted in his diary, a comment on his species.

··

J had not seen Fleur again for over a year now. They talked briefly on the satellite cell-phone but there was no response on the last solar checkpoint. They had closed their camp and moved on when he checked last year and he assumed they were forced to move toward the lake by the current drought. J was disappointed, for he had decided to seriously consider Fleur's offer of matchmaking. He would check again the next spring.

*The difference between stupidity and genius
is that genius has its limits.*

Albert Einstein

Ch 4.4 Encounter At the Tree

J had been reading in the library about midmorning of a still spring day when he first became aware that something was out of the ordinary. It came upon him as a slow double take, as though his senses mused over the situation before sending a signal to his brain. The feeling was almost immediately confirmed when the hollow sound of the hooves of a running gazelle rose and fell nearby.

J placed the bookmark, shelved the book and marked its spot. He didn't want to upset his routine too much. He was often roused by a false alarm, which was anything deviating from the norm. Still, caution was the order and rather than open the library windows, he headed for the sky room.

Before he started up the stairwell he pushed a large yellow button on the nearby panel. This stopped the main generator and switched to silent power sources, checked that all entrances and windows were secure, and ran a test to see that all extraneous functions, such as antennas, were in security position. This was the first time in weeks that the yellow button had been pushed except for testing. During the first years, it had been used much more often.

He climbed the tightly wound circular staircase that rose from the side of the room. As he passed through several darkened rooms, the white noise of hundreds of hooves striking the delta broke over his home like surf over a sandcastle. The vibration traveled up the steel stairwell as the herd apparently split around the oasis.

J hurried up to the observation room, quickly swung the big chair over the terminus of the stairwell, sat down and took a deep breath. He wasn't winded. A regime of seven bottom-to-top stair climbs daily kept him fit. The breath was more a sigh. He had reached the point where a small break from the daily routine was very welcome.

He activated the window lever to halfway open and looked over the vista through a wide angle of window. J could see the herd gliding over the plain, half a kilometer away. He swung down the field glasses. It was necessary to push the floor to ceiling dark screen around like a revolving door to look in the opposite direction from the retreating gazelles. J could see nothing. But his mind told him that there was something out there. Something that was a threat.

He tried to analyze the feeling. There was certainly nothing unusual about fleeing animals in this part of the world. He was personally practiced in it. Fleeing was a part of life. But usually at fairly well regulated times. The big cats generally hunted in the evening and night, occasionally in the early morning, and rarely around noon. During the past year, not once could J recall seeing running animals at this time of day.

Those sounds were common enough to his senses. There must have been something more to the excitement, or was it fear, that presently was activating his nervous system. He knew from experience during his first years that there were many primitive adrenaline reactions to sounds, sights and even smells that were valuable when he was outside but unnecessary when safe in his house. But his intuition integrated peripheral inputs that could be subliminal. He took a deep breath and went over his defenses in his mind. This relaxed him, and in minutes, he was eagerly anticipating some form of engagement.

With the large binoculars, J began scanning the far eastern edge of the plain. There were more clumps of greenery associated with local springs, often with smaller brush and trees surrounding the central baobab tree like serfs surrounding a king. There wasn't a sign of life.

The nearby points were checked. Walking up to the window J spotted two more animals. A Thompson was leaping in great bounds in the same direction the herd had disappeared. A leopard was slinking swiftly through the long grass in the same direction as the Gazelles but totally without regard of the one bounding twenty meters away. Hunting seemed to be forgotten; escape was the order of the day.

Moving to the northeast, the sparsely spaced trees joined to give a partial blind spot. Here, the plain merged into a forest in a few kilometers although it did not deserve the name until further away, on the slopes of the mountain.

Visibility increased tremendously as J continued searching around to the Southeast. Here, the slope of the plain gave a grandstand view over the tops of the isolated baobab trees. J checked where the stream that paused at his pool emerged once more, marked by trees and greenery for as far as he could see. The scene was just as it should be at this time of day.

But something was different. His good companion monotony was gone today, chased by apprehension. His mind was working, picking and sorting the possibilities, choosing each likelihood on the merit of its improbability of being true, until only the one was left — his fellow species.

There was time to relax and plan. To savor the threat as only the confident can. There could be no real danger to him as long as he remained within the tree. So, J opened the mini-bar, made some popcorn, opened a beer, and settled in the big chair to wait.

They were there on the horizon the next time J peered through the large glasses. Six bipedal figures.

It was likely that they would come close. His home was at a focal point. Paths for kilometers around led toward him, or more correctly, toward the clear, cool water that began twenty meters to the east. It was without the hazards of crocs or hippos.

They would want water and shade. And whatever else they're here for.

J could tell little about them other than their number. They were walking with strong posture, fairly healthy judging by their quick progress. This motivated him to close the windows even more except for a small section facing the intruders. When they were closer, he could switch to the many carefully disguised portals designed long ago for just such occasions.

He saw with disappointment that they were heading for the northern water hole. This told him that they were wanderers, not familiar with the area, or they would know the superior oasis was here.

They reached the far water in the afternoon. Then, apparently deciding quickly that it was too dangerous to camp there, they followed the path of the stream that pointed toward his oasis.

It gave him a sort of pleasure to evaluate them in the same manner as he did so many other creatures. He got the logbook and recorded the observation. It certainly qualified as a 'rare' sighting; the last entry for Homo sapiens was over a year ago.

This line of thought lent confidence, and dulled the edge that fear had honed. J really began to anticipate their arrival. He was happy. Like a soldier who is constantly training for war- it was almost natural to be relieved that it was not all in vain.

He wondered why they were here; if there were women with them; did some people have the leisure and means to safari once again? Thousands of questions welled to his mind and frustrated him even more, as he knew that he should not contact them. But still, it would be stimulating to observe, and perhaps listen to them. He wondered if they would speak one of his languages.

In the past two years he had picked up only a few short-wave transmissions in English, none were long enough to establish any broad concept of conditions outside. The regular English broadcasts had halted, and although there were still occasional transmissions, they were in an eastern language that he could not understand. He had books and self-teaching records in his library, but he hadn't been able to generate sufficient interest to learn Chinese or Arabic.

The last person J had talked to was Fleur and that was months ago. J probably just needed to talk. To someone, almost as a compulsion. To hear their grunt or murmur that indicated they were listening. And to listen to them; measure them. Debate, argue, and grow angry. To give vent to emotion! To test his ideas in the environs of another brain. The gift of communication demands exercise. These were powerful incentives for J to make contact.

They would have to be awfully strong reasons though, as he wasn't here because he desired the company of fellow humans. He just didn't trust them, and if he were going to make contact, he would have to be damn careful about it. The problem was to manage the meeting without losing the secret of his sanctuary. He would have to craft a good story.

He finally decided that there was just no way he could safely interact with them. No, he would just observe them- look and listen. Panzaic reality. With this decision, he relaxed into his chair and waited the hour as they approached.

When they were at a few hundred meters, the binoculars revealed that there was one woman, maybe two. But there was obviously, one. It annoyed and excited him that he found such interest in the sex of the visitors. The small things that distinguished a female, the walk — loose and hippy, were classic in this one.

The other possible female had just the opposite walk, minimal body movement, as though she were carrying a jug of water on her head. Of course, the first could be a male with aberrant hormones; the second a male with poise. He would enjoy finding out. It was late in the afternoon, and he was sure that they would camp here.

And so they did. As J watched, he could also listen with the hidden microphones. Unfortunately, he was afraid to expose the parabolic sound receiver that brought the sound of birds from hundreds of meters away.

It was too large and recognizable. He would have to rely on the array of hidden miniature microphones.

As they set up camp, the obvious female spoke often. However, the other one did not speak so he couldn't positively identify her. Not that he paid that much attention to the second one, since the first deserved maximum attention. He considered giving her the designation of Juliet's nom de guerre, 'sex bomb'. She released a small flood of blonde hair when she removed her helmet, so he settled for 'Blonde'.

She seemed to be attached in some way to the person who appeared to be the leader. J realized that he should focus attention on that person rather than being sidetracked by gender. This was the person who would determine the character of this small troop.

They spoke English, German and French almost at random. He couldn't hear very well from the hidden microphones. But he listened carefully, and made notes on each person's demeanor and the few statements that he could decipher.

They set up a camp with four tents. Two of the troops shared a rather large tent, the leader and Blonde shared a two-person tent, and the other two had their own small tents. They were apparently tired, as all retired early. J decided that he had better do the same, since he wanted to arise at the same time as they.

He looked at his notes. There was an obvious leader, apparently by dint of stature since he was an impressive specimen. The others gave him maximum elbowroom and generally assumed subservient postures around him. This wasn't characteristic of an intellectual leader. J caught a couple of interactions with Blonde that suggested to him that her attachment was more of obedience than love. It was a fascinating soap opera for J. He had to take a melatonin to get to sleep that night.

♦

The next day started slowly, the two troopers leaving early to go hunting. J named the second likely female 'Slim', watched her sit on a rock at the edge of the plain and busy herself with a couple of gadgets. The binoculars revealed a GPS and a notebook computer — and apparently a solar charger and enough batteries to run them. She made notes on what looked like a map. They apparently had a destination.

Blonde emerged from the tent wearing what J remembered as a 'Barbie-doll' outfit, startling attire for a trek. She spent a long time at a washbasin, in a complete sitz-bath that mesmerized both J and the other male, who sat at a folding table drinking a hot drink.

A shout, 'breakfast' crackled over the speaker. It came from the Leader's tent, and Blonde quickly moved to the mess tent and soon emerged with the leader's meal, which she dutifully delivered.

J broke from observing for only a few minutes to get minimal subsistence, tea and muffins. He recorded all the conversations and took many pictures. He managed to get a close-up of the map when Slim spread it out on the table to discuss with the Leader.

That evening after all had retired J looked at his many pictures, digitally zooming the images. There were some great photos of Blonde that he put aside. He blew up the map to where he could make out their route. They were headed for an area at the edge of the Serengeti that J knew well. He called it the Outpost area because of the large tree house that existed there. This was a small hotel, supported in a grove of about ten baobabs, built for tourists by a local entrepreneur. It had an illustrious record of famous visitors. J and other primates had been its only guests for the past several years. It had been trashed by natives but J had restored it to a livable campsite and used it as a base in his Serengeti forages.

He couldn't imagine why these people were headed there. More likely they were headed for another nearby attraction. Possibly they were taking a scenic route to a not-too-distant town that had a comfortable hotel and airfield. It was the stepping off point in the days when wealthy people came to 'rough it' in the wild. It was abandoned, as were all of the small townships in the region when the mushroom grew over the coastal capital of Dar es Salaam over five hundred km to the south. That event had forced another cloister from radiation on J.

In any case J was elated. He could be discovered living at the Outpost and interact with this group. He was a bit apprehensive over the survivalist militia demeanor of the leader and the troops, but the lure of conversation and the Blonde allowed enough rationalization to overcome these fears.

He didn't need to rush. He could leave a day after them, taking the ultralight. He had a safe storage place a few hours from the Outpost. He considered the land rover, and decided that he couldn't risk it; it was too noisy, too visible, with a smell of gas. He would need the speed of the aircraft, since they would travel the direct route that would be pointed by the GPS.

J was up at dawn; he didn't want to miss any chance to gather more information about them from eavesdropping, and ogling. They didn't get up early. Finally, the leader was up sounding like a drill sergeant hassling his troops to move along. They broke camp after lunch, leaving a mess that J noted he would have to clean up later. J watched them for a kilometer; worried that this would be his last sight of them; that he had misread the map, or that Slim had miscalculated. There was a small canyon on the straight-line route that would delay them. They appeared to be in no great hurry so it would take them at least a couple of days.

The rest of the day J prepared for the trip. He had to take along material to make it look like he lived there. He had stashed some supplies there and he hoped that it hadn't been raided again since his last visit, over six months ago. Raiders were not necessarily natives; the baboons loved the place. His final load was about seventy pounds, all he could carry to the hanger. This didn't count apprehension, which weighed heavily on his decision to meet these people.

In the end, he set out for the Outpost, come what will. He flew far enough north that there was no chance of them seeing him. The route was exciting for animal life. The plains changed radically with the seasons; the usual hot parched land, dead grass and dust changed in November to the rainy season to quick green grass and ample water. Now, the plains had settled into equilibrium between the two. The young prey animals had months of growth and were no longer easy marks. The new crop was only days away. For now, the culling of the old and infirm was the order of the day for the predators.

At the slow, steady pace of the ultralight, it was late afternoon when he landed and secured the plane in its hiding place. He had an hour's walk to the Outpost. The sun set at seven but it was hot into the night. It would be an exciting walk across the Serengeti Plain. Herds of wildebeest, zebra and gazelle began to appear. He knew that the cats and hyenas would be present and stirring in the late evening hours as he approached the Outpost.

Excellent binoculars gave J an advantage in spotting the clear paths, and the big gun gave him courage to shave the distances between him and threats. At first he had loved to observe the cats hunting. But he had tired of seeing the kill. If life was just to eat and be eaten and create more of the same to repeat the process ad nausea, it was a dull place. And he had to add, a dull god who "intelligently" designed it. As anatomical details revealed in the Gnome showed, it was quite apparent that the design of Homo sapiens left much to be desired, with many miss-directions like the appendix. And the gene to produce a tail had lost its punch. Evidently the evolution of life was a result of random perturbations.

But he still had to appreciate how glorious a step it was to create a creature that could even ask itself; what's it all for? Too bad they never found a viable answer.

He paused for a late dinner amidst house-sized boulders and baobabs. He sat on the top of a high boulder and watched the animals grab one more mouthful of grass before the yellow, orange and red sunset. There were cumulous clouds, hinting that the dry season might not yet be in full swing. The clouds were in long streets pointing to the heart of Africa. They were kilometers apart, converging at the western horizon. High above was cirrus, laden with ice crystals feathering the sky. A front was probably near. J was hoping that the rain would hold off.

Just as the red of the sky darkened in the last burst of color, J spotted the Outpost. He was always relieved to see something intact. It looked to be in good shape, this two-star hotel in the sky. He was tired and anxious, so he barely managed to spot the lioness crouched to the side of his trajectory. He stopped, but too late to avoid detection. She was about fifty meters away, and apparently quite willing to shift her attention from the tough oxen to the soft Homo sapiens.

She moved in a crouch toward him. J looked around. It appeared that she was alone. He didn't want to shoot the lion. J had developed a technique for these occasions. In his belt, one pouch was filled with powerful M-80 firecrackers. A butane lighter quickly fused one, and J hurled it toward the advancing lioness. He jumped too, in symmetric dance with the cat, as the loud report sent the animals in the area into fright mode.

As the cat disappeared in the grass, J cursed his luck. If there was anyone at the Outpost, the doorbell had been rung.

After five minutes of observing the windows through his binoculars, J moved to the base of this Treehouse. His markers set on his last visit were unmoved. He untied the ropes that let him lower the staircase. The sturdy stairs were strewn with a year's debris. He climbed them quickly and gave a quick look around. There was no sign that any creature had been here since his last trip. He cleaned the stairs, then slowly cranked them up. After a quick inspection of the place, noting that the luxury larder was still there, he fell quickly asleep in the comfort of a bed with a plastic covered mattress. He had a lot of housecleaning to do the next day.

Ch 4.5 The Outpost Tree Hotel

J looked out over the edge of the Serengeti from the verandah. The local environment was one of the extraordinary places in the world. When J was a child he had read about this Treehouse, built by an entrepreneur for the rich safari tourists. It had probably inspired him to build his own. This one was very crude in comparison to his, no high tech, but very comfortable by other standards.

There were half a dozen bedrooms, a kitchen/dining room and a loo — a galvanized pipe to a deep hole in the ground. The place had been in terrible shape when J visited two years ago. He had spent several trips sprucing it up and suffered only one setback when baboons had trashed the place.

The windows were open, the doors easily bypassed, so safety was only guaranteed with the gun. In addition to the baboons, leopards could easily visit, and lions would walk up the big stairs when they were down.

There were doors to each room, so a sense of privacy was available. J had stocked the larder with freeze-dried foods in a locked chest and they had lasted. He brought with him some delicacies. He settled in as a guest, reading an old book remnant found in the storage closet.

On the next day he was getting anxious. He arose at dawn, ignored the elephant herd in his front yard, and cleaned the place. In the afternoon he climbed to the rickety lookout that had been fashioned in the topmost branches of the biggest tree. Visible to his binoculars was the wonder of the Serengeti, with hundreds of animals, life and death sagas, and breathtaking vistas. Yet he trained his binoculars on the eastern horizon, straining to spot the one mammal that presently consumed his interest.

Eventually, he was rewarded with several thin vertical specks moving along the horizon in the far distance. They would be here in an hour. J's pulse raced. Homo Sap was the biggest game, the biggest unknown, producing risk and adventure.

Looking at them again, he finally registered that one was missing. As J adjusted his position, he looked down. The sixth one was fumbling with the stairs to the hotel. Once again, reflected J, his caution was inadequate. The edge was difficult to maintain. He hastened to descend to the hotel, arriving on the top deck just as the visitor entered the front door.

J decided to make the effort, shouting 'Hello', at the same time that the man shouted 'Bonjour'.

Damn, J thought, the one language of those he knew that he had real difficulty speaking. He tried a quiet 'Bonjour', since they were only feet apart, simultaneous to the man's 'Hello'.

"Wonderful, you speak English," spoke J calmly, noting that the man had moved his rifle to a non-threatening position. He was a classic point man, sent out to reconnoiter because of his stealth and cunning. He had the sharp features of a hunter, closely spaced eyes peering past a pointing nose, dark hair pulled straight back. A ponytail didn't surprise J. He wasn't very appealing, physically. His kind didn't propagate by beauty, but by survival.

"And so do you. The first person we've encountered in a year that does." There was a French accent.

"Yes, the language has become rarer in this part of the world. As have people. Won't you have a seat?" J took a position at the card table, and sat down as the other man sat across from him.

Pointman seemed friendly. "There are few of us left. We are always pleased to find another civilized person in this world. There are mostly savages."

"We?"

"There are six of us. The rest are coming. How many live here?"

"There is just me." J didn't feel comfortable with this answer, but it was the simple truth, and he considered that was the best way to relate to these people. Up to but not including the existence of the Tree of course.

"A pity. I hope that you don't mind visitors. Mostly civilized."

"It certainly breaks the monotony." They were sparring, learning, revealing.

Pointman tried to up the information ante, "Is this where you live? Have you been here long?" They seemed like natural questions to ask.

So J answered, "Yes, here, and houses in the abandoned town south of here. Over a year now." He had changed his mind a bit about the truth, noting the man's 'mostly'. He had better pay attention that he was consistent.

J wove a story of being on a safari in Kenya when the global meltdown occurred. He first tried to wait it out in the luxurious tourist camps in the Masai Mara. Eventually the natives arrived and weren't friendly to "those who wrecked the world". He fled to the sparsely occupied regions of Tanzania. He avoided displaying much knowledge of African countries with the realization that it could easily be the homeland of these people. A good guess, it turned out.

The man seemed congenial. But remembering the lessons of the new age learned from listening to the radio during the past years, J was careful. Finally, Pointman looked at his watch and almost apologetically explained, "My group, with the boss, should be here soon. I wonder if you mind if I look around — my job is to case out the area to be certain that it is safe."

J smiled tolerantly, "Be my guest, as I assume you all will be."

"Thanks."

J looked out the window at the approaching group as Pointman toured the hotel. He returned shortly — it was a small hotel — and looked down to where the group was nearing the stairs. "I found a black mantra in one of the rooms. You don't do a very good job of housekeeping."

"I hate housekeeping." J mused that Pointman was probably considering that J was not here for long periods.

Pointman leaned out the window and hollered, "Come on up. There is a single occupant who seems harmless," glancing and winking at J, "and the view is terrific."

In less than a minute, not bad for four stories, the Leader burst through the front door. He headed straight for J, extending his hand, "Mr.?" Leaving J to finish, "J, and you?"

"I'm the Boss, for some reason. Most likely because I fund the expedition. And I'm biggest, strongest, smartest, and best looking."

"Four out of six isn't bad." J was just naturally aggressive, and quixotic.

"What's the six?"

"I was thinking of Gandhi's description of perfection: Big, strong, smart, good-looking, honest and humble."

The boss eyed him with interest. "Yes, maybe only four. Most people seem to value looks above humility and smarts above honesty."

"Different strokes for different folks."

"How long have you lived here alone?" A non sequitur caught J off-guard.

"Too long, seems like forever." J knew the man would wonder why he was so coy. Take the offense. "And who is it that I am welcoming to my hotel?"

The other four had by now entered and were standing around, evaluating the new person in their midst. The boss struck his head, "Of course, forgive me, there are so few encounters anymore that one forgets the civilities. Permit me to introduce my companions, We got together in the South after the Revolution. Pete is a hunter and cook, Priest is our priest, Jane 1," who J called Blonde, "is in charge of entertainment and cooking, and Jane 2," who J called Slim, "is in charge of logistic decisions. She came to South Africa with Peace Corps III from the US South. For some reason she has studiously eliminated her southern accent, so you'd never guess her origins. You've met our reconnaissance, we call him our Scout. What is your profession?"

"Survivalist. Philosophy. Geophysics."

"Esoteric. But perhaps a good combination for living alone." This came from the Blonde. Her smile and eye contact reminded J of what he had missed for the past three years.

"Isn't it terribly lonely and frustrating to live alone?" This was a clinical question from Slim. No smile, but good-looking eyes. Nice average features and ramrod erect posture. There was a nasty scar on her right cheek that she tilted toward him as though it was badge of honor.

J nodded and shrugged. "You must all be tired. There is running water depending on the rain, a toilet, a little food to share and several empty bedrooms. They are probably in a barely tolerable state. I wasn't expecting guests. But for this special occasion, we might as well share some wine that I found here. There was quite a bit from the days it was a three star hotel, but it's disappeared fast. I've been saving the last for just such an event. It should go well with the dehydrated chili." He headed for the locked larder in the kitchen.

Pointman quickly got up and followed, "Let me help."

Later, after one of the daily world-class sunsets, mellowed by a few glasses of wine — only the Boss, Priest and Blonde drank — and growing comfortable with friendly conversation, J was feeling good. They knew about the effect of the holocaust on the region better than he did. He did not let on how much he knew lest they wonder how he knew it.

These people knew of pockets of survivalists, from militia to Mormons to isolated tribes who could manage well for a while, until they were often overwhelmed by neighbors who had reverted to the law of the jungle.

South Africans, who were proud of being the only first-world country on the continent, paid the price of technology dependence and went under more quickly than other African nations.

There were few nuclear strikes to the Southern Hemisphere cities. However, the germs and the anarchy eventually reached them all. Aids, Ebola and influenza could be cured, but without organized medical response, they were pandemic. Hunger was catholic, with agriculture suffering under the thumb of global warming. They didn't know of a single functioning city.

It was a depressing but interesting tale. It reminded J a bit of his conversations with Deman, except they were usually speculating; these people were relating real history. Still, J reveled in the conversation, whatever the topic. They seemed to accept him, impressed that he had survived the degenerate period.

♦

The next morning he was up early. Two people were sitting on the verandah savoring some of his hoarded coffee. Pointman and Slim were early risers.

"I like to take an early morning walk," said J, as he picked up his rifle that was still leaning against the wall in a corner. It had been moved he noted, since it wasn't precisely on the floor crack where he placed it. He checked the magazine. It was full. It wasn't like he was unarmed without it anyway. He had his pistol.

"OK if we join you?" from the Pointman.

"Of course."

"I'll go," said Slim. It was said resignedly like someone had to be a chaperone and she volunteered. Pointman gratefully sat back down to his coffee, "Well, I'm still tired from yesterday's reconnoitering. I'll watch you from here."

"Just a minute." Slim went to her individual room down the hall, emerged with a multi-pocketed jacket and bush hat, and headed for the stairs.

They walked straight out onto the plains, a course taken by J for the benefit of the eyes above.

J mused on the fact, "It has been a long time since I've talked to a woman."

"It is best to just think of me as one of the guys." Slim was matter-of-fact.

"Fine with me. I'll send that message to my hormones."

Slim glanced over at J for the first time. He was a no-nonsense type of guy, just as she was. "Where are we going? You must have some beaten paths."

"Yes," that was no problem for J, three months maximum and he still had several beaten paths. "We'll take a short two-kilometer hike to a lookout. There's still some hunting going on this early in the morning."

"You're not worried?"

"I'm always worried. So I'm always prepared. I have my gun and I'm proficient."

Slim laughed. Rather, she snorted, "You're all proficient with your guns."

J understood the attitude. "Well, I'm ambivalent about that. I love my gun when walking the plain. There is a primordial fear that is assuaged only with the gun. This tool makes Homo sapiens the equal of any beast."

"Yeah, you all love your guns."

"It would be foolhardy to walk on the Serengeti without a gun. I also carry firecrackers and a percussion grenade so that I might scare an animal away before I have to shoot it.

"On the other hand, on an intellectual level I truly believe that the proliferation of guns and man's love affair with the gun and other weapons were fatal flaws in the attempt to establish a civilization. I suppose that's no longer a question, having been proven. Today we just have to worry about the other beasts. You should be safe."

"I don't give a damn about that much anymore. Life is just existence."

J looked for Slim's expression. She was certainly a downbeat dame. "I suppose that's all it ever has been. And procreation."

"Yeah, and now having babies doesn't make any sense. Who'd want to bring a kid into this world?"

"My daughter said that a long time ago, reflecting on the overpopulation, pollution and crime of that time. It seems she was right."

Slim warmed to the compatible conversation, "I guess the word 'existence' is too fricking fuzzy. Existence is a lot of things. Some of it is enjoyable. I was raised in what used to be Alabama before the US revolution, deep in Dixie, and it was a nice existence. But now, when you have to work like hell just to get through the day there's no energy left for enjoyment."

J said; "I'm ambivalent about that. I saw most of my colleagues and friends in exactly that situation. In contrast, the African bushman, working one full day a week and sitting around the other six observing the world ten hours a day may have gotten more pleasure in life. Now, we are all Bushmen. Some know how to be happy with that, some don't."

"You think it's all in the mind?"

"Fifty-fifty. Depends on the individual's chemical stew."

"Whatever. In my opinion, it can all be said in a few ideas. I got these from a class on evolution at Tuscagee College. First, we lucked into a damn nice environment for evolution of our ancestors. I guess that it started here, right where we are now. I learned that we made it through the first million years by doing a good job at breeding and hiding out from all the animals that wanted to eat us. At some point we had to move on, finally checking out the whole planet. Everyone has to move on sometime. I don't know why. Probably trying to find a nice place to live, or just a place to survive in, and probably to escape from those predators that we're worried about right now. I suppose you think it was a big plus when we got your beloved gun and killed off the other predators."

"For good or bad, it made us number one."

She nodded; seemed to be reveling in talking to a new listener. J didn't feel that it was for his benefit, but for her own. He was a little startled at her college, which started as a black college but later became integrated. He decided to ignore it. She brought it up, so she will probably explain it.

"It's weird, talking about it now with all the disease going around, you can't shoot a germ."

J smiled. "Well, germs have always been a big part of wars. Even when it was inadvertent, like when the explorers from EurAsia, which we finally realized was the relatively New World, visited the Old World of the Americas, inadvertently, they brought their cultivated germs, namely smallpox. The diseases arrived with the first visitors and quickly spread to entire civilizations. A hundred years later when the Europeans came to settle, they found the continents nearly empty. Not realizing their germs had caused the greatest mass extinction in history, it became a New World for them." J had taught this course. "So before we knew it, we evolved into the age of the computer, woman's equality and gladiator football. But they say that we still answer to our basic instincts, formed according to our needs a million years ago."

"Yeah. So presto, the whole shebang was brought down by you guys' lusting for power and sex."

J accepted being lumped in with the majority of his gender. He wondered how she came to accept this philosophy. That was an excellent summary of OC's creed. Substitute a little erudite syntax for colloquialisms and Slim would have fit right in there. "I agree. Wish I'd had that course. You got a lot out of it. Maybe everyone should have had that course."

"It was more than the course. Some students didn't get much out of it. It was my mom's teaching. She prepared me for accepting the put-down of human importance that we learned in that course.

"She hated being called 'black' when no one in the city could tell by looking; even my white father did it. They kept track of your ancestry in the South. Part of the reason I'm here. Ma hated cooking, babies and men. Taught me to expect nothing from others, and everything from myself. She said women had no chance of escaping their flunky destiny. As for men, she taught me that right now, given the choice, you'd much rather be humping me then talking philosophy."

J wasn't shocked by this assertion as she probably expected. He threw out a question in the free association method of OC. "It's not possible to do both?" But he felt that it came from the loins, not the cerebrum.

"Proves my point." Said as she turned her attention to the surroundings. Low rumbling sounds emanating from the plain rocked the brainstem, and the original priorities governing survival took over.

They had reached a knoll, with rocks and stunted trees bonsaied by elephants. J was wary, for this was a kopje favored by lions for the vistas. He liked it for the same reason.

When they had carefully threaded their way through the trees, the plain sloped gently away in front of them. There were many zebra a few hundred meters away. J knew from the nervous attitude and the lofty circling vultures that some hunting cats were in the vicinity. They got out their binoculars and scanned the plain.

Soon, J whispered, "Over to your right, about an equal distance as the zebra and a hundred meters from them, do you see them?"

"No," a pause, then "yes a lion, or two. Whoa, she's up and running."

J watched as the lion closed in on the zebra herd. He couldn't see any laggards, "I don't think she is going to be successful this time. She probably has been at it all night and lacks energy."

Another hundred meters and the lion gave up. She looked around frustrated, and J thought she looked right at them.

"She's looking at me," said Slim.

"Don't move. You probably know, most animals detect mainly motion."

They listened to each other's increasingly loud breathing. J slowly surveyed the area, and found several elephants heading toward them from the left. The lion also saw these imposing intruders and decided to call it a day, trotting off in the opposite direction.

Slim also sized up the situation, "Should we worry about the elephants?"

"Probably not, if they get our scent they'll head off. Or if they see us, they'll give us enough time to slowly back away. Let's eliminate any third possibility by just returning the way we came, I'm hungry for breakfast."

On the way back, Slim probed J for his life story, so he told her one. He got it from some book that he had read a few years ago. There was enough of him in it to interest her.

♦

That evening, the Boss noted the decks of cards on a shelf and asked if J played bridge. He was delighted when J said yes. Not as delighted as J, but then J hid his pleasure --- always keeping competence hidden until needed. They might play for the new currency that had replaced money — bullets.

The visitors had made it clear that this was one of the scarcest commodities, desired everywhere. Soon there would be a world full of guns and no bullets. That would make it more comfortable for J, as long as he had his bullets, carefully stored.

Apparently, this was the reason that they were out in this remote place. Some information made them think there was a large store of ammunition around here. One of the many military dictators had stashed it. Plenty for J too, if he could help them find it.

They knew, or decided, that J didn't have access to the ammunition they sought, since his game hunting rifle and ammo were not the right type. J reflected on the fact that he had randomly chosen this rifle from several. He wondered what would have happened if he had chosen a wrong one. He did have a likely one, an AK-47 assault rifle that he never used. Ultimate firepower to ease the ultimate fear. Then there was the sniper rifle, with 50mm ammo that would have really raised eyebrows. But his chosen rifle was all part of his 'dressing-down' for this occasion.

To J's further delight, the other two bridge players were Blonde and Slim. They were both quite good, although with radically different styles. The Boss was a shark. He played with Slim. They played standard conventions, nothing fancy, but extremely precise.

J was surprised when Blonde asked if he knew a slightly offbeat system, an aggressive bidding style that was J's favorite. It was the European favorite and probably imported to South Africa. He said that he had played it once or twice, and they adopted it. She had played it a lot, learning from her mother.

Although the opponents were getting dealt the strong cards, J and Blonde managed to steal or bluff their way to stay nearly even. When they finally got some good cards, Blonde bid to the hilt, putting J into a commitment to take all the tricks. This he did with methodical efficiency.

Boss was impressed. But he liked to win. "It's time to switch partners. I'll try the new guy." Trading seats with Blonde, "We'll play your system since it worked so well against me."

Apparently, Slim was limited to American standard, and since Boss had also been exposed to the European system in South Africa, he and J had an advantage. Fine with J as he managed to allow Boss to play and win a slam. He was playing for bigger stakes.

It was a special evening; they played for hours. Like a bunch of adolescent kids in a rickety old Treehouse removed from the world's cares. J fit into this group like a tin drummer in a Calypso band. It was a nice feeling. Escape, some would say. Escape from what, J would say. He knew Sancho Panza would say there probably wasn't much more to life. Just the moment-to-moment enjoyment of being alive.

♦

The Hunter accompanied J on his morning walk the next day. He didn't say much. That was fine with J. He wasn't in the habit of talking on these ventures. J took him straight to a popular game spot on the plain, although they had to traipse through grass that reached to both of their chins. It was a place for surprises. But they moved safely on to the short grass of the plain and were a few kilometers out when they came to a dry ridged area with little vegetation.

On the edge of the grassland, there was a small herd of impalas. The hunter aimed quickly and brought down a young buck. "The young ones are better." They were easier to butcher and to carry, so J often went this route himself. There would be venison for a day or two. As they were in the process of rendering it, a female lion burst out of the grass twenty meters away. Startled, following the scent of blood, she stopped to see the new creatures. Fatal error, Hunter placed a bullet between her eyes, "Best not to take any chances." J showed no sign of his inner revulsion to such wanton killing.

They carried the meat back in their packs, keeping a wary eye for other predators that might smell the blood. They hadn't touched the lioness carcass. Looking back, J saw a dozen vultures zeroing in on the spot. They were quick to exploit an unexpected bonanza. Gratuitous killing was not the order of the day in the balanced ecosystem of the Serengeti. J didn't like to be part of it. But he would enjoy the impala steaks.

At dinner, the conversation over the steaks turned to the wonderful benefits of the hunt. Blonde was particularly pleased with the Hunter's prize, "We are so lucky to have such a good hunter with us. He has kept us well fed."

J followed his usual bent and introduced some philosophy. "Right here in the Serengeti, man or near man hunted a few hundred thousand years ago. That would mean that Homo sapiens's tenure of dominance on earth was almost a hundredth as long as the dinosaurs'."

The Priest snorted, "You don't really believe that balderdash about man being related to the apes, do you?"

"I believe the DNA mapping has shown the branch of life that we belong to in pretty good detail. It shows that some fifty million years ago, there was a great ape type critter that possessed much of the DNA that we now carry. We can delineate the time ten million years ago where the gorilla branched off from this line, carrying a little bit different DNA stream. Then Homo sapiens branched off, and a few million years later, the chimpanzees and some of their cousins remained. The shared DNA, some ninety-seven percent with the chimp, is like a tape recorder over millions of years. What's not to believe?"

The Priest smiled tolerantly as though accepting the naiveté of a small child. "It is difficult for most of us to be so facile with time spans of millions of years. Since scientists can't even forecast the weather next week, how do they find it so easy to see back so many millions of years?" He was gentle, with a friendly countenance and sonorous tonal quality that vouchsafed certainty. And probably determined his profession.

J couldn't be aroused. He had been inoculated with cynicism by the holocaust. "Can't even do the weather the day after tomorrow."

The Priest pursued this line. "So if you can't even forecast the weather, how do you see what happened so far in the past?"

"Well, for one thing, it has happened, and left a trail. But I can also be pretty accurate predicting some aspects of weather a year in advance — that summer will be warmer than winter. The 100,000-year cycle of the glacial-interglacials is simply related to orbital dynamics. The greenhouse warming was correctly predicted decades in advance of it being noticeable.

"Anyway, I can still easily understand that events transpired on a gigantic scale compared to my short lifespan. The evidence is all around us. Some things yield to physical analysis, some don't."

The conversation was an entropy gainer. J had traversed this beginning mental gymnastics long ago and he was well-known for getting bored with talk that was an order of magnitude more sophisticated. He listened to the Priest pontificate for a while, and then excused himself to walk on the verandah.

Blonde soon appeared at his side. "You weren't overly polite to Priest. He was enjoying jousting with you. Why did you leave?"

"When he said that after one science class he knew that he couldn't be bothered with that if he wanted answers to the big questions, I knew that a meaningful conversation with him was impossible."

"That's interesting. He prides himself on his intellectual score. And you feel that he isn't up to your level. You have a lot of confidence. I like that."

"If you like that, then you'll love the scope of my confidence. I feel that my discussing evolution with him is similar to him discussing how many angels can dance on the head of a pin with the local chimpanzee." Said with a temporizing smile.

"I love that all right. Can I come with you on your morning walk tomorrow?"

"I'll see you at seven."

Someone has to watch him, and he figures that Blonde is relatively non-threatening. J is definitely poor at predictions.

*She isn't a bad bit of goods, the Queen! I wish
all the fleas in my bed were as good.*

Don Quixote

Ch 4.6 Blonde

During J's trip to the Outpost he had managed to really think about what
he was doing. He realized quickly that hormones drove his actions. They
weren't going to stop, but at least he could review the situation and perhaps
set some logical goals.

There were certain rules for his life that he tried to follow. He was
successful half the time. So far, he had been lucky the other half. The two
regimes could be separated into cerebrum driven and hormone driven.
The latter arose in the teens and didn't rest until about 30. The cerebrum
driven periods were present only by default — at times when the hormones
rested. Even then they lurked beneath. Any cerebral success depended on
prior preparation to allow some manipulation of the hormonal imperatives
when they rose to do their thing. Tripwires were set in place in his brain
to alert the cerebrum whenever hormones were being released. He didn't
have to know anything about the details. For instance it was obvious that
the set of hormones that drive the sex interest could rise steadily to the
point where they were in command. They managed to turn off circuits to
logic centers. Some other hormonal drives could supersede them, like those
governing survival, but only temporarily.

J had learned this slowly from experience. In the sexually obsessed
culture in which he grew puritanical forces were strong enough to forbid any
sex education in schools. Their main way to suppress hormonal imperatives
was to ignore them, fear them. Still, a general reading of literature reveals
most simple facts. But this wasn't literature frequented by most people. It
was science — anthropology, biology and zoology.

It was simple for him to see these facts in his daily life. After participation
in a sexual act, real or artificial, there is a flood of canceling hormones,
almost instantly after climax in the male, to the consternation of the
female but probably enhancing survival in the male. These testosterone
suppressors would dull the sexual imperative for a period. That period was
minimal at about twenty years of age, increased slowly to a few days at J's
present age. These were simple observations that were never discussed and

examined in the inhibited popular culture that Homo Sap had contrived. Too bad, it might have helped avoid a lot of misunderstandings.

J had occasionally used this knowledge. He had learned a lesson from his wife in an innocent way. She would always take care to make love before he went on a trip. It was like a vaccination. It could be self administered if one didn't have the strained cultural repression against masturbation.

But the inhibitions often prevailed, a tribute to his childhood education his mother would say. An affront, J would say, since one cannot rid the brain of the cobwebs woven by well-meaning simplistic teachings in youth.

The popular culture's interest lay in the other direction from hormonal suppression. There were accolades for the hormonal sexual enhancer pills. They made large fortunes for the creators.

The drug that produces the suppression of sexual interest had later been isolated and made available in pill form. It made little money. However, it was salvation for some poor souls whose unchecked hormonal drives had made them outcasts. It was a handy tool for those who wanted to be rid of sexual distractions for concentration on more 'important' things in life. There was even a movement to install this drug in everyone at puberty or before. Then an antidote hormone would be available to properly prepared parents-to-be. It didn't sell of course; not a politician would touch it. Another 'logical' solution on the trash heap.

J hadn't been thinking along those lines these days. He had no pills and no preparation in this arena. But he was considering it now. Too late.

♦

J was up at his usual crack of dawn. They had been together a week. Each night the ponderous ladder to the Treehouse had been raised. The system of pulleys allowed it to be slowly cranked up by one person. It provided a nice sense of security from the nighttime prowlers.

Every morning he found Pointman in the same place, studying the dawn on the plain. Even when J arose half an hour before dawn one-day, Pointman was up. J wondered if he ever slept. This morning he made some coffee, and soon Blonde emerged to join them. She was very appreciative of the coffee.

"I heard that you guys had coffee every morning. It's a treat, worth getting up early for." She had the gift of making whomever she was talking to feel that they were the center of her existence.

"I found a stockpile in the town south of here. I don't drink it very much, so it lasts." Continuing in the vein of telling half-truths. He had a great store of vacuum-packed coffee at the Tree.

She looked at J, and he felt that she knew just what part of that was true. He was happy that in his life he had one more chance to see a real live gorgeous woman like Blonde. She, as Peter would say, was perfectly average. Her teeth were an ad for toothpaste, her nose for the local plastic surgeon, and her eyes were jumping-out blue. Her hair was almost too blonde to be real. J didn't even consider whether it was real or not. These days, dying hair was probably ridiculous, although anyone could probably pick up a ten-year supply of dye in an abandoned store in any city.

Pointman seemed immune to her charms. He looked out the window at one of the world's best views and yawned, "I am sleepy." J was glad to hear it. So he was susceptible to human weaknesses. He couldn't help injecting, "So you sleep?"

Pointman didn't smile. He took it as a criticism. "Briefly, and only when there's nothing else to do."

"I'm afraid that there's not much to do around here." J was now in the political habit of saying what was expected rather than what he thought.

"Right. I'm not anxious to accompany you on your morning constitutional." Pointman had walked with J on his last three early morning sojourns. Camaraderie had been struck between the two men. But Pointman didn't have J's need for getting out to exercise.

"Well, I am certainly used to going alone." They had a tacit understanding that the Boss had ordered J to be watched on these outings.

"But I would like to accompany you this morning, if you don't mind." Blonde's smile was guileless, and removed the dilemma between the stated and ordained positions of the two men.

J didn't care if this was a demand or request. He wasn't about to do anything except say, "I don't mind at all."

He walked to the corner and picked up his gun, checked the magazine, and asked Pointman, "If you want the staircase raised, you can do it."

"Sure, the Boss really loves defense mechanisms like that. I could cite you several occasions where that is the reason we're alive today."

J understood that, considering the myriad of defense mechanisms at the other Tree.

◆

One of the last storms of the rainy season had washed the plains early this morning. It was now moving to the West, leaving in its wake a nearly complete set of two rainbows. J moved off to the North, skirting around the dry ravine that marked the edge of the plain. "That is one of the clearest rainbows I've seen. The colors of both inner and outer bow are sharp and the region in between is so dark." J described the scene with the same reverence a museum guide gave to a Leonardo da Vinci painting.

"I have never noticed that before. It certainly is pretty." Blonde was truly without pretensions.

J reflected on the inadequacy of 'pretty'. He pushed the intellectual at the same time he admired the contours of Blonde's khaki blouse. "The physics of light bouncing off the water droplets explains the order of the colors and the darkness between the two rainbows. I'm not sure whether knowing that makes it prettier or not."

She was certain. "I'm sure that it is no prettier." And what more was there to it?

They continued on a path that J hadn't taken for a long time. There was less chance of encountering animals this way and he didn't want to be distracted. He figured that Blonde wouldn't miss them, as she hadn't shown great interest in looking out from the Treehouse.

"You must not have talked to a woman for a long time." She looked at him with the force of an electric discharge.

"Well, Slim and I walked the other day." A logical exception.

She smiled and nodded her acceptance of J's nickname for her companion. "But Slim's one of the guys, so she says. Was that fun?"

"I'm not sure what you mean by 'fun'. It was good company."

"I mean did you get intimate?"

J was unsure what that term meant to Blonde. It could simply mean did they get personal in conversation. It was also one of a hundred terms for the basic sexual function. He was startled by Blonde's frankness. But he was sly enough to forget his devotion to the facts. Intrigue was called for here; he intuitively knew it. "I'm a gentleman. We don't answer those questions."

"Sure you don't. You just did. Anyway, I know Slim, and your chances with Slim are less than slim." She seemed to like J's nickname for her companion, and enjoyed the play on it.

"Yes. Frustrating."

"I'm sure. But not for Slim. I think the brutal things she has been through turned off her desire switch. She had a family. They're all gone now. And a woman, unless they have a lot of protection, like we have, is just an easy mark these days. Matter of fact, we didn't do too well in the old days."

"So you haven't had the same bad experiences?"

"No. Boss was a friend of my dad's. I was off in England at school, having a ball, when I came home for a break. It was then that someplace in the USA got the first bomb. Before I could even consider returning, London was hit.

"We were OK for awhile, but we had our share of terrorists in South Africa. So we all retreated from Johannesburg, with just a few days to spare before it went mushroom. Months later my dad went to look, and caught some kind of germ. He lasted four days. Boss has taken care of me since then."

J marveled at how he had Blonde's life story so succinctly. Most people were too careful to be so open any more. Blonde was a breath of fresh air.

J had packed the essentials, to include a salami sandwich with crackers instead of bread. This had attained the stature of a Dinner at Antonio's. He also had a bottle of wine, the last one at the Outpost. They sat for a break and snack at a Kopje off the beaten track.

The wine was not something Blonde was used to, especially for a late breakfast. She lounged back in the grass, "I've a wonderful feeling of peace."

So had J. He lay back beside her, and she moved perceptively toward him. The touch of her body at two or three spots was electrifying to J. He was about to make a move to see if she was receptive when a loud noise brought him upright.

He didn't have to look far to see that several elephants had snuck up on them. He mused to the thought of how distracted his bodily senses were to let a herd of elephants approach within fifty meters without his knowing.

He pulled Blonde up by her hand as she grabbed his arm. She wasn't afraid, but enjoyably awestruck. The matriarch was standing thirty meters away now, looking their way. About a dozen others, females and juveniles, were strolling in their direction. J supposed that they were intent on checking out the trees and shrubs in this very Kopje.

He slowly picked up their pack and backed away toward a large clump of rocks. They arrived amidst the boulders without alarming the big leader. They ducked back into the cracks and found a narrow path they could climb to the top of one of the larger rocks.

By now, the rest of the elephants had reached the edge of the Kopje, and were soon engaged in playful foraging. There were four youngsters that were extremely rambunctious. They ran out from under the biggest of their aunts, who assisted them with a lifted leg if there wasn't room. It was a loving community. Even J felt good watching the lively action. Blonde was enamored. She laughed out loud with glee at the baby elephant antics.

She was having such a good time that J couldn't suggest they go elsewhere. A half-hour went by, and he was worried that they were wasting their time watching elephants. But Blonde couldn't get enough of the interaction of the elephant family.

Finally, J insisted that they leave although he knew they had hours left before anyone really worried. The Boss, who stayed up very late, arose for lunch and wouldn't be up for hours. They moved quietly away from the Kopje in the direction away from the herd's activity. J was happy that Blonde had such a great time, but his hormones were still aroused and frustrated.

He led the way back, cutting directly toward the Outpost. This took them across a glen with grass taller than J, a nervous area. He stopped to listen carefully often, and on the third stop, Blonde bumped hard into him. She spoke into his ear from three centimeters away, "Do you think that elephants get more pleasure out of being in a family than humans?"

"It would seem to be the same," J turned to make the five centimeters separation between noses. But he had to add, as an uncool scientist is wont to do, "Elephants have nice family units, probably because they kick out the males, keeping a female fraternity."

She ignored his motion. "I would like that. I'd like to be a mother in a herd of human mothers with many babies around."

"They seem to have a nice life. But you probably wouldn't enjoy the twenty-two months gestation period, or the up to eight months nursing."

"You don't know. Do you think that it is possible? I mean, for humans to live like that?"

"Well, we have, in many cultures. We change it a little, include the male, but there are many examples of mankind living harmoniously in family units for generations." J petulantly realized that he had changed a romantic mood into a discussion.

Blonde seemed pensive for a moment, then, "I wish that we could try it." She moved into J.

The tall grass seemed like a shelter now. Maybe no carnivores would wander through. Even the animal sounds from Blonde were damped in a short distance. Their coupling was inevitable to Blonde, and to J, and probably to Pointman. But J did not expect Blonde's pensive intimacy. She didn't want to end it. "Let's not go back. Let's go off somewhere and raise a family." J hadn't really thought about it.

It really wasn't impossible. Even in the post coition flush of cold logical attitude, he figured that they could just take off. The ultralight wouldn't carry two. It would take several days hiking. But he knew where to get food and drink; he had his gun and pack with basic survival tools.

So he said, "If you want." And picking up his gun and pack, throwing a come-hither smile, and walking back from whence they had just come, he committed himself.

Blonde followed closely, without another word. They didn't say much as they placed as much distance between themselves and the Outpost as swiftly as possible.

They ate rations from the pack for lunch, finished the water, and skipped sex. By the evening, J figured that they were untrackable. He knew that Pointman was a superb tracker. But he had also studied the art and was confident in the trickery he had employed to disguise their sign. Now his only problems were food and survival. They spent the first night in the upper branches of a baobab tree.

J wasn't willing to shoot game yet; the noise might carry too far. He could fix snares, but wasn't willing to wait around long enough to bag a quarry. He resorted to tricks taught him by his native friends. He handed the last sandwich to Blonde.

"But shouldn't we share it?"

"Not necessary. I can find some grubs. I suspect that you are not into that fare just yet?" Said as a question, but assumed as a statement of fact.

"Like what?"

"Well, you see that mound over there? Inside are thousands of termites. A delicious treat to many of the animal kingdom. Chimpanzees love to fish for them and lick them off a stick like a lollypop. The assassin bug disguises itself in dung and debris from the outside of the nest and grabs workers that pass. The Masai love to roast them; they taste like popcorn. With a crowbar, I could break inside, where the huge queen, equal in size to ten thousand workers, is busily producing a hundred eggs per hour. She would furnish enough protein to last a person days." J was a little reluctant to eat something that might live for over thirty years, but there was an abundance of termite mounds on the plains. "Some think that the queen has magical properties, including of course, as an aphrodisiac."

"Well, I haven't noticed that you need that."

"No, but I'll sit on the mound and use the chimps technique to get myself enough food to survive until I can do better."

The next day he caught a fish, by hand, and starting a fire with his flint starter. They had delicious roast trout. J was feeling comfortable enough now that he began to revel in the wonderful sexual creature that was Blonde. She seemed intent on starting a family right now, and taking all steps that might bring her that way. J didn't know enough to question how she had avoided it up to now, but was happy to join her in family planning. They found taro roots, berries and fruits, plenty of water, and didn't reach the tree until the fifth day. J took a lot of time and effort to obliterate their tracks.

J had a great time showing Blonde the wonders of the Tree. She was in heaven, constantly stating that she was 'free at last'. They had a royal feast the first night, a bottle of Champagne, and the best sex J had had in years, if ever.

He spent a day carefully checking and rechecking the defenses, obliterating any evidence of their passage. He figured that they should spend at least several weeks safely ensconced in the tree, before they ventured outside. The confinement was made palatable by the frequent sexual tournaments.

After a week, he was beginning to wonder if the restrictions were going to be worth it. Would he ever be able to wander about again? Blonde was fantastic food for a sexually famished body. But the conversations left something to be desired. J was expecting this, of course. Although she was a naturally clever woman, he knew that Blonde had little education beyond the brain stem. She had attended one of those English schools where form was tyrant over substance. Her gentle, politically correct conversation was always feminine and acquiescent. Her smile was her statement about life. The few tentative forays that J made into meaning of life conversations always mutated to the wonders of a family and Blonde's hope to begin one soon.

There was no question that she was bright. With a lifetime in front of them perhaps she could catch up with a lot of tutelage from J. He resolved to start her intellectual education the next morning.

*'Tis all a Chequer-board of Nights and Days Where Destiny
with Men for Pieces plays: Hither and thither moves, and
mates, and slays, And one by one back in the Closet lays.*

Omar Khayyám (1050?–1122),
Persian mathematician, astronomer, and author.

Ch 4.7 The door was open...

J was sleeping in, sprawled out on the bed alone. It was a deep sleep. He
didn't respond very quickly when he was awakened rudely. Sleeping with
a young woman takes it out of the over fifty crowd. But a familiar voice
was intruding on his dreams; warning him to get up. He turned his head
and opened his eyes with great effort. Then they opened wide.

Pointman was standing on the stairs, shouting for him to get up and
get presentable, he was having guests — the entire party of Boss. "What
do you expect, when you leave the front door open?"

Laughing, and adding, "Boss might not take kindly to your running
off with his girl." Pointman took a look around, saw no weapons, and
continued climbing the stairs in his exploration of this fantastic structure,
as he was heard to keep exclaiming as he moved up.

J was wide-awake now. He pulled on shorts and a shirt before moving
to the stairs, where he heard others below. He poised to step onto the ladder
and descend. But someone was on the stairs, perhaps two levels below. He
wasn't going down. He wasn't going up.

He quickly crossed the room and pulled open the cabinet door that
led to the laundry chute. As soon as he opened the chute door, he could
hear shouts floating up from the basement. Someone was standing near
the exit of the chute in the basement. They were 'securing' the lowest level,
and the 'only exit'. The voices seemed knowledgeable and he assumed that
Blonde was coaching them. J grimaced; once again, the gonads screw the
cerebrum. They must be mightily ahead in this cross body rivalry.

At least he thought clearly when planning for circumstances where
he might falter. Knowing the susceptibility of his logic to his emotions,
and the inevitability of mistakes in both realms, he was able to allow for
them. It was a way of life, and had worked its way into the design of the
Tree more than once.

Reaching inside and up to a sliding switch, he moved it in a certain way. A noise occurred behind him on the stairway and without looking he swung from the shelf and his feet entered the chute just as a bullet entered his back.

He was ready for the rough detour at ground level, and the bouncing landing in pitch darkness. At least there was a cushion. It was the first time that he had tried this exit. He rose, to see if he could, and felt for a bullet exit site in his shirt. It was there; the bullet must have been smooth and passed through him, apparently without hitting anything fatal. He turned to the wall and felt around for a light switch; soon he was bathed in low-level amber light. He attempted to stand and felt a wave of nausea, sitting down immediately.

He was feeling faint. But he couldn't pass out just yet. Rising to his knees, he punched a number into the keypad near the light switch. It opened up a large panel and he weakly reached to a red button sheltered under a protective cover. He pushed it as he felt a wave of nausea and had to sit down again.

The emergency button set a program into action. Several of the exposed switches, and their accompanying panel lights blinked on or off. The detour in the slide was closed and the laundry chute reconnected to the basement. Control of the critical security functions and most of the exotic aspects of the tree were disconnected from the interior panels and put in limbo.

There was a loud thumping from the other side of the wall, and J surmised that his assaulter had just taken the slide. There would be some startled reactions when he came shooting out of the ceiling in the basement. He would have a rough landing, since the huge pillow that J used wasn't there, just a small plastic laundry basket. From the shouts over the intercom, someone may even have been looking up the opening when he arrived. It was an amusing conversation, but J was losing interest. He slumped dizzily down to the floor mattress and contemplated his sorry state.

The chamber he was in was the back door. It was an escape route. With the detour of the laundry chute closed, there was almost no way they could find him. Even though they would know that he disappeared down the chute, when they tried it they simply ended up in the basement. And even if they found the hidden switch, it had now been disabled.

He imagined Boss's chagrin, nay, wrath, directed toward Pointman when they could find no sign of him. He liked Pointman. Well, he would soon know — if he could stay awake — as the sounds from each room were emanating from the console beside him. "This place is a prize." "This is the fortress I've been dreaming of, we can live here forever."

But J was fast falling asleep. His injury was worse than he thought. He rolled across the narrow passage and reached a first aid kit on a shelf there. Fumbling slowly, he applied ointment with great pain to the holes in his body. Bleeding didn't seem to be too serious, and he applied compress bandages. He then took a couple of pills and tried to settle comfortably on the floor. He vaguely remembered that he had something to think seriously about.

The 'disaster switch' that he had thrown on the panel above his head did many things besides disabling security access from inside the tree. It disabled most electrical. It locked some rooms in the basement. And more. J was struggling to think about this. There was something that he had to do. But by now he was unconscious.

♦

Sounds continued to emanate from the speaker on the panel. The Boss had found J's liquor supply in the kitchen. They were partying with their first good liquor in years. The search went on for J to no avail. The Hunter was certain that his shot had hit J. Still, a guard and a trap were set up at the inside of the front door.

They felt secure in this fortress. They spent a long evening exploring the tree. Boss and Blonde had a lively discussion about the plan to seduce J and just how much did Blonde enjoy it. Late at night the whole group fell asleep one by one scattered from basement to library. Pointman sat awake savoring a cup of real coffee from a beautiful cup at the table in the kitchen.

At two in the morning, the panel click was too dim to awaken J. In the Tree, the slightly open windows in the library and kitchen smoothly closed. Pointman was startled by the window click. He rose and started looking around.

The air conditioning continued, but switched to interior air only. Upstairs in the library, inside a heat outlet, a small valve clicked open. Very slowly a colorless odorless gas seeped out into the Tree.

♦

J awoke with a start. He didn't know how long he had been out. His shoulder was numb. He felt alert, but events came back to him slowly, a slow motion horror movie. His mistake was made in the tall grass of the Serengeti. Many an animal had perished from mistakes in that grass. Why should he be different?

He couldn't tell if it was night or day. There was nothing over the sound system. The panel lights were still a warm yellow. But the silence was complete. His mind slowly caught up with the events of the day before. He struggled to remember what was happening when he faded. Only then did he remember that fumigation was a part of the consequences of the panic switch that he had pushed. He looked at his watch. It said 2200 hours. The switch wasn't scheduled to activate until two in the morning, so he figured that he had time to turn it off.

When he checked his watch more closely he was horrified to see the date. He had been out for thirty-six hours.

He wondered if the defensive flood of carbon monoxide had activated. Would he want them all dead? Well, not exactly. J would have had a difficult time with that decision. But he was out cold and taken out of the loop.

He listened and dozed for another hour, then reached slowly upward and reactivated the functions of the tree. Still no sounds. He noted that the tree was still shut tight. Sitting up, he searched the console for the switch that opened the hatch to the lookout and another near the base. He could hear the top one open over the study mike. Still, nothing else. The air-conditioning was switched to maximum and to accept outside air. He closed his eyes and dozed.

He jerked to wakefulness. He couldn't wait much longer. He could feel his strength ebbing. Needed to get to his medical supplies. It would be a large effort. He dragged himself up a short ladder with his one good arm. Latches were released on a panel and he peered into the superstructure of the lowest meters of the tree. He listened for a while, and heard nothing.

He climbed into the tree, getting weaker by the distance. He walked very slowly to the staircase, entered and descended. His medical room and supplies were next to the downstairs bedroom.

As he slowly walked to the medical cupboard, he saw that two people were stretched out on the bed. He looked carefully, but there were no signs of breathing. Carbon monoxide was the silent killer. He wondered if his nausea was due only to the injury. But the air-conditioning had been on for a while, and the outside vents had been open for hours, so the gas should be gone.

He proceeded to the cabinet and found medicine and bandages. He took quinine, another pill for 'gunshot wounds', ascertained that the slug had passed smoothly through his shoulder area, dressed the wound and then felt the need to lie down. He pulled one of the men by the arm until he fell to the floor. There was a loud thud, as of deadweight, a sack of potatoes. The Priest was no great loss. He flopped down in his place. After fifteen minutes, he planted his feet in the back of the hunter and shoved him to the floor. He thought, 'I'm the only nestling surviving in this nest'.

It was late at night when he next awoke. He felt better, but not up to climbing the stairs. He did think to move to the bedroom console and check the place out, including closing the top-venting hatch. He could look around the outside of the tree, and the pond, but he didn't have the capability to look inside the tree remotely. Couldn't anticipate everything.

There was food down here, everything he needed to convalesce could be found in the basement. It was another day before he felt well enough to move upstairs. He was feeling much better, on the road to recovery, and began the climb up the tree. It was a long haul just up to the library. Everything was almost as he expected.

He had a moment's hesitation when he reached the kitchen and found it empty, with a half-eaten biscuit and coffee in his favorite cup sitting on the table. Had someone escaped? He remembered that it was the early morning hours when the lethal gas was released. He climbed the ladder. The Boss and Blonde were where he expected them to be, in the bedroom, peacefully asleep together for the last time. He had no interest in even looking at Blonde.

It was a long climb up the central ladder to the Lookout room. When J carefully poked his head up the hatch he found Pointman. His eyes were wide open, fixed on J. He had expected J to emerge from the stairwell. His rifle was pointed straight at J.

J reflexively withdrew into the stairwell. There was no sound. He slowly peeked up again. Pointman was in the identical position. He was dead. J's emotions bounced from fear to sadness. More so than at finding the Boss and Blonde. He felt that Pointman and he could have had an interesting relationship. Between them, long-term survival chances would have more than doubled.

Five bodies. But there were six at the Outpost. J slowly descended the tree, searching for Slim, just as they had done the night of their arrival, looking for him. He could see the evidence of their search. He had months of repair work to do.

He thought back to the first night. He couldn't recall hearing Slim's voice amongst the cacophony over the speakers. But she never had much to say. Still, J figured that there was no way she could have left if she had been here. She must never have arrived.

The next day, with the help of the laundry chute, J moved the bodies down and outside. They were beginning to smell. He didn't have the energy for digging graves. Finally, he just dragged them a few hundred meters away and left them for the elements and animals. Once more he had survived.

Ch 4.8 Mzima Springs

Months passed. When J checked, even the bones of his recent visitors had disappeared. Slim never appeared, and the rainy season moved in. There was work to do to eliminate all traces of that event. J relaxed back into his old routine. But the missing Slim revitalized his interest in defensive caution. He tuned the tree's defenses over and over again. It kept him alert.

It was a little difficult to settle back into a hermit's existence. 'Better to have loved and lost than not to have loved at all' kept going through his mind. An interesting hypothesis, he thought, but probably untrue. He had experienced full spectrum love — from chemical to logical — twice in his life. Each time he thought of either his wife or Kay there was only a resurgence of pain at their absence. For Blonde, he missed the sex.

J needed a diversion from going over his encounter with the Boss and crew. Slim was a loose end, and he decided to look around for where she had diverged from the group. She was the most interesting of the group, when you thought of it, anyway. Interested in evolution, independent, and could think for herself. Maybe she hadn't been willing to take part in a hijacking. He supposed he was being unrealistic again. She had been remarkably cynical. Probably she just got tired of the Boss and drifted away, with the computer and the GPS. Maybe she was in one of the nearby towns. But J talked himself out of making the same mistake, chasing after a woman. He put them out of his mind for a while.

He hadn't yet retrieved the ultralight. He was loath to go near the outpost. So he decided to go snorkeling at Mzima Springs. His strength had returned, and he was anxious to affirm it. This meant a five-day journey to Mzima Springs.

He packed for a week's journey. A scoped long-range sniper rifle and a 44mm pistol were selected. It was dangerous out there. In addition to the lions, there was still the planet's most dangerous predator. J was determined to be number one amongst them. Based on his recent experience, he was definitely of the attitude that only the top predator survives.

As he left, there was a sense of trepidation as he activated the intruder

341

defense program. This was the program that included the doomsday switch, as he called the fumigation procedure. It would activate automatically if not turned off in time. He had fallen out of the habit of using it routinely every time he left the tree in recent years. Mainly because he was always in dread of forgetting to disarm it when he returned. The recent inadvertent use of this feature added to the apprehension. He modified the system with several warnings in the form of lights and sounds to alert him that it was on and about to be activated.

This trek was a foot journey toward the east. It skirted the southern flank of Kilimanjaro. He walked across very old lava plains that rapidly drained the moisture from the slopes. There were isolated strips of fertile regions where the water pooled near the surface. He could see coffee plants on the slopes. J figured to harvest some of them if his supplies ever ran short. As he passed, he pruned a section to prepare for this possibility. It was very satisfying to renew his gardening habit.

The density of animals dropped off. There were still a few that had survived and even thrived in the great Homo sapiens' kill-off. In fact, to J's right lay huge plains in Tanzania where elephants were restoring the population that historically numbered in the hundreds of thousands before it was reduced to a thousand by the ubiquitous human poachers.

The region near the coast in Kenya's Tsavo National Park, east of Kilimanjaro, had always been a dangerous place for man. At the turn of the twentieth century when the railway was thrust through swamp and savanna, hill and plain, scrubland and forest, there had been a several month delay because the lions of Tsavo were dining on the workers. Scores of workers and local Africans became victim to these lions who learned to specialize in hunting Homo sapiens. The carnage was halted only when a renowned hunter from London came to meet the challenge. Guns were not so easily available then.

The lions were soon dispatched by the marksman, placing man-with-a-gun at the top of the food chain. So it remained. Now there were not enough people for lions to learn to make them their chief prey. But J would not enter this area without the tool that made the difference.

The area had become too dangerous for tourists when poachers moved in. Ivory brought them to the hapless elephant herds. The poacher had been branded a horrific criminal by the Western world, but the demand for ivory came from the same place. Since they were branded criminals, they decided there was not much to lose by taking a more direct access to the foreigner's money. They took up highway robbery and kidnapping of tourist parties.

It was an illustration that when a species obtains the power to destroy beyond the power to reason, anarchy follows. The relatively few poachers destroyed a tourist industry that had benefited a large majority of the country. Belatedly, the government forces then destroyed most of the poachers. But with a broken economy, protection for the animals in the parks also disappeared at this time. Fortunately for the animals Homo sapiens self-destructed before they vanished completely.

It was a hot, dry and fairly boring journey. Always to J's left rose the snow-covered slopes of Kilimanjaro. J felt the cold regions above mocking the heat in the plain below. The mountain had a broad, almost top hat summit, with two peaks several kilometers apart. It used to have large glaciers.

Without water, the herds were sparse, the predators absent. He was getting near the half way point to the port of Mombasa, a possible home to renegades. J would have to stay alert.

He moved quickly, and on the fourth day, the green region that surrounded Mzima Springs came into view. He was several hundred meters above it on the mountain flank. Beneath his feet the permeable ash absorbed the water like a sponge. This made a semi-circle around the mountain far to the north. There could be three meters of rain per year above him where the clouds were wrung dry by the heights of Kilimanjaro, but few plants had deep enough roots to live at the level where J sat.

A river of water flowed a hundred meters below him - in a hundred-kilometer square region fifty million gallons of water per hour rushed to percolate to the surface in a series of pools at Mzima. These pools were up to four kilometers long, one kilometer wide and a remarkably constant one to two meters deep. The river then disappeared, not to appear again until near Mombasa.

Wildlife from hundreds of kilometers in every direction came here to drink. His log from previous visits included sightings around the periphery of monkeys, baboons, warthogs, impalas, zebras, lions, leopards, and elephants. In the water he saw monitor lizards, otters, darter fish, gray headed kingfishers, crocs, pythons, eels, snakebird and, of course, the hippos. Kenya's oasis; it had become a big tourist attraction before the poachers and terrorists prevailed.

J was always apprehensive when here. But so far he had found that apparently he alone had inherited the magnificent visitor center and facilities. On his visits they were undamaged and apparently of no interest to surviving marauders.

J camped above the main springs. He wanted to observe from a distance before entering the wooded area. He saw lots of animals in the evening and heard noises of many encounters, probably between the drinkers and the crocs. It was the business of evolution as usual.

As he sat having dinner, there was a flash of iridescent green in the scrawny tree nearby. J recognized the scarlet-tufted malachite sunbird. He knew of this bird long before he saw it. It had been used as an example of evolution's vagaries at OC. It fed on the nectar of flowers and insects that it caught on the wing. The male had two long beautiful tail streamers. Females preferred the males with the longest streamers. Consequently some birds had developed extra long tails and enjoyed much success breeding — if they lived long enough. This feature was not aerodynamically desirable and they were slower in flight. This made them more susceptible to predators and less able to catch insects. Just another case where female sexual preferences constitute a hazard to the male. It made him wonder just what aspect of Boss it was that made Blonde prefer boss over him.

J reflected that if there was a priest amongst these birds, he would convince them that the tail was sacred, and that the god bird had a humungous tail. What they needed was a biologist bird that told them the female's gene-driven preference was killing them off and perhaps they should devise an alternate strategy. They could trim all their tails to the same length. Dream on; Homo sapiens couldn't do it.

In the first light of day, J was already moving down toward the densest area. A paved road could be seen departing from the opposite shore, merging into the mist toward the coast. Hidden near the water's edge, J found the dugout canoe he had stashed there almost two years before. He ferried his equipment across a hundred meters of crystal-clear water. He could see fish darting away from the big shadow of his boat, and an occasional slither of an eel, or the slow motion ripple of a snake.

There were signs of the park development in covered bridges stretching between some of the islands. He cruised under one bridge and headed slowly for a dock. He left the dugout tied under the dock and began the final approach to the main center with stealth. He found a position where he could observe the station, sat down, and made a cup of instant coffee on his micro-burner.

When he reached the door, he found a hair superglue between door and sill just as he left it. With increased confidence, he entered and made himself at home. So far, the park was his alone – plus a few thousand animals. They made a lot of noise. J welcomed the signs of life. The relative silence at the Tree was particularly heavy on his loneliness the past month.

The visitor center looked as new as when he first found it. There was a side room with scuba and snorkeling gear. The latter included the modern version with an extra long tube that enabled the snorkeler to swim a half-meter under the surface. There were the necessary belt weights to make the average person neutrally buoyant. A bank of windows overlooked the spring. The door was heavy and J locked it. He slept well.

He was up early and anxious to explore the springs. It was necessary to put the snorkeling gear on before entering the water. Getting in was the most dangerous step. The crocs favorite approach was to grab an animal by the legs, or a drinking snout, and drag it under. Apparently, legs all looked like prey to them. Most Africans wouldn't dare enter the water.

But J had read that a swimmer underwater presented a new apparition and didn't appeal to the crocs. J had also been taught not to believe everything one read. It was an anxious moment when he was swimming under the water and came face-to-face with a fast moving croc for the first time. But the croc did an abrupt somersault and whirled away. Knowledge is power, J enjoyed the triumph.

So it was important to get under the water and moving quickly. He moved with agile speed this warm tropical morning. When he had his mask half-above, half-below the water, the view was clear in both mediums. His favorite procedure was to hang out, breathing through the tube, and wait for a hippo to come lumbering by. These obese beasts sprinted like an astronaut on the moon, with their enormous weight buoyed to nothing by the water. To J, they even began to look beautiful; they fit into their element so well. He spent the entire morning exploring the springs for the neighboring kilometer.

The biggest thrill was a five-meter python as thick as his thigh. When it spotted a goggled swimmer it retreated too quickly for him to get his fill. The pool was a warm, safe place to snorkel. He grabbed a fishing spear that he had left on the pier and had a fresh fish in hand for a late lunch.

It seemed to J that the superbly balanced eco-system of the Springs was prospering more now that his species was gone. This seemed all right to him. He sometimes wondered why he didn't feel like a traitor in his appreciation of how much nicer it was without them. He hoped that it was only because of their unchecked, overbearing numbers that they spoiled their nests.

But that wasn't all of it. Something in their nature led to these problems. He regretted that the OC campus wouldn't be able to try to sort this out. He missed the philosophizing about how good it could have been, were a few major sociological factors successfully tweaked. In the aftermath of the world collapse, he had learned a few things.

The purpose that drove him, to his profession, to the development of OC, to find a meaning of life in the cosmos, was quixotic and unattainable. The meaning of life as Deman and Peter preached it was sensible and attainable. The concept that a quixotic principle was dangerous had been proven beyond a doubt. The premise that a panzaic attitude was logical and survival-oriented was confirmed. Too bad it took such a devastating experiment to prove it. Just like it was too bad that the consequences of global warming became so disastrous before mankind faced up to it. It was a potent 1-2 punch that did his species in.

He was getting into the 'Last of the Mohicans' mood too often. After his last brush with his fellow humans he felt he might be permanently alienated to the point that solitude was his only fate. As a check on this, he decided to attempt to see another of his species. The nearest likelihood of this was right down the road out front of the visitor center. It led to the coastal city of Mombasa. Soon after he thought of it, he was packed and ready to go.

He didn't take the road. Rather, he fished out his GPS and map. He was gratified that the device still acquired several satellites to give him his position. Many of Mankind's accomplishments might outlast their creator.

He set a path directly for the port city. It was about three days away. J had a Geiger counter stashed in his cache at Mzima. But he had no way to detect the various germs that had been a big feature in the apocalypse. He remembered Blonde's story about the death of her father. There were many things that he had to fear. He probably shouldn't go into the city to explore. Still, it was exhilarating to once again see the accoutrements of civilization as he drew near.

Mombasa was on the only bay on the continent that was hospitable to ships sheltering from Indian Ocean storms. There was a large island that harbored the first city, built sometime in the eighth century. Arab, then Portuguese, and finally English explorers made it their headquarters for African adventures. The old city and deep-water port, Kilindini, remained on the island. Bridges and causeways connected to the modern city on the mainland.

J recalled the stories he heard of Kilindini's last days. It sounded like a small bomb went off in the bay and damage was mainly from the monster waves and the radioactive rain that resulted. Months later, people were still broadcasting from the area, but something finally silenced them. J could recall the last feebly powered broadcasts of the local ham operator.

From a parched hill several hundred meters to the northwest he could see most of the city and bay. He decided to camp here in a sheltered area amongst the dead grass and trees, hoping that whatever killed them was now history. He got out his binoculars and began a long period of surveillance.

There was no sign of a working boat in the harbor, which had been severely damaged by the waves. The causeways and bridges were gone except for one road presently awash in the high tide of a rising ocean. A long survey of the island revealed nothing. He viewed the main avenues of the new city frequently. Much of it looked undamaged, farther from the water. There was occasional movement down there. But each time it proved to be an animal; usually dogs, or perhaps hyenas. Then he saw a few small game animals and realized that this was now a nice little hunting area. He wondered if the big cats visited. It would be so odd to see lions ranging into the quiet town. One might expect that new lions of Tsavo would range here.

Then he noticed a couple of patches on a bare lot directly below, and a few large containers on some roofs that suggested remedial cultivation. Someone likely was maintaining a meager garden. Then he noticed a clothesline on the top of a three-story building practically right in front of him. It had neatly hung khaki shirts and pants and underwear pinned to it. This wouldn't last long without tending. There were other items on the roof that made it look lived in. He located two other rooftops that looked inhabited. There were probably more outside his range of vision.

The next day J saw a khaki-clad figure emerge to tend the plants on one of the roofs. By the evening he had identified three groups that may or may not have been families — they were all in unisex gray; located in three places separated by a few blocks. He couldn't determine whether there were any humans over on the island. He noted that the road connected the island at low tide, but vanished quickly on the incoming tide. He thought it strange that the people didn't live on the island, taking advantage of this Mont St. Michel style defense.

As he made his evening meal, he thought about whether to visit them. There was a strong attraction. They all looked to be quite peaceful. His recent experience gave him pause, however.

Then, as he finished his meal, two people appeared, crossing the causeway from the island, it looked like one had an AK-47. Maybe they were wardens, or military. He lost sight of them for a few minutes but then they appeared on the street directly in front of his location. He ducked.

They headed for one of the occupied buildings several blocks away. There were faint sounds of shouting, a long quiet, then what may have been a scream, then quiet.

In the morning they left, moving back toward the center of the city at low tide. Everything was back to normal. J wondered just what was normal. This couldn't have been the first visit by that patrol. Is there a new culture where the possessor of the gun is the local baron who does as he wishes with the serfs? Are they managing with this? J considered that he didn't want any interaction with this dilemma.

Still, his loneliness drove him to seek a little more observation before he gave up on this place. He left for a day to hunt and get water. When he returned he cautiously occupied his observation post.

One day later, a patrol that may have been the same twosome, moved down the street to the nearest residence where J had seen several people. This time after a period of shouting and a scream or two, one person ran to the rooftop. She — since she had no clothes J could tell — fell victim to the man chasing her. Apparently the forages were for sex. After one had his way on the roof, the other joined him and they dragged the woman downstairs and vanished for the night.

J had spent enough time there. Same old Homo Sap. He would leave immediately in the morning.

During the night, he slept only fitfully. He kept thinking how some Homo Sap such as Fleur's band managed a peaceful existence and a just and amiable society. Yet far too often — the evidence was writ large — when constraints of civilization failed, a significant group reverted to savagery. The gun helped.

Why were some driven to exert power over others? How did others avoid this self-destructive lure? It didn't require respect for the other person's brain, beauty or even compatibility. It did require a respect for their right to exist and live their own life, provided only that they didn't impose on others. The human animal embraces the entire spectrum from saint to beast. The more he thought about it, the more his fury rose at the two who clearly fell into the latter category. In this limited domain they appeared to be the difference between peace and savagery.

In the morning, he was up early and finished packing before the intruders emerged. He had decided to go with his gut feeling. The fifty-caliber sniper rifle that he carried fired a flat trajectory for over a kilometer. It was an easy shot. He waited until the two terrorists emerged and started down the street. Breath, aim, squeeze and he dropped the rifle bearer, and then another shot before the second man even realized what was happening.

But the second shot only wounded the man and he rolled to the side of the street out of J's sight. J pulled off three more rounds, bouncing the AK-47 along the street, destroying it. That was the essential evil here. The thought occurred to him that the tyranny allowed by the shattered assault rifle had now been replaced by that of his own rifle.

J waited a few minutes and was about to move to a new position where he could see the side of the street where the terrorist had crawled. He had named them terrorists, to justify his sentence of them.

A figure emerged from the building that they had just left. The person looked around, walked to the dead man and kicked him. The person moved on to where the wounded man lay, and dragged him into the center of the street. One more look around, apparently not expecting to be shot, and the figure retreated to the building. J took careful aim and put the renegade out of his misery.

Two people came out of the building and walked to the center of the street. They turned toward his position. It was probably evident where he was from the trajectory of the AK-47 along the street. They got down on their knees and bowed as a Muslim does to Mecca.

J moved back to remain invisible to them and sat contemplating them. His heart was fluttering a little bit. He could understand why it bothered him more to be treated with religious respect, than to take human life. They arose and entered a building nearby, reemerging with a wheelbarrow. They placed one of the bodies on it, added the AK-47, and the larger of the two began up the street with it. He turned down the next street heading for the harbor two blocks away.

The man presently returned with only clothing in the wheelbarrow that he delivered to the house. The other person emerged, helped him with the second body and another trip to the water was made. It was done calmly and methodically and led J to assume that they weren't worried about retaliation from any friends of the two.

J was still trying to sort out what had happened. It wasn't only his indignation at the assault. He recognized that he had a deep-rooted fear of the renegade survivors. These were two who would no longer be a threat to him.

He considered going down and talking to the people. They would obviously welcome him. There might be a dozen or more people like them in town. There were possibly other terrorists around, too. He could be their equalizer, their protector, their teacher, their savior. He remembered the bow toward Mecca. Huh uh.

It was too big a job for him. He picked up his pack and headed inland. He carefully picked his way through outlying suburbs for a kilometer before he stopped for a quick lunch. He hadn't seen anyone, or any evidence of anyone. An afternoon of travel put him many kilometers from Mombasa. He finally felt his tension ease. He was back in the jungle where all he had to fear was the lion, panther, hyena, snake and hippo, to name a few. His foray into humanity hadn't provided the companionship he craved.

It continued to bother him that he probably had just wiped out a significant part of the population of Mombasa. What a shame that as civilization crumbled, the crassest, and most animalistic of the species often survived the best. What was he doing surviving best of all?

He wouldn't return to that place for a long time. He didn't get over his depression until he finally came into sight of the Tree a week later.

I've looked at life from both sides now,
From win and lose and still somehow,
It's life's illusions I recall I really don't know life at all.
Joni Mitchell (1943–): Canadian singer and songwriter

Ch. 4.9 Another year

The winter passed uneventfully. There were no more radio transmissions when J searched the bands. The sky was clearer and the weather was getting warmer.

This spring seemed to herald a reawakening. The earth sighed like an antelope after escaping a lion's pursuit. It began in January, and now, two months later, every living thing celebrated. Well, nearly every living thing. J was still feeling isolated.

He decided to take an early camping trip to the Serengeti, leaving early in the morning to hike to the gorge where he kept his vehicles. An hour was spent servicing the recovered ultralight aircraft. He enjoyed flying more than driving. But the threat of an accident — inconvenient in the vehicle, most likely fatal in the aircraft — usually made him decide to stay on the ground.

He had taken short trips to the north in the Rover where he spent weeks amongst the large groups of wildebeests, zebras, elephants, gazelles, lions, hyenas and many other animals that migrated northward during the dry season in bands of a dozen to thousands. Abundance of life had certainly returned rapidly to the area.

He left the gorge on a road that was camouflaged by being six inches deep in the creek. J headed west. He was always happy to return to the central Serengeti, where a balance in population always seemed to be quickly struck. Driving in the Rover was secure enough to pass closely by a pride of lions. They had gotten less used to seeing a vehicle and were reverting to being spooked and fleeing. He stopped soon after nightfall and fell asleep in the back of the Rover. Sometime in the middle of the night a dozen lions climbing around the vehicle awakened him. Apparently they didn't have fear of the parked vehicle. He jumped into the driver's seat, gratefully acknowledged the roar of the engine, and drove for an hour with his lights piercing the plains. He headed south, toward the Outpost.

Early in the afternoon he arrived at the Serengeti hotel, stopped a quarter mile away and hiked in to check for habitation. He wasn't certain just how much looking for signs of Slim was behind this early spring jaunt, but he couldn't fool himself that this wasn't a partial impetus. He felt a primal caution around the place.

There was no sign of anything except leavings of a baboon visit. He tided up and spent one mildly nostalgic night there. In the morning, animals were everywhere, and he carefully chose his time to hike to his vehicle. Many of the new generations of animals were not shy of this small creature. The rules were changing.

In his search for Slim, as J now recognized this part of the trip to be, he went south toward the town of Olduvai. Perhaps she went on herself looking for the cache of bullets. First he had to pass the Ngorongoro crater. He was anxious in his quest, but he couldn't pass so close to this unique wildlife region without taking a look. He took the road that cut through a pass in the three thousand meter rim of the ancient crater.

The grass covered crater had for centuries sheltered large herds of wildebeests, gazelles, zebras and other animals. The main predators here were the hyenas. There were lions that didn't hunt but lived off the commandeered kills of the hyenas. Being isolated, this area remained in the equilibrium of the past thousand years.

There was a comfortable cabin left from National Geographic expeditions. J parked next to it since there was no place to hide the Rover on this immense flat grassland. There was an uneasy night spent listening to the whooping calls of a gathering pack of nighttime marauders.

In the morning he picked up a can of gas that he remembered from his years ago visit. There were certain advantages to being the only tourist on this vast freeway. There was no sign that anyone had been here since his last visit. The second night, the hyenas were noisy and curiously scratching at the door of the cabin. He was glad to see the dawn. As soon as it warmed a bit, the predators all returned to their daytime lethargy, and he took the opportunity to leave.

As he headed east toward Olduvai he detoured a bit south to get a look at Lake Eyusi, a flamingo haven. He could see a pink cloud rise from the edge of the lake as the sound of his vehicle reached them. It put him on notice that his arrival in the Rover was like ringing a doorbell, so he stopped at the outskirts of the town. He very carefully approached this area, since there were people living here at his last visit about two years ago. The town was intact; everything just as it was when it thrived with thousands of people. But now there were no signs of life, no fresh tracks, no temptation to enter the town.

J was beginning to feel the isolation. He drove into the night toward home, catching fiery eyes of hyenas even in the barren lands north of the lake. He felt safe with no Homo sapiens to worry about, so that he didn't even worry about the sound and light show that he produced in this journey across the plain. Was he thinking, if Slim is anywhere around, I want her to notice me? As he slept in the vehicle, he caught himself listening for a knock on the window. He even left a butane light burning through the night. The only disturbance came from early rising rhesus monkeys exploring the vehicle.

Only when he neared his gorge garage did caution return. He slept in the garage, and spent most of the morning erasing tracks in the vicinity before returning to the Tree for lunch.

It had been a year without human contact; J was feeling the edges of acute loneliness. Yet he could be satisfied with his situation at times. He enjoyed his existence, loved the location and the Tree, and had decades of food and drink without the need for hunting or gardening. But these he did, just to interact with the earth. Life was returning to a set rhythm.

◆

A month later he decided to see if he could find Fleur's new camp. It was early spring. When he arrived at the last site he knew, there was no one there. However, there were signs that they had been there until quite recently. It was the time of year when they migrated to the lakeshores to the west. He decided not to search for them. He was doing all right on his own. But it was nice to know that this option was available. He had ambivalence over his visit, because he realized that his motivation was most certainly to take Fleur up on his offer of a bride.

He would return in late summer, after his regular solstice satellite call to Fleur. Chances were even that Fleur would remember to turn on his cell-phone. He figured to stay with them for a week or two and make his own choice. Although, on further reflection, he was probably content to defer to Fleur's superior matchmaking ability. This decision was influenced by his recent colossal error.

◆

This exuberant spring was a delightful time. As it merged into summer, J was up on the lookout early in the morning, tinkering with one of his miniature planes. These were products of Homo sapien's acme of technology. Miniaturization had been promising to be the next revolution in technology. They would have had tiny machines to do everything from keeping the place clean to operating inside a person's body.

He had just gotten around to assembling this kit. The mini-plane he had in his hand was the size of a large Frisbee. It had a small, thimble-sized, whisper-silent motor, a propeller spin the size of a silver dollar, and could fly for half an hour up to several kilometers away. J held the radio control.

It was for surveillance. A tiny monitor camera sent pictures back to the large viewing screen on a stand in front of J. He fueled it, flicked the motor on, and set its autopilot for two hundred meters altitude. It launched like a glider. He was thinking of an overnight hike to the northern oasis and points west. This flight was simply doing a preliminary check of the surrounding area before departing. He loved gadgets, and it was good to get back into them. He was trying to think of a science project he could initiate, as well. He needed to engage his brain in something compelling, all consuming. He wasn't designed to be a hermit without occupation.

The camera showed the usual pride of lions was lazing about in a familiar spot to the south. He always avoided their territory. Everything looked clear to the east — a small herd of impalas were lazily grazing there. To the north, the hippos were out on the plain, foraging. The last of the spring rains had produced the final fresh growth before the golden dryness of summer. He would have to avoid them, and reconsidered his afternoon plans.

The west was wide-open plain, with only a gazelle and warthogs. He banked the plane to turn toward home, its half-hour nearly up. As the camera tilted, he saw two figures on the horizon.

J was so startled that he nearly lost control of the plane. Then he frantically maneuvered it, turning it to move closer to where he saw this unbelievable sight. It had to be seen again to verify it. He wasn't worried about losing the plane; it could land and be picked up later. It wasn't likely they would see it.

When the camera passed unnoticed several hundred meters away from the couple, J recognized Fleur. The other figure was stocky, dressed in fatigues. Strange, not many people had the wherewithal to get fat these years. The plane's fuel alarm sounded. He had thirty seconds to land it. As he turned to look for a landing site, he saw Fleur gesture toward the east, in the direction of the tree.

He concentrated on setting the plane down and taxied it to a safe place between some rocks. This was a wonderful toy and he didn't like to risk it. Only after this maneuvering of the plane did he allow himself to contemplate a new threat. Everything was a threat. He felt that Fleur was a friend, but he certainly didn't recognize the other person. J went into his defensive mode.

At only a couple of kilometers away, they would be at the oasis in less than an hour, even allowing that the visitor seemed to be in poor shape. J was dumbfounded that Fleur would be directing someone toward his home. Who would know about it and want to come here? It certainly wasn't Slim. There was a rifle slung over the person's shoulder. Could it be one of the tree's builders or a mafia minion — J was desperate to guess.

In the lookout room, he had the powerful binocs trained on the west. He expected to see the figures immediately since he had a good view of the horizon. A single figure emerged, very clearly the rotund shape. Fleur must have turned back. J hurt to think of Fleur's betrayal. This would leave him alone in the world.

The figure moved along the northern edge of the plain. When it spotted the grazing hippos, it turned southerly, directly in the direction of the Tree. The person knew to avoid the hippos, and had evidently gotten good directions to the Tree site. He was making good time for so much excess baggage. The pace was strong; the posture erect, and there was actually a little skip in the stride. When the person was only a few hundred meters out, heading directly for the tree, he took off the safari helmet. Auburn hair flowed.

J was down the laundry chute — the pillow was in place — out the corridor, past the blasted security procedures, and now running toward the figure. When the person saw him, she started running too, even discarding the rifle to facilitate her bouncing gait.

J closed the distance as quickly as humanly possible. He wanted to see for sure who it was. He stopped when they were ten meters apart, just to let his eyes focus, to let his mind reassemble, to prolong the moment.

Kay didn't stop. She hit him so hard that they fell locked together. Nothing was said for many minutes. She was laughing, and then crying, and then collapsing as the weight of her three-year journey came to an end.

J didn't question it. The extraordinary tale would be told eventually.

Her presence was in need of constant verification. J's caution finally reawakened, and he escorted Kay into the Tree --- remembering to recover her gun.

As soon as they were inside she announced that she was hungry. They made their way up to the kitchen. J recovered a remnant pizza from the refrigerator. As he was moving to the microwave to heat it she grabbed it and wolfed it down cold. She washed it with a beer. Then she sighed and relaxed. She got a twinkle about the expression on J's face. He was checking out her new figure. The results of this ravenous appetite?

Anticipating this thought, Kay smilingly asked, "How do you like my new image?"

Looking at her face, which looked as it did when last he saw it, "I love your image."

"Can you hardly wait to take me to bed? I notice we blazed right past the bed downstairs."

"You had another hunger, I believe."

"Now that one is satisfied, time to work on another."

J was willing. He beckoned her to follow him up the stairs. She actually had a little difficulty squeezing by in the narrow stairwell. When they reached the bedroom there was another lengthy round of necking. J was concentrating on Kay's face. She laughed at him, sat down on the bed, and said, "You seem to be hesitant about confronting my new pleasingly plump persona. Here, let me help you," starting at the buttons that reached to her neck. Under the buttons there was a long zipper.

He knew that he could love a plump Kay, but his apprehension was involuntary. Then it dissolved, as Kay could not be seen even under the long zipper. This was a fake body, made to discourage the men whom she encountered in her travels. Underneath, she was just as she was the last time J had been with her. Or nearly, she had lost about ten pounds. She had a big scar on her right arm. Otherwise, it was as though they hadn't missed a beat.

♦

Later Kay told her story, "It was a nice day." J remembered it well. "I was practicing my thesis presentation and had gone to the physics classroom in the hill to practice delivery. I decided to let you get from the airport on your own. There were no classes; no one else but me. You know how that room is built into the ridge so you can't even see it very well from the East.

The big windows that look out to the Strait to the northwest were behind me when the room got bright.

"I turned around as the light was fading, and still hadn't registered what it was. It must have gone off close to downtown, right by the Sound, about a hundred kilometers from me as I rehearsed my talk. Several seconds later, the shock wave washed over the ridge like a flood tide goes over the levee. The rush of wind blew down trees."

They moved up to the sky room, she in the captain's chair over the stairwell, he was in a pull down seat at the side where Pointman had spent his last moments. The first day was spent on celebrating each other, and by Kay celebrating the new larder. Apparently, one of her biggest problems for the past year was finding enough to eat. It was the next day before they even got started on the huge catch-up stories.

"I realized what it was. Our education made me stoic. I thought, 'what the hell, Homo sap, you're self-destructing already. I wonder if you escaped.' Your plane wasn't due for another half-hour. You would probably assume that I was at the airport. My mind was racing.

"Survival genes take over, please. The only way I would find out what the situation was, whether I would ever see you again, was to survive. By chance, I was in an ideal place to sit it out; first the blast, then the fallout.

"I had thought about this scenario. I turned on the water immediately and stored as much as I could. Wouldn't want any after the radioactive rains came. Food was going to be a problem. But there were emergency stores in the building.

"I was anxious to go outside to look for other survivors and see the extent of the damage to the east. But fortunately, I was in a physics room with a physics lab attached. There were Geiger counters galore, so when I ventured out the next day, that little counter really screamed. I went back inside and didn't test it for a week, then another week. Finally, I detected when the rain was no longer dangerously radioactive.

"I let another week pass before I explored the campus. I later regretted that. The Olympic peninsula was far enough from the bomb that there were many survivors. But nearly all of the able had left a few days earlier for Canada and Alaska, away from the civilization that had done this horrible deed.

"Many people who had survived the blast got radiated in a splash-like wave of warm rain that engulfed all of the coastal cities and the campus. And there were quite a few people who had been in sheltered areas but ventured out too soon. They were still around since they were too ill to travel. I cried a lot as I looked for our friends. I found Professor None, that tough old guy. He knew that Peter, Nicole and Deman were all dead. None was planning on heading out when he regained his strength. There were a few of my student friends in the band of survivors. I was tempted to head north." She looked at J to see his reaction.

J shook his head in awe. "I am so glad you didn't." But he felt again that 'ye of little faith' applied to his decision not to search for her. He could have gotten back there after a few weeks somehow. But how could he ever guess that she would be one of the few survivors. Or where she would be. He probably would have arrived days after she left.

It wasn't logical, and Kay laughed at his lament that they could have been together these past years. She wondered whether they would have even tried the long journey to Africa. "I just knew you were here. I had to get here. But you really picked the farthest point on earth from Seattle to retreat to."

Kay listened to the radio reports that told her that Seattle had been the initial example. She heard the slow progression of disasters from city to city, nation to nation, and finally continent to continent. It was clear that J had time to flee to the African oasis. He hadn't discussed it specifically, but hints had started at the Verandah. She could make a pretty good guess at its location.

From the radio reports she learned that transportation over large distances had become nearly impossible. No planes, trains, buses, or any organized transportation remained. The highways were dangerous; fuel was precious. During the first year there were a few jets making last trips for super-rich persons. But the rich were soon victims; the population blamed them for the cultural collapse. Their currency quickly became worthless. Finally, there were just a few pilots who took off for a last trip to some final destination. Kay couldn't fly a plane although she was confident that she could quickly learn. But it became clear that difficulties in finding safe landing sites and fuel made this a very chancy plan.

Only a boat remained as a possibility. It was the obvious solution. She had her own, with lots of experience; and she wasn't intimidated by an ocean voyage. She wanted to get started as soon as she could, but months went by before she could get the provisions and the nerve to sail out the strait into the ocean. The isolation of the campus and a small band of friends made it a relatively comfortable place. The rest of the world was not.

The Atlantic was quite doable in her experience, but the vast stretch of the Pacific daunted her. Down the Americas' coast and around the tip of South America was intimidating.

She finally decided to go north, through the Northwest Passage. The Arctic ocean had lost its ice cover and this was a quick way to the Atlantic. Global warming had also made the climate in this region more reasonable. She left in late spring, took the inside passage to Alaska, then struck across the Gulf of Alaska, through the Aleutians and up through the Bering Strait. She saw a few bands of people, mostly men, and fled from them. Her ship was fast and she knew how to get the most out of it, so no one came close to her. Apparently gas wasn't available for speedboats. She learned to scrounge for food and supplies, made easier by the sparse population.

The Canadian coast was pleasant with no sign of pack ice. The trip down the East side of Greenland was quick with a favorable current. There were a few signs of people in the newly thawed valleys there. This wasn't the case for the coast of the US – she saw no signs of life, although her mode was more to avoid any such meetings.

The next steps were difficult to decide. She listened to the astronauts' reports from the space station, and it became clear that the Mediterranean and the Suez Canal were impossible to transit by boat. Pirates had re-established their dominance. Although there were significant surviving populations, most had degenerated into anarchy. Another problem was the hurricanes. There would be no forecasts. The Mediterranean might be passable, but the Red Sea would undoubtedly be very dangerous. These civilizations had always been only a step away from anarchy. Up the Congo was tempting from the map — the shortest distance — but she had read of the dangers of this trek too often to attempt it. That left sailing the Southern tip of Africa. At least it was farther north and consequently had better weather than the Magellan Strait. But all storms had been getting worse and more frequent over the past two decades. The final plan was to go along the South American coast to the region of the westerlies, sail across the South Atlantic and then work her way around the Cape of Good Hope

Although the USA couldn't exist without the computer and electricity, neither technology was missed as much in the backwaters of South America that had now become the forefronts of civilization. The usual dictators were still in charge. There weren't as many bombs, but the revolutionary forces had all joined in the worldwide mob frenzy. A semblance of civilization remained but slowly decayed- as refugees, renegade armies and small-scale militia groups roamed the world. It was not easy to avoid these dangerous predators.

She lost her boat when it was boarded at night off Brazil. Her attackers were looking for food and goods, which they found and consumed. By the time they considered the sexual treat they had encountered she had slipped overboard and swum away. It was a game of hide and seek for an hour, but they couldn't find her in the dark.

She hid easily in the sparsely populated area, met some women who were gathering roots and seeds and was allowed to join their group. They were several families of mostly women and they readily accepted her. The women were definitely in charge. This was the land of the Amazons and these ladies were organized and armed. It was such a comfortable place that she ended up joining them. She adopted her overweight masculine identity here with help from the women for whom this had become a cottage industry. She had considered a disguise as a man, but the women persuaded her that this was too common and easily checked; and anyway men quickly killed strange men. A fat woman had a better chance of being ignored, or at least underestimated. The village was an isolated safe haven and she spent her time helping them establish a viable community.

It was hours into Kay's narration before she even got to the South American part of her story. J could see that this was going to occupy a few weeks. They would take turns at telling stories, savoring the telling. They would also record them, in case posterity continued to exist.

J enjoyed demonstrating the many gimmicks of the Tree to Kay. She particularly loved to watch the animals from the many vantage points. There was so much to do and learn that they relegated the story telling to evenings only. It would take a month at this rate before they were caught up.

Her next installment addressed the crossing of the Atlantic to the African coast. One of her great fears was running into a freighter while on autopilot at night. This probably wouldn't be the greatest danger as there were not likely to be any other boats in the middle of the oceans these days.

She knew the wind patterns from her studies. She managed to acquire several GPS systems and was gratified that they still worked. This remnant of civilization would guide her across the ocean.

A several-month search finally yielded a splendid twelve-meter sailing ship. The trip across the Atlantic occupied a year of her life and a week of telling. It was mainly boredom, spiced with enough terror and narrow escapes to write a book, which she eventually did from the tapes they made of their stories.

She learned to trust the GPS and traveled mostly in at night, when the stars and the moon were her friends. She loved the many storms and their winds as they hastened her along. Still, she had more than one encounter with pirates as she probed the coastal cities of Africa. They had big lumbering boats however, and could not compare with her sleek and fast sloop.

She landed near Mombasa not too long after the time that J was there. She encountered some peaceful people, heard extraordinary stories and got some provisions. She heard of the 'savior' and the destruction of the only gun with bullets in town. When J heard this, he was finally persuaded that he had done the right thing in eliminating those deterrents to civilization in Mombasa. It would have been horrible if Kay had stepped into their trap after all her success. But then J considered, with her confidence, maybe she could have saved them some other way. Still, he was glad she didn't have to be involved in that. Just imagine if she died when she was so close. J's throat closed. That would have been more like life.

After a week of travel, saved by her gun more than once, she arrived in Arusha. J figured that she must have passed within a hundred kilometers of the Tree. During these tales, J was impressed that the will to survive within Kay was scarcely less than his own.

She didn't know what to do next, since she didn't know the exact location J would choose. She wondered if she would have to wander in circles at random, hallooing. They both grinned. She camped in Arusha for a week with no sightings of people. Then on an excursion out from town she encountered members of Fleur's tribe. In their broken English they indicated that someone in their camp might help her. In desperation, she followed them to their village. She couldn't believe the rest — Fleur and astoundingly good communication; news of J! Fleur was pretty aware of what the Tree was, although they had never discussed it. Kay felt satisfaction well up, and justification of her journey.

After a month of this story telling, J and Kay took a mini-safari. But it wasn't much of an adventure. J was cautious; he wasn't going to lose Kay to some misadventure after miraculously finding her again. It would be years before he could relax his protective cocoon. And it was a very thorough protective nest, with all the survival paraphernalia provided by the Tree. They could go on for a long time, simply living for the day.

I have always heard, Sancho, that doing good to base
fellows is like throwing water into the sea.

When thou art at Rome, do as they do at Rome.

Well, now, there's a remedy for everything, except death.

Miguel de Cervantes (1547–1616)
Spanish novelist and dramatist.
Don Quixote (1605)

It is not the strongest of the species that survives, nor the most
intelligent, but the one more responsive to change.

Charles Darwin

5.0 Epilog

Years passed into decades. All monitoring of airwaves from the tree's sophisticated capabilities had come up empty. It looked like mankind was back to the stone age or before.

The tree had turned out to be a decent place for Kay and J to raise a family. They had to connect to the future despite its uncertainty. But they established a firm footing in the philosophy of Sancho Panza. Based on their life's experience, both were planted in Panza's Plea. It was an essential philosophy in order to face the day bearing the knowledge that they had of the frailties of human attempts at creating an advanced culture. Whatever that was.

Fleur had naturally evolved a very similar view and his group of natives was prospering, they established a close relationship. It was grounded in Panzaic purpose. Quixote was comatose but not forgotten. Not least of the reasons for this was their knowledge that ideologies could do immeasurable harm.

The children, of the Tree and those in Fleur's band, were infused with a desire and reverence for Knowledge. They got the message that the brain was their species unique claim to fame. The cerebral mass was nourished from birth. Evolution was manifest. Their faith was in agnosticism and observations. There would be no Crusades or Jihads or suicide campaigns from them. They were all learning at the OC level. Science in the scrub brush. That was the extent of their quixotic enterprise.

They knew survival was a long shot. And they would never know the outcome. They knew that genetics — the way of the flesh — was a significant component of their makeup, their panzaic side. They knew too, that nurture could develop cranial components that could override those inclinations of the flesh that were often destructive to self or society. Well, maybe. J had his reservations. The genes were very strong. He'd found that out the hard way many times. But they did retain a slight hold on their quixotic side. Society needed both.

It was recognized that the brain-stem demands toward sexual reproduction could not be stilled. But a complete awareness of its roots in evolution and biology allowed one to minimize its impact. While the pleasures of hormonal appeasement were accepted, logic was strong in the choice of mate. The posturing macho male or sultry siren was viewed by all as critters subservient to their glands. It took a lot out of the wow.

The freedom from having to hear the constant failures of mankind over the media, the isolation from the politics that were necessary for the nation-state, and from the hypocrisy that such power elicited, allowed concentration on existence; on maintenance and meaning thereof. It was a delightful way to live. They celebrated serenity, and joy in each other's affection. J was so relieved not to be living alone, to have his chance again at rewarding mutual affection, he cherished the opportunity every day. This gave meaning to life. But it did not extend beyond death.

Cooperation and respect were natural. A positive attitude resulted from being at the top of the food chain, tempered with the knowledge that it was a precarious position. This led to a contented life. There was no racial prejudice; the individual was too valuable. The children of the Tree each mated with a Fleur tribe member. They all understood eugenics and biology and the continuum of racial characteristics. They didn't ignore it. They studied it.

Recognizing a successful appeal to human needs, Sundays were kept for communal meetings on philosophy of the meaning of existence, often exploiting the unknowns in biology, physics or another natural mystery. They recognized the limitations of evolution and this was a time to speculate. The need for spiritualization --- the god gene --- was a recognized human characteristic. But each theory was naturally subjected to critical thought. Faith-based fantasy religions were simply, inevitably, joyously rejected. J called it Quixote day.

There were happy decades for the extended family. Perhaps the planet was meant to support only a very limited number of sophisticated Homo sapiens. Their territorial demands were immense. One of the children learned to range far with the ultralight and built others for the tribe with parts, and precious gasoline, scrounged from the old cities. Fortunately, the automobiles were more difficult to reproduce, and would require too much gas to be practical anyway. Oil, gas and the internal combustion engine were rarities in this age, and the group did their best to make them no-nos.

On their excursions, they encountered huge explosions in the populations of many animals that had been bordering on extinction during the dominion of Homo sapiens. They didn't see many humans. That species seemed to need a critical minimum number and a societal structure to survive in a dangerous world. They encountered a few small bands living in a primitive tribal state. For now, they were treated as a dangerous animal and best avoided. There were no radio transmissions although the airwaves were still monitored.

But they knew they were there — other pockets of Homo sapiens surviving under new rules. Culturally, there were Neanderthals here, Homo erectus there. They would diverge under diverse pressures from dissimilar ecological niches. Perhaps they would meet, generations down the line, and compare notes, or do battle.

Their next generation seemed to be on the right track. A gamble. But what the hell, the last experiment was a big failure. Back to Evolution.

♦

One day Kay approached J with a new woman at her side. "I'd like to introduce you to Celeste. I believe you might have met."

J regarded Celeste critically, noting the GPS on her belt. "Hoo boy, a visitor from the past. A past that I have mixed emotions about."

Slim laughed to diffuse his anxiety. "You're OK. I'm OK. We're both survivors, I guess."

She added a lot to their enclave. Kay and she got along really well.

In this culture, guns were a carefully controlled commodity. They were valuable, perhaps essential, in Homo sapiens' struggle for survival. But bullets were in short supply and difficult to fabricate. Fortunately, knowledge of the bow and arrow, sphere, crossbow and other early weaponry were documented. Still, the male role of hunter and protector from the many predators in Africa took a small but significant toll on the men of Fleur's tribe. There was a shortage of men, and genetic diversity.

Fleur had suggested to Kay, "You know, from a so-called scientist's point of view, it might be beneficial if J could spread his seed. This is an important ingredient in maintaining a healthy gene pool." Fleur was logically pure, unfettered by the Western world's odes to monogamy. He had three wives in the African manner.

Kay was inclined to say, "Those are my seeds." She was quixotically motivated to save the species but she was a creature of her nurture. She thought about it. After all, they were about regenerating the Homo sapiens' race. Together they approached J.

"Of course my hormonal drives are for it. But I've a big wall of culturally instilled inhibitors that are concerned only with Kay's attitude," said J.

Kay looked him in the eye. "I'm confident you love me. I also know men can detach sex from their cerebral thinking with the slightest rationalization. I won't say 'go for it', but I will look the other way."

One Quixote day, before the assemblage, the three of them had a freewheeling conversation on how the sixties flower children had some correct assumptions about sex. The hypocritical and culturally disruptive policy of preaching sex as a sinful distraction while permitting it to be pervasive in almost every aspect of culture had given sex the role of the dominant force in that society. The evolutionarily naïve free love solution of the children of the sixties had been a too severe yielding to the hormones and failed on the tines of disease and psychological trauma.

But the simple adage might have been right — diffuse the dominant power of sex by making it less important. The notion of sex as a tool and not a hormonal edict must be taught to the young psyche. If there was to be a new era of the intellectual Homo sapiens the scientific rationalizer, the generation fettered with Old World ideologies must strive mightily to suppress these judgments. It isn't easy, but it's worth a try.

Hence in an era of panzaic practicality, J fathered two more children from women in the Fleur band. However they couldn't be considered concubines, since the matings, in the best tradition of the old religions, were for progeny. Kay was flexible, but a 9-month commitment kept her reproduction to "not more than three" with her mate.

The children were wed under tutelage of Fleur, J and Kay. These were often arranged matings that seemed natural, since the children had the main voice in the choices. These hormone-plagued teenagers were at least aware of their own limitations in applying logic to the impulsive chemical bond. There would be no Romeo and Juliet stories in this era.

The new attempt at creating a culture centered on Fleur and his tribe.

There were many storehouses of knowledge available to this embryo civilization. Just in case, J and Kay wrote a treatise on the accumulated knowledge of ten thousand years- carefully edited by the native philosopher. It formed the basis of thought for generations of successful progeny. Beyond that, it is difficult to look.

◆ ◆ ◆ ◆